VANISHING TEARDROPS

VANISHING TEARDROPS

TAMARA'S TEARDROPS #4

P.D. WORKMAN

ISBN: 9781989080245 (IS Hardcover)

ISBN: 9781989080238 (IS Paperback)

ISBN: 9781989080207 (KDP Paperback)

ISBN: 9781989080214 (Kindle)

ISBN: 9781989080221 (ePub)

pdworkman

ALSO BY P.D. WORKMAN

Tamara's Teardrops:

Tattooed Teardrops

Two Teardrops

Tortured Teardrops

Vanishing Teardrops

Medical Kidnap Files:

Mito

EDS

Proxy

Toxo

Pain

Between the Cracks:

Ruby

June and Justin

Michelle

Chloe

Ronnie

June, Into the Light

Breaking the Pattern:

Deviation

Diversion

By-Pass

Stand Alone YA novels

Stand Alone

Don't Forget Steven

Those Who Believe

Cynthia has a Secret

Questing for a Dream

Once Brothers

Intersexion

Making Her Mark

Endless Change

Gem, Himself, Alone

AND MORE AT PDWORKMAN.COM

To those who have chosen the greater good.

ONE

TAMARA SAT IN FRONT of the parole board, feeling like a bug under a magnifying glass. Everyone in the room had watched her enter the room. She stumbled, suddenly forgetting how to walk normally, too conscious of her feet and legs. Gomez directed her into the lone chair waiting front and center, as if she might not know where she was supposed to go otherwise.

She was in her orange uniform. They didn't get civvies for appearing in front of the board. It wasn't like she had anyone to fool, anyone who would think that she was not a convicted felon. Not like when she appeared in court and they were concerned that the jury not be influenced by the fact that she was a criminal. Though that had never turned out well. Her court appearances had been unmitigated disasters.

They had trusted her to appear in court to testify against the monsters and she had failed, her psychosis worsened by the stress. She didn't know what the verdicts had been in the cases against Mr. Baker and Glock, but she hadn't helped the prosecutor like they had expected her to. But that was all in the past. There was nothing she could do about it months later.

"Tamara French," one of the parole board members said crisply, looking down at the papers in front of her. She was an older woman, probably a retired judge, deep frown lines carved in her face. Tamara had wondered whether she would know anyone on the board, but the faces were unfamiliar to her. People who didn't know her personally and wouldn't care whether she stayed in juvie or got out on parole. They were supposed to be unbiased, but Tamara didn't suppose they would be starting with the opinion that she was a good little girl who had just gotten mixed up in something that was beyond her control. "Convicted of two counts of murder. Released on parole last year, but violated and returned to custody," the woman summarized.

Tamara nodded stiffly and swallowed, a lump in her throat.

Everyone was silent. Tamara looked around, waiting for someone to say something. Her first parole board had been pretty warm toward her. She'd had an exemplary record before her release a year before. But that had all changed and the board undoubtedly knew it.

As awkward as it had been to have them all looking at her when she entered the room, it was worse to have them all looking at their papers and files as if she weren't sitting right there in front of her. Why wouldn't they look at her? Had they already decided, without even talking to her, without even hearing any evidence from anyone else, that they were going to turn her down? If they had already decided, why didn't they just say so and send her back away without going through a charade first?

"Why don't you tell us why you violated last time?" the frowning woman inquired. The way she said it made Tamara feel stupid for not offering up the information herself without prompting. But she had been following the rules she had been given when her lawyer had tried to prepare her to testify in court. Don't offer anything. Wait until a question is asked. Only answer what is asked and nothing more.

"Uh..." Tamara cleared her throat. She needed to sound

confident, not like a little girl, so she forced some strength into her voice. She imagined she was talking to one of the guards or one of the other juvies, not someone who controlled where her life was going to go for the next year. "I made some mistakes... I was contacted by an old cellmate and I didn't say anything to my PO. I was afraid he'd send me back." She shrugged helplessly. "I made a lot of stupid choices. I... didn't think it was going to be so hard."

"And how are things going to be any different this time?" It was a man who asked this; short, balding, peering at his papers through his glasses and then at Tamara over the rims.

Tamara concentrated on not saying 'uh' or 'um' again. They wanted her to be clear and concise, to give the impression that she was being honest and up front and was intelligent enough to change what had gone wrong the last time and over the last year of her incarceration.

"I know I need to use my PO as a resource. Not to treat him as an enemy. I know that he's there to help me, not just there to slap me back in juvie the first chance."

Tamara closed her eyes briefly, fighting back the memories of Glock telling her the system was rigged against her. That the whole thing was just a way to make it look like they were giving felons a chance when all they intended to do was revoke her parole and send her back at the first opportunity. She couldn't believe that. She had to believe Mrs. Henson and Zobel and the other people who wanted to help her. Collins was the one who had told her he would speak for her when she came before the parole board again. He'd had to send her back to juvie after everything she had done, but he said he'd speak for her.

But Tamara had taken a quick glance around the room as she was directed to the hot seat in the middle of the room. Collins wasn't sitting up at the front with the board and he hadn't been sitting in the spectator seating. Tamara's eyes had been drawn to a woman there, square jawed, her blond hair pulled back into a ponytail, who Tamara didn't recognize. She hadn't been able to see the woman's face, only the back of her head, but she wasn't familiar. Mrs. Henson was there. But there was no long-legged, bald black man. If Collins had been there, he would have been obvious. Tamara fought back the disappointment over his no-show. Would the board still consider giving her a second shot at parole so soon if he weren't there to speak up for her?

"Miss French."

Tamara opened her eyes and looked at the board members. The frowning woman was speaking again.

"Your record since you were returned to custody has been interesting... and not in a good way."

"Yes, ma'am."

"I'm surprised that you would even apply for parole again after what's taken place over the past year."

Tamara swallowed and shifted in her seat. It would have been nice if they'd at least given her a drink of water. Surely everyone who sat in that hot seat must have a mouth as dry as hers. Were they intentionally making her as uncomfortable as they could?

"The staff encouraged me to apply," she said. "There should be letters there from Dr. Sutherland about my... problems... and from other administrators..."

A couple of the board members shuffled papers, but everyone had undoubtedly read them already.

"Dr. Sutherland suggests that your psychosis was triggered by your pregnancy. A pregnancy that you kept a secret until it was too late to deal with it."

"I didn't know I was pregnant."

"I see. I've never heard of psychosis being triggered by preg-nancy before."

Tamara shrugged. "It's rare." What else could she say about it?

"So that means you're not responsible for any of the

violent incidents on your record during the past year?" challenged another woman on the board. She had long hair in a straight, severe style and slashes of red blush along her cheekbones. She reminded Tamara a little of one of her fifth-grade teachers, a dragon of a woman who had scared Tamara to death.

Tamara looked down the line of the parole board, trying to analyze their reactions. Things were not going well. Dr. Sutherland and the others had assured her that once the board knew that her problems had been the result of psychosis with an identified trigger, there would be no problem. They could ignore those incidents completely.

"I know I did a lot of things that were wrong or bizarre..." Tamara said slowly. "It's hard to explain what was going on in my head at the time... but my thoughts weren't right. I saw and heard things... hallucinations... and I was really paranoid. I thought... there were plots against me... I couldn't control my reactions..."

She had expected further probes from the dragon-woman. Snide comments, disdain, and disbelief. But the woman was quiet, making notes along with the rest of the board members.

"Which brings us to the next point," the balding man said, looking down his nose at his papers and readjusting his glasses. "Your pregnancy."

"If I get out on parole, my foster mom from last time, Mrs. Henson, she wants me to go to her house and to try to take care of my baby," Tamara told him, diverting him from any questions about how she had managed to get pregnant during her incarceration. She turned slightly in her chair to nod to Mrs. Henson, sitting in the chairs behind her. "That's her."

The board all looked up from their papers and notes to study Mrs. Henson. Mrs. Henson smiled and nodded.

"You have discussed this with Social Services?" the man questioned, his brows drawing down as he stared at Mrs.

Henson. "They will approve a plan to put an infant into the arms of a girl convicted of murdering two young children?"

Tamara opened her mouth, unsure what to say. But Mrs. Henson had already been dealing with the prison officials and Social Services on the matter and she spoke up. Her voice was calm and measured.

"Yes, we have been in consultation with Social Services and already have a Safety Plan in place. There is nothing to indicate that Tamara would be a danger to her baby. In fact, even dealing with the psychosis triggered by the pregnancy, Tamara tried to protect him. She asked for help several times when she felt she might be a danger to him."

The balding man's expression didn't change as he stared at her. "This is aside from when she tried to commit suicide or tear the baby out with her bare hands."

The room was silent. Tamara could hear herself breathing. She hadn't been sure how much information the parole board would be given on what had happened over the past year. Obviously, they had been given plenty of ammunition against her.

"Yes," Mrs. Henson agreed. She was still calm and confident, but there was an extra bite in her voice as well. "They changed her meds after that to try to get better control over her psychosis. But more than that, Tamara learned how to ask for help. She learned how to judge when she was losing control and to ask the appropriate people for help."

Mrs. Henson actually made it sound good. Like Tamara had improved and progressed, rather than spiraling further and further into darkness she couldn't cope with. The balding man nodded and wrote something down. Tamara felt like something had shifted in the mood of the room. Maybe the board would actually consider granting her parole?

There were more scribbled notes. Murmurs between the members of the board. Tamara let her eyes roam around the small, warm room. The board. Mrs. Henson. The unknown woman. The rest of the audience she could see without turning her head. She could still feel Gomez's presence somewhere behind her.

"It says here your former parole officer wishes to make a statement?" the frowning woman said, looking up from her papers to spear Tamara with her gaze.

Tamara nodded. She swallowed and cleared her throat. "I don't know where he is…"

"Call Mr. Collins in."

Tamara heard the door behind her open. She didn't turn around to look, afraid they would judge her as easily distractible, impulsive, and unable to control herself. There was another guard there; it wasn't Gomez's voice that called in the larger waiting area for Mr. Collins. Footsteps sounded, the guard and Mr. Collins entering the room. Consuming more of the air in the already-close room.

She wasn't sure whether he was going to sit behind her or stand in front of the board with his back to her. As it turned out, he stood at an angle to Tamara, so she could see his face in profile as he addressed them. He gave Tamara a nod. He gave a casual, confident greeting to the members of the board. It appeared that he knew them. Tamara supposed it wasn't the first time he'd given a statement.

"You were Miss French's parole officer last year," the frowning woman said.

Collins gave a nod. "She had a number of problems, but I believe that if she's willing to communicate with her parole offi-cer, she can successfully reintegrate with society. She did turn herself in. In fact, she has twice. That shows me she has what it takes. With a better understanding of the challenges she is going to face once she's left here and more open communication with her PO, she can succeed."

"Do you really think that things have changed that much since her last release?" the dragon lady demanded, tapping the end of her pen on the papers in front of her. "I'm not sure her behavior since returning to custody shows a positive turn."

"I don't think she had to change much to be successful," Collins said smoothly. "She had a lot of pressure from a previous acquaintance. She was, at times, physically prevented from complying. With Glock Spielman now incarcerated, Tamara's chances of success go up a hundred percent."

"You don't think she's going to allow herself to be influenced by someone else this time?"

Collins turned his head slightly toward Tamara, considering. They hadn't spoken since she had returned to juvie. He didn't know all that had happened to her since, though he had likely seen some of it on TV.

"I think she has the ability to resist pressure. She has a desire to do the right thing, which isn't something that can be said of all of the parolees I've supervised."

The little, balding man wrinkled his brow. He scratched out a few words in his notes. "Do you think she knows the difference between right and wrong?"

Collins didn't hesitate. "Yes."

Tamara waited for him to prevaricate, to temper his statement. Each of the members of the board looked at him, apparently waiting for the same. But Collins didn't qualify it.

"Thank you, Mr. Collins," the frowning woman said.

Collins stood there for a minute longer, waiting to see if any of the other board members had any questions for him. Then he nodded, and he walked behind Tamara to sit in the chairs and watch the rest of the proceedings.

"Is there anyone else who wants to make a statement?" the frowning woman asked, closing her folder.

"I do," Mrs. Henson offered quickly, before the proceedings could be closed.

"You've already had your say," the woman countered, clearly ready to go on.

"No, I only answered your question regarding Social Services' opinion of Tamara taking care of her baby."

The woman rubbed at the lines around her eyes, sighing and nodding tiredly.

"Okay. You've agreed she can be placed in your home, so clearly you believe she can be reformed and is not a danger. Do you have anything else to add?"

"It's important for Tamara to be able to bond with her baby. She hasn't had the opportunity to do that. She hasn't even held him. If she's going to have any involvement in his life, she needs to be given the opportunity to care for him. For his mental health and hers. And caring for a baby means she'll be motivated to make it work. She'll want to succeed for his sake. A baby can have a huge influence on a young woman."

Tamara suppressed a shudder at Mrs. Henson's words. That baby had already had a huge influence on her, taking over her brain for the months before he came into the world. She knew that he wasn't actually evil, but she remembered thinking he was, during her breaks from reality. She had been sure he was a demon, something she needed to fight back against. She struggled to keep her expression blank and not let the board see her thoughts.

"With a baby to take care of, Tamara isn't going to be out partying or looking for excitement. She'll stick close to home. She'll have the opportunity to make friends with other young mothers. She'll have plenty of social supports. We have been working with teen moms for years. Not all of them are cut out for it... but I believe Tamara is. I think she could be a great mom and this could be her path back into productive society."

The dragon lady turned to the others on the board, whispering. Did she think Mrs. Henson was full of hot air? That she didn't know what she was talking about? Mrs. Henson had a lot of experience, but Tamara still had a hard time believing Mrs. Henson knew what she was talking about as far as Tamara's parenting skills went. She didn't know what a pitiful job Tamara had done taking care of Corrine and Julie. It wasn't just that she had killed them while suffering from the psychosis of an earlier pregnancy. Even before that, the Bakers had criticized and berated Tamara, shouted at her for putting the children in danger, and beat her for her errors. If Mrs. Henson knew what a screw-up she had been with the Baker children, she wouldn't be so quick to say Tamara would be a good mother to her own baby.

But it was Tamara's one slim chance of getting out instead of a delay of another year, trying to show everyone what an exemplary juvie she was. If they could be convinced that she wanted to be a mother to her baby, they had to let her out. The baby was already a few months old. In another year, her chances of being able to bond with him properly would be that much lower. Earlier was better. Mrs. Henson kept emphasizing how important it was.

"My baby needs a mother," Tamara said. "I don't want him having to go from one foster home to another his whole life. I don't want him to not have any parents, like me." Tamara blinked tears. "Lots of the girls in juvie didn't have a real mom in their lives. I don't want my baby to end up somewhere like this."

The board members looked at her for a moment, then resumed whispering. Tamara could hear Mrs. Henson shifting in her chair back behind Tamara. She knew Mrs. Henson wanted to be there beside her, holding her hand to encourage her and show the board how sure she was and how much she would help and support Tamara. Mrs. Henson was used to getting her way with Social Services, but Tamara wasn't sure she would have as much sway with the parole board.

Tamara closed her eyes, focused on keeping her breathing steady. She waited for the board to announce their decision.

TWO

"YOU DID IT!" MRS. Henson cheered, giving Tamara a squeeze around the shoulders. "I told you we could get you out. I knew we could do it!"

Tamara put up with the hug for a moment, then wriggled to extricate herself. "Yeah. I didn't think it was going to go my way. I just figured, after all the stuff that happened... there was no way."

"You should pat yourself on the back. It wasn't easy. You did a great job advocating for yourself and telling them you could do it."

"It was all you," Tamara disagreed. "You and Collins. I didn't say that much."

"You don't have to say a lot. You handled yourself really well. Give yourself the congratulations you deserve. If you'd just sulked and not spoken up for yourself, do you think they would have approved it?"

Tamara shrugged. But her face got a little warm thinking about it. Mrs. Henson was right. She had done something for herself for once instead of just withdrawing and saying it was never going to work out.

Mrs. Henson gave her another hug around the shoulders, but Gomez was getting anxious for Tamara to be on her way. "You'll have plenty of time for that later," he said. "If you want to get out of here, everything has to be processed properly. I'm not supposed to be letting you hang around and socialize."

Tamara already had her hands cuffed in front of her, ready to be escorted back to her housing unit. As nice as it would be to just walk out of the parole board hearing and go home, that wasn't the way it worked. There would be paperwork to be processed, interviews with Dr. Sutherland and someone in administration, getting her release date approved and her parole officer onside, and a dozen other moving parts before she actually got out the door and was free.

"Yeah, fine. Let's go," she agreed.

The other woman who had been watching the parole board hearing was standing nearby, watching Tamara and Mrs. Henson closely. She had a hard face. Not unattractive, but not, Tamara thought, used to smiling much. Tamara wasn't sure who she was. Maybe a news reporter, seeing if there were a story to be told. Maybe some victim's advocacy group, though she hadn't spoken up against Tamara being released, so Tamara didn't think that was the case. Maybe it really wasn't anything to do with Tamara or her case; the woman was just a new guard or staff member and wanted to see how it all worked.

She didn't look away when Tamara looked at her. Tamara was used to some measure of respect in juvie. It wasn't respectful to just keep staring at her like that. It was a challenge, and Tamara didn't like to be challenged, especially by someone she didn't even know.

* * *

Mrs. Henson had asked if she could be the one to pick Tamara up from juvie and to take her home but, for some reason, protocol forbade it. Tamara had to be picked up by her social worker, who had initial custody of her, and then transferred to Mrs. Henson like a courier package. So, just as she had a year earlier, Tamara sat in the receiving room, staring down at her dingy white tennis shoes, waiting for the social worker to sign her out and take her away from juvie.

The social worker had said she would be there at noon. Tamara sat in the hard plastic chair watching the second hand make its way around the wall clock over, and over, and over again, until two hours had passed. Social workers were always dealing with emergencies and were notorious for being late, so she wasn't sure why she had thought the one picking her up would be any different.

Tamara hadn't eaten lunch, and she was annoyed and angry by the time the social worker finally showed up.

She was cut from the usual mold. In a skirt suit, hair pulled back away from her face, a narrow, stern face. Tamara bit her lip and looked away from the social worker. It wouldn't do to start out on the wrong foot. Snapping at the worker for being late was not going to win Tamara any awards.

"All ready to go, Tamara?" the woman asked briskly.

"Yeah." Tamara looked toward the reception counter. "You gotta fill out papers?"

"All done. We can go."

Tamara got stiffly to her feet. The social worker was watching her face. Tamara wasn't sure what was in the woman's eyes. Curiosity?

"You don't remember me?" the social worker asked.

Tamara frowned and looked over her. There was no name tag to help her to recall. But the woman's face did look a little familiar. Tamara couldn't remember where she knew her from.

"We met at the hospital. When I picked up your baby."

Tamara squinted at her, trying to force recollection. It had been a bad time and her memories were foggy and disjointed.

"Sorry," she said finally. "I was pretty doped up."

"I'm Mrs. Arbiter. I have to say, I was surprised to hear that you were going to go back to Marion and try to raise your baby. You were pretty adamant at the hospital that you didn't want him."

Tamara shifted back and forth, uncomfortable with Mrs. Arbiter's keen gaze. "I was going through a lot of stuff," she explained. "I didn't know what I wanted."

"You seemed to have a pretty good idea!"

"I guess." They started to walk toward the door. "But things changed... and I didn't think back then that I'd be able to get out and have anything to do with him. I didn't think there was any point in trying."

Mrs. Arbiter nodded, accepting this. She led Tamara out to her car and didn't try to keep her talking on the drive to the Hensons' house.

Tamara watched out the window as the scenery changed, getting farther and farther from juvie and closer to the house where she had spent those few weeks the last time she was released on parole.

She would do better this time.

She had to.

THREE

T HE HOUSE WAS WEIRDLY familiar. It had been only a year since Tamara had been there, but it seemed like a lifetime had passed in that short time. Mrs. Henson gave her a brief hug in greeting. Tamara was starting to adjust to physical contact, but she was still guarded. She appreciated the occasional comfort, but she was hypervigilant, always defensive at first, until she could consciously quiet her body's reaction. Tamara pulled back. She looked toward the stairs.

"Is it the same room?"

She knew it had to be. Nita and Deshawn were still there. They would not have changed rooms. Tamara's room had been the one with a crib, the one normally used for teen moms who needed support and coaching in learning to care for their little ones.

"Yes, same one," Mrs. Henson agreed with a smile. "Go ahead and get settled in. Then we can talk."

Tamara indicated her plastic bag containing one change of nondescript clothing. "This is all I've got... I don't exactly need to unpack." She looked toward the kitchen. "I actually didn't get anything to eat."

"Oh, well go ahead, then," Mrs. Henson encouraged. "You know where to find everything, and if you don't, just keep opening cupboards until you find it."

Mrs. Henson didn't say she wanted to talk to Mrs. Arbiter alone, but it was obvious. Tamara complied, going into the kitchen to see what she could find. She couldn't hear what Mrs. Henson and Mrs. Arbiter had to say when they put their heads together.

After eating slop in the canteen for so long, being able to go to the fridge and pick out her own food, real food, felt like a gift. Tamara pulled out bread, crisp lettuce, a tomato, and cold cuts. She picked out her own condiments. And instead of some indescribable stew of mush and gristle, she had a real sandwich, like on a sub shop commercial. She sat down at the dining room table by herself, and savored each tangy, crunchy bite.

* * *

Mrs. Henson called up the stairs to let Tamara know her parole officer was there. Tamara looked at the bedroom door, waiting for Mr. Collins to appear. She was doing her best not to look at the crib or to think about having to take care of an infant again and was almost looking forward to seeing Mr. Collins. She needed to thank him for speaking up for her at her parole hearing as he had. She would reassure him that she was going to stick to her parole rules this time. She wouldn't be talked or pressured into disobeying the rules he set out. If she'd just followed them to the letter last time, she wouldn't have ended up in such trouble and would have avoided all of the horrible stuff that had happened since then. But she'd gone full-circle and was back, ready to try again. She was going to make it.

But it wasn't Mr. Collins who appeared in her doorway. Tamara gasped to see the blond, square-faced woman who had been at her parole hearing. Tamara had known that she might not get Mr. Collins back as her PO, but she had figured he would somehow arrange it. He would want to carry through where he had failed before and see her successfully reintegrated.

Tamara quickly sat up, knees to her chest to form a barrier, instinctively protecting herself from the new threat. The woman stopped in the doorway.

"Mind if I come in?"

Tamara nodded her permission. She bit her lip and faced her new PO, unsure what to say.

"My name is Wanda Brisk. As you know... I'm your parole officer."

It didn't come as a shock to Tamara that she was a parole officer. She looked like a policewoman. Tough, straightforward, no nonsense. Someone who had dealt with a lot of crap from her parolees in the past and wasn't about to fall for anything.

"Uh, hi. I'm... Tamara."

Of course, Wanda already knew that. But Tamara didn't know what else to say to her. Tamara hugged her knees close, reminding herself that she was strong. She was going to make the right decisions, so she wasn't going to end up in Wanda's bad books. She wasn't going to go back to juvie. She was going to succeed, just like Mr. Collins, Mrs. Henson, and Dr. Sutherland all said she could. If she put her mind to it, she could make it.

"Can I sit here?" Wanda pointed to the end of the bed, away from Tamara but still uncomfortably close. There wasn't a chair for her to sit in, and Tamara wouldn't feel comfortable with Wanda standing over her, so there really weren't any other options.

"Uh... yeah. I guess."

Wanda sat down. She fixed Tamara with a hard stare.

"Let's get one thing up front. I'm no pushover. I expect you to do everything you're told. I'm not going to put up with a bunch of lame excuses. You break rules, you're going back. I'm no cream puff."

"No," Tamara agreed, shaking her head. Collins hadn't been a cream puff either. Tamara had been afraid of him, terrified he would revoke her parole and send her back. But instead of keeping Tamara from breaking the rules, her fear had only kept her from telling him the things she should have. She needed to do better this time. She had to be open and to ask for help.

Wanda was staring at Tamara as if she could see right through her into her brain and analyze everything that was going on there. She didn't smile. At least Collins had tried to be reassuring. Tamara bit at the skin around her thumbnail, already tender and inflamed.

"What are the rules?" she asked. "Are the rules the same?"

"I'm not sure what your rules were last time. You've got a curfew of nine o'clock. That means you're here and you've checked in with one of your foster parents. No alcohol or drugs. Any prescriptions need to be approved by me. Anything. I want the names of anyone you're spending time with outside this house. I don't care if it's an old friend or someone at your parenting class, if you have coffee with them, I want to know about it. And you *will* be attending parenting classes."

Tamara nodded. That was something she'd already talked about with Mrs. Henson before ever appearing before the parole board. It didn't matter that Tamara had taken care of children before, she had to go to a class just like it was her first time and she didn't know what she was doing. Tamara had acquiesced. What did it matter if she had to take a boring class?

"Yeah, I know."

"I honestly don't know what Social Services is thinking, letting you take care of an infant. That is the last thing I would have allowed if it was up to me. You shouldn't have any access to children."

Tamara bit her nail, then tried to distract herself by running her nails along the seams in the jeans she was wearing.

"I'll have help. Mrs. Henson will be here if I need a break or don't know how to handle something."

Wanda glowered at her. "I'm not exactly worried about your poor feelings."

"But that's why before... I got overwhelmed... I didn't know what to do..."

"You did not kill those children because you needed a nap."

"No, I..." Tamara searched for words. She didn't want to give excuses and she didn't want to have to tell the whole story to a stranger. But she wanted Wanda to understand that the baby wouldn't be in danger from her. Tamara wasn't going to let that happen again. "It wasn't just that..."

Wanda made a cutting motion with her hand. "That's all beside the point. That decision isn't mine to make. You're here, they've already agreed to let you care for your baby, so that's that. I don't have any say there. But that baby had better be fed and dry and happy if I come by for a check, or I will be making a report."

Tamara's throat tightened She shook her head worriedly.

"Sometimes babies aren't happy," she protested. "If he's sick or tired or just got up... what if he's just had his shots? Or he's teething?" She could already feel panic rising. She needed to be like the nurses and everyone else had been at the hospital, calm and collected even when the baby got grumpy. They had kept reassuring her that there was nothing wrong with letting him cry for a while. It wouldn't hurt him.

"He'd better be fed and clean," Wanda said grudgingly. "If there is any sign he's neglected or abused, I am not going to stand by. He'll go straight back to his own foster family. Understood?"

"I'll take good care of him. Mrs. Henson will help. I'll make sure he has everything he needs."

Wanda didn't look impressed by the promise. Her face said that she'd heard plenty of promises from her parolees before and they didn't mean squat. But Tamara didn't know what else to say. She couldn't prove herself until she'd had some time.

"Is that all my rules?"

"You need to be under a psychiatrist's care, seeing them regularly. They need to have my name and number, so they can report anything to me that might indicate a problem."

Tamara nodded. "I need your card."

Wanda reached into one of the pouches on her belt and came out with a small stack of business cards. She tossed three or four onto the bed between them. "Memorize my number. Don't just put it into your phone, I want you to know it by heart, so you can call me any time from any phone. Your psychiatrist gets a card. Your foster mom. Everybody needs to be able to reach me. Any time, day or night."

Wanda stopped talking. Her mouth went into a straight line, lips pressed together thinly. Did the parole officers come up with the rules themselves, or were they dictated by the parole board or someone further up the administrative ladder? Tamara imagined that if Wanda was the one making the rules herself, Tamara would be locked down more tightly than she was in juvie. A lock on the door. Tracking anklet. Eyes on her at all times. But that wasn't the way it was. They were trying to get her reintegrated. They wanted her to look and act just like anyone else, as if she were normal.

"At your hearing, you said that you'd had hallucinations. You saw and heard things."

"Yeah."

"Did you know that they weren't real?"

Tamara frowned. She scratched the back of her neck, thinking back to the months of darkness at juvie, and before that, when she was at the Bakers'.

"I didn't know what was real and what wasn't," she said slowly, "but I knew not everything was."

"And you haven't had any hallucinations since having the baby?"

"For a few days after. But they started to go away pretty quickly."

"And none since then."

"No."

"I want you to really think about it. Any hallucinations at all?"

"No." Tamara shifted uneasily and looked away from Wanda.

"What?" Wanda demanded. "What else? You tell me the whole truth, not just the part you think is technically true."

Tamara chewed a jagged piece of skin on her lip. "I have PTSD. So sometimes I have flashbacks."

Wanda swore. "Is this on your medical records? Everybody else already knows this?"

Tamara nodded.

"What's the difference between a flashback and a hallucination? Dr. Sutherland says you're cured because you're not having hallucinations anymore, but you're still having flashbacks? What's the difference?"

Tamara squirmed. "A flashback is a memory. Not... something new... not... twisted thinking."

"But you still see or hear something that isn't there."

"Um... yeah. Sometimes. Usually, it's just anxiety... just a feeling... panic... but sometimes I see and hear things, like it's happening again."

Wanda shook her head angrily. "And they think you're a candidate for mom of the year. Unbelievable. How often?"

"What?" Tamara stalled.

"How often are you having these flashbacks?"

Tamara chewed on her thumbnail again.

"I want the truth," Wanda said. "Don't try to obfuscate by telling me something that is *technically* true. I want the reality."

"I don't know... it will be different here than at juvie. There are different triggers. Different memories. I don't know... how often."

"How often at juvie? Once a month? Once a week?"

"Yeah..."

"Tamara."

Tamara cleared her throat. She wanted to lower her voice to a whisper. She didn't want to have to tell Wanda everything. She wanted to just go back to juvie and hide her face in her pillow. It wasn't fair that she should have to tell Wanda about her own private thoughts and reactions. Wanda wasn't a doctor. She didn't know what it all meant. Dr. Sutherland knew, and he said it was safe for Tamara to be on the outside. He said it was safe, so why should she have to tell Wanda the details?

"Most days," Tamara finally admitted.

"You have flashbacks every day."

"*Most* days."

"But that's okay," Wanda said in a sarcastic, mocking voice. "Why should that be any concern?"

"Lots of people have PTSD."

"They aren't under my supervision and taking care of help-less infants. What about Mrs. Henson? Does she know about this?"

"Yes..." Tamara frowned thinking it through. "She knows I have them... she's seen a couple bad ones, so she knows..."

"Does she know they're happening every day?"

Tamara bit the inside of her cheek, resisting the urge to correct Wanda again. "I... don't know."

But she did. Mrs. Henson didn't have a clue Tamara had flashbacks every day. Dr. Sutherland didn't know she had them every day. No one else had demanded to know that.

Wanda shook her head. "People have no common sense. None. You are hallucinating every day, and they say it's fine because it's flashbacks, not...?" She looked for a word to finish her sentence, not familiar enough with the medical lingo.

"Psychosis," Tamara filled in. She swallowed. "It's not a psychotic break. It isn't the same thing."

"I'll need to discuss this with Mrs. Henson and my boss. I really hate it when the quacks do stuff like this. You're on meds?"

Tamara nodded.

"I want to see them."

Another invasion of her privacy. Even in juvie, she hadn't had to show anyone else what she was taking; how defective she really was.

Swallowing her anger, Tamara unfolded herself from the bed and went to the dresser where she had stowed her meager belongings. She pulled out three bottles of pills and handed them to Wanda. Wanda took out her phone, and while Tamara watched, she took a picture of each label and then the pills inside of each bottle.

"You are to keep the pills in their original prescription bottles. If I find pills loose in your pockets, you're in violation. I don't have to identify whether they are legal or not. If they're not in their original containers, they are illicit. Not even an aspirin. Got it?"

Tamara could just imagine the scenarios Wanda had been through with previous parolees to lead to this rule. She nodded. "I don't do drugs. I wouldn't even take these if I didn't have to. They forced me to."

Wanda's eyes narrowed. "You'd better keep taking them, too. You go off your meds, it's a violation."

Was there anything that *wasn't* a violation?

"I don't need them. They are low dose, just in case stress or something other than being pregnant might trigger me. But I've never had a psychotic break any other time."

"Are you on birth control?"

Tamara blinked at her. "No."

"See a doctor and get fixed up. I don't want you getting pregnant again."

"I'm not even *seeing* anyone!" Tamara was suddenly short of breath.

"By the time you decide you need it, it will be too late. Just like last time, right?"

Tamara tried to close her mouth and answer properly but couldn't explain to Wanda. She didn't want to explain to Wanda. "I didn't—last time—it wasn't..." She rubbed her forehead, the pressure building. "Okay, yeah. All right."

Wanda nodded. "Don't put it off. I'm serious."

"Okay."

Wanda got up from the bed so that she was face-to-face with Tamara, though a good head taller. Tamara found herself immediately assessing Wanda as a threat. She was powerfully built. For sure she lifted weights. Tamara would need to be quick. Move fast, grab a weapon, use her lower center of gravity to sweep the woman to the floor and cut and run.

"Take it easy," Wanda warned, watching Tamara's face.

Tamara took a deep breath. She relaxed her hands and tried to assume a casual stance. *Stand down, French.* Wanda was just like one of the guards at juvie. There to make sure Tamara followed the rules, but not someone who was going to attack her. She was safe. Tamara breathed out.

"You know what's going to happen if you screw up?" Wanda demanded. "You get what's at stake here, don't you?"

Tamara nodded. She'd tried once before. She knew the risks better than Wanda.

"If you screw up again, you're going to adult prison," Wanda said. "You're sixteen and still have one to six years left on your term. No more juvie for you. You think you're tough enough to face those women?"

That's where Vernon had gone. Not only would Tamara be facing older, tougher women, but she would be known. Olivia

Vernon might have liked or respected Tamara at one time, but Tamara was the reason Vernon was back in prison. Tamara would be lucky to survive a week at the women's facility.

She licked dry lips. "No. I don't want to go there."

Wanda looked grimly satisfied. "Good. Then you're going to work with me to stay out, aren't you? You're going to follow the rules and not violate them, right?"

FOUR

TAMARA WAS SHAKEN LONG after Wanda left her room. She remained in her room, listening for Wanda's departure. The probation officer stayed and talked with Mrs. Henson. Was she pumping Mrs. Henson for information? Telling her what all of Tamara's rules were and the tidbits she had learned in the interview? Reminding her that she was responsible for the baby's safety? It was a long time before Tamara heard the front door close again. She didn't go down to talk to Mrs. Henson.

She lay with her face buried in her pillow, remembering things as they had been the previous year. There had been good things. Her excitement over having a real friend. Playing on the volleyball team. Hot showers. Nita and Deshawn, eager to play the role of big sisters and to help her with her clothes, makeup, and hair, as if she were just a regular sister. She thought of how Mrs. Henson had visited her at juvie and kept returning, in spite of Tamara's anger and instability. Now they would be able to talk to each other without the presence of a guard, able to say and do whatever they pleased. Tamara could be part of a family, if she could just follow the rules to avoid being sent back to juvie. Or to the women's prison.

She hadn't realized how late it was when she heard the front door open and heard several people arrive. Tamara rolled over and looked at the clock on her bedside table. School was out. It would soon be suppertime. Tamara sat up and rubbed her face, making sure it was free of sweat and tears. She heard girls' voices downstairs, so she figured Nita and Deshawn would be up to greet her in short order.

She was right. There were footsteps on the stairs, and then a quick knock on the door. Nita's perfectly plucked eyebrows and classic Mexican features peered through the crack. "You up, Tamara?" She broke into a grin when she saw Tamara standing beside the bed. "How are you doing, girl? Oh, it's good to see you again!" She opened the door the rest of the way and entered. Deshawn was close on her heels, smiling her brilliant white smile, cornrows cascading around her dark face.

Nita stopped short of Tamara and made a little gesture, reaching her arms wider. An invitation for a hug, a query whether it was okay. Tamara swallowed and braced herself, putting her arms out. Nita pulled her into a vigorous hug, pressing her cheek against Tamara's and giving her a squeeze; then she let go. Tamara was relieved it hadn't lasted too long. She didn't know what she would do if Nita held it uncomfortably long. Was it acceptable to pull away? Did it have to be mutual, timed so they both withdrew at the same time? Tamara hadn't ever had any friends who had hugged in greeting. She looked at Deshawn, ready for a hug from her as well. Deshawn was less ardent, reaching around Tamara's shoulders with one arm, not squashing her. Tamara nodded and stepped back, trying to hold a smile steady on her face.

"It's good to see you again too. It's good to be back."

"Missus said she was going to get you back," Deshawn said.

"She kept saying it... I didn't know if she could! But here you are!"

"I wouldn't have thought it," Tamara agreed. "I didn't think there was any way I was making parole this time. After everything that happened..."

"You've had some adventures," Nita chimed in. She rubbed Tamara on the back. "Man... it's just so good to see you!"

Tamara nodded, not sure what else to say.

"We're supposed to go back down to set the table and help get dinner on," Deshawn advised. "You coming?"

"Yeah, sure." Tamara was relieved to have something to do. It wouldn't be so awkward if she had a way to keep her hands busy.

Nita ran her hand along the rail of the crib as she walked by it. She looked at Tamara, eyes twinkling. "And you've got a little one of your own this time? When is he coming?"

"Uh... tomorrow, I think. Missus didn't exactly say."

"I'll bet he's just the cutest. Does he have your beautiful hair?"

Tamara ran her fingers through her limp blond locks. It would look better once she'd had a chance to condition it and use the blow-dryer and curling iron, like Deshawn had shown her the last time. It was impossible to keep nice in prison, with the harsh, electric-orange shampoo that looked like it had been shipped from a nuclear facility and nothing but a comb to style it. Nobody in prison cared. They all looked equally drab and pitiful.

"I don't know what he looks like."

"Babies change so fast," Nita allowed. "Their hair and eyes can change after they're born too, you never know what they're going to look like after a few months."

There really wasn't any reason for Tamara to point out that she'd hardly even looked at the baby when he was born and that she hadn't seen him since. Nita probably already knew that. She was just being polite and giving Tamara an excuse for not knowing what her own child looked like.

She didn't say anything as they went back down to the main floor and got to work. Mrs. Henson passed out jobs and everyone pitched in. Soon the table was set, a salad and vegetables prepared, and a couple of pots bubbled on the stovetop. Deshawn looked at her watch.

"Can I put a load of laundry in? Nobody's going to need to shower until later. Tamara, you weren't going to, were you?"

Tamara shook her head. A hot shower sounded like a wonderful idea, but she could wait. Deshawn headed for the stairs. "You need anything washed, Nita?"

Nita shrugged. "Just whatever's in the hamper... or on the floor." She made a face at Tamara, then glanced over her shoulder to where Mrs. Henson was writing out a grocery list. "I *sometimes* don't get them all the way to the hamper..."

"Sometimes?" Mrs. Henson echoed, not even looking up from her list.

Nita giggled. She grabbed Tamara's hand. "Come on. You can pick out some clothes to put in your closet and free up some space in ours. Tell us everything that has happened since you left."

Tamara went with her, but with no intention of telling the other girls everything that had happened to her. The year since she had last been released on parole had been... eventful. Too traumatic to discuss casually with girl friends. So, she didn't give any details while they went through the closet and drawers in the girls' room, pulling out the items that caught Tamara's eye. The room was so overstuffed with clothes, it was like having free rein in a department store.

Nita paused when the front door opened, cocking her head to listen. Tamara listened to the footsteps climbing the stairs. "That's Dirk," Nita offered. "He's new. He wasn't here last time you were out, right?"

Tamara shook her head. "No. Harry was still here."

"Oh, Harry," Nita sighed. "I miss him!"

"Doesn't he still come visit?"

"Yeah. But it's not the same as having him here. He was always so handy if we needed something done. Or a listening ear that wasn't, you know, a parent. We get him over for dinner sometimes, but it's not the same as when we had him here."

"Yeah. That makes sense."

Tamara wondered as she flipped through some blouses hung on the doorknob how it was Nita knew which of the boys was home. Dirk wasn't the only boy living with the Hensons. Unless Mrs. Henson had forgotten to tell Tamara about the most recent changes.

The front door opened again, and this time was shut so hard that it shook the windows in their frames. The feet that made their way up the stairs sounded like they were wearing combat boots.

"And that's Jason," Deshawn observed. She and Nita exchanged a look and shook their heads. "Jesse should be home soon, then we'll eat."

Tamara pulled out a blue shirt. She held it up to herself, eyeballing the size. It had been a year since she'd been able to pick out what she wanted to wear. And three years before that. Four years of orange day uniforms and pink nights. The blue was soothing to look at. The cut might be generous on her, but should look okay.

"You like?" Nita asked. "That's a great color for you."

Tamara nodded. "I think I'll try it on. Then... maybe I'll take a break until we eat."

She appreciated the friendliness of her two foster sisters, but found it challenging to be around both of them, trying to be social and say and do the right things, for more than a few minutes at a time. They were both so high-energy, Tamara felt like they were sucking the life out of her. If she were going to make it through supper without any problems, she was going to need some time to breathe and regroup first.

"Take these," Nita reminded her, piling the hangers full of clothes that they had picked out into Tamara's arms. "Then you have a few things to choose from and we'll have a little more space."

But looking around the room, it didn't look like Tamara had made even a dent in the stores of clothing.

* * *

Tamara had a good half-hour before supper, which helped her to calm her body down a little. With things so different from juvie, everything she did seemed to take more energy. She had to make choices. She had to think about her interactions with the others in the family. All of the schedules and routines were different, pulling her attention ten different ways. She had to keep telling herself it was good. It was a nice place to be. Safe and secure. But she felt like she had to be constantly vigilant.

"Hey."

Tamara pulled her face out of her hands and looked at the door, where Deshawn was poking her head in.

"Oh... what? Is it supper?"

"Yeah. Missus called. Come on down."

Tamara rubbed her temples and stood. "Coming."

Deshawn nodded and let Tamara trail behind her. The kitchen and dining room were bustling with last-minute activity. Tamara remembered the first time she had been there, how it had felt like a whole mob of people.

Jesse, Mr. Henson, still looking boyish with his short red hair, smiled at Tamara in greeting.

"The prodigal has returned," he declared. "Kill the fatted calf."

"What?"

He chuckled and didn't try to explain. "Come find a seat. Right down the end there," Jesse pointed out the corner he wanted Tamara to take. Tamara looked at the high chair. The next day when she sat there for supper, she would have the baby beside her. Was he old enough to sit in a high chair and eat? Or would she have to give him a bottle before supper, so he'd be quiet and give the family some peace and quiet? Tamara tried to swallow the lump in her throat and took her seat.

Jason and Dirk fought their way over to the chairs on the opposite side of the table. Tamara remembered Jason. Dark skin, short hair, taller than she remembered. They hadn't exactly been on friendly terms, but Tamara didn't have anything against him. They had just been living very different lives.

The boys pushed and shoved each other, competing for attention. Dirk was white, a handsome boy around Tamara's age. Someone she might have been interested in getting to know in another time and place. But he was also a foster brother, so even if she had the time and energy for a relationship, he was out of bounds.

They eventually settled into the chairs. Dirk looked across the table at Tamara and looked surprised, as if he hadn't known someone new was coming to the house.

"Oh, hi," he said with a cool casualness that was obviously put on.

"Hi."

"Dirk, this is Tamara," Jesse introduced. "Tamara, Dirk. You remember we told you she was here for a few weeks last year?" Jesse reminded Dirk. "All of us have met Tamara before, other than you."

"You're the one with the baby," Dirk said. He gave a laugh. "Well, lots of the girls who come through here have babies, I guess. But yeah, I guess they did say they were expecting you." Dirk looked around. "Where is the baby? Sleeping?"

"He'll be coming tomorrow," Mrs. Henson advised. "We

wanted to at least give Tamara a night to catch her breath. And you can never actually be sure when things will happen with the juvenile facility. Sometimes they take a day or two longer than expected."

Tamara nodded. She looked around at the dishes on the table, not wanting to look at all of their faces. She needed to just take it slowly and not get overwhelmed.

"Cool. It's a boy? How old?"

Tamara closed her eyes and shook her head.

"I think maybe Tamara needs a minute," Mrs. Henson said. "Let's give her a bit of breathing space for a minute."

Dirk stopped asking questions and the dining room got too quiet for an awkward minute. Then everyone started talking again.

"Do you need anything, Tamara?" Mrs. Henson asked, leaning closer to her. "Your meds?"

"No. I'm fine," Tamara snapped. She was irritated that Mrs. Henson would mention her meds in front of the others. She wasn't sick. She wasn't having an episode. There was nothing wrong with her. She just didn't want to be interrogated.

Soon, Mrs. Henson started passing dishes around. Tamara wasn't sure how much she could eat. She had eaten her lunch late, and with the claustrophobic feeling of having everyone sitting around the table, her stomach felt tight and heavy. She took a little bit of each of the dishes and then looked at the little mounds of food on her plate, trying to decide what to have. Her inertia lasted until Nita gave her a little nudge, indicating that everyone was watching her, wondering why she was sitting there like a statue. Tamara forced herself to scoop up a forkful of peas and to put them in her mouth.

The burst of fresh, sweet flavor surprised her. They occasionally had peas at juvie as their vegetable of the day, but they were mushy, tasteless things from a can, usually stirred into a stew. The peas tasted like they used to on the farm, when she lived with Gram. Tamara chewed and swallowed and had another bite. She was oblivious to the conversations going on around her until raised voices from across the table demanded her attention.

"I didn't have anything to do with it!" Jason was shouting. "Do you think I pay any attention to rumors at school? You could be dating half the cheerleaders, for all I know. Why would I care?"

"You're the one spreading the rumors," Dirk insisted. "You think I don't know that? You're jealous because they pay attention to me and they don't give you a second look!"

"Boys," Jesse attempted to intervene. His voice was pitched to be low and calming. "Let's just cool it a little, okay...? We're trying to have dinner here, we don't need to have—"

"I didn't do anything!" Dirk shouted at Jesse. "I'm just sitting here minding my own business! He's the one who brought it up! He's the one causing all this trouble for me at school—"

"Dirk," Mrs. Henson tried as well. "It's okay. We can talk about it and sort things out later, okay? Let's not let a little disagreement ruin dinner for everyone."

"Why is everyone picking on me?" Dirk's voice was aggrieved. He jumped to his feet. For a moment, Tamara thought he was going to flip the dining table into her and the other girls' laps, much like Tamara had done to Lewis in juvie. But his hands didn't close around the edge of the table. Instead, he whirled around and left, knocking his chair over with a clatter. He stormed off up the stairs and to the boys' bedroom, slamming the door when he got there.

Tamara sat there, her heart hammering in her throat, not sure how to react.

"It's okay," Mrs. Henson soothed. "Just a little temper tantrum. He'll be fine in a few minutes."

Jason was shoveling food into his mouth, but Tamara caught his self-satisfied expression. She tried to release her death-grip on her plate. She could relax. No one was going to flip over the table. It was just a minor argument. Just a skirmish in the house full of hormonal teens. Everyone else went on eating as if nothing had happened.

"I suppose I should go talk to him," Jesse said, laying his fork down.

Mrs. Henson shook her head. "Give him a few minutes to cool down." She looked across the table at Jason. "You want to tell us exactly what happened at school today?"

Jason shrugged and chewed a large mouthful of casserole. He swallowed it down. "I don't know why he thinks I had anything to do with it. I got nothing to do with his social life. If he's got girl trouble..." He gave a little snort of derision. "It's got nothing to do with me."

"I just wonder what happened to set this off."

"He's a sensitive little cupcake—"

"Jason," Jesse warned, "that's not helpful..."

"We should be supporting each other," Mrs. Henson agreed. "I wish the two of you would make an effort to get along together."

"I'll make an effort to get along with him when he gets his head out of his—"

"Jason!"

Jason shook his head and stuffed his mouth full of potatoes. He chewed through them for a few minutes. "It's not like with the girls," he said, nodding toward Nita and Deshawn. "We're not going to get all buddy-buddy. We don't like each other. He's a stupid, self-centered white boy and he's got no idea what real hardship looks like. He's got no idea what life has been like for me and the kind of crap I have to put up with at school. He thinks his little problems are so awful and that he's the center of the universe—"

"Okay." Jesse stopped him. "Let's just stop there. You guys don't have to be best friends. You're both very different, that's obvious. But it's time for this rivalry to end. It isn't about who's had a worse life or who's been here the longest. You can do better."

Jason scowled. He scraped together the last forkful of food from his plate and looked around at the dishes on the table. "Is there dessert?"

FIVE

TAMARA HADN'T SLEPT WELL. It wasn't because the bed wasn't comfortable. Tamara didn't know how many girls had slept on the mattress over its lifetime in the Henson home, but it was still thick and supportive, nothing like the thin, lumpy slabs on the bunks at juvie. She'd spent many nights trying to find a way to get comfortable with her hip grinding into the bunk platform or her ear pulsing with pain. When she woke for the reveille bell in the morning, her body was often stiff and sore, her joints swollen.

Maybe it was the unfamiliar comfort of the bed that made her so restless. Maybe it was the dim light from the street making the baby crib glow palely in the darkness.

Her stomach clenched in a tight ball, sick with anticipation. Mrs. Henson had talked her into agreeing to parent the baby. She had rightly guessed that the only way Tamara was going to get out on parole was if they pointed out the benefit to the baby. Tamara needed to pay society back by nurturing the life she had brought into the world. It was her one chance for restitution. To redeem herself in society's eyes. But Tamara had no actual desire to see her baby or to raise him. The pregnancy and the birth of her son was a cruel joke fate had played on her. It was not something she had sought; in fact, it was something she had done everything in her power to avoid.

Night marched inexorably on and eventually the room began to brighten. Tamara's body had moved from restlessness to exhaustion, unable to doze for more than a few minutes at a time. Finally, she couldn't lie in bed any longer. She looked at the clock—just in time for the reveille bell at juvie—and got out of bed.

First one out of bed, she could take a few minutes to have a hot shower and to lather up her hair with something other than neon orange shampoo that smelled like floor cleaner. She took the hair dryer and curling iron out of the bathroom with her, so she could do her hair without tying up the bathroom for the next person who wanted it.

By the time she was done fiddling with her hair and deciding what to wear, her stomach was growling angrily for food. Her entire morning routine at juvie—shower, pulling on a clean uniform, and running her comb or fingers through her hair—took a total of about five minutes. Her stomach protested having to wait so long for breakfast.

Coffee was already on and Jesse was reading his morning paper. He looked up from it to greet Tamara.

"You know where everything is, right? Just give me a shout if you can't find what you're looking for."

"Yeah, thanks."

She went about quietly getting her breakfast ready. She didn't need a lot, but she needed something.

As Tamara was eating a bowl of cold cereal, Mrs. Henson made her way into the kitchen, dropping a laundry basket at the top of the stairs to be done later and stopping at the little writing desk to make a few notes in her planner before getting to the coffee.

"Morning, Tamara, sleep well?"

Tamara swallowed a mouthful of cereal. "Uh... it's a real nice bed, but... I was pretty restless."

"I would imagine so. Looking forward to getting that sweet little boy of yours today?"

Tamara grimaced. "No."

Mrs. Henson gave her a sympathetic smile. "It's normal to be nervous about it. You don't need to feel guilty about being anxious."

"Uh-huh."

"We're all here to help you. You won't be on your own. We can show you what you need to do."

"I know what to do. I've taken care of babies before."

A silence fell over the room. Jesse looked up from the newspaper at his wife. Neither of them said anything.

Tamara couldn't eat anything else. She went to the garbage to dispose of what was left of her breakfast.

* * *

She was back upstairs when the doorbell rang. Tamara didn't move. She heard Mrs. Henson answer the door, her excited tones, her call from the bottom of the stairs. "Tamara, come on down!"

Her stomach a lead weight, Tamara forced herself to go down the stairs.

It was Mrs. Arbiter, the same social worker who had picked Tamara up from juvie. She'd been hoping it would be someone she didn't know.

"Here he is," Mrs. Henson sang out.

Tamara focused on the baby carrier at Mrs. Arbiter's feet. Her baby. The baby that she'd been sentenced to take care of for the foreseeable future. She no longer saw him as something evil, a threat to her, but she knew the reality. She'd taken care of three children. Two of them were dead. And she had twice tried to kill the baby as he'd been growing inside her. That didn't bode well for her ability as a mother or caregiver.

"Come and meet him," Mrs. Arbiter invited.

Tamara dragged her feet like she was wading through wet concrete. She bent down to examine the infant. He was foreign to her. His face had changed since he'd been born. He had round, full cheeks and downy black hair. His eyes had changed from baby blue to a dark brown. He looked at her with interest, waving his fists and burbling.

"Hey, little guy," Tamara said softly. She knew she should reach out and pick him up, show some maternal attraction, but she didn't. She just crouched there, looking at him, afraid to do anything.

"His name is Oliver," Mrs. Arbiter said.

Tamara shot from her crouch to a standing position, looking at Mrs. Arbiter in shock. "What? Who named him that?"

"Well, the child had to have a name and you wouldn't pick one out."

"Oliver?"

"If you don't like it, you can always change it, but that's what he's accustomed to right now."

Tamara staggered blindly to the couch and fell into the seat. Mrs. Henson sat down beside her, putting a hand on her back and peering into her face.

"Tamara? What's wrong? What is it?"

"Olivia... that's..." Olivia. Livy. Vernon. "Olivia Vernon and Sly... they were the ones who..." She cast her eyes toward the baby, trying to block out the memories that flooded through her brain. The night Sly had assaulted her. They had pinned her in the bed between them and she'd been unable to defend herself. "Olivia Vernon and Sly," she repeated, unable to move beyond their names. What kind of cruel joke was it to name her baby after her abductors? She saw the baby's dark eyes and dark hair and thought of Sly's features. Vernon's name and Sly's face. How was Tamara ever going to be able to look at the baby without reliving what they had done to her?

Tamara held her arm across her stomach, trying to keep her breakfast down. Mrs. Henson looked at Tamara, then at the baby and Mrs. Arbiter, gradually grasping what Tamara was trying to tell her.

"Olivia is the name of the woman who took you hostage," Mrs. Henson said.

Tamara nodded confirmation.

"And her partner, is he the one who...?" Mrs. Henson nodded to the baby.

Tamara nodded again, arm tightening over her stomach.

"What a horrible coincidence," Mrs. Henson sympathized. "But you have to remember, he's a completely different person. He isn't either of them. He's just an innocent baby. If you want to call him something different, you can. It can be legally changed down the line. Or you could give him a nickname. Call him Olly or call him by his middle name. Or just Bug or something affectionate. A lot of babies have nicknames. They take a while to grow into their names."

"Okay."

"Do you want to hold him?" Mrs. Arbiter asked.

Mrs. Henson shot her a look. Tamara appreciated it. She wasn't feeling anywhere near being able to hold the baby.

"Just... I need a few minutes. Can I..." Tamara looked for an excuse to leave the room. "I just need to use the bathroom. I'll be right back."

The two women made no objection. Tamara hesitated between using the bathroom by the back door or the one upstairs. She decided she needed the distance and maybe to be able to sneak into her room for a few minutes to calm down, so she mounted the stairs and left the baby with the horrible name behind.

Did she really have to take him? Was it part of her terms of parole that she had to look after him or, now that she was out, could she just say no and live her own life without having to worry about taking care of someone else? Would they send her back to prison if she didn't follow through on her agreement to parent the baby?

She cupped cold water in her hands and splashed her face. She no longer cared about the makeup and hair she had prepared so carefully. She didn't care what she looked like. No one else cared what she looked like. Mrs. Arbiter and Mrs. Henson would not be judging how good a mother she was by her makeup.

The shock of the cold water helped to still the flashbacks. Tamara tried to focus on something calming. She stared at the picture of a sailboat on the wall and tried to imagine what it would be like to sail out on the ocean on a calm day and hear nothing but the noise of the waves and the sea birds. She stared at the white sail against the clear blue sky and tried to slow her breathing. Dr. Sutherland was always walking her through visualization exercises, trying to teach her how to calm her anxiety with the power of positive thinking. Tamara let the water run to drown out any other noises.

She was afraid that any minute they would come knocking on the bathroom door, demanding that she hurry up and take care of the baby, but they didn't.

Tamara wasn't sure how much time had passed before she finally left the bathroom and headed back down to the living room where the women and the baby awaited. She looked at them, waiting for the recriminations for abandoning her baby there while she just wasted time, but neither of them criticized her. Tamara breathed through her mouth, pushing back the angry replies she had ready. She looked at Mrs. Henson, who gave her an encouraging nod, and then back to Mrs. Arbiter.

"Ready?" Mrs. Arbiter asked.

"I don't know."

"Let's give it a try, shall we?"

Tamara didn't get any closer. Mrs. Arbiter bent over and pushed the carry-handle back, unbuckled the straps, then gently slid her hands under the baby and lifted him out of the carrier. Tamara tensed, waiting for him to cry. She remembered his deep, hoarse cry from the hospital. It had gotten under her skin like fingernails on the blackboard, making her panic that much worse. But he didn't cry. He looked around with interest and, when he saw Mrs. Arbiter's face, his expression blossomed into a gummy smile. The testy social worker smiled back at him, her expression softening.

"Hello, little man," she greeted. "How would you like to meet your mommy? Come on over here, Tamara. Sit down with me."

Tamara took the long way around the room to sit on the couch near Mrs. Arbiter. Mrs. Arbiter adjusted her hold on the baby to turn him toward Tamara. The baby's eyes met Tamara's and he gave another big smile and a deep chortle. Tamara couldn't help laughing in response.

"He has such a funny voice."

"It's very deep for a baby. Very unique," the social worker agreed. She inched closer to Tamara, not making her take the baby, but clearly intending to move things along.

Tamara swallowed and took a strangled breath.

"There's your mommy," Mrs. Arbiter told the baby in a soft voice. "Say hi, mommy."

Tamara wasn't sure whether Mrs. Arbiter was telling the baby to say hi to Tamara or Tamara to say hi to the baby, but since the baby was too young to talk, Tamara took it as an instruction to her.

"Uh... hi, there," she whispered, looking into the baby's face.

He was very different from the Baker girls. They had all been blond and fair and the Bakers dressed them in very feminine dresses, pink lacy things that were bound to get spilled on or spit up on in the first ten minutes. Tamara's baby had dark features and he was dressed in a dark blue t-shirt and fat baby sweatpants with snaps on the insides of the legs. He looked at her intently, animated whenever she met his eyes. Tamara gave a little smile in response.

Mrs. Arbiter lifted the baby up and set him into Tamara's lap. She instinctively clutched at him, not wanting him to fall. Mrs. Arbiter let go.

For an instant, Tamara experienced a whiteout. Not a blackout, where everything went dark and she couldn't remember what had happened afterward. Instead, everything flashed brighter and there was a loud buzzing in her ears like white noise that drowned out anything the women said to her. Tamara closed her eyes, trying to reset her brain. It was okay. It was okay for her to be holding the baby. He wasn't crying or fussing. She wasn't angry and overwhelmed. All she was doing was holding a baby in her lap.

"Tamara?"

Tamara looked over at Mrs. Henson, who was looking at her inquiringly.

"What? What is it?"

"Are you okay? I was asking you what you wanted to call him. Did you want to try out a different name?"

Tamara looked at the baby's face, trying to imagine what name matched his face and personality. The Bakers had always called their children by their real names. Corinne, Julie, Amy. No silly nicknames. Sybil had called her little sister Boo, for no reason apparent to Tamara. She had a bad feeling about taking the baby's name away. It seemed like it would be a bad omen. She was the one who had refused to name him when he was born. She would have to deal with the consequences.

"Olly," she said finally. "I guess I'll try that out."

* * *

For a long time, they sat and visited in the living room. Tamara appreciated that the two women didn't rush her into anything. Mrs. Arbiter could have dumped the baby on her and left. Mrs. Henson could have forced her to start taking her job seriously, giving her immediate full responsibility for the baby boy in a sink-or-swim proposition. But instead, everyone seemed to be of the opinion that it was better for Tamara to take her time and to get used to it gradually. They chatted while Tamara held Olly in her lap, getting to know his face and the way he reacted to her when she smiled or talked to him. The way that he would get agitated if she looked away from him and didn't give him the attention he wanted.

When he started to fuss, Tamara automatically looked around for a diaper bag. She'd taken care of babies before. She knew what she was doing.

Mrs. Arbiter had the diaper bag near her, and at Tamara's look, she picked it up and put it between them on the couch. Tamara moved things around and pulled a bottle out. It was already prepared and didn't need to be mixed. It was slightly cool from the fridge, where it had obviously been stored until Mrs. Arbiter had picked Olly up from his foster family. Tamara glanced over at Mrs. Arbiter.

"It doesn't have to be heated up, does it?" she asked. "He's big enough I can just give it to him like this?"

Mrs. Arbiter nodded. "Yes, that's fine," she agreed.

Tamara snuggled Olly into the crook of her arm and he took the nipple of the bottle eagerly.

"Sh, not so fast," Tamara told him. "You'll get gas."

He was too little to understand her words, but she thought that maybe he did relax and slow down a bit. Still, the bottle was drained in a few minutes. Tamara put Olly up to her shoulder, patting his back and rubbing it. She stopped to look for a flannel burp cloth or receiving blanket in the diaper bag in case he spit up.

"You look like an old pro," Mrs. Henson said.

"I told you, I've done this before."

Mrs. Henson and Mrs. Arbiter looked at each other.

"Yes," Mrs. Henson agreed.

No words passed between her foster mother and her social worker, but Tamara understood the message without any words. Mrs. Henson couldn't get casual in her supervision because Tamara knew how to feed and burp a baby. She needed to pay close attention to Tamara's mental state and to be sure she didn't do anything to harm him. The danger wasn't that Tamara didn't know how to take care of a baby, but that it might become too much for her, that she would become too frustrated or her psychosis would come back due to the stress, and she would do something to intentionally harm him.

None of them could let that happen again.

SIX

W HEN THE GIRLS GOT home from school, they immediately wanted to see the baby and to know all about him. Tamara had put him down for a nap in the crib, but he was starting to stir, so she obligingly picked him up and showed him to Nita and Deshawn.

"Oh, isn't he just the cutest little thing!" Nita exclaimed. "What a precious baby boy! He looks a little bit Hispanic to me." She lowered her voice, "Is his daddy Hispanic?"

Tamara coughed, trying to come up with an answer. The girls obviously didn't know many details about how she had gotten pregnant with Olly in the first place. To them, he was just a baby, not the result of a traumatic assault.

"I dunno," she said finally. "His hair and eyes were dark."

Vernon had looked more Hispanic than Sly, but she couldn't judge what Sly's ethnicity was just by looking at him. His skin was pale, but that didn't mean he was Caucasian.

"Well, I think he's just a cutie," Nita said, blowing a raspberry on Olly's cheek and making him laugh. "I could just eat him up!"

"I want a turn too," Deshawn reminded them. "You have to let me hold him."

Nita gave him a few more cuddles and talked baby nonsense to him, then reluctantly passed him on to Deshawn. Deshawn pressed her cheek against the baby's silky hair. "He smells so sweet. It would almost be worth getting pregnant to have one of my own."

"He won't smell so sweet after a stinky diaper," Nita laughed. "They don't stay that way, you know."

Deshawn looked at Tamara's face. "Oh." She pressed her fingers to her cheek as if it were hot. "I'm sorry, Tamara. I shouldn't have said that. I was just being silly..."

Tamara ground her teeth and did her best to shrug and look unbothered by Deshawn's thoughtless comment.

"No, really. I'm sorry, Tamara. I know you didn't have an easy time when you were pregnant with him. It was a stupid thing to say."

"Didn't have an easy time?" Tamara snapped back. For a moment, she was too stunned to find words to express her outrage. "You think I just didn't have an easy time? It was hell having him grow inside me! I lost my mind. I tried to kill myself. I tried to kill him. I tried to rip myself open to kill him, did you not get that?"

Deshawn looked hurt. Tamara knew she should stop, but she was so furious at Deshawn just brushing her experience off as a tough pregnancy that she couldn't stop the waves of rage.

"No," Deshawn protested, her eyes wide. "I... I didn't know, Tamara."

Tamara stopped, her mouth open mid-rant.

Nita shook her head in agreement. "They didn't tell us," she said. "Missus never gave us any details. Just said that you weren't feeling well. That things weren't going very well."

Mrs. Henson had tried to protect Tamara's privacy. But in doing so, she had left the girls with the wrong impression. Tamara's anger drained away. She sat down on the edge of the bed, deflated by this revelation.

"I thought she told you."

"No, sweetie, never any details."

Tamara shook her head. She didn't know where to begin. The girls should know her history, so that they knew what to watch for. So they could help watch Tamara and keep the baby safe.

"When I get pregnant... I get psychosis. Things are different... I can't tell what's real from what's not. I get... I..." She shook her head, unable to tell her foster sisters how she had killed the two Baker children. But of course, they knew that already. When she had been on TV because of Amy's kidnapping, most of the story had come out. Nita and Deshawn knew she had killed the two children. "That's what happened... before."

"I thought that was because they were abusing you," Deshawn said. She looked down at Olly, rocking him back and forth. "I thought it was... retaliation."

Tamara felt sick. But she couldn't deny it. She no longer knew what her motivations had been. She didn't know how much had been carefully reasoned out and how much of it had been psychosis. How much had been to get back at the Bakers, how much to protect the babies from further abuse, and how much was pure, unreasoning rage. It was like a recipe she had lost. She didn't know the breakdown of the ingredients anymore.

Nita stroked Olly's hair as Deshawn held and rocked him. "What's his name? We can't just keep calling him baby!"

"Olly," Tamara offered, glad to have something that was easy to answer.

"Olly!" Deshawn squealed. "Isn't that just the most darling name? Oh, he is just too precious, Tamara. We're going to have so much fun spoiling him."

"You can't spoil him," Tamara said. "Then he won't behave. You can't just give them everything they want."

"Maybe we won't spoil him all the time. But we're his aunties! We have to do something!"

Tamara looked at Nita. "Is she like this with all of them?" she demanded. The Hensons specialized in teen moms, so they must have babies there a lot of the time.

"The girl is baby crazy," Nita admitted. "I'm telling you, if she wasn't on the shot, she'd be—"

At Deshawn's wide-eyed look, Nita caught herself.

"Uh. I mean... yeah. Deshawn loves babies. She's the best auntie in the world, aren't you?"

Deshawn smiled sunnily at this compliment. "I am," she agreed. "And you're the second-best auntie."

Nita chuckled. "You got it, girl. We are the two best aunties in the world, and we are going to spoil little Olly rotten." She flashed a grin at Tamara. "Just a little. Every baby needs to be spoiled rotten sometimes."

Tamara shook her head. She didn't know what to think about how crazy Nita and Deshawn were over the baby. Tamara wanted nothing to do with him. She couldn't fathom what it would feel like to actually want a baby. To hold a baby in her arms and long for one like Deshawn was.

Tamara had never felt that way.

* * *

Tamara looked at the clock as Olly appeared to be getting tired and ready to fall asleep again. Holding him against her shoulder, she went to find Mrs. Henson, who was in the kitchen making a list or writing a letter or report of some kind.

"Do you think I should put him down for bed?" she asked. "Is he ready to go to sleep, or should I keep him up for a while? Is he just going to nap and then get up again? Or go down for the night?"

Mrs. Henson glanced at her watch. "I don't know his usual schedule, but it's probably getting late enough to try putting him down for the night. He probably doesn't sleep through, though, so be prepared to have to get up and feed and change him."

Tamara looked down at Olly as he gave a big yawn, his dark eyes squeezing shut, a little tear appearing in the corner of one.

"What if he doesn't sleep? What if he only goes to sleep for a little while and then wants to be up again?"

"We'll figure out his schedule in a day or two, and then we'll be able to plan better or try to adjust it a little. For now, just go with the flow. Realize that you need to get attuned to each other's rhythms. You'll be amazed at just how quickly you adjust and are able to anticipate his needs."

Tamara shook her head. "I don't think I'm ever going to be able to do that." She rubbed her eyes and the center of her forehead, pounding with pain. "I didn't sleep good last night and I'm not going to sleep good tonight. Dr. Sutherland said that I might get triggered by being overtired. I need to make sure I get the sleep my body needs."

"Then go lay down now," Mrs. Henson said. "Put him in his crib to sleep and lie down and have a nap. If you wake up later and aren't ready to go to bed yet, that's fine, you can stay up later. But you might as well at least get a nap in now if you're feeling that tired already."

"What if he wakes up?"

"If he wakes up and you can't handle it and need me to help with something, just give me a shout. That's what I'm here for. Okay?"

Tamara wanted Mrs. Henson to say something else. That she would take over for Tamara, or that Tamara didn't have to take care of Olly after all. She took a deep breath, trying to push down the panic bubbling in her chest.

"Okay," she agreed finally.

"Call me if you need me. It's okay."

Tamara nodded. She went back up to her room and jiggled Olly until he was closer to sleep. She laid him down in the crib very carefully, worried about waking him up. But he didn't rouse. Tamara hovered over him for a few minutes to make sure. She stared down at him.

"I don't know if I can do this."

SEVEN

OLLY DID WAKE SEVERAL times in the night, but he didn't get up for good until later in the morning after Tamara's internal reveille alarm had rung. Tamara was lying in bed, wide awake, waiting for him to stir. She was tired and hungry, but she couldn't go back to sleep or get up for breakfast.

Olly started off making a grumbly noise, then moving his arms and legs. Tamara swallowed hard, tense waiting for him to finish waking up. She'd always dreaded Corrine and Julie waking up, knowing they were fussy in the morning and that she had to keep them quiet all day. When Olly started with his loud, hoarse cry, Tamara jumped out of bed and hurried over to the crib. She reached down to pick him up and was suddenly thrown into the past. Instead of Olly in the crib, she saw Julie.

Julie was flaccid and still, her skin gray, the sharp smell of vomit rising into the air. Tamara's guts were tied in knots. She was going to be sick herself. Julie was going to die. It was too late to do anything for her. Unless Tamara could hide her. If she could get rid of the body, keep Mr. Baker and the cops from finding her, maybe she could avoid being sent to prison.

"Tamara?"

Tamara blinked. She turned her head and looked at Mrs. Henson, standing in the doorway.

"Are you all right?" Mrs. Henson asked.

Tamara stared at her, trying to reorient herself in the present.

"Olly's been crying," Mrs. Henson said. "I thought maybe you were still sleeping."

Tamara was reaching out, hands toward Olly, ready to pick him up, as she had been before she'd flashed back to Julie. She focused on him. Olly, not Julie. Dressed in the cute little mail truck jammies the foster mom had sent with him. Tamara closed the distance between her hands and the baby. She felt his bulk under her fingers and picked him up, feeling far removed from herself.

"You're okay?" Mrs. Henson prodded.

"Just tired," Tamara said faintly. "I was up a lot last night."

"Do you need me to feed him, so you can go back to sleep for a while?"

"No. I can't sleep."

Tamara trudged to the door. Mrs. Henson opened it the rest of the way and stepped back. She followed Tamara down the stairs to the kitchen. She stood by as Tamara prepared a bottle for Olly, who was still grumbling, but not full-on crying. Tamara glanced at her, waiting for the criticism to begin. Jesse was in the kitchen with his coffee and newspaper and Tamara watched him with equal wariness. It was just like being back with the Bakers again. Foster mom and dad and the baby Tamara was supposed to be looking after. It was only a matter of time before they were beating her for some slight infraction. For letting Olly cry too long. For falling asleep when she was supposed to be watching him. For putting her hand over his mouth.

Tamara's own stomach felt hollow, a great yawning hole inside her. But she couldn't worry about her own breakfast. She needed to get Olly fed first. Then he would be happy and satisfied for a few minutes, so she could put him down and get something in her own belly.

Olly's cries were getting more urgent again. He'd been comforted by Tamara picking him up, but she was taking too long to get him fed and he was impatient. Tamara tried to jiggle him as she was getting the bottle ready, which only made a bigger mess.

"Take your time," Mrs. Henson suggested. "Nothing is going to happen if he cries for a few more minutes. He's okay. If you want, you can put him in the high chair so that you have both hands free to get the bottle ready. Or I could hold on to him for you."

"I can do it! I'm getting it ready!"

Mrs. Baker would make Tamara put Julie down, so she could discipline Tamara. It was the only time she would ignore the babies crying. Tamara wasn't going to put Olly down. She wasn't going to open herself up to being hurt.

Her movements became jerkier, even more clumsy in her panic. She knocked the filled bottle over, sending formula racing across the counter and dripping off the edge onto the floor. Tamara tried to watch Mr. and Mrs. Henson at the same time. Either one of them could strike. Tears leaked out the corner of her eye and Tamara berated herself for showing them weakness. It would only make her more of a target.

"I'll clean it up!" she told them, her voice louder than she had intended. Not a voice that said she was calm and in control and wasn't a victim. Instead, she had let it communicate her fear. They would smell it like sharks scenting blood in the water. Olly's voice got louder. He was crying in earnest, his face getting red and sweat starting to collect in the hair around his temples.

"Put him in the high chair," Mrs. Henson ordered.

Tamara edged away from her.

"Tamara," Mrs. Henson tried again. "Give him to me."

Tamara didn't obey. "I'll clean it up," Tamara repeated, "and I'll feed him. He's just hungry. Once I feed him, he'll be quiet…"

"I'm not worried that there's anything wrong with him. I'm worried that you're getting so agitated over feeding him. Just let me hold him for you while you get ready."

Tamara refused.

Jesse turned the page of the newspaper. His unexpected movement nearly made Tamara jump out of her skin. She looked from him to Mrs. Henson and back again, assessing threats. Mrs. Henson remained the bigger concern.

"Let me do it," Tamara insisted. "I can do it."

Mrs. Henson took a step toward her. Tamara's grip on Olly tightened. He squawked and squirmed in protest.

"Marion," Jesse spoke without looking at either of them directly, still, by all appearances, engrossed in his newspaper. "Maybe you should just give Tamara some space. Let her handle this her own way."

Mrs. Henson's brows came down. She opened her mouth to argue with him. He was far enough away from her to be out of reach, so he didn't seem concerned about her hitting him. Mrs. Henson closed her mouth.

"Okay," she said finally. "I'll be close by. Just give me a shout if you need me."

She walked out of the room. Tamara breathed out, loosening her grip on the baby. She shot a glance toward Jesse, but he continued to read, not looking at her. Tamara swayed, soothing Olly. His cries quietened and slowed, but he didn't stop, his hunger still unsated. Tamara looked at Jesse again. She glanced toward the door to make sure Mrs. Henson wasn't still hovering there and hadn't changed her mind and decided to come back. Then she wet the dishcloth and started wiping up the milk.

It was another ten minutes before she had everything cleaned up and a full bottle of formula ready for Olly. Tamara's anxiety was soaring, but Jesse hadn't made any move to put his newspaper down to deal with her and Mrs. Henson hadn't returned to the kitchen. Upstairs, the shower went on and there were sounds of movement from both bedrooms. Tamara tipped Olly back and plonked the bottle into his mouth. He was startled and didn't stop crying immediately, milk leaking out of his mouth around the nipple. Then his sobs slowed and stopped as he gave the bottle his attention. Tamara stood there with him, still jiggling and swaying to comfort him, even though he had quieted. She looked over at Jesse, who looked up from his paper.

"There you go," he observed. "That's better, eh?"

Tamara nodded.

"He's fine," Jesse reassured. "It doesn't hurt him to cry. He's not going to starve if you take a few minutes to get his bottle ready."

"I know."

"Then why were you getting so upset?"

Tamara just looked at him. He knew very well why she was worried.

Now that Olly had his bottle, she was free to go back up to her bedroom again. She didn't need to stay in such close proximity to Jesse, putting herself in harm's way. She left the kitchen. Mrs. Henson was sitting in the living room folding laundry.

"Why don't you come sit in here?" she suggested. "If you spend all of your time in your room, you're going to end up feeling lonely and isolated."

Tamara stopped and considered. Mrs. Henson didn't get up. She didn't appear to be angry or upset. Eventually, Tamara decided it was safe. She sat down in the living room in an easy chair across from Mrs. Henson. She rocked slightly, looking down at Olly's peaceful face.

"I didn't mean to make you more upset," Mrs. Henson said. "I was just offering my help."

Tamara didn't trust these overtures. She wasn't sure what Mrs. Henson was planning, but she didn't want to get trapped by her words. She kept her mouth closed and said nothing in response.

"Do you want to tell me how you're feeling?" Mrs. Henson suggested. "If you can help me understand what's going on in your head, we can work together better. I can give better advice and suggestions."

"Just leave me alone. I cleaned up the milk and he's not crying anymore. I did what I'm supposed to."

"You did just fine. I'm not criticizing you. I'd just like to understand what's going through your mind. I don't know what happened in the past, Tamara, but I'd like to understand where you're coming from. You don't need to tell me all of your private thoughts, but could you share a little bit more?"

"What's to understand?" Tamara snapped, making Olly startle. "I'm just trying to do my job like I'm supposed to."

Mrs. Henson went back to folding laundry, letting it go. Tamara gradually started to relax, the tightly-wound coils of stress loosening and relaxing. Jesse finished his breakfast and joined them to say goodbye to his wife before heading off to work.

"Can I get you anything, Tamara? You want your coffee?"

Tamara's stomach felt like a bottomless pit.

"Uh... yeah, coffee would be good," she admitted.

He went back to the kitchen and in a minute returned with a steaming mug for her. He put it on the side table close by so Tamara could help herself.

"Thanks."

"No problem. I'll see you later."

He gave Mrs. Henson a hug and kiss, whispering something to her that Tamara could not hear.

EIGHT

T AMARA, WHERE'S THE BABY?"

Tamara rubbed her eyes drowsily. Why was Mrs. Henson trying to wake her up when she'd just dropped off to sleep? She hadn't previously done that in the weeks since Tamara had arrived.

"Tamara!" Mrs. Henson shook harder. Normally, she was such a gentle woman; the hard grip she had on Tamara's arm was surprising. Tamara tried to pull away.

"I'm up," she said. "I'll get up. Just a second…"

"Tamara, now!" Mrs. Henson was insistent. Her grip hurt. Tamara forced her eyes open and blinked, trying to jump-start the waking up process.

"He's in the crib," Tamara said.

"He's not in the crib. Don't you think that's the first place I'd look?"

Tamara looked over at the crib. A modern design, there were no bars where a baby's head or leg could get stuck, so she couldn't see through the side. She forced herself to roll over and put her feet over the side of the bed. She shuffled over to the crib to confirm what Mrs. Henson had said. Olly wasn't there. Tamara rubbed her sticky eyes and tried to remember.

It was daytime, sunlight streaming through her window. The angle it was filtering through the trees suggested it was late afternoon. Tamara had just lain down for a short nap while Olly slept, exhausted by her child-care responsibilities. How a baby who couldn't even crawl or walk yet could take so much energy, she didn't know.

"I... I think maybe he fell asleep while I was watching TV. He's downstairs, in the living room."

But what was Tamara doing upstairs if the baby had fallen asleep downstairs? She wouldn't hear him wake up.

"He's not in the living room," Mrs. Henson growled. "I would have seen him in the living room."

Tamara made her way toward the bedroom door, starting to grasp that something was wrong. She turned and looked back at her bed to make sure that Olly wasn't there, nestled snugly in the blankets beside where she had lain.

"What do you mean?" she asked faintly.

If Mrs. Henson answered her, Tamara didn't take it in. Alarm bells were starting to ring in her head. Tamara was sleeping in the bedroom and Olly wasn't in the crib. Mrs. Henson said that he wasn't downstairs. There were only so many places that she would have put Olly down to sleep.

She stumbled down the stairs anyway and looked around the living room like Mrs. Henson might have been mistaken. There was no sign of the baby. There was a blanket on the carpet where Tamara had lain him down for some tummy-time that she'd hoped would lead to a nap. But Olly wasn't there. He wasn't sleeping on the couch or anywhere else in the room. Tamara had the urge to begin looking under and behind the furniture, at a loss as to where her baby was.

There was laughter from upstairs. Tamara and Mrs. Henson both looked up toward the source. It was Nita's voice.

"Nita has him," Tamara said with relief.

"She's home from school early," Mrs. Henson said. "I didn't know she was home!"

Mrs. Henson immediately mounted the stairs to go check on Nita and Olly.

Tamara stayed in the living room, rubbing her eyes and trying to get her sluggish brain functioning again. She didn't normally sleep so heavily in the afternoon, but Olly had been teething and fighting a cold over the previous couple of weeks and Tamara was desperately short on sleep.

Mrs. Henson was coming back down the stairs, and Tamara looked up to see Olly in her arms. But he wasn't. Mrs. Henson was looking even more alarmed.

"Nita doesn't have him," she said unnecessarily.

Nita was coming down the stairs behind Mrs. Henson. Her eyes were wide. She had on her Bluetooth headset, and Tamara guessed she had been laughing with a school friend on the phone, not playing with Olly.

"Where is Olly?" Nita asked, looking back and forth between Mrs. Henson and Tamara, clearly baffled.

Tamara looked around the room again. Panic was rising inside her, seething and spreading like steam over water nearly at the boiling point.

"Missus...?" She wanted Mrs. Henson to reassure her. To say that it was all a joke or a test. That she had put Olly in her own bedroom to teach Tamara a lesson. Tamara had left him alone while she slept, and Mrs. Henson was showing her that anything could happen while she slept.

Mrs. Henson stared at Tamara, not cracking. Tamara saw her swallow hard.

"I'm going to call the police. You two start a room-by-room search. Stay together. Don't touch anything. Do you understand?" She looked at Tamara and Nita fiercely. "Do you understand? Stay together. Search every room."

"Okay," Nita agreed. She grabbed Tamara's hand and looked around the empty living room. "Let's start in the back with the bathroom and work our way up."

Tamara let Nita pull her to the back of the house. Olly was, of course, not in the bathroom. He wasn't in the dining room and he wasn't in the kitchen. They'd already checked the living room. Tamara paused at the door to the basement.

"He couldn't be down there," Nita objected.

Tamara remembered a news story she'd seen about a baby picked up with the laundry and put in the washer by her junkie mother, the mistake not discovered until it was too late. She felt nauseated.

"We have to look," she whispered.

Nita conceded, and they went down the basement stairs in single file. How many times had Tamara heard stories of missing children discovered dead in the basement, killed by someone in the home? She couldn't bear to find Olly's still corpse in the basement.

She'd always hated the Hensons' basement. Undeveloped, lit by just a couple of bare bulbs, full of broken furniture, washers and dryers that never worked properly, and with lots of shadowy corners. Her throat constricted painfully, Tamara walked around the basement. She forced herself to open each washer and dryer and check inside, Nita standing behind her and swearing.

"Don't look in there, Tamara. He can't be in there. Tell me he's not in there."

After checking each one, Tamara's knees buckled in relief. She had to hold herself up on one of the washers, trying to breathe and keep from blacking out.

"No. Not here," she confirmed to Nita. Nita sobbed and nodded, tears streaming down her face. Nita was always so upbeat and cheerful. Tamara had never seen her cry.

Fortified with a few deep breaths, Tamara nodded. They went back up to the main floor, then climbed the stairs to the bedrooms. Tamara checked the bathroom. All the while, her brain kept objecting, demanding to know how Olly could be any of those places without her knowing. But she didn't know where he was, so he could be anywhere.

They went into Tamara's room. Nita went immediately to the crib and gazed down into it, sniffling. "Where is he, Tamara?" She wiped at her face with the back of her hand. "What the hell happened?"

"I don't know. I just... I was asleep, and Missus woke me up and wanted to know where he was. I don't know what happened. I was asleep."

Nita shook her head. They looked around the room, even in the closet and under the bed. They went down the hall to Nita's room.

"I was just in there. He's not there."

"We're supposed to check every room together." It all seemed so bizarre, she couldn't wrap her mind around it. The only things she had to cling to were Mrs. Henson's instructions.

Nita hesitated, then pushed her door open and they went into the room together. Tamara looked at the messy beds, closets full of clothes, and mounds of laundry on the floor. A baby could be anywhere. She started moving piles of clothes around, looking desperately for Olly.

"She said not to touch anything," Nita said.

"But he could be..." Tamara stopped. She knew Olly wasn't under any of the piles of clothes. She sniffled and nodded. "Okay."

They crossed the hall to the boys' room, which was a bigger disaster area than Nita's and Deshawn's room. But there was no sign of the baby and no sign either of the boys had been home during the day while Tamara had slept. The room was close and still, not like someone had been in it recently. Tamara did the best she could to look around, but there was no sign of the baby.

"Last room," Nita said reassuringly, and they went down the

hall to the master bedroom. It was tidier, but still lived-in. There was a pile of clothes on an armchair waiting to be put away. There was makeup on the dresser, stacks of books and papers, shoes falling out of the open closet. Tamara caught a glimpse of herself in Mrs. Henson's mirror, white as a sheet, eyes so wide she looked like a little child. One that had been watching ghost movies. She and Nita looked around the room, not expecting to find anything. They didn't. As they finished their search, Tamara could hear a siren getting closer and closer until it pulled up outside the house.

She and Nita went back downstairs to the living room, arriving at the bottom of the stairs as Mrs. Henson opened the door for a couple of police officers.

"You reported a missing child?" one of the officers demanded.

Mrs. Henson nodded, seemingly unable to find her voice for a minute. She motioned for them to enter. She looked out the door searchingly, as if she might find Olly out there. But what would he be doing outside? How could he not be inside?

Tamara studied the officers closely. Would they be able to help? Would they be able to do anything more than Tamara and the others had done, wandering around the house looking for the missing child? One was young with the look of a college student. Open, friendly face. The other was obviously the senior partner, closer to retirement, a face that was deeply lined as if all of his experiences had been etched into it.

"My name is Magrit," the older one introduced himself in a rough, gravelly voice. "And this is Scott. You said in your phone call that a *baby* was missing. How old is the child?"

"He's just a few months old," Mrs. Henson said in a voice that was breaking. "Just... four months."

"Is there any custody issue? Do you know who took him?"

Mrs. Henson looked at Tamara and shook her head. "No."

She continued to shake her head. "No, I have no idea who would do something like that. Do you know, Tamara?"

Tamara bit her lip. "No. No one. There wasn't anyone here. It doesn't make any sense."

Magrit's and Scott's heads swiveled to look at Tamara. They tried to make sense of the situation. "Who is the mother? One of you?"

Tamara raised her hand like she was at school. "Me. He's mine."

They narrowed their focus to her. "You were home alone with him?"

"No, I wasn't alone..."

"Just for a few minutes," Mrs. Henson said, looking guilt-stricken. "Tamara was here, in the living room, looking after Olly. Everything was quiet. I went out for a few minutes to the store. When I came home, Tamara wasn't in the living room anymore. I figured she'd taken Olly upstairs to put him down in his crib for a nap. When it had been a couple of hours, I went to check to make sure everything was okay."

Mrs. Henson looked at Tamara, waiting for her to explain and fill in all of the blanks. Tamara couldn't add anything else.

"The crib was empty. Tamara was sleeping, but Olly wasn't there."

"Have you searched the house?"

"I had Tamara and Nita search while I called 9-1-1."

Magrit looked at the two girls. "You searched the whole house? Everywhere?"

They nodded mutely.

"We didn't touch anything," Nita said. "But he's not here. We looked everywhere."

"The first thing we need to do is make sure," Magrit said. "You'd be amazed the number of missing child calls we get where the child is in the house."

He didn't say, though, whether they found them alive or dead. Tamara couldn't get the horror stories out of her head. The baby in the washing machine. Corpses discarded in basements, garages, and garbage bins. Olly had been right there. What could have happened to him? Who had taken him? Tamara looked at Mrs. Henson and Nita in confusion. What reason could either of them have for taking Olly? Nita would be happy to play with him, but she wouldn't have done something to hurt him. She wouldn't have taken him out of the house or hidden him somewhere.

"I want all three of you to stay in this room," Magrit said sternly. "No going to get coffee or to the bathroom. All three of you stay here. Understood?"

Then, just as Tamara and Nita had done, the policemen toured the house, looking for Olly or some sign of what had happened to him.

"We didn't look outside," Tamara said. "Should we have looked outside? In the yard and the alley?" She couldn't make herself say 'in the garbage bins.' Her mind made a sudden jump back. A year ago, Tamara searching for something else in the shed. Discovering the tortured body of a neighbor's cat. Her first clue that Glock was there, living somewhere close by, keeping tabs on her. Tamara grabbed her stomach. She'd been sick that night. She'd thrown up again and again. But Magrit had told Tamara she couldn't go to the bathroom. She needed to keep her body under control, something she'd never been good at.

"Tamara!" Nita grabbed at Tamara as she doubled over, trying to help control Tamara's descent as her legs gave way.

She just wanted to curl up in a ball and let her mind go somewhere else. She couldn't face the thought of something happening to baby Olly. She couldn't think of him being gone and the bloody, maggoty body of the cat both at the same time. She couldn't connect the two of them together.

Mrs. Henson and Nita helped Tamara over to the couch, murmuring soothing words to her. The police would figure it out.

They would find Olly. It would all be okay. But how could they? If someone had come into the house and taken Olly away, how could they ever find him?

Tamara was barely aware of the police officers walking through the living room, on their way upstairs to the bedrooms as she sobbed on the couch, trying to get some control over her emotions. She hadn't thought that she even liked Olly. She hadn't, at first. But as the days and weeks passed, she found herself growing more attached to him. She felt proud when he did something new, sad and frustrated when he was teething, and she couldn't comfort him. He was becoming a real person to her. She had started to forgive him for his origins and what he had done to her and to think of him as his own person.

The police officers returned to the living room, looking so grim Tamara was sure they were going to tell her they had found Olly's body.

"I need to call in," Magrit said. "We'll need to get some detectives here, get a search started. The earlier the better, in cases like this."

"Cases like what?" Tamara asked.

He turned his eyes on her, assessing her again, trying to classify her as either suspect or victim. "Cases of a missing child," he said simply. "A four-month-old didn't just walk away. We know that someone was involved. Somebody did this."

He left Scott there with them while he made his call in the kitchen, speaking quietly so they couldn't hear him. Tamara didn't want to know what he was saying. She didn't want to know that she was the prime suspect in the disappearance of her own child. She didn't want to hear that he figured the baby was already dead.

Tamara stared at Scott, standing just a few feet away from her, as if she could read him. If she looked hard enough, she would be able to see every thought and every motivation. Whether or not he would be able to solve the case and bring her baby back safe. Her eyes focused on an embroidered badge over his pocket. *This officer is wearing a body camera.* She would have to stay cognizant of the fact that he was filming everything she said and did. Every move she made and word she said was on the record.

"It will be okay, Tamara," Nita said, rubbing Tamara's back.

"How could it be?" Tamara argued. "This isn't right... what could have happened?"

"I don't know."

Magrit returned to the room. He looked around at them all. Looked at his partner to see if he had anything to report. Scott shook his head.

"We didn't look outside," Tamara pointed out. "None of us have looked in the yard... or the shed..."

Mrs. Henson made the connection immediately, turning from pale to green. "Oh, Tamara... don't even think it."

"I'm not," Tamara insisted. "It's just that... someone should look."

Magrit's brow wrinkled. He shook his head. "What's this all about? What is or isn't in the shed?"

Nita looked just as lost as they did. Tamara didn't want to say anything in front of her. She didn't want to give Nita nightmares. Nita hadn't seen the cat. She'd been able to forget what had happened.

"You don't think it's Glock, do you?" Mrs. Henson asked Tamara. It was strange to hear Mrs. Henson call Glock by her nickname. The rest of the adults all called her Spielman, refusing to call her by her street name. Mrs. Henson didn't say 'that girl.' She remembered Glock's name.

"It couldn't be," Tamara insisted. "She's in prison."

"Unless she was released."

"They wouldn't. They wouldn't release her."

"Or she escaped."

"We would have heard. It would have been on the news. Someone would have called."

Mrs. Henson didn't look convinced.

Magrit's face was getting red. "What's this all about? Who is Glock and what does she have to do with all of this? And the shed?"

"Glock Spielman is… someone Tamara knows. She once left a dead cat back there and Tamara discovered it."

This news had a definite effect on Magrit. He hadn't been in a big rush to go outside and check the yard and the shed but, hearing what had happened, he acted quickly.

"We need to check. Is the shed kept locked?"

"There are two sheds. The keys are on the rack at the back door. If someone got into the house, they could get into the sheds."

"Where the cat was, though." Tamara said, her stomach turning queasily, "it wasn't actually in the shed, it was beside, sort of shoved into a pile of junk."

The two policemen left the room again. They didn't warn everybody to stay put this time, but they all did anyway, watching each other and trying not to think horrific thoughts about what fate might have befallen little Olly. Poor little Olly, who was innocent of any crime and had barely begun life. Magrit was talking on his phone as they walked through the kitchen. Calling for current information on Glock Spielman.

They wouldn't have let Glock out. Tamara was sure of it. They knew Glock had been the one who had assaulted Coach McClure, nearly killing him and leaving him with irreversible damage. They wouldn't let her out. And after Vernon's prison break, every facility in the area would have undergone safety audits to make sure the same thing couldn't happen again.

NINE

BY THE TIME MAGRIT and Scott returned to the house, other cars were pulling up to the house. Marked cars, unmarked cars, flashing lights, people in uniform, people in black jackets. Everyone either ignored Tamara and the others or repeated the warnings for them to stay where they were and demanded a recap of how Olly had disappeared.

Tamara kept hoping against hope that one of them would simply find Olly and return with him in their arms. But that didn't happen.

Eventually, the traffic through the living room slowed, and two cops who must have been the detectives assigned to the case sat down with Tamara, Mrs. Henson, and Nita. They introduced themselves gravely as Timmons and Bowen. Tamara was surprised to meet Bowen, a woman, who was apparently the senior of the two of them. It gave Tamara pause; she had never thought that a woman could be a detective or realized that she had that prejudice. And Bowen was not just a detective, but senior over her male partner. She was tall and full-figured, but neatly tailored, with her brown hair pulled back from her face and secured in a professional bun. She leaned in when she spoke, making Tamara feel like she was being included in on some secret.

"I understand how scary this must be for you," she told Tamara. Tamara was pretty sure she had no idea at all what it felt like. "But we're going to figure out what happened. We're going to find your baby for you, okay?"

Tamara nodded. She didn't believe it, but she nodded anyway.

"I understand a search has already been made of the property. We will probably do a couple more. You wouldn't believe how many times children are found hiding in cupboards or places you never would have thought they could squeeze into."

But Olly wasn't a child playing hide and seek. If he were squeezed into a hole or a box, it was because someone had put him there, not because he had crawled in of his own volition.

"We're going to have a K9 unit come in to see if he can pick up a trail. Is there something we can give the dog that would have your baby's scent on it? Something he's worn recently?"

Tamara looked around the living room. She indicated the blanket still on the floor. "That's where he was laying... this afternoon... before..."

"That's great. I'm sure that will be very helpful. Now," Bowen leaned back slightly to take all three of them in at the same time, "we would like to interview each of you separately so we can learn everything you remember without any interruptions or distractions."

She wanted to get their stories separately to see if they all matched up. To see if they contradicted each other.

They all dutifully agreed. What else were they going to say? That they didn't want to talk to the police? That they didn't have anything to say? Of course they would cooperate. They would pretend that they weren't all suspects and hope that something they had to say would lead the police to Olly. Some small details would blow the case wide open, and the police would know exactly where to go and what to do.

"Tamara, I'd like to talk to you. Would you come with me up to your bedroom, and we can talk where it's quiet?"

Tamara nodded. "Yeah. Of course."

She had to show them that she wanted to find her baby. She had to make them believe it. There could be no doubt that the baby was taken from her. To show them that she hadn't done anything to harm him.

She went with Bowen to her bedroom. Bowen had already been through the room once, but she looked around with interest as if it were the first time. She looked into the empty crib.

"Can't be easy, being a young single mom," she commented. Her voice was neutral, not accusatory or buddy-buddy.

"No," Tamara agreed. "But that's why I'm here... Mrs. Henson helps girls out, teaches them how to take care of their babies. I don't have to do everything myself, if I'm tired or over-whelmed."

It wasn't the full story. She wasn't just there so Mrs. Henson could teach her how to take care of her baby. Tamara already had experience taking care of babies. She knew that Bowen would find out, if she didn't know already, that Tamara was a parolee, recently out of juvie, with a record of having killed two children in her care. As much as Tamara wanted to keep that information from her, she knew it wouldn't be possible.

"How have things been going?"

"Uh... okay, I guess." Tamara wasn't sure how to classify her experience thus far. It hadn't been easy. But she'd managed to stay out of prison, which meant she'd done better than her previous parole. Her chest hurt when she realized that Olly's disappearance meant she was going back to prison sooner rather than later.

"Is that what Mrs. Henson and her husband will tell me?"

"I don't know. They tell me I'm doing good, but that doesn't mean I don't screw up. Like you said... it's not easy."

"Tell me about what happened today. You were downstairs watching TV when Mrs. Henson went out to run a quick errand."

"Yeah... Nothing happened, though. I played with Olly a bit and watched TV. He fussed because he's teething and was tired, then he fell asleep."

"Then what happened?"

Tamara tried to break through the fog to remember.

"I... I don't remember. I've been so tired, because he hasn't been sleeping well and it's a lot of work to take care of him. I just... I just had a nap as well."

"In the living room?"

"No... I was sleeping in here. I thought... when Missus came in to wake me up, I thought he was in the crib."

"Did you put him in the crib?"

"I can't remember doing it. But... I wouldn't just leave him downstairs in the living room and come up here to sleep."

"Maybe you didn't want to take the chance of waking him up by picking him up and putting him in the crib."

"Well, yeah... but then I would just close my eyes on the couch. I wouldn't leave him in the living room and come up here to sleep."

"Are you sure that's not exactly what happened?"

"No... sometimes the days are just a blur, everything on autopilot... it will be three o'clock and Clifford is on the TV, and I can't remember what happened since Olly got me up at five in the morning..."

Bowen thought about this, her eyes roving around the room. Did she have kids? Did she understand what it was like to lose big chunks of the day to routine stuff that barely even registered? Surely even in her job, there were times when surveillance or patrolling were so routine that an hour or two passed on autopilot and she couldn't remember any specifics later.

"Are you on any medications, Tamara?"

Tamara took a deep breath. She had known this question was going to come up at some point. She had hoped to delay it as long as possible, but she felt curiously relieved to have it out in the open. Something she wouldn't have to spend energy hiding.

"Yeah," she admitted. Knowing that Bowen would want the exact details, Tamara went to her drawer and pulled the pill bottles out. She handed them to Bowen, remembering how Wanda had taken pictures of the labels and the contents. Bowen looked at the labels and gave no sign of whether she recognized the prescription names.

"What are they for?"

Tamara tapped each one. "Antipsychotic. Anxiety. And... depression, ADHD, PTSD..."

"You don't remember which they are supposed to treat?"

"They're supposed to help with everything. But... they don't seem to do much."

"You don't think they're working?"

Rather than taking a photo, Bowen painstakingly wrote each one down in her notepad, adding her own notations.

"I don't know. Doesn't seem like they make much difference."

"And..." Bowen was staring down at the page in her notebook, "an antipsychotic...?"

"I had some trouble when I was pregnant with Olly." Tamara shrugged, minimizing it. 'Some trouble,' like she's just had insomnia or trouble concentrating on her schoolwork. Like it wasn't full-blown psychosis that had taken over her entire life. "It's gone now, but the doctor wanted me to continue taking low-dose antipsychotics just in case... if it might be triggered by stress or something else."

"But you haven't been having any symptoms?"

"No."

"The stress of taking care of an infant hasn't triggered anything?"

"No. It's been hard, but I haven't had any hallucinations."

Bowen shook the third bottle. "If these don't help, then that means you're still having depression and focus issues."

Tamara opened her mouth, looking for a way to deny or minimize it. Then she shook her head, realizing there was no way out of what she had already said.

"Yeah."

"And PTSD... what does that mean? Flashbacks?"

"Sometimes. Sometimes just... panic that comes out of nowhere... trouble sleeping..." She didn't add anger or mood swings, reacting to a stimulus before she could stop herself. Bowen needed to focus on finding who had taken Olly. Not on Tamara's problems. Tamara wasn't the reason Olly had disappeared.

"Do you often have memory blackouts? Times like this, when you're unable to remember what you did?"

Tamara struggled with an answer that was both true and didn't make her sound guilty or like some weird freak.

"No... sometimes if I have a flashback, I don't know what was really happening to me at the time, because I was back there, in the past... and sometimes, like I said, when I'm just following a boring routine... it's not a blackout, it's just that... it was routine... my brain just sort of shuts off."

"Is that what happened today?"

Tamara tried to swallow the lump in her throat. "I... no... I can't figure it out. If I had left him downstairs and came up here, that wouldn't be routine. I must have just brought him up with me and put him in the crib. That's where I thought he should be when I woke up..."

"How did you put him down?"

Tamara frowned trying to make sense of the question.

"What?"

"Did you put him down on his stomach or his back?"

"Back to sleep," Tamara said automatically. She closed her eyes and tried to remember actually doing it.

"I beg your pardon?"

She opened her eyes again, unable to access the memory. "It's a phrase to help you remember... you're supposed to put a baby down on his back to go to sleep. Because of SIDS. If you have a baby who won't go to sleep on his back, you're supposed to turn him over once he's asleep or prop him on his side."

Bowen nodded slowly. "Where did you learn about that?"

"I go to parenting classes for new moms. They teach all that kind of thing."

"Good. That sounds like a really smart idea."

Tamara let out her breath, relieved. She finally had at least one point in her favor. After all of the negatives she had felt piling up, it was like having the sun break through the clouds to finally have one positive.

Bowen looked again at the labels on the pill bottles before reaching out to pass them back to Tamara. Then she stopped, mid-reach.

"What?" Tamara reached to take them back, but Bowen didn't release them. She kept looking at the labels.

"These were dispensed at the juvenile detention facility."

"Well... yeah," Tamara admitted, letting go of the positive point in her favor and plunging hundreds of feet into a black abyss.

"You were in juvie. What for?"

Tamara put her hands over her tired, aching eyes, and pressed. She mumbled her answer into her hands.

"Tamara. Speak up. What were you incarcerated for?"

"Murder. Two counts." Tamara didn't want to finish answering what she knew Bowen wanted to know. "Two little girls I was looking after."

TEN

T AMARA WAS NUMB AS Bowen Mirandized her and put her into handcuffs. Bowen checked her pockets and did a quick pat-down. She escorted Tamara down the stairs, to the living room where Timmons, the other detective, was speaking to Mrs. Henson. Nita was not in evidence. Tamara didn't know whether she had just been sent to her room to wait, or whether there was another detective who had been called in to talk to her. Mrs. Henson looked up, alarmed.

"What's going on?"

Timmons raised an eyebrow at his partner. "You've already made an arrest?"

"I'm taking her in as a material witness. She's not under arrest *yet.*"

"But..." Mrs. Henson made a helpless movement. "What makes you think Tamara did anything?"

She didn't protest that Tamara was innocent.

"Her history," Bowen snapped. Her eyes were full of fury. "While we're at it, tell me why the first thing you said when you called the police wasn't that you were harboring a girl previously convicted of murdering two children?" Her voice was dripping with venom.

Mrs. Henson's mouth worked as she tried to come up with an appropriate answer. Timmons's eyes got wide. He looked Tamara over afresh.

"We've wasted more than an hour," Bowen said, "when all along you knew exactly who the likely culprit was." The police detective shook her head in disgust. "We're not looking for a kidnapped infant. We're looking for a body."

"No!" Tamara couldn't stop the word from escaping her lips. She shook her head vehemently. "I didn't do anything to Olly. I didn't hurt him. I didn't kill him. I don't know what's happened to him, but I didn't have anything to do with it. I didn't hurt him!"

Bowen looked like she would like nothing better than to slap Tamara's face and tell her to shut up. But she needed to act like she believed Tamara. She needed to be friendly and nonjudgmental to get Tamara's trust. Being a woman, she had to act empathetic. Tamara looked away, not wanting to see any more in Bowen's eyes.

"You can tell me all about it at the police station," Bowen said, her voice flat and unemotional.

"There's nothing to say. I didn't hurt him. I already told you. Someone took him while I was asleep."

Mrs. Henson didn't know what she should do. "You'll need a lawyer, Tamara. And... I'll need to contact Mrs. Arbiter. And Wanda Brisk."

"Yeah, call in the dogs," Tamara agreed. "But don't worry about a lawyer. They've never done anything for me."

"Who are they?" Bowen asked. "Mrs. Arbiter and Wanda Brisk?"

"Olly's social worker and... Tamara's parole officer."

Bowen nodded. "Yes, we should probably notify them." Her gaze shifted to her partner. "I want *you* to call them. And not with Mrs. Henson in the room. I want to get first reactions from them. Any concerns they might have. Any... background they might not have shared with the foster mom."

Mrs. Henson's face was pale and pinched. She didn't look like she liked people talking about her as if she weren't even in the room either.

"I know Tamara's background," she insisted.

"And Timmons is getting your statement. I hope you're more honest with him than you were with the police dispatcher."

Bowen gave Tamara a shove toward the door, taking her off guard. Tamara stumbled. She half-turned, anger flaring, to confront the detective, then forced herself to stop. If she added resisting a police officer, they might just use it as an excuse to hold her while deciding whether to charge her with kidnapping or murder. It took an effort, but she turned back toward the door and just walked ahead of Bowen.

The detective took her by the arm as she stepped out the door to escort her to the correct car parked out on the street. The neighborhood looked like a parking lot, with cars double-parked all up the street, vans pulled up onto lawns, and police and technicians with cameras and crime scene tape swarming over everything.

Bowen directed her to one of the unmarked cars, opened the door, and pushed her head down as she climbed in.

* * *

As Tamara had expected, once in the police station interview room, Bowen did her best to appear sympathetic.

"Taking care of a baby is hard," she acknowledged. "Especially when they're fussy and teething. It's frustrating."

It was. Sometimes Olly's fussing filled Tamara with inexplicable rage. But she wasn't about to share that with Bowen. She knew how the system worked. If they didn't have enough evidence, they needed a confession. They would push as hard as they could to get it. They would say anything and do anything to persuade Tamara to admit her hand in Olly's disappearance.

"You need to talk to me about it now," Bowen urged. "If you wait until we find him, it will be too late to cut a deal. It was an accident. You just got too overwhelmed. It happens more often than you would think."

"I didn't do anything. He was asleep. Then when I woke up, he was gone."

"That's the way you would like to remember it," Bowen agreed. "He was just peacefully asleep. He just disappeared without a trace. That is what you would like to think happened. But I think you and I both know that is not true."

Tamara rubbed her temples. She had a splitting headache. "Can I have a drink of water?"

"I'm sure we could find you something," Bowen said, but she made no move to get up or to call someone to get it for her.

Bowen said nothing for several minutes, waiting for Tamara to fill the void. Eventually, she spoke.

"What was it like, taking care of Olly?"

"He wasn't a bad baby. Missus said he should have been sleeping better by his age... but not all babies do. It was a strange place for him, people he didn't know... it wasn't like he was born drug addicted. I was never on anything other than the prescriptions they made me take."

"Could those have had an effect on him? Maybe they affected brain development."

"They said no. But they were experimental drugs, so what would they know? They were only guessing."

"I bet it was frustrating, having a baby that didn't sleep very well."

Tamara didn't say anything. She wasn't going down that road. Bowen wasn't going to get her to admit what a difficult time she was having taking care of Olly.

* * *

Tamara spent a lot of the day sitting, staring at the wall and waiting. Bowen would leave to go talk to the other investigators, Tamara supposed. Or to have her supper, while Tamara still waited for a glass of water. Bowen must have to coordinate with the people at the house, or to talk to Mrs. Henson and Nita. Tamara supposed that they'd want to talk to everyone else in the family too, whether they had been around when Olly disappeared or not. Get their perspectives, background details on Tamara, what they had seen and heard in the days leading up to the disappearance.

Where was Olly?

Tamara had been terrified when she and Nita searched the house that she was going to find him dead somewhere. Did that mean that he was dead? Did she know something unconsciously, or was it just what she dreaded finding out? But he hadn't been at the house. The police hadn't found anything in the yard, the shed, or the garbage bins. The dogs should have been there within an hour or two of Tamara being escorted out of the house, and if Olly had been stashed somewhere on the property, a scent dog would have discovered him.

Then where had Olly gone? He hadn't wandered off by himself. He was rolling over, but he couldn't yet crawl or walk. He couldn't get out of the house under his own power, and that meant he'd been taken, either by someone inside the house, or by someone outside.

It didn't make any sense that someone walking by, some stranger, would just happen to walk into the house and find Olly and Tamara asleep. No stranger was going to just walk in, pick up Olly, and walk back out again. She couldn't suggest it to Bowen.

Tamara had thought about Glock, wondered if there was any way she could have possibly gotten out of prison and had taken

Olly to get back at Tamara. But the police would have told her if they had found out Glock was free. They would want to know about any grievances between Glock and Tamara or if Tamara had any idea where Glock would take the baby. Other than the apartment Glock had rented when Tamara had last been out on parole or the warehouse where she had stashed Tamara and the dog, Tamara had no idea of where Glock would have taken a baby. But Glock wasn't still paying for an apartment on the outside and the owner of the warehouse would have figured out that something was going on inside his building and would have replaced the big padlock with something more secure.

Tamara had a better idea of *what* Glock might have done to Olly, given the chance, but she couldn't let that worm its way into her mind.

It wasn't Glock. She was still in prison.

ELEVEN

BOWEN RETURNED TO THE interview room to talk with Tamara. She looked fresher. She had changed her shirt, had something to eat, maybe even had a nap. The smells of cigarette smoke and coffee clung to her. Probably her worst vices. Tamara had been tapering off her cigarette use before getting out on parole and she hadn't had one since she had been released. Coffee was another story. She was drinking a lot of coffee. She took a deep breath, inhaling the scents.

"I need water," she told Bowen.

The dull ache in the back of her head and neck was, Tamara was sure, the result of dehydration and low blood sugar. Lack of sleep, caffeine withdrawal, dehydration, and low blood sugar—it was no wonder she was feeling so rotten.

Bowen made a flicking gesture. "It will be here soon. Meanwhile, we need to talk."

"I'm not talking," Tamara growled. "I need a drink."

Bowen looked at her, eyebrows raised. She shrugged again, unconcerned. "Soon, I said."

"I need it now. I'm not feeling well. I had to go to the hospital for dehydration once, you know. I just about died. I know what it feels like!"

"Then you know that you're not that dehydrated." Bowen gave a brief laugh. "You aren't going to get life-threatening dehydration sitting around in here talking to me for a couple of hours."

"But I did. I got—"

"You don't lose that much fluid in a couple of hours. Not in an air-conditioned room."

Tamara had to admit that they weren't the same conditions as she had been in at the court house when she had gotten so dangerously dehydrated. It had been sweltering and she had sweated heavily for several hours before getting sick.

"I'm not talking," she repeated stubbornly. "I haven't had anything to eat or drink. I'm feeling sick."

Bowen rolled her eyes. "We've been talking to your foster mom about the way things have been going. How you've been managing with Olly."

Tamara closed her eyes. She folded her arms across her chest. She leaned back in her chair, putting a wall up between her and Bowen. She couldn't see anything. She couldn't hear anything.

"Tamara."

She didn't give any sign. She couldn't see anything. She couldn't hear anything.

"Tamara!" Bowen shouted.

She still didn't respond.

Bowen slammed her hand down on the table with a slap so loud it sounded like a gunshot. Tamara couldn't help jumping. Her eyes flew open. Bowen leaned forward into her space, so close Tamara could feel her breath and smell the remains of pizza behind the pungent coffee. "Don't you try to ignore me," Bowen growled. "I've dealt with thugs much worse than you in my time. You are a cupcake compared to the criminals I have dealt with. A little girl who doesn't even have enough gumption to take care of a baby."

"I did too! I was doing a good job, Mrs. Henson said so!"

"You didn't know how to properly look after a kid. I looked at your history. I have no idea why they would let you anywhere near a kid even if he was your own. You had no idea how to be a parent."

"I did it before. I took really good care of Corinne and Julie. I did! And I was taking classes, I told you. Mrs. Henson could help me out with anything I needed, but I didn't need her help. I was doing it all by myself!"

"You're a pitiful excuse for a mother."

"No, I was doing a good job!"

"Then where is he? Where is your baby now, mama?"

Angry tears sprang to Tamara's eyes. "I didn't hurt him! I didn't do anything to hurt him! I swear it!"

"If you were such a good mother," Bowen's nose was almost touching Tamara's, "then why did Mrs. Henson report to your parole officer that she had concerns?"

Tamara's growing anger collapsed. She tried to keep her assertive posture and the self-righteous feelings of having done well for Olly, but it was an act instead of what she truly felt.

"That was... a misunderstanding."

"A misunderstanding. The Hensons have a lot of experience with teen moms and their babies, don't they?"

"Yeah."

"It was Mrs. Henson who was instrumental in getting you out on parole and getting you access to your baby."

"Yeah."

"Then why did she report you? If she thought you were doing such a good job and she wasn't inexperienced at what she was doing, why would she tell your parole officer otherwise?"

"She wasn't telling her I was doing a bad job. She was saying... she was just asking for advice."

"But she was the one used to dealing with teen moms, not Wanda Brisk."

Tamara tried to find the words. Bowen was making it sound like Mrs. Henson thought she was a danger to Olly. It wasn't an accurate reflection of what had happened.

Bowen withdrew, relaxing into her chair. Her expression was softer. Encouraging.

"Why don't you tell me what happened, then?"

Tamara took a deep breath to try to calm the pounding of her heart. She licked her dry lips. "I need a drink." She wiped her mouth with the back of her hand. "I need a drink, or I can't talk."

This time, Bowen went to the interview room door and opened it. She talked to someone in the hall and stood there with her foot propping the pneumatic door open while she waited. In a few minutes, she returned with a plastic bottle of water.

Tamara cracked it open and wet her lips. She took a few gulps of the cold, sweet water and let out her breath in a sigh.

"So, tell me," Bowen said. "What did Mrs. Henson report you for?"

"She didn't report me. She talked to my parole officer. That's not the same thing."

Bowen raised her brows and waited.

* * *

Tamara had fed and changed Olly, but he was still fussy. Grumpy and crying when she put him down, but squirming and kicking when she tried to hold him and calm him down.

"Just put him down with some toys," Mrs. Henson suggested when she came into Tamara's room. "He'll either find something to occupy himself with or he'll get tired and fall asleep."

Tamara rolled her eyes. "That's not going to work," she insisted. "As soon as I put him down, he cries to be picked up. If I don't pick him up, he'll just scream."

"If you let him cry for a few minutes, he'll sort himself out and be okay. You don't have to pick him up every time he cries."

"Yes, I do!" Tamara insisted. "I can't stand it when he cries. It makes me want to... I want him to stop. I just want to hold him and calm him down. It's not good to just let your baby cry, they said that at my parenting class."

"You can't just let your baby cry and ignore his needs," Mrs. Henson agreed. "But that's not what I'm talking about. I'm talking about five minutes, not neglecting him for hours. You give him five minutes to decide whether to play with a toy or put his head down and close his eyes to sleep. If he's still crying after five minutes, give him a little comfort, pat his back, and see if he calms down. He doesn't need to be held all the time. He needs time to squirm around on the floor and explore."

Tamara grimaced and tried to think of a way to explain to Mrs. Henson just how painful it was for her to listen to Olly crying. Even if she wasn't having hallucinations about Mr. and Mrs. Baker appearing to make her shut up the baby, she still remembered the way they had treated her with Corrine and Julie. If they heard either of the children crying, Tamara was in trouble.

"Just try it, why don't you?" Mrs. Henson suggested. "What could it hurt?"

Logically, Tamara knew that Mrs. Baker wasn't going to break through the barrier to the past and whip her for letting the baby cry, but her anxiety level rocketed whenever Olly started to wail. It would trigger flashbacks, and she would be back there again, being beaten for letting one of the children cry.

Tamara jiggled Olly, but he continued to fuss and squirm to be put down, until Tamara couldn't stand to hold him anymore. She put him belly down in the crib and picked up a few toys to scatter within reach. Olly lay there and looked around for a few moments, then his face wrinkled up and he started to cry as if Tamara had abandoned him.

"No," Tamara murmured, too low for Mrs. Henson to hear.

Olly's big head wobbled on his neck and he laid it down for an instant. Tamara held back. Was he going to go to sleep? Maybe he was so tired that he would just rest his head for a minute, and that would be enough for him to fall asleep.

"Just leave him for a few minutes," Mrs. Henson advised again. She patted Tamara on the back and left the bedroom. If she noticed Tamara flinch at her touch, she didn't say anything.

Tamara tried to focus on something else as Olly cried. Five minutes wasn't long. She could read a few pages of the book she'd picked out from Mrs. Henson's shelves. She could close her eyes and pretend she was sleeping. She could play a game of solitaire.

Her heart pounded at the sound of Olly's deep cry. It was easy enough for Mrs. Henson to say to just let him cry. She'd left the room. Tamara was the only one who had to put up with the full force of Olly's distress.

She went to her drawers and pulled out her anxiety meds. She tipped two into her hand and swallowed them. They wouldn't calm her anxiety in under five minutes, but she didn't know what else to do. She had to do something about her heart pounding so hard it felt like it was going to push right through her chest wall.

"Olly, stop," she pleaded. "Sh, just stop."

But of course, he didn't. There wasn't even a pause in his cries.

Maybe a bath would soothe him. He always liked to splash in the water. It would make him relaxed and tired, so maybe he would go to sleep earlier than usual. Tamara always resisted bathing him, reminded too much of Corinne in the bathtub, but she was determined this time. It was the solution to all of her problems with Olly. She picked him up and removed his sleeper, trying to keep jiggling him to calm him down. Then she took him into the bathroom and laid him on his back on the bath mat while she started the water running. She focused on the water, making sure that she got the temperature right, stirring it with her hand to make sure the water that had started out cold got mixed around so that it was all a homogeneous temperature. Jesse had the house's water temperature turned down so that it couldn't be turned hot enough to scald but, even so, it could still be too hot to be comfortable on the baby's skin.

Kneeling beside the tub, Tamara picked Olly up. He was still crying, but the noise of the tub faucet blocked some of it out so that his cries were muted and didn't upset her quite so much. She pulled back the tabs on his diaper to remove it and put him into the tub. Olly quieted for a moment when she picked him up. His skin was so soft and smooth under her fingers. But she wasn't thinking about how soft and sweet his baby skin was. Instead, she felt Corinne's body under her hands, remembered putting her in the tub that day and holding her still, struggling to keep her down under the water while Corrine's body bucked and fought with more strength than Tamara would ever have guessed a four-year-old's body could possess.

"Tamara!"

The exclamation went through Tamara like an electric shock. She jolted back to the present and saw Mrs. Henson in the bathroom doorway, her lips pressed into a straight line. Mrs. Henson was never angry. She always stayed calm and even-tempered, even when one of her foster kids was shouting or threatening or slamming doors. Tamara's gut clenched, and she looked around her, quickly assessing how she could defend herself or escape. She had the baby to think of; it wasn't just her own safety she had to worry about.

"I... I thought maybe a bath would calm him," Tamara squeaked.

"You know you're not supposed to bathe him without supervision."

Never mind that Tamara had bathed him numerous times

over the previous few weeks without incident. They still didn't trust her.

"I wasn't going to. I was going to get you."

"No, Tamara, you weren't."

"I..."

"Where were you just now? A flashback?"

Tamara rubbed one of her eyes. "I'm just tired. I was distracted for a second. No big deal."

"It was more than a second. Don't lie to me."

"It's true, I was just—" Tamara turned and reached for the lever to turn the bathtub faucet off and broke off when she saw how full the tub was. She wasn't supposed to fill it higher than two inches for Olly's bath and it was almost up to the overflow drain. "I was just distracted for a second." She pulled the plug to let the extra water out. Olly was squirming and fussing in her lap, still sobbing at irregular intervals.

"Tamara, look at me."

Tamara reluctantly looked back at Mrs. Henson, avoiding her eyes.

"You need to follow the rules. This isn't something you can skate by on. You know you're not supposed to have Olly in here alone, and you know why."

"I'm not going to do anything to hurt him."

"You are frustrated with him crying, you bring him in here without supervision, and you fill the tub too high. When I came in here, you were totally gone. I don't know where. Tell me you weren't thinking about..." Mrs. Henson swallowed, unable to finish.

"No. I told you, I wasn't going to hurt him!"

"Put his diaper back on and give him to me."

"I'm going to give him a bath, see if that calms him down so he'll go to sleep."

"No. You're off-duty tonight. You get a break. Go read a book or have a nap or whatever you need."

Tamara laid Olly back down to put his diaper back on. He kicked and hollered, furious and red-faced. Tamara was just as angry as he was. She had been doing a good job. She hadn't been doing anything to hurt Olly and hadn't been planning on doing anything that would harm him. Mrs. Henson was treating Tamara like she'd caught her red-handed.

As she stood up to hand Olly over to Mrs. Henson, she had a sudden memory of Mr. Baker taking Julie from her when he thought that Tamara had been trying to hurt her. The slaps that had snapped Tamara's head back. Waking his wife up and claiming Tamara had been trying to kill Julie.

Mrs. Henson had never treated her that way, but tears welled up in Tamara's eyes as she handed Olly over, the memory triggering emotions she had tried to bury deep down.

"I wouldn't hurt him," she reiterated, handing Olly over to Mrs. Henson.

"I hope not. Take a break tonight. Tomorrow will be easier if you can get a good rest."

Tamara went back to her room and shut the door, wondering what the next day would bring.

* * *

Tamara looked at Bowen, sure that knowing the details, she would understand Tamara hadn't done anything wrong. She had, after all, just been doing her best to look after her baby. Bowen was sitting back in her chair, considering the story.

"And that's when Mrs. Henson called your parole officer."

Tamara nodded.

"I can see why she was concerned."

A wave of heat washed over Tamara's face. "I didn't do anything wrong," she reiterated.

"Really. You drowned one of your other victims in the bathtub."

"I... yes—but..."

"And because of that, you weren't allowed to have Olly in the bathroom alone. You weren't allowed to bathe him without supervision."

"He's *my* baby!"

"What about the pills you took?"

"What?" Tamara was thrown off balance by the change in direction.

"You said you took a couple of pills when Olly was crying. What did you take?"

"My prescription! Not anything illegal."

Bowen looked at her steadily.

"What?" Tamara demanded.

"I looked at those prescriptions."

"Yeah. I showed you which one was for anxiety. That's what I took. To help me stay calm when he was upset."

"None of those prescriptions said 'take as needed.' They were all daily doses."

"Yeah...?"

"Were you supposed to be taking two more when you got upset? I assume you'd already taken your morning dose, since it was evening when this happened."

"I could take more if I needed them."

"Really?"

Tamara chewed on the inside of her cheek. She had never been explicitly told that she could take more pills if she needed them. But it only made sense. If she was anxious, she should take more of the anti-anxiety medicine. It would help her.

"What are the side effects? Do they make you drowsy?"

"No. Well, maybe a little. But I wasn't too tired to give him a bath. I didn't fall asleep in there." Tamara remembered falling asleep while Corinne was having a bath. She'd been so exhausted living with the Bakers, in the end. Mrs. Baker had been furious and had screamed at her for putting the four-year-old's life in danger.

Mrs. Baker had no idea how hard it actually was to drown a four-year-old.

"How often did you take extras?" Bowen asked, shattering the memory and bringing Tamara back to the present.

"I don't know. Sometimes. But they never made me too tired to take care of Olly."

"Did you take extras today?"

Tamara's stomach twisted. She didn't snap back a denial immediately. Bowen wouldn't believe her if all she did was deny it. Instead, Tamara thought back. Although she was getting better at anticipating Olly's needs and was bonding with him, Olly's unreasonable cries still set Tamara's anxiety skyrocketing. She had been taking a lot of extra doses. She tried to remember everything that had happened before Olly's disappearance. She shook her head.

"No. Just my morning dose. Nothing extra."

"You're sure? Because I'm thinking maybe you could have taken an extra dose and forgotten about it. Maybe even more. And that's why you fell asleep so soundly and can't remember what happened."

Tamara shook her head.

"It could have happened that way," Bowen said.

"No, it didn't. I didn't take any extra today. I didn't take anything."

"I'm not saying it did happen, I'm saying it could have happened that way. It's logical. It makes sense."

"It didn't!"

"It could have," Bowen pressed again.

"It could have," Tamara finally agreed, "but it didn't."

Bowen nodded.

"What did your parole officer say about you disobeying the rules?"

Another disorienting jump in the direction of the conversation. Tamara wondered if Bowen was deliberately taking illogical leaps to throw her off balance and make her say the wrong thing. Tamara took a minute to think back. She didn't need to be in a hurry to reply. She didn't have to let Bowen throw her off with her tricky twists and turns.

"She didn't send me back. She just told me to be more careful."

"Did she take Mrs. Henson's concerns seriously?"

Tamara didn't think either alternative was going to reflect in her favor. "They talked. They told me to just be more careful. Follow the rules. Get help if I needed it. I didn't need help, I was doing just fine."

"You didn't need help?"

"No."

"Then explain what happened to your baby."

Tamara tried to shove herself back from the table in frustration. The chair was bolted securely in place. "I want to go home." She stood up. "I don't know what happened to Olly. But nobody is going to find him here. We should be looking for him. Is it on TV? Did you put one of those Amber Alerts on so people know to look for him?"

"Amber alerts are for children we know have been kidnapped. Where we have a suspect and can tell people who to look for, or a vehicle to watch for. That's not the case here."

"I don't know who took him, but someone did!"

"Glock Spielman?"

"I never said that. Glock's in prison; she couldn't have had anything to do with this."

"You tried to make the first officers at the scene think that she might have been involved. What was the reason for that misdirection?"

"I didn't! I was just remembering... when she'd been out before. I was scared of what happened to Olly, and I remembered when Glock was out last time, and she was... doing what she does."

"Torturing and killing animals."

"Yeah."

"Sit back down."

Tamara paced a few steps and back again. "I can't sit right now. I want to go home. I can... I don't know what I can do. I want to help. Someone should be looking for Olly."

"Where should we be looking for him?"

"The dogs didn't find anything? I thought you were going to have scent dogs looking for him."

"And what do you think they're going to find?"

"I don't know! I have no way of knowing what happened or where someone took Olly. I don't understand why anyone would take him."

"What makes you think someone took him?"

"Because he's gone!"

"Sit."

Tamara didn't. "You can't hold me. I can go home any time. You didn't arrest me."

"You're the suspect in a felony. Your parole is revoked."

"You can't do that!"

"There will be a hearing and a judge will decide. We can hold you until then."

"Well... I don't have to answer any questions. I don't have to talk to you anymore."

"I told you your rights," Bowen agreed. "But I thought you wanted to help us to find Olly."

Tamara hesitated. "Yeah... but I don't know anything. I don't know where he is or where you should look. I just know that I didn't do anything and you're wasting your time railroading me. I don't care if you send me back to juvie—" though Tamara knew it wouldn't be juvie she'd be going back to, it would be the women's prison. Where Vernon was. "You're looking at the wrong person. If you're talking to me, you're not finding out who really did this!"

Bowen pointed to the chair, staring at Tamara fiercely. "The only way we are going to solve this crime is by talking to you. Whether you did it or not, you are the key. This wasn't random. Babies are not just randomly stolen from cribs in their homes. If it wasn't you, then it was someone else in the home, or you were targeted. You are the only one who can provide those clues and motives."

Tamara was silent, thinking it through. Finally, she went back to the chair and sat down.

"It wasn't me," she said. "So, what do you need to know to find out who it was?"

Seconds ticked by, Bowen considering the question. She drummed her fingers on the table. "Who do you think it was?"

"I don't know. Everyone in the house loved Olly. They wouldn't hurt him."

"Everyone? No one reacted negatively to having a fussy baby in the house?"

Tamara shook her head. Mrs. Henson and the girls were gaga over Olly. They always wanted to hold and spoil him. Jesse wasn't home a lot, but when he was, he was calm and didn't seem bothered by the baby's fussing when he was teething or tired. Tamara imagined they'd had so many babies in the house that he probably didn't even hear it anymore. He probably just blocked it all out.

TWELVE

TAMARA HAD JUST BARELY sat down at the table when Olly's cries broke through the busy conversation of everyone sitting down to eat. Tamara couldn't believe it. She groaned in frustration.

"Go get him," Mrs. Henson said. "He can sit with us in the high chair."

"I don't want him in here," Jason whined. "Can't I even eat without listening to the little brat scream? He drives me crazy."

Tamara rolled her eyes. Jason thought he was hard done by with the baby's crying? He had no idea what it was like trying to take care of Olly twenty-four hours a day. If Jason didn't want to hear the baby cry, all he had to do was shut the door of his room. Tamara had no such escape.

"Jason, that's enough," Jesse warned. "Go ahead and get him, Tamara. He'll be fine."

Tamara went back upstairs to pick Olly up from his crib, showing him her angry face and holding him more tightly than usual so he would know how upset she was at her supper being interrupted.

"Why can't you stay down for ten minutes?" she demanded.

"Why can't you just go to sleep and let me eat in peace for one meal?"

He continued to sob, grasping her shirt and clinging to her. She automatically patted his back and bounced him, trying to comfort him even though she was angry.

What right did Jason have to be complaining about Olly crying? His complaint was another irritant, worming its way into Tamara's brain.

She took Olly downstairs, trying to quiet him along the way. She did as Mrs. Henson said and put him into the high chair but, of course, Olly didn't like this treatment. He immediately held out his hands to be picked up, his face getting red with anger. Mrs. Henson handed Tamara a small container of Cheerios cereal to put on his high chair tray. He wasn't really eating solid food yet, but he was showing an interest in it and, every now and then, managed to get one of the O's into his mouth.

Olly looked at the cereal in his tray and just smacked at the tray with his hand, stiffening his little body into a board to scream louder at this treatment.

"He'll settle down" Mrs. Henson said calmly. "Just ignore him and he'll get over it."

"I can't hear myself think!" Jason shouted over the baby's cries.

"Why would you start now?" Dirk taunted.

"Hey!" Jason punched Dirk in the arm, and for a minute everyone's attention was taken by the two boys arguing and tussling at the table. Tamara was on her feet, prepared to protect herself and the baby from the two brawlers.

Jesse managed to get them settled back down. Tamara didn't know why the two were still allowed to sit together at the table. It would have made more sense to separate them, so they couldn't cause any more trouble. But that solution didn't seem to occur to Jesse or Mrs. Henson.

"Tamara, it's okay. Why don't you sit down?" Mrs. Henson

suggested. "You need to relax and eat even if Olly is fussy. You need to take care of your own body, or you won't have the energy and patience to deal with him."

Tamara glared again at Jason and Dirk, warning them not to cause her any more trouble. Jason smirked at her.

"Well, she's got the *mom look* down! Too bad the rest of her maternal skills are—"

Tamara blew. She took one step closer to him and shoved his shoulder, toppling him over, chair and all.

"Whoa, whoa, whoa!" Jesse grabbed Tamara to prevent her from doing anything else. Jason took a minute to right himself and get to his feet. He swore angrily. Dirk was on his feet to try to hold Jason back, and Mrs. Henson inserted herself between Jason and Tamara. Not the brightest place to be in the middle of an altercation.

"Enough. Both of you. This is not how we act at the table! I can't believe this behavior. Everybody sit down and stop provoking each other!"

She put her hand on Jason's chest, keeping him back from Tamara. "You're going to hit a girl, Jason? Really? Is that the kind of man you want to be?"

Jason didn't fight back against her. He withdrew, looking down in shame or embarrassment.

"No, I'm not going to hurt her. I'm just mad! There wasn't any call to do something like that!"

"I agree," Mrs. Henson said, giving Tamara a stern look. "You all know better than to put your hands on each other."

"He said I'm not a good mom!"

Mrs. Henson just looked back at her steadily. She didn't jump in and say that Tamara *was* a good mom and not to worry about what Jason had to say. She just stood there looking at Tamara and waiting for her to do what she was told.

Jason eyed the food on the table, clearly trying to decide

whether to stay and finish eating or to withdraw to his bedroom, slamming the door to express his anger and disgust.

"Sit down," Mrs. Henson told Tamara. "Look after Olly."

It was completely unfair that Tamara had to take care of the baby and no one else had any consequences for causing trouble. She resented being hobbled to Olly all day long, responsible for making sure he had everything he needed while everyone else was free as a bird.

"I don't want to sit down—"

"Olly needs your attention."

Tamara looked down at him, crying and red-faced in the high chair. She wanted to just take him back upstairs and plop him in his crib and let him cry it out. It wasn't like he was hungry or wet. He was just being crabby for no reason.

But she hadn't eaten lunch and, as Mrs. Henson kept reminding her, she had to take care of her own body. She picked Olly up and held him against her, waiting for him to calm.

"You need to eat," Mrs. Henson reminded her.

"I know."

Tamara pulled angrily away from Jesse, who was still holding her arm. She sat in her chair and bounced Olly. His cries started to subside. Jason picked up his chair, glaring at Tamara the whole time. She ignored him. Nita made a comical face at Tamara, rolling her eyes over all the drama. "Boys," she mouthed.

Mrs. Henson and Jesse both stayed on their feet a little longer, watching to make sure they weren't going to start up again or begin some new mischief. Tamara, Jason, and Dirk all sat sullenly, waiting for the dishes to be passed around.

"Let's just have a pleasant dinner," Jesse said, sitting back down.

"I think that plan is all blown to hell," Dirk pointed out.

"Enough, Dirk. I don't need any more smart comments."

Mrs. Henson sat down. The serving dishes were started on their courses and everyone dished up. There was no pleasant dinner conversation. Nita and Deshawn, being the only ones not involved in the drama, made some quiet comments to each other, but the usual cheerful family atmosphere of meals at the Henson home was absent. Tamara let Olly suck and chew on her spoon while she ate one-handedly.

* * *

"So, there *was* some resentment around the baby."

Tamara shrugged. "Nobody threatened to hurt him. We were just... arguing with each other. No one intended any harm."

"The rest of the time, Jason has been perfectly happy to have Olly around the house?" Bowen pressed.

"Well... no. He still complained and tried not to be around Olly. But... Jason didn't kidnap him. Jason wasn't even home when Olly disappeared."

"As far as you know."

"It was during school. He was nowhere near the house."

"Again, as far as you know."

Tamara looked for a way to argue it. But what was she going to say? She didn't have proof that he'd gone to all of his classes and been sitting at his desk when Olly disappeared. She couldn't say who it was that had come and taken Olly while she slept. If she could, she wouldn't be in an interview room at the police station trying to defend herself against accusations of kidnapping or murder.

"Okay... but I don't think he'd ever do anything about Olly crying. They've had other babies at the house. Plenty of them. And none of them have ever disappeared or had anything happen to them. It couldn't be Jason."

"The same holds true of everyone else in the house."

All except Dirk, Tamara realized. He'd come to the Hensons while they still had Cecelia and her baby, but the overlap had not been long, and Dirk had just been getting settled. But he hadn't been the one to complain about Olly. Tamara was sure neither of them could have had anything to do with Olly's disappearance.

"Somebody must have come into the house. It couldn't have been anyone in the family."

The door to the interview room opened and Tamara looked expectantly at the woman who stuck her head in, hoping it was news about Olly. They had found him. They knew it wasn't Tamara, he was okay, and everything could go back to normal. But of course, it wasn't. It wasn't going to end that way.

Instead, the woman entered and bent over to speak to Bowen, whispering in her ear so Tamara couldn't hear. At the same time, she placed a plastic bag, a wipe, and a cup with an orange lid on the table. Tamara stared at it in dismay, waiting for Bowen and the woman to finish talking. The other woman nodded, then left the room. Bowen looked at Tamara, nodding to the cup while raising one eyebrow.

"You know what to do with that, I assume?"

Tamara rolled her eyes upward. She'd done enough drug testing to recognize a urine collection cup. "I assume I'll actually see a toilet at some point."

"You haven't asked for one before now. But yes, I'll be escorting you to a restroom."

"I'm not on anything."

"Good. Then the test will rule that possibility out."

"What if I refuse?"

"Then we'll assume that you are drug positive. What did you take? A little something other than your anti-anxiety prescription?"

"No, I didn't take anything. I just don't want to pee in a cup."

Bowen shrugged. "You're probably not going to like a lot of what's going to happen to you in the next few days. Are you going to cooperate and give a sample or not?"

There really wasn't any point in refusing. Wanda would terminate her parole, if she hadn't decided to do it already.

Tamara knew the test would be negative. It was better to prove she hadn't taken anything than to let them assume she had. They could at least confirm to the judge at her hearing that she was clean.

"Yeah, I'll do it."

"Good. Let's take a walk, then."

Tamara stood up. Bowen motioned to her hands to cuff her again.

"I can't do it with my hands cuffed. I've tried before, and it just makes a mess."

Bowen gave her a level stare, weighing the risks, then nodded. "Come on then. But if you try anything, I'm going to take you down."

"What am I going to do?"

"Just be warned."

Tamara let Bowen escort her out of the interview room down the hall to a single-toilet restroom.

"You gonna watch?"

"Just a pat-down and then you can have your privacy." Bowen's eyes assessed the small bathroom, making sure there were no hazards. Unless Tamara were going to drown herself in the toilet bowl, there wasn't much to worry about.

Tamara put her hands on the wall and Bowen performed a careful search, feeling for any fluid bags or tubes Tamara could have taped to her body. Tamara had been in juvie, she knew packing clean urine was the easiest way to get around drug testing. But she would have had to have known she was going to be tested to be prepared for it.

"Satisfied?"

"All clear. Do your stuff."

Tamara went into the bathroom and shut the door, flicking the deadbolt closed, in spite of the fact Bowen was bound to have a key to unlock it again if she wanted to. Tamara was going to take every second of privacy she could get.

THIRTEEN

TAMARA WASN'T SURE WHAT time it was, but she was getting tired. They finally provided her with something that could have been called dinner and Tamara picked at it, her hunger fighting against her gag reflex as she tried to get down the lumpy, bland stew.

The door opened again. Tamara looked up, hoping it was Mrs. Henson or someone who would give Bowen the word that Tamara was to be released. It was the same woman as the previous time. She gave Bowen a thumbs-down.

"Negative," she announced. "Both tests."

"Good." Bowen nodded. She turned back to Tamara. "So, you didn't take any recreational drugs. Then explain to me how someone could walk into the room where you're sleeping and take the baby. And why you claim you can't remember the events surrounding Olly's disappearance."

Tamara rubbed her eyes. Any benefits that might have come from her afternoon nap were long since gone. Her body was exhausted, and she just wanted to know where she was going to be for the night.

"I already said I don't know."

"Do you have a boyfriend?"

Another question that nearly gave Tamara whiplash with the change in direction.

"What? No."

"No one you're interested in?"

Tamara's cheeks grew warm. "No... not really."

"Why not? You can't exactly tell me you're not interested in boys when you have—had—a baby."

Tamara wanted to argue that there wasn't any correlation between the two, but she didn't have the energy to pursue it.

"I just... I barely got out of juvie and I haven't had time for anything except taking care of Olly. I can't exactly be out dating."

"Mrs. Henson might have taken Olly to give you a break one night, like she did the night you nearly drowned him. Or you might have been interested in someone... closer to home."

Tamara wondered how much Bowen already knew.

* * *

Tamara had been up half the night with Olly, walking him to put him to sleep, sitting down or trying to put him down, and then pacing again when he reawakened. She had finally been able to sit down with him, sinking into the soft couch, and she was watching an old sci-fi movie on the TV, starting to doze off.

"Hey, you still up?"

Tamara startled. She looked immediately at Olly instead of the source of the voice, worried that her sudden movement might have woken him back up again. He was still slumbering peacefully, so Tamara looked into the shadowy recesses of the stairs and saw Dirk standing there watching her.

"He just got to sleep," she whispered.

Dirk stepped down from the last stair and drifted across the room. He sat down beside Tamara and peered into Olly's face.

"They look like such little angels when they're asleep," he said. "You can forget about all of the stuff they did during the day and think they're just perfect."

Tamara snorted. "Perfect isn't the word I'd use to describe him."

"I know. But when they look like this..."

Tamara had to admit, Olly did look like an angelic little cherub with his fat round cheeks and long dark lashes. He was breathing evenly, with just a little bit of a snore. She thought he might be fighting a cold. That would account for the difficulty settling.

"Okay, yeah. He looks cute."

Dirk frowned slightly. Tamara looked at him, trying to read his expression. He wasn't pleased about something.

"What is it?"

"He's your baby. You don't... you sound like you don't even like him."

"I don't." The words were out of her mouth before Tamara could stop them. She put one hand over her mouth. "Don't tell anybody that. You can't tell anybody I said that."

His brows knotted, Dirk shook his head. "Why are you taking care of him, if you don't like him? He was with another foster family before; why didn't you just leave him there?"

"Because to get out of juvie, I had to say I was going to take care of him. That it was important for me to get out this year so that I would have a chance to bond with him and to be a good mom. If they kept me in juvie for another year and didn't give me the chance to bond for another year, he might not. And because I was taking care of him, I wouldn't be a flight risk. They'd know where I was going to be, because I was going to want to stay with him. See?"

Dirk nodded slowly, but she wasn't sure he really understood.

"I had to take care of him if I wanted to get my parole," Tamara repeated. "That was the only way I was getting out."

"So, this is all for show?"

"What is?" Tamara asked. "I am taking care of him. I'm doing just what I said I was going to do. I'm not... I'm not *pretending* to take care of him."

"But the whole concerned mom thing. You don't actually care if he's crying or teething. You just want everyone to think you're being a good mom."

"I don't like him crying."

"Neither do I, but that doesn't make me his mom. You don't really care about him."

Tamara looked for a way to argue with his assessment. "I care. I'm here. I'm looking after him."

"You just said that you're only taking care of him because you have to. You don't care about him."

Tamara shook her head and looked at the TV. She watched the extra-terrestrial invaders.

"I take good care of him," she reasserted.

"But not because you gave birth to him. Not because you love him."

As much as Tamara wanted to say that she did, she didn't love him, and she knew Dirk would read the lie in her face. He'd already seen too much. Dirk watched the movie for a few minutes.

"You like this?"

Tamara shook her head. "It was just on. I was falling asleep watching it. I just want this little guy to stay asleep."

He put his arm casually along the top of the couch behind Tamara's neck. Though he wasn't touching her, his movement electrified her. How many times had she seen that move in TV shows and movies? He was seeing whether he could put his arm around her. He wanted to know if she had any interest in him. Tamara shifted a fraction of an inch closer to him, studying his face. He was good looking. Her age. Not afraid of the fact that she'd been in juvenile detention, but not obsessed with it either. He knew what it was like not to want other people knowing all of the details of the past. Dirk matched her shift in position and let the hand on the couch behind her brush past her hair, light as a butterfly.

"You were here on parole last year," Dirk said. "Jason told me."

"Yeah. For a few weeks. Didn't work out so well."

"Doing better this time?"

"Yeah. I guess so. I'm still here."

"So, you think you'll stay? For how long?"

"Long as I can. In a year, I'll have served five. I can ask for a hearing to review my sentence. If they decide I'm rehabilitated... I could be free."

"You think they'll do that?"

"No." His hand on her shoulder made Tamara jump, and she looked down at Olly again to make sure she hadn't woken him up. "I think... they won't want to count the last year, because of how much trouble I had. They'll want me to serve another year, at least... keep me on parole for another year, maybe without so many restrictions..."

"Uh-huh."

He wasn't listening to her anymore. He was staring into her face, but he wasn't in rhythm with her speech patterns. He was leaning closer.

Tamara patted Olly's back nervously. Dirk leaned in farther, his warm breath on her neck.

"You could put him down," he suggested.

His closeness and the whisper in her ear made her shiver. "I can't. He'll wake up if I do."

"He'll be fine."

"If he starts crying again, Mrs. Henson will be down here to check on him. Making sure I'm doing everything I'm supposed to and not doing anything to hurt him. You want her down here?"

"No."

He rubbed her shoulder. Tamara tried to control her reaction to him. It was too dark for him to see the goosebumps on her arms, but he'd be able to feel how rapidly her heart was beating.

"You're very pretty."

"I look like a wreck right now."

"No."

"Then it's too dark."

He laughed. His fingers drifted from her shoulder to the back of her neck, making her squirm.

"It's so quiet," Dirk observed, looking around the dark room. The only sound was from the dimly glowing TV.

"That's because Olly isn't crying."

"It's peaceful. It's not usually like that around here. I like it."

Tamara leaned into him, feeling the warmth of his body spreading into hers. The house was peaceful, and Olly was peaceful, and Dirk might have been feeling peaceful, but Tamara's thoughts and feelings were anything but. Her heart hammered hard in her chest. Her thoughts were whirling a mile a minute. She knew nothing was going to happen between them. Nothing could happen with Olly there, bound to wake up as soon as she shifted to stand or to put him down. Men referred to marriage as a ball and chain, but Tamara couldn't think of anything more confining than having a fussy baby to care for twenty-four hours a day. She'd been in prison, but the restrictions she faced trying to take care of Olly were worse.

Dirk accepted Tamara's move to lean against him as permission to proceed further, and tightened his arm around her, pulling her closer.

"You sure you can't put him down?" He breathed into her hair and kissed the top of her head.

"The minute I think I can put him down and he'll stay asleep, I'm going to sleep too."

"I could join you."

Tamara couldn't help but laugh at his boldness. "No, you couldn't," she asserted. It wasn't just the Hensons' rules or Social Services' rules that held her back. She was enjoying Dirk's attention, but they barely knew each other. They weren't even to first date level. Tamara had had enough of people demanding intimacy; she wasn't about to jump into anything with Dirk.

He withdrew slightly so that he could look her in the face. The TV was bright enough for them to see each other, but not well.

"I was just kidding," he asserted, though Tamara was pretty sure he was not. "I don't move that fast."

Was it just a line or was he really agreeing to slow down and take things at Tamara's pace? Sly had had an agreement with Vernon too, until he had gotten too impatient and everything had changed in an instant. Dirk wasn't Sly, but Tamara didn't have any reason to trust him.

FOURTEEN

YOU CAN TELL ME, Tamara," Bowen encouraged. "If you want me to help you, you need to be honest and up front with me. You know that, right? I just want to help you."

Bowen didn't want to help her; she knew that. Bowen wanted to find Olly and to lock Tamara up.

What kind of stupid idea had it been for Tamara to get out on parole and try to take care of her baby? She hadn't done it out of maternal instinct. She hadn't done it because she'd wanted to. She should have said no. She should have told Mrs. Henson that it was a bad idea and she wouldn't do it. She knew what had happened in the past and she wasn't convinced that it had all been the result of psychosis triggered by the pregnancies. Deep down, she suspected she really was a monster. She kept it hidden from everyone else and especially from herself, but what kind of person did the things she had done?

"I don't have a boyfriend," she asserted. "I'm not seeing anyone. All I had time to do was take care of Olly."

"You've had a lot of trouble with him."

"Him? Olly?"

"That's who we're talking about, isn't it?"

Tamara tried to focus her thoughts on Olly again. "Yeah. I mean, taking care of a baby isn't easy... especially when they're teething or sick."

"Before you got out on parole, he was with a foster family."

"Yeah. The first couple months."

"His foster mother says he was an easy baby. Calm, good sleeper, good eater. Not a problem at all."

Tamara felt a chill. It had started. They were building a case against her. She might have passed their drug testing, but that wasn't going to make them believe her. The foster mother said Olly was an easy baby. Tamara said he was a difficult baby. The foster mother said he slept well. Tamara said he didn't. He didn't settle easily, he awoke too many times. The foster mother said he was a good eater. The doctor said that while he had put on weight since his last visit, his weight percentile had gone down. Nothing alarming, but something to keep an eye on. They were going to use all of those things to say that Tamara was a bad mother. They'd say that she neglected or abused Olly. They already had Mrs. Henson on record saying that she had concerns about Tamara breaking the rules and not listening to her.

"He wasn't teething then," she pointed out. "He was just a newborn and his teeth weren't coming in yet. Not until after he came to the Hensons."

"To you."

"What?" Tamara chewed on her thumbnail, not following Bowen's train of thought.

"You said 'not until after he came to the Hensons.' Don't you mean not until after he came to you? He wasn't just living with the Hensons. They weren't the ones who were supposed to be looking after him. You were."

"Yeah, that's what I meant. When he came to me at the Hensons' house. When he left that foster family to come to the Hensons instead."

"You're still doing it. When he left his foster family to come to you. You were the reason he was moved."

"Yeah. I know."

She had been taking care of Olly for weeks. Did Bowen think that reality hadn't settled in yet? Tamara was fully aware of the weight of responsibility on her shoulders. She hadn't wanted it to start out with, but she'd been able to romanticize it, to make believe it was going to be idyllic. Even though she kept telling Mrs. Henson that it wasn't going to be like that. Babies were messy and demanding, not peaceful little cherubs.

"You think that is the only difference? How long did it take for him to go from a cheerful, normally-developing baby to one who was grumpy and fussy and not meeting all of the growth and development milestones he was expected to? You think that was just because he was cutting teeth?"

"I don't know." Tamara snapped the words out, irritated she had hit so close to home. Did Bowen think Tamara hadn't noticed the change in the baby? Did she think that Tamara didn't care that he was miserable? "Maybe it wasn't just teething. If he was bonded to his foster mom, then moving him to the Hen—to me—might be hard for him. I... I know how hard it was for me to move when my Gran died... and I kept getting shuffled from one place to another... Olly might just be a baby, but he still knew I wasn't the mom who'd been taking care of him before."

Bowen nodded. "Everything about you would have been different. That could be very disconcerting to a child."

"They talk a lot about bonding at my parenting classes... it's really important for the baby's development."

"And he wasn't bonded to you."

Tamara tried to bury the anger that rose up in her at this assertion. What did Bowen know? She was only guessing. She was just trying to goad Tamara. Or had Mrs. Henson or someone else from the family or the circle of professionals constantly monitoring Tamara told her that? Had someone said something out of genuine concern for the baby? Or was it malicious?

"He was. I think he was starting to. And I was..." Tamara searched for words that wouldn't sound cold or calculating, "I was getting... attached to him."

* * *

Tamara changed Olly's diaper and also put a fresh shirt on him, even though it was almost time for supper and he would probably either spill or spit up on it, forcing her to change it again after the meal was over. Nita had come home with a t-shirt with a tuxedo and bow tie printed on it. It was so cute, Tamara had to put it on him right away.

Olly was satisfied with a full belly and a dry diaper, and he laughed when she pulled the shirt on and his head popped through the hole. After Tamara got his arms through the sleeves, she playfully pulled the bottom of the shirt up to cover Olly's eyes and played peek-a-boo with him as he chortled away and waved his arms in excitement.

There was a knock on her door, even though it was standing open. Tamara turned her head to see Deshawn.

"Dinner's on," she said. "Didn't you hear?"

"No." Tamara picked Olly up and held him to her. "We were playing."

Deshawn looked at Olly and gave him a big smile. "Were you playing with your mama?" she asked him in her baby-talk voice. "Is your mama playing games with you?"

Tamara smiled. "Do you like his new shirt?"

"It's darling! I just can't resist a man in a tux!" Deshawn leaned in and gave Olly a noisy, sloppy kiss on the cheek, making him squeal.

Tamara pulled him back and headed down the stairs ahead of Deshawn, not sure she was comfortable with anyone kissing

Olly without her permission. Of course there was nothing inappropriate about it, but Tamara felt territorial. Deshawn should have asked.

Everyone was already settled at the table, which was obviously the reason Deshawn had made a special effort to get Tamara there. Tamara gave an apologetic smile. "Sorry, didn't hear you call."

She plopped Olly into the high chair and slid into her seat. But as soon as Olly's butt hit the chair, he started to slap the tray of the chair and fuss.

Tamara did as Mrs. Henson always said and ignored his noise, filling her dish. But it was rare for Olly to settle on his own like Mrs. Henson said he should. Tamara wasn't patient enough to give him the time to settle, especially when the others started to complain and get annoyed with his noise. Mrs. Henson said that Olly needed to learn to self-regulate and he wouldn't if she kept picking him up too quickly, but Tamara couldn't stand to listen to him cry. Once she'd finished dishing up, she reached over and pulled Olly out of his chair and into her lap. He started to quiet almost immediately. But he kept reaching for her food, which made it almost impossible to eat. When Nita was finished her dinner, she held out her hands toward Tamara.

"I'm done. Let me hold him for a few minutes so you can eat."

Tamara passed him off to Nita, but almost the instant she did, Olly started to complain again. Tamara ignored him and ate a few bites of her meal. She tried to just let Nita deal with Olly. She was good with babies. Nita walked Olly, jiggling him and talking to him in an unnaturally high voice, smiling her big, friendly smile and trying to find something that would calm him down again. Olly wasn't in full-blown crying mode, but he wasn't settling down for Nita, either. Tamara polished off her dinner as quickly as possible, knowing that she was being rude and that her stomach would likely protest this treatment later. Then she stood up.

"Here, I'll take him back."

"I don't know what's wrong," Nita said. "He's not hungry or wet…"

She passed Olly back to Tamara. He cuddled against her and his sobs chugged to a stop. Tamara looked down at him and grinned. It was the first time that she'd been sure he knew who she was and differentiated between her and the others who occasionally helped to care for him. At her smile, Olly babbled and jammed a fist into his mouth, mumbling around it.

"Hey, Rollie-Ollie," Tamara said to him. She blew a raspberry against his cheek to make him laugh. "Why are you being fussy for Auntie Nita? Huh?"

He seemed to be perfectly happy back in her arms. Tamara was delighted by the signs that he actually knew she was his caregiver, not one of the others. She looked over at Mrs. Henson, who gave her a thumbs-up at this progress.

Olly knew who she was and being with her made him happy.

FIFTEEN

BOWEN HAD LEFT TAMARA alone again. Tamara wondered whether they had discovered anything or made any progress in the case. They weren't going to find out what had happened to Olly as long as they focused on Tamara. She didn't have anything to do with Olly's disappearance. Had they finally turned up some clue at the house? Had they talked to someone who knew something they shouldn't or was covering something up? Maybe there had been a known kidnapper in the area or some rash of disappearances similar in some way to Olly's.

Tamara couldn't help wondering where Mrs. Henson was.

Mrs. Henson had been there for the last year, the person always stepping in to advocate for Tamara, even when Tamara's mental health was so bad that she was incapable of distinguishing reality from imagination and didn't want Mrs. Henson or anyone else helping her.

So where was she? Why wasn't she there insisting that Tamara not talk without a lawyer? Why wasn't she there saying that she was Tamara's guardian and the police weren't allowed to talk to her?

Was she staying away because she didn't believe Tamara's story?

Did she think that Tamara had been negligent in watching Olly? Or worse, that she had done something to harm him?

Bowen returned to the interview room. She started to slap photos down on the table in front of her. Fear gripped Tamara's heart, sure they were going to show her Olly's body, recovered from some cupboard or cistern where everyone had failed to look to begin with. She was afraid to even look at the pictures.

"What is it?" she demanded. "What's going on?"

"I just want you to look at these pictures. Tell me if you see anything out of place."

Tamara looked at the closed door of the interview room, waiting for Mrs. Henson to come in. But she didn't. Was that because they were keeping her away? She was Tamara's guardian, so they couldn't keep her from Tamara, could they?

"Look at the pictures," Bowen insisted. "Tell me about the scene. Anything that wouldn't be where you expected it."

Tamara forced herself to look down at the grid of pictures Bowen had laid down on the table. Mostly pictures of her bedroom and the living room, the places where she had been taking care of Olly earlier in the day. The places he should have been. Full-room shots followed by close-ups of the cluttered top of the dresser, the blanket and various surfaces in the living room, the diaper bag dropped carelessly by the front door. Tamara scanned everything quickly to make sure they weren't trying to ambush her with a picture of Olly's corpse, then went back to the beginning and looked over them one at a time.

She rubbed her eyes, gritty and sore. "I don't know. I don't see anything weird."

"Is there anything missing? Something that should be there that isn't?"

Tamara closed her eyes to visualize the rooms, picturing

them with as much detail as she could. She opened them and looked back at the photos again.

What would someone taking Olly need? They hadn't taken the diaper bag. That was the first thing Tamara had grabbed when she had taken Amy. If they wanted to take care of Olly, they would need bottles, clothing, and diapers, at the very minimum. Tamara started chewing on the skin around the nail of her index finger. Her thumb was stinging, already completely wrecked with her nervous biting.

"I don't know. Did they take bottles? Diapers? You don't have pictures of those things."

Bowen made a note in her notepad. "Anything else?"

"Clothes? Blankets?"

"Where would you take him, Tamara?"

"What?"

"If you didn't want to take care of Olly anymore, or if something happened to him, where would you take him?"

"I... I told you I didn't take Olly anywhere. I didn't do anything to him."

"But he's not there. You were his caregiver. You can't tell me that someone walked in from the street and took him while you were sleeping. That doesn't happen, Tamara. You know it and I know it. Nobody came into that house to steal Olly. So where would you take him? Where would you feel safe and comfortable leaving him?"

"I didn't!"

"I didn't say you did. I said hypothetically, if something happened, where would you feel like you could take him? A church? Hospital? Friend? If something happened to him, would you take him to a cemetery? Everybody has places they would be more comfortable with. If you were starting to feel closer to Olly, then you'd want it to be somewhere he'd feel safe. And that means somewhere you felt safe."

Bowen was silent, waiting for Tamara to take it in and

consider the question. Tamara didn't answer. There was nothing for her to say. She didn't have any safe places. The only safe place was at the Hensons'.

What if something had happened to Olly when Tamara got too frustrated or had a psychotic break? Dr. Sutherland said it was still possible for her to have a psychotic break, even without being pregnant and while taking the antipsychotics. If she couldn't remember because she'd had a break with reality, what might have happened during that time? Was there anywhere she could have taken Olly? Anywhere she might have gone instinctively?

"I don't even know anywhere else in the neighborhood. You need a car or bus to get to the hospital or the doctor's office. Even to get to the school. There isn't anything close by."

Bowen scratched several more words into her notepad. "You don't have any friends in the neighborhood? Someone you could go to for help if you were in trouble?"

Tamara shook her head. Her thoughts went to Sybil, but she hadn't talked to Syb since she'd gotten out on parole again. Sybil didn't even know she was back. The other girls she knew at school the year before were on the volleyball team, Tamara didn't know where any of them lived. Even if she did, none of them had been great friends. She didn't particularly want to see any of them again.

"Any places you hung out when you were not taking care of Olly? Or where you hung out last year when you were on parole?"

"No." Tamara tried to remember any neighborhood hangouts from the previous year. "We went to the mall once, but that's near the school. And there was a youth rec facility. But I didn't know anyone there." Tamara's mind went to the warehouse Glock had held her in. To Glock's apartment.

She had been in a bad state when she was at the warehouse. Would her brain have taken her back there if she were sick again? When she'd been sick and exhausted with Amy, she had returned to the neighborhood, to the Hensons' house, so she could give Amy to someone who would take care of her and turn herself in.

"The Hensons' was the only safe place," she said, trying to leave the images and feelings of the warehouse behind. Sick almost to death with pneumonia, chained up, wrapped in foul, stinking blankets.

And the dog. What if she'd relived rescuing the dog when Sybil had come to get her?

Bowen must have seen something in Tamara's expression, because one brow went up. She leaned close. "What? Where?"

"There was... I don't know where it was. I was only there once..."

"Where?"

"A... a dog food store..."

Bowen's confusion couldn't have been more obvious. "A dog food store. What dog food store are you talking about, and why would you take a baby there?"

"No, it's just... I sort of... saved a dog. It was hurt and lost, and I left it outside the door at a pet food place, so it would be found and taken care of."

"Where was this place?"

"I don't know... I don't know if I could even find it again if I looked for it. I just thought... if I did have a psychotic break... my subconscious might remember taking that dog back there to be taken care of... maybe I'd think..."

"That your baby was a dog? That a dog food place would be a good place to take care of your baby?" Bowen's voice was sharp and sarcastic instead of sympathetic. Her real feelings showing through the facade.

"I don't remember anything. I'm just saying, if my brain jumped to that being a safe place, a place where they would help..."

"What else can you remember about this place? Was it near the Hensons' house? How are we supposed to narrow down to one dog food shop in a city this size?"

"It wasn't real far from the Hensons'. Not... not real far, but it wasn't in the neighborhood. It was... sort of a trendy place. In a strip mall. Not one of those big chains. They bake doggie biscuits by hand, you know?"

Bowen jotted it into her notepad. "I need to get someone to run this down. You stay put. Look at those photos. Really focus on anything that might be out of place."

Tamara shook her head. "The only thing out of place is that Olly isn't there. I should be there with him. Not here. Not... whatever happened to him."

"Yeah, whatever happened to him," Bowen agreed, the sarcasm slipping out again. She left the room. Tamara looked back down at the photos. She stared at them hopelessly. She had no idea what had happened. She didn't know how she could fall asleep with a baby and wake up without one.

* * *

"There's someone here to see you."

Finally, Mrs. Henson had come or had sent a lawyer to help Tamara get out of the situation. She hadn't abandoned Tamara at all. She would get everything sorted out. Even if they didn't know yet who had taken Olly, she would be able to prove to the judge that Tamara hadn't done anything, and they would let Tamara go home.

But when she looked expectantly at the door, it wasn't Mrs. Henson. Nor was it the unfamiliar face of a lawyer.

It was Harry.

Tamara had always liked Harry. When she had been there the year before, he had still been living with the Hensons even though he had officially aged out of foster care. He worked and paid them a little rent and they helped him to get on his feet. Something many foster families wouldn't have done. His face looked like a mix of races, and Tamara had never had the courage to ask him what his heritage was. He was laid back and easygoing, but according to Nita, when he had gotten out of juvie he had been angry and volatile. The Hensons had stuck with him through his outbursts and issues, and he had settled in to become one of the most stable and level-headed young adults Tamara knew. Knowing that he had gone from being angry and aggressive like many of the girls Tamara knew at juvie to the nice guy he was gave Tamara a little hope for herself. Maybe someday she would be able to overcome her own problems and become a normal, happy person as well.

"Harry?"

Tamara didn't know whether to stand up to greet him, whether to shake his hand or hug him, or just to say hello. Why was he there instead of Mrs. Henson? He couldn't speak to anyone on Tamara's behalf.

Harry approached the little table where Tamara was sitting. He glanced down at the photos as if worried they might be graphic crime photos. He attempted a reassuring smile that Tamara didn't find at all reassuring.

"Hey, Tamara. How are you holding out?"

Tamara shook her head. "Not so great... why are you here? Did Missus send you?"

"Yeah. I brought you a change of clothes." He put a plastic shopping bag on the table. "So, you have something fresh to wear for your court hearing." He looked at his watch. "That would be in a couple of hours, I guess."

"I thought it wouldn't be until the morning." Tamara wasn't sure whether to be happy or worried. Was there any chance she wouldn't go back to prison? Not likely.

"It is morning."

That would explain why Tamara felt so weak and exhausted.

She had been there all evening and night being interrogated about one part of the case and then another. It was morning and she hadn't had more than a few minutes to rest her eyes since she got there.

"Oh."

"You look beat," he observed.

"Yeah. I am." She wiped her eyes. "I've been up all night."

His expression was veiled. "At least they're taking the investigation seriously. Putting their resources into it."

"I guess."

"Mrs. Henson didn't want to leave the house. But if they don't revoke your parole, she'll come and pick you up. Just call her."

Tamara shifted in her seat. Her butt and legs were stiff from so many hours of sitting. She rested her elbows on the table, rubbing her face.

"Harry...?"

"Yeah?"

"Missus... she knows I didn't do anything, right? She knows I didn't hurt Olly."

Harry didn't answer immediately. He rubbed the bridge of his nose.

"Harry? She knows that, doesn't she?"

Harry shook his head slowly. "She doesn't want to think that you did anything. But there's no way for her to know. She wasn't home."

"But I wouldn't! I... I was doing better with Olly. She told the cops that, didn't she? I know she told my parole officer she had concerns, but she told the cops I was doing good and taking good care of him, right? And that he was bonding with me? I wouldn't just... I wouldn't do something to him."

"I don't know all of the details," Harry evaded. "From what I gather... she couldn't trust that just because you were trying or just because it looked like you were managing better that you wouldn't... do something."

Tamara blinked, hot tears welling up in her eyes. Mrs. Henson had done so much for her that she was sure Mrs. Henson would know that she hadn't done anything to hurt Olly.

"I fell asleep," she told Harry, her voice rough and a hot lump in her throat. "He went down for a nap, and I fell asleep, and when I woke up later... he was gone. He was just... gone!"

Harry nodded.

"I'm still on my meds. I've been taking them like I'm supposed to. I didn't have a psychotic break and hurt him or forget about him."

"Okay."

"You believe me, don't you?"

"I believe that *you* believe that."

"So, you all... you all think I'm crazy. You think I did something to him."

Harry shrugged. "We don't know, Tamara."

Tamara slumped back in her chair, swearing. Tears released from her eyes and streamed down her face. "My baby is gone, and you think I don't care? You think I did this myself?"

He just looked at her. Looking into his dark eyes, Tamara was transported back several weeks, to the first Sunday dinner Harry had come home for after her release.

* * *

Tamara had left the dinner table with Olly, frustrated with his fussiness and unable to keep him quiet enough that everyone else could visit and enjoy a nice family meal together. She sat on the couch in the living room, frustrated to tears. She cradled Olly against her body and encouraged him to take the bottle, even though she knew he'd already had enough and if she kept feeding him, he was just going to throw it back up again.

Nothing else seemed to soothe him. She had tried a pacifier numerous times, hoping that the sucking would calm him just as much as actually drinking a bottle. But Olly was not to be fooled.

Mrs. Henson could often quiet him by singing or humming to him, but when Tamara tried to sing him *Hush, Little Baby*, the one lullaby Gran had taught her, he would howl and kick like she was torturing him.

Harry was the first to finish his dinner and leave the table. He sat in the easy chair close to Tamara, giving her a sympathetic look.

"Not having a great day?"

Tamara choked back a sob. "No, not a great day! Not a great week! I don't know how this is better than being stuck in juvie!"

"Well..." He considered. "The food is better."

She gave a short laugh. "Yeah, it is."

"And I don't imagine he cries all the time."

"Ugh. Yes, he does. He knows I'm not his mom. Or not his foster mom. Not who he's used to. He's teething." Tamara brushed his red cheek with one finger. "It seems like the only time he's not crying is when he's eating or sleeping, and he doesn't do either one for very long."

"We've had lots of babies through this house. They all grow up, sooner or later."

"Sometimes I wonder whether he's going to make it that long," Tamara growled, trying to cajole Olly into keeping the nipple in his mouth just a little longer.

When she looked back up at Harry, he wore a concerned expression. "Tamara... if you're feeling like that... you need a break. You need to let Mrs. Henson know that you're feeling overwhelmed and need some help."

"She knows."

"I don't think she does. If you're feeling like you could harm him, you need to get someone else to step in."

"I'm not going to hurt him."

His eyes were piercing. She looked away from him.

"I won't."

"Even if you love someone, that doesn't mean you couldn't hurt them. A lot of parents do hurt their children, even when they say they love them. Kids are a big responsibility. I've seen Mrs. Henson teach so many girls how to love and care for their babies... and honestly, they're not all up to it. Even though you love him and have the best intentions, it takes more than that."

"I don't love him."

Harry's eyes widened. That obviously wasn't the answer he'd been expecting. Tamara looked down at Olly, pressing her lips together tightly.

"I'm trying. But I don't even like babies. And Olly... I try not to think about all the bad stuff that happened before he was born... that's not his fault... but I don't love him."

"Then why are you taking care of him? Especially when it's this hard? Why didn't you just leave him with his foster family and work on yourself? Parole is hard enough without throwing a baby in the mix."

"I have to. It was the only way I could get parole."

Harry shook his head slowly. "Probably Mrs. H's idea, right? She always wants to save the babies. But you know if something happens to Olly, you're going to end up back in juvie anyway, right? If you can't handle it, you'd better talk to someone before you do something."

"I'm not going to do anything. I'm going to be a good mom to him and stay out of prison and it's all going to be okay."

"And then what?"

Tamara looked down at Olly's face, hoping he would drift off to sleep while he still had the bottle in his mouth.

"What do you mean?"

"I mean... so you succeed, and you have him for a year, or two years, until they release you from parole and you're a free citizen again. Then what? Are you going to say you're done and send him back to foster care? Or be a single mom for another sixteen years?"

She looked back up at Harry's face in dismay. Up until then, she had only thought about staying out of prison. About successfully caring for Olly to avoid going back. All she had worried about was what would happen if she failed; she'd never considered what would happen if she succeeded.

She was only sixteen herself. She couldn't fathom having to care for Olly until he was an adult. She'd somehow been able to focus on the next year or two, and then Olly disappeared from her future. She hadn't thought about how the rest of his life was going to unfold when she was finished her parole.

"He's a person, Tamara. He's going to grow up, and then you're going to have a toddler to deal with. A school kid. A teenager. He's not going to be a baby forever."

* * *

"You're tired." Harry's voice dragged Tamara back to the present. "That's why you're getting emotional. I'll see if I can talk them into at least letting you have a nap before your hearing, but they're going to have to transport you to the courthouse soon. Have some breakfast. Get on your new clothes. You'll feel better."

"Harry!" Tamara stood up as he turned away from her.

Harry looked at her.

"I didn't hurt Olly. Things were getting better. He was getting attached to me. I was getting... I liked him. I was getting attached to him. He was my baby. Mine. It wasn't the same as when I was taking care of other people's babies. We had—have— a connection. I really did like him."

She had meant to say *love*, but at the last minute, she couldn't follow through. She cared about her baby and what happened to him, but she wasn't sure she could claim to love him and be believable.

Harry studied her, his face still a blank mask. Tamara was pretty sure he didn't believe her. He thought it was all an act and she was just trying to cover for herself. He and everybody else were sure she had done something to Olly.

Finally, Harry spoke. "Then where is he?"

Tamara wished she could answer his question. She was Olly's mother and she should be able to answer that question.

"I don't know."

SIXTEEN

S HE DIDN'T GET A nap before her hearing. As Harry had predicted, they soon brought her breakfast, not much different from the fare she was accustomed to at juvie. Bowen probably had coffee and donuts, but Tamara was consigned to stale toast dipped in lukewarm oatmeal. Not that she would have been able to get much down anyway, but she could have used a hit of caffeine. And nicotine, even though she hadn't had a cigarette in the weeks since getting out.

Bowen also brought Tamara her meds. She didn't give Tamara the full bottles, but dispensed her morning dose as directed on the labels. They probably didn't want her getting her hands on a full bottle of pills and taking the chance that she would overdose.

They let her wash up and change into the fresh clothes Mrs. Henson had sent. Tamara splashed cold water on her face, trying to wake herself up to face her hearing. Before long, she was transported to the courthouse, where she had been a number of times before. She was taken directly to a courtroom where the judge was going through the stack of offenders who had been arrested the previous night. Tamara joined the rows of detainees.

Most were in their street clothes and weren't even handcuffed. Because of her history, Tamara was in full ankle and leg shackles with waist chain and the noisy chains joining everything up, so she was secure. She felt the curious gazes of the other prisoners and the spectators in the court room upon her.

Some of the spectators would be reporters looking for a story. She didn't know whether they would already know about Olly's disappearance and her history. Hopefully, they had been featuring Olly's disappearance on the TV, so they could find the person who had taken him. But she had a suspicion the police weren't looking for additional suspects.

She saw Wanda Brisk there, looking impatiently at her watch and then over at Tamara every so often to make sure she hadn't managed to wander off.

When her case was called up, Wanda Brisk outlined Olly's disappearance to the judge and introduced Bowen. He looked at the papers in front of him.

"Do you have a recommendation?"

"She is one of my parolees. It would appear from the circumstances that she has violated the terms of her parole and should therefore be returned to custody."

"It would appear...? I assume there is evidence that Miss French was involved in the disappearance of her child?"

"She was alone with him."

"That's hardly an admission of guilt. She was in compliance with the terms of her parole up until the disappearance?"

"There were a few bumps along the way... but we hadn't seen the need to return her to custody up until now. She appeared to be settling in and managing her son's care better."

The judge studied Tamara. She tried not to squirm or look away.

"She was not being directly supervised on these visits with her child?"

"Uh... she wasn't having visits. She was his primary caregiver. Officially, he was in the custody of Tamara's foster mother, Marion Henson, but his care was Tamara's responsibility."

"Ah." He rubbed his chin. "And the foster mother felt that it was safe to leave her alone with him?"

Bowen jumped in with the details. "She was only out briefly to run an errand."

"I assume she knew the child's life was more important than a gallon of milk and she believed everything was fine when she left."

"Yes. Of course."

"How long was she gone?"

"Just an hour, your honor."

He frowned. He took off his glasses and wiped them, then returned them to his face and stared at Detective Bowen.

"And in the space of an hour, you believe things escalated from there being no concerns about the child's safety to the point that she harmed her child, left the house, disposed of the evidence, and then returned, without alerting Mrs. Henson to the fact that something was wrong."

"Yes. Tamara may have been out of the house for longer than that. Her bedroom door was shut when Mrs. Henson returned home, and she assumed Tamara was napping. Tamara could have returned sometime in the next two hours without Mrs. Henson being aware of it. At some point after Tamara returned, Mrs. Henson went to wake her up and discovered the baby was missing."

"Mrs. Henson woke her up. You think she was playing possum?"

"She gave the appearance of being more deeply asleep and difficult to awaken than would be normal for a daytime nap. It's quite likely she was faking it," Bowen asserted, nodding vigorously.

"The house and property has been searched?"

"Yes. No sign of the baby."

"No woods nearby? Scent dogs been out?"

Bowen nodded, less vigorously. She had doubtless faced judges before and sensed that her case was not standing up as well as she had hoped. "We are following up on leads to other sites where she might have dumped the baby. Sites that were suggested by our interviews with Tamara."

"How long will that take?"

"It will take some time. These are large sites, some distance from the house."

"Not sites she could have reached in, say, fifteen minutes."

"No, but if she wasn't in her bedroom when Mrs. Henson got home..."

"You are still looking at a very narrow timeframe. She had access to a vehicle?"

"No, not that we know of. She could have an accomplice who helped her dispose of the body."

"Do you have any other suspects?"

"Tamara is our primary suspect at this time. We're asking that she be remanded without bail—"

The judge looked down at his papers. "This is not a bail hearing. You don't have the evidence to charge her with anything, and you know it."

Bowen flushed pink. The judge turned his attention from Bowen to Wanda Brisk.

"You didn't have reason to violate Miss French's parole before today?"

"No. But given the circumstances..."

"I haven't heard any evidence that Miss French was negligent or had the opportunity to harm the child and dispose of his body anywhere but on the property, which has been searched." He lowered his pen to the page and scribbled something on the papers before him. "It's almost unheard of to reject a parole officer's application to revoke parole. But that's exactly what I'm going to do. I've heard no evidence that Miss French has done anything in violation of the terms of her parole, nor that she has committed a felony. It would be a miscarriage of justice to punish her for the disappearance of her child if she had nothing to do with it." He looked again at Bowen. "One of the primary tests for a suspect in any crime is *opportunity*. Miss French does not meet that requirement."

"We don't know how long she had—"

"I would advise that she be returned to her home without delay. Widen your net, detective. If she did this, it would have had to be premeditated and with an accomplice, not in a moment of anger or impatience."

Bowen nodded slowly. The judge banged his gavel, handed the paperwork to the brown-suited woman standing by, and went on to the next case. Bowen and Wanda both turned to look at Tamara. Neither appeared to be in a particularly cheerful mood.

"You lucked out today," Wanda said in a flat, emotionless voice. "I've never had a judge turn down a recommendation to return someone to custody before. Don't expect it to happen again."

Tamara nodded. She was still too stunned by the judge's words to really take in what had just happened. Bowen produced a key for the shackles and proceeded to remove Tamara's chains. Tamara felt instantly lighter, but also completely exhausted.

"What do I do now?"

"Go home." Bowen looked at her watch. "I'm going to revisit the scene. You want a ride?"

Tamara bit back an angry retort. She didn't want anything from Bowen. But it would be ridiculous to turn down the officer and make Mrs. Henson drive to the courthouse to get Tamara, when Bowen was driving to the house anyway. She clenched her fists.

"Do I get the front seat this time?"

Bowen gave her a stare, eyes half-closed. "I suppose that could be arranged."

Tamara followed the detective out of the courtroom. Several of the cons she passed on the way out nodded to her or murmured a few words of respect. Walking into the courtroom in chains and walking out a free person didn't happen very often.

* * *

They did not converse in the car. Bowen didn't seem sullen so much as thoughtful. Maybe the judge had actually gotten through to her. Tamara struggled to keep her eyes open and her mind alert. She hadn't felt like herself since Mrs. Henson had woken her up. It was a waking nightmare. But it wasn't like her psychotic episodes. She just had a sense of unreality and disconnection. And blank space where she should have been able to remember what had happened to Olly.

They pulled up to the Hensons' house. Tamara sat looking at it for a moment. She didn't know what to think of it. Was it home? Was it a safe place? Would they even want her there anymore? It was still the only familiar place she had to go, but the yellow tape and strong police presence were an uncomfortable reminder of what they thought of her.

Tamara got out of the car and walked up to the house. She didn't ring the bell, but just went straight in.

"Tamara?" Mrs. Henson, dark bags under her eyes, saw Tamara enter. "Are you—they let you go? Are you okay?"

Tamara looked at her, anger and bitterness rising up, a foul taste in her mouth. Mrs. Henson hadn't even shown up at her hearing. She hadn't even been the one to drop the clothes off for Tamara, sending Harry instead. "I didn't do it. I didn't do anything to Olly."

"Okay."

"I don't know what happened to Olly. I want to find him. I want to know he's okay."

Mrs. Henson just nodded, for once at a loss as to what to say or do. Tamara expected some kind of reassurance or a hug, but Mrs. Henson just stood there.

"I have to lay down." Tamara turned and went up the stairs.

Behind her, she could hear Bowen approach Mrs. Henson. "Excuse me, Mrs. Henson... I need to talk to you."

SEVENTEEN

TAMARA SLEPT RESTLESSLY. SHE was too exhausted to sleep properly. She would drift off quickly, but then awaken with a start, disoriented. She kept telling herself that she was okay. She was safe. She wasn't in prison or in a jail cell at the police station. They didn't have any evidence to put her away. They hadn't been able to find any blood or other signs that indicated she had hurt Olly when the frustration and anger just got to be too much for her. There was no sign that she had wrapped him up and disposed of his little body somewhere. There wasn't a single thing that suggested foul play.

But she was still sure that Bowen was going to come up the stairs at any minute and arrest her for real, take her down to the police station and confront her with horrific pictures, and send her on the prison bus back to juvie or to the women's prison. She wouldn't be safe if that happened. She had to keep herself out of prison.

Maybe, too, part of her body was waiting for Olly to start crying. She had become conditioned to listen for him while she slept. She was used to having to wake up over and over again to calm and soothe him, never getting more than a couple of hours at a time to sleep.

But Bowen didn't come up the stairs to arrest her. Mrs. Henson didn't come into the bedroom to talk to her. There was no apology for not believing in Tamara's innocence. As far as everyone was concerned, she had hurt Olly and was just trying to cover it up. They figured all they had to do was wait or catch her in a lie, and then they could break her.

Tamara found herself lying on the bed with her eyes open, staring at the side of the empty crib. She couldn't tell from her position that it was empty. It could all have been a dream, and baby Olly was sleeping there soundly, for a few more minutes, and then he would wake up again and need to be fed or changed or comforted.

The sun was getting low in the sky when Tamara finally got out of bed again. She could hear voices downstairs and knew that the Hensons were busy getting dinner prepared. In a few minutes, they would call everyone to eat.

Tamara paced across the room. Her thoughts kept whirling around and around, and then bumping up against the blank space where her memories of the previous day should have been, like a balloon filled with air.

If she hadn't been the one to remove Olly from the house, then someone else had.

It could be someone in the house, or someone outside the house. She went through the names and faces of everyone who lived there. Was it possible that Deshawn had taken Olly, wanting to care for him by herself? She wouldn't hurt him, not intentionally, but what if she hid him somewhere unsafe? What if she smothered him trying to keep him quiet, or propped a bottle for him and he choked on it? What if she had put him into a nest of soft clothes and covered him up, and he had not been able to get enough air or had overheated?

She couldn't think of any reason Nita would have to take

Olly. Then there were the boys. Jason had been irritated with Olly's crying. He had complained about it and didn't want the baby around. But Jason had never shown any violence toward Olly. He wouldn't have done anything to make Olly be quiet.

Tamara was suddenly overtaken by a memory of putting her hand over Julie's mouth to stop her from crying. She had been so scared of the consequences of letting the Bakers' baby cry. She had done it more than once, but she had always chickened out in the end and removed her hand, letting Julie take a big breath and begin to wail again. The one time that Mr. Baker had seen her put a couple of fingers over Julie's lips, trying to cue her that she needed to be quiet, he had blown his top. But that hadn't stopped Tamara. Mrs. Baker screaming at Tamara for falling asleep while bathing the little girls had not stopped her. In the end, there was no beating severe enough to keep Tamara from doing what she had to do to escape their tyranny. She had been more afraid of them than she had been of the consequences she would face if the police figured out she had killed the children.

But that was Tamara, not Jason. He was vocal about his objection to Olly's crying. He had let it be known that it bothered him. That had been his release valve. He wasn't the kind who would hold it all in and then throttle the baby in a fit of rage.

Not Dirk.

She was sure that he wouldn't do anything to harm Olly.

Jesse, then? He had always remained calm around Tamara. Like Mrs. Henson, he was able to tune out the baby crying, to tell her that it was fine for him to cry for a while and learn how to soothe himself. Despite Tamara's distrust of foster fathers, he had never made any overtures toward Tamara or tried to be alone with her. He was like one of the fantasy fathers on TV, the ones who knew how to handle everything and always gave their kids valuable advice. She couldn't fault him for anything. He'd been at work when she had taken her nap. He never came home unexpectedly during the day, never came home early in the afternoon.

He was home for supper every night and spent the evening with Mrs. Henson or fixed things up around the house. He was very handy and seemed to know how to do everything. Except keep the washers and dryers running.

And Mrs. Henson? She was the only one who had opportunity equal to Tamara's. She had been home while Tamara slept. She had the car. She had been the one to wake Tamara up and demand to know where Olly was. Had her behavior been at all odd or suspicious? Had she been too quick to think that something had happened to Olly? Too slow? Had she sent Nita and Tamara off to check all of the other rooms while she did something with them out of the way? Stowed the baby in the trunk of the car? Disguised his smell with something that would throw off the dogs?

A knock on the bedroom door nearly made Tamara jump out of her skin. She whirled around to see Deshawn crack the door open a few inches and peer through.

"It's supper, Tamara."

"No, I can't eat," Tamara objected.

"You need to have something."

Tamara shook her head. She was too focused on trying to figure out what had happened to Olly to stop and eat and to have to be surrounded by the family, all awkward and watching her. All suspicious of her while she looked around at them, trying to figure out who was really to blame.

"I can't go down. I can't face everybody. Can you just bring me up a plate? Can't I just eat in here for once?"

"It's against the rules. We always have to go down for dinner."

"Can't you tell Mrs. Henson that this is different? I can't go down and face them all after all of this. I just can't."

Deshawn grimaced. "I'll give it a try, girl. But I can tell you now, they're not going to like it."

"This is different. They haven't ever had something like this happen before. I need time. I just can't deal with family right now."

"I'll try."

She withdrew, shutting the door behind her. Tamara continued to pace back and forth. She stopped and looked into the empty crib. So many times, when she had looked into that crib, she had seen Julie in her memories. Gray and flaccid and breathing her last breaths. The image had haunted Tamara. But now she saw Olly. What would she have done if she had found him in the crib, his skin blue, not breathing? What if she had accidentally laid him on his stomach and he had died of SIDS? Or what if he had squished himself into a corner and smothered on the padded mattress? What would Tamara have done if she had found him like that? Would she have broken? Would she have been able to admit what had happened? Or would she have blocked it all out, wrapped him in a blanket, and gotten rid of the evidence, preferring to imagine that Olly had been stolen away by some stranger who had come into the house?

What about Mrs. Henson? What if she had come home and Olly had been sleeping in the living room on the blanket, where Tamara remembered him lying earlier in the day? What if Olly had been there and Tamara had been nowhere in sight, and Olly had stopped breathing? What if he'd put something in his mouth and choked on it? What if he had just passed away without a cause, but Mrs. Henson thought it was something that Tamara had done? Would she confront Tamara with the evidence, or would she quietly clean it up and get rid of all of the evidence? Would she prefer that everyone thought Tamara had done something than that an accident had happened while the baby was in her care? Did she realize that suspicion would be thrown on Tamara, or would she think that she could blame it on an unknown subject? She hadn't accused Tamara outright. She hadn't pointed Tamara out as the culprit to the police. She hadn't even told them about her history or that she was only out on parole.

There was another knock on the door and Tamara looked guiltily toward it, anxious at being caught hanging over the crib, staring into it like it could reveal its secrets to her.

Deshawn didn't ask Tamara what she was doing or if she was the one who was responsible for Olly's disappearance. She just entered without a word and put a plate of food down on the dresser for Tamara.

"Thanks," Tamara whispered, unable to find her voice.

Deshawn nodded and tried to raise a smile, but didn't manage it. She looked like she wanted to say something, to reassure Tamara that everything was going to be okay. It would all work out in the end, somehow. But she didn't say that she knew Tamara hadn't done anything. She didn't say everything was going to be okay. She just left the food and went downstairs.

Tamara went over to the dish and took a bite. It stuck in her throat, and for a moment she was afraid that it wouldn't go down and it wouldn't come up, and she would just choke there silently to death. It would be fitting. To die there like Olly had.

But she didn't know that was what had happened. The food went down, forcing its way down Tamara's esophagus, scraping as it went. Tears came to Tamara's eyes at the pain. She hadn't cried for Olly. He was her baby and she hadn't cried for him. What kind of a mother was she? The social worker had said she would become more attached to Olly, and she had, but she still wasn't the kind of mom that she should have been. She still didn't have that mother's heart everyone talked about. That unconditional, pure love of her own flesh and blood. Instead, she was easily irritated by him. Didn't like him when he wouldn't settle and just screamed and screamed no matter what she did for him.

She poked at the plate of food.

Mrs. Henson hadn't insisted that Tamara had to go downstairs to eat with the family. Tamara was no longer part of their circle. She wasn't family. She was just someone who lived there. A murder suspect. Someone they couldn't kick out until a new home was found for her. They didn't want her there.

Tamara sat down on the edge of the bed. She didn't lie down, and she didn't get up and resume pacing. She sat there soaking in the silence of the room.

If everybody else thought that she had harmed Olly, that meant that no one was looking for other suspects or for what had really happened to him. The police detectives just kept looking for evidence that it was Tamara. Mrs. Henson thought that it was Tamara because she had a history and she was the only one who had been home. Even Tamara herself was starting to wonder what had happened to Olly and why she couldn't remember, wondering if she could have done something on a psychotic break and just blocked it all out.

If no one else were going to look for the real culprit, then Tamara needed to. She had to figure it out herself. She held the key to what had happened. She was Olly's mother. She owed it to him, in spite of the dismal failure she was as a mother, she had to find out who had hurt him or, if he were still alive, who had taken him away.

* * *

Family dinner was still going on when Tamara opened her door. She listened for a moment to make sure everyone was still downstairs. Waited until she could account for each one of their voices. She went into Nita's and Deshawn's room first.

Nothing had changed. It still looked just the same as it had when Nita and Tamara had searched for Olly the day before. Had the police even bothered to move the piles of laundry around to look for evidence or the baby? If he'd been in the room, the dogs would have been able to smell him. Tamara couldn't see or smell anything that would have fouled their noses. Olly wasn't there. He never had been. There was no sign that Deshawn had been trying to take care of Olly herself. No baby things. Nothing out of place in the clothing-strewn mess. It all looked just as it should.

Tamara tiptoed out of the girls' room and into the boys'. She avoided the areas of the hallway where she knew the floorboards creaked. She didn't need anyone downstairs hearing a stray creak and thinking she was up to something. She opened the door as quietly as she could and went inside.

Like the girls' room, it was messy, but she didn't spot anything suspicious. She looked at Jason's bunk and the things he had collected on his shelves and dresser over the time he'd lived with the Hensons. Foster kids didn't usually have many possessions, and they tended to become packrats. Jason had baseball cards, some old kids' games, ball caps, and trophies he had earned at school. He must have been a pretty good athlete.

She was reluctant to look at Dirk's side, but she finally dragged her eyes over to examine his things. His side was a little neater than Jason's, with far fewer possessions. No trophies. No collections. He had some clothes and his school books. A second pair of runners. Tamara didn't know much about where he had come from, but it was obvious he hadn't brought much of anything with him. Like Tamara, he had come to the Hensons with nothing.

"What are you doing?"

Tamara jumped and whirled around, her hands up defensively. Dirk was standing in the doorway looking at her. His voice wasn't outraged, but it was clear that he didn't like her being there. Tamara kept her hands up, her heart slamming against her ribs. What if he had been the one to take Olly? What if he now thought she knew something? If he thought she was a threat to him, she could be next on the list. But she was in a house full of people; he wasn't going to do anything with everyone else there. A shout or a scuffle would bring the rest of the family in an instant.

"You're supposed to be eating," she told him.

"Is that why you wouldn't come down? So you could search my room?"

"I'm not searching it... just looking..." Tamara said lamely. "I thought..." She was going to say she thought she heard something, but she trailed off, knowing that wouldn't cut it. She'd heard something? Like what? A baby crying?

She looked around again, paranoid. What if there were a clue in the room, and she missed her one chance to see it? What if Olly were there?

But he wasn't. The police had looked. The dogs had sniffed. Everybody had been in there at least once, looking for the baby who had disappeared. They wouldn't have missed him. If there had been anything of his, even one of his tiny socks, kicked under one of the beds, the scent dogs would have found it. Tears prickled in Tamara's eyes. She blinked, wanting to rub them away, but not wanting to move out of her defensive stance or show weakness in front of Dirk.

"You thought what?" Dirk's voice was growing more confrontational. "You thought I had something to do with your baby disappearing?" He stared at her, his eyes getting wider. "Really? That's what you thought? You think I took him?"

Tamara shook her head, trying to swallow the lump in her throat and keep her breathing quiet and steady. "No. How could you? You weren't here."

"No, I wasn't," he agreed. "And the cops have already searched this room and checked my alibi, so what do you think you're going to find that they didn't?"

He had an alibi. The police had already checked. They knew for sure that it hadn't been Dirk. Tamara's shoulders relaxed. Her fists lowered slightly.

"I'm sorry. I just... had to know."

Dirk looked around the room, spreading his hands wide. "Well, what do you think? You see anything? You think if I did do something, I would leave some kind of clue in plain sight?"

"No..."

He shook his head and stepped toward her. Tamara tensed in readiness. Dirk watched her carefully, taking another step. "You really think you could do anything about it if I wanted to hurt you?" he challenged, eyes on her raised fists and tense face.

He was bigger than she was. Taller and heavier. But Tamara had fought plenty of people who were taller and heavier. She knew how to use her size to her advantage. She was quick and had a lower center of gravity. All she would really have to do would be to hold him off. The noise of any altercation would bring Jesse and Jason up in seconds.

Dirk took another step toward her. Tamara readied herself.

But when Dirk reached toward her, it was with open hands and he moved slowly, telegraphing his movements, like she was a skittish horse and he didn't want to frighten her. Tamara flashed back for just an instant to life on the farm with Gran. She'd had a horse at one time. A beautiful, mischievous paint pony that had been the center of her world. That life was so distant, it could have belonged to another person altogether. Tamara had changed too much from that horse-crazy little girl to ever go back to that life.

Dirk reached toward her, and Tamara didn't move. Her heart raced, and her breathing rasped, but she didn't move away from him and she didn't punch him in the face, which was what her body kept telling her to do. She stood still while he wrapped his arms around her. She remained rigid in his embrace, not moving.

"You really think I would have done something to your baby?" he whispered near her ear.

A shiver ran through Tamara. Would he? Was the romantic approach just a smokescreen? He had wanted her, and she had turned him down because of the baby. Olly had been her excuse for not engaging with him. What would he do to clear that obstacle?

"Do you?" he repeated, when she didn't answer.

"I don't know. I don't know you."

He squeezed her against him. Tamara pulled her hands out from where they were pinned between them and, for lack of any other idea, put them around him. Her body melted against his, craving the comfort of another warm human being. Her arms ached for Olly, but she held Dirk against herself instead.

"I wouldn't do that," Dirk assured. He loosened his hold on her, transferring his hands instead to her head, tilting her face up toward his so he could kiss her.

Tamara's mind flipped between the past and the present. She thought of other people who had taken control of her body without her permission. Had she given Dirk permission? Was she giving it to him by not fighting back when his lips pressed to hers? She didn't know whether she wanted his attentions or just the comfort of being held.

Dirk paused and pulled back from the kiss, his eyes measuring the distance to the bed. Tamara shook her head.

"Everybody's going to be coming upstairs."

She put her hands on his chest and pushed away from him. She was having trouble catching her breath. Dirk didn't stop her when she turned to the open door and left him in the bedroom alone. She was at her own door when Nita reached the top of the stairs. Tamara could have just been returning to her room after using the bathroom. There was nothing to give away that she had been in the boys' room. Except maybe her flushed cheeks and heavy breathing. Nita smiled. If she guessed that anything was amiss, she didn't say so.

EIGHTEEN

T HE PERSON WHO WAS at the top of Tamara's suspect list was Glock. Kidnapping a baby right under Tamara's nose was just the type of thing she would delight in doing, and she had reason to resent Tamara and want to hurt her.

Tamara was the reason Glock was back behind bars.

Tamara had testified against Glock and tried to kill her the last time they had seen each other.

Glock was back in prison; she couldn't have been the one who had taken Olly. But Tamara had to be sure she hadn't escaped or been released. Glock always found ways around the system. The police had said they would follow up on her, but Tamara didn't trust them to look at anyone other than herself, and they certainly weren't giving her any information about what they had found out. After agonizing over it for a while, Tamara sought out Mrs. Henson. She found her in the living room, folding laundry. Olly's blanket and any other bits Tamara had left in the living room while looking after him were gone, taken away by the police as evidence. Tamara didn't know what clues they thought Olly's slobbery toys and spit-up-on blankets provided.

"Oh. Hi, Tamara. Did you get enough to eat?"

"Yeah." Tamara's plate was still up in her bedroom, barely touched. "Do you think you could help me with something?"

Mrs. Henson laid down a folded shirt in a stack and didn't look at her. "I supposed that depends what it is."

In the past, Mrs. Henson would have always told her yes without knowing anything about Tamara's request. Her new caution irritated Tamara. She wanted to just snap 'Forget it, then!' and walk away. But that wouldn't help her. It wouldn't help Olly. She stood there for a minute, weighing her words, trying to figure out how to approach the problem. Mrs. Henson finally glanced over at her to see what the problem was.

"What is it, then? What do you need help with?"

"It's about Glock."

Mrs. Henson's brows drew down, creases appearing between them.

"I want to make sure... she's still in juvie."

"The police would have told us if—"

"I want to get in to see her."

Mrs. Henson stared, mouth open. After a minute of stunned silence, she pulled herself together and spoke. Her voice was calm and measured, but Tamara sensed something different behind it.

"Why would you want to visit her?"

"I want to see her. In prison. To know that she's there. And... to make sure she didn't get someone else to take Olly. If she's in prison still, she couldn't have taken him. But she could have been friends with a girl who was getting out. If she wanted to get back at me, she could have someone else do it. She'd know they could never trace it back to her..."

"How could she hire someone to take Olly? And why would

she? I know the two of you ended up at odds, but really... do you think she would hold a grudge against you? Enough to care about doing something to hurt you? And how would she know about Olly? The fact that you had a baby hasn't been advertised."

Tamara rubbed her aching forehead. "I don't know... stuff spreads on the prison grapevines... I just want to talk to her to make sure."

"I don't think that's a good idea. And that's not the only issue..."

"What?"

"You're not allowed to have contact with her. With any of your old associates."

That fact had not even occurred to Tamara. She looked at Mrs. Henson, frustrated. "But couldn't you... I wouldn't be doing anything with her, just making sure..."

"I can't okay it. You'd have to get permission from your parole officer."

Tamara swore. The last thing she wanted to do was call up Wanda Brisk to find out if she would okay Tamara going to talk to Glock.

"But I'm trying to help the investigation."

"You should leave that to the police. There's nothing you or I can do. They know what they're doing. Let them do their jobs."

"They don't know! They're only looking at me. They won't believe that I didn't do anything. All they care about is railroading me. Even the judge said so—if they had any evidence against me, I'd be in prison. But I'm not!"

Mrs. Henson considered this, her eyes wide. "Did the judge really say that?"

"He said they never go against a PO's request to remand a parolee. Ever. But here I am! Because he didn't think I could have done anything. They don't have any evidence."

"You were the last one with Olly."

"That's true whether I'm guilty or innocent."

"You never sleep that soundly. You always waken at the slightest sound."

Tamara closed her eyes. "I don't know. I was tired. I can't explain that. He keeps me up a lot at night and I just couldn't wake up."

Mrs. Henson folded a few more items of clothing, thinking about it. "I can call the prison and see if Glock is still there. But if you want to see her, you're going to have to call Wanda."

"I don't want to ask her about it. It's not like I'd be associating with Glock. Just talking to her at the prison. We wouldn't be out drinking together or getting in some kind of trouble."

"You know the rules. And you know that if you break them, Wanda will take the first opportunity to put you back in juvie. You embarrassed her once. She'll be looking for a reason to prove that she was right all along."

Tamara sat down in the easy chair, hunching over and putting her hands over her face. The room was too still. Too quiet.

"I miss Olly," she said. "I never thought I would."

"I know." Mrs. Henson sighed. "The house always feels empty when one of my babies moves out."

She said it like Olly had just graduated to other living arrangements, like the other mothers and infants Mrs. Henson cared for. It pierced Tamara to the heart to know that wasn't true.

"I want to find him."

"If you want to talk to Glock, you'll need to get permission."

* * *

Mrs. Henson was right, and she was wrong. Tamara did need to talk to Wanda to get permission to go to the prison to talk to

Glock, who everyone assured her was still incarcerated and not out snatching babies. Tamara also needed permission from the prison and to get on Glock's visitor list. And if Tamara were going to talk to someone who might have given orders to have the baby kidnapped, the police wanted to be in on it. Bowen helped to grease the wheels both with Wanda and with the prison officials, indicating that it would be beneficial to the investigation if Tamara could talk to Glock. She was the one who was most likely to be able to get information out of Glock. The older girl wasn't going to talk to anyone else. She wasn't known for being cooperative.

So, it wasn't Mrs. Henson or even Wanda who took Tamara to the juvenile facility several hours away. Instead, she had to go with Detective Bowen. Glock had been sent upstate to ensure that she and Tamara didn't have anything more to do with each other. Putting them both back into the same juvenile facility would have been disastrous. Bowen arrived at the house to pick Tamara up. When she got to the detective's car, Tamara found that Bowen's partner, Timmons, was sitting in the driver's seat, which meant that Bowen was going to be riding shotgun and Tamara was going to be in the back of the car. She stopped short. Bowen scowled at her.

"What? You forget something?"

"I don't want to sit in the back."

Bowen let out a bark of laughter. "Too bad about that. Get in."

"But I don't want—"

"Did you think you were getting the royal treatment? We're taking you to see your friend. We're taking a whole day to make the trip, let the two of you talk for a few minutes, and come back again. It's not a college road trip."

Tamara stood her ground. She didn't know what else she expected them to offer, but she didn't want to be treated like a criminal.

Timmons leaned over the back seat and opened the door, pushing it open for Tamara to get in. When Tamara didn't move, he looked at his partner.

"What's the problem?"

"Kid doesn't want to sit in the back of a police vehicle. Thinks she's a princess."

Tamara bristled at being called out as a princess. Hadn't she proven enough times at juvie that she wasn't a privileged little white girl?

"It's not a marked vehicle and we won't be traveling with the lights on," Timmons reasoned. "No one is going to know."

Tamara nodded to the open car door. "There are still bars in the window."

"No one is going to take a close enough look to notice. Hop in, we've got a long way to go. Let's get this show on the road."

Tamara looked around. No one was obviously watching her, but there could have been neighbors watching through their windows. People who would easily recognize Bowen as a cop and think that Tamara was being arrested or taken in for further questioning.

"Would you prefer to be transported in handcuffs?" Bowen asked, leaning in too close to Tamara, in her personal space. "You want us to really put on a show?"

"No!" Tamara snapped back. "I'm helping you out, not going in for more interrogation!"

"Then climb in, princess. Unless you've decided you don't want to go after all. We both know this is just a wild goose chase."

Acid burning at the back of Tamara's throat, she climbed into the waiting vehicle. Bowen at least refrained from pressing Tamara's head down and shutting the door behind her, letting her do it herself so it looked more natural.

"Seatbelt," Timmons instructed, as Bowen got into the front seat.

Tamara grudgingly found the seatbelt and fastened it. The back seat of the vehicle was more of a bench, hard molded plastic with dips for seats, polished and slippery. Something that could be easily removed and hosed off, instead of upholstery that would soak up whatever filth and bodily fluids the passengers baptized it with. It was going to be a long, hard ride.

They drove for a while without speaking to Tamara, exchanging comments between themselves in lowered voices and making reports on the radio. When they hit the highway and were away from the din of the traffic in the city, Bowen turned partway around in her seat to look at Tamara.

"You know that all communications between you and Spielman are going to be monitored. We will be watching and listening to everything and will review it all afterward. You want to find out whether she had any involvement in Olly's disappearance, so just say what you would naturally. There's not going to be anyone whispering in your ear telling you what to say. You know Spielman better than any of us. Get her talking and get whatever information you can out of her."

"I don't have to wear a wire?"

"You'll be in a visiting booth. Glass between you, talking over the phone. Spielman is a dangerous offender and you're not going to be in the same room where she can get her hands on you."

Tamara closed her eyes, seeing and feeling Glock close to her. Impinging on her space. Touching her. Pulling her in. But not this time—this time, Glock wouldn't be able to put one finger on Tamara. She could laugh and mock and bait Tamara all she liked.

"Good." Tamara breathed out, trying to keep her body and brain quiet. No flashbacks. She could just stay in the present and experience what was really happening to her. She didn't have to go back.

Bowen gave her a look. "I gather that the last time the two of you got together, you were the one who attacked Spielman."

Tamara nodded. "Yeah... that was before they put me on the antipsychotics... I kind of... tried to kill her."

Timmons apparently hadn't heard the story. He looked at Tamara in the rear-view mirror. "You tried to kill her? In juvie?"

"No. In a courtroom. I was supposed to be testifying against her, but I... figured killing her would be a better solution. I wasn't in my right mind."

"Sounds pretty logical to me. Exactly how did you try to kill her? Criminal trials are usually pretty secure."

"The judge had a pen... I was in the witness box. I grabbed it and tried to kill her."

Timmons chuckled, shaking his head. "I guess they probably stopped you before you got very far."

Tamara stared out the car window. "Depends what you call very far. I didn't kill her, obviously."

"They caught you before you could get to her."

"No. Stabbed her once in the neck and once in the gut. Sent her to hospital. Didn't kill her."

"Seriously? Remind me to put away the pens before interviewing you."

Sometimes what Tamara had experienced during those breaks with reality was muddled and far away. Other times, it was sharp and clear as crystal. Sitting there in the car, it was one of the clearer times.

"I thought afterward... I should have stabbed her in the eye instead of the belly," Tamara told him. "Might have been able to kill her if I'd done that."

"Maybe that would have been better," Bowen said. "Get rid of Spielman *and* keep you off the streets. You wouldn't be out on parole if you had killed her."

"I wasn't in my right mind," Tamara reiterated. "Sometimes you're not guilty if you were on a psychotic break."

* * *

Tamara was stiff and sore when they reached the prison. She had to go through various security checks, but none as invasive as what she'd had to go through as an inmate. Everything seemed to go in slow motion like they didn't care if it took all day for Tamara to get in to see Glock. There was a lot of resistance at first, as the administrators asserted that Glock wasn't allowed any visitors and then that Tamara wasn't on the approved visitors list. Bowen kept reiterating that the visit had been preapproved and that Tamara was assisting in an active police investigation. Tamara could only imagine what had happened if she had just shown up there with Mrs. Henson.

Finally, Tamara was moved from the last waiting room and taken to a restricted visitors area, where they explained one more time that for the safety of the visitor and the prisoner, they would not be allowed to touch or communicate directly, but would have to use the phones in the special visitor booth. Then they finally led her to the booth and told her to sit down. Tamara sat, reading over the many scratched signs and notices that were arranged around the booth, indicating in big bold letters that all communications could be monitored and recorded, that anyone who was disruptive would be removed, that prisoners had the right to end the visits at any time, and a long list of rules that were supposed to be followed during a visit, including remaining in her seat, not being abusive toward the security staff, and remaining clothed at all times. Tamara snickered, wondering what incident had provoked the posting of that last rule.

Glock was escorted in on the other side of the glass and sat down in the booth across from Tamara. Tamara's heart raced and her breathing became more labored, being in such close proximity to Glock. She had to remind herself that even though Glock was close, she couldn't do anything. Tamara was safe.

Glock's skin was sallow. Her dark hair was uneven like it had been cut with a knife. Her eyes were bloodshot and red-rimmed. She had been one of the biggest girls in the block when she and Tamara were in juvie together. Big Glock Spielman and little Tamara French, opposites in every way.

"Well, look who's here," Glock said, smirking at Tamara. "I guess that means you made parole again."

Tamara nodded. She swallowed and cleared her throat, and tried to speak in a strong, confident voice. "Yeah. They decided to give me another chance," she said as casually as possible.

"After all of that trouble you and Vernon caused and trying to kill me in court, they thought it was safe to let you out free?"

"I'm here."

"Yeah, you are, Princess."

"I was sick when I attacked you. So that didn't count."

Glock fingered the place on her belly where Tamara had stabbed her. "It counted for me! Got a freaking infection. Couldn't eat for a month."

Tamara tried to suppress a smile. It warmed her heart to know that she had caused Glock more than a few minutes of pain. While she couldn't see the stab wound under the prison jumper, she could see the one on Glock's neck, still red and angry. It shouldn't have been so vivid. Prisoners were slow to heal, their bodies in poor condition at the best of times.

"So, what are you doing here?" Glock demanded. "Come to tell me you're sorry?"

Tamara shook her head. "I'm not sorry. I might have been on a psychotic break, but you were buggin' me."

Glock laughed. "Man, I miss the times we had, Frenchie. You were such a kick to have around."

Because Tamara entertained Glock, or because Glock liked having someone to kick? Either way, it hadn't been much fun for Tamara. She had done her best to keep Glock calm and satisfied, but even a contented Glock could be dangerous.

Tamara forced a smile as if she too were reminiscent about

their old times together in juvie. It had been two years since Glock had been released, leaving Tamara behind in juvie. Two years was plenty of time to color those memories.

"What would you do if you were out?" she asked.

Glock raised her brows. She leaned back in her chair, pressing her knees against the cubicle counter to tip herself back on two legs.

"What would I do? You bored already? Guess I might call on old friends."

"Yeah?"

"Sure, why not? Stir up a little excitement. Go out on the town." She rocked back and forth on the back two legs of the chair. "Stretch my legs. Get high. Let loose."

None of that seemed to lead to kidnapping an enemy's baby. The first reassurance Tamara had felt since arriving.

"You know anyone who's gotten out recently? Heard anything from anyone?"

"Prison grapevine, there's always some news." Glock's eyes narrowed as she studied Tamara. "Where's all this going, Princess? Who do I know on the outside? What kind of connection are you looking for?"

At first, Tamara thought that Glock was on to her. Then she realized that Glock meant connection in the sense of a supplier. Connections to underworld or black-market contacts. A drug dealer or purveyor of some other product Tamara needed.

"I'm looking for someone..." Tamara picked her words carefully. "Someone who could take care of a little problem for me."

Glock drummed the fingers of her free hand on the counter. "What kind of problem?" In a covert gesture, Glock pointed to one of the warning signs on the cubicle wall.

All conversations may be monitored or recorded.

"I need someone to... stop bothering me. If they would just... disappear from my life..."

Glock shook her head. "You're always attracting these types, Frenchie. Why don't you tell him to get lost yourself? Why don't you just take care of it?"

"It's not like that. It's someone... who wouldn't understand. Someone smaller."

"Smaller?" Glock repeated, not getting it.

Tamara made a small movement with her free arm. A slight rocking movement. Glock got it and her eyes widened.

"Really? You dealt with that yourself before, haven't you? A couple of times, if I remember right." Glock laughed. She tapped the skin just below the corner of her eye, the place where Tamara had two black teardrop tattoos, memorializing what she had done.

"Yeah, and how did that turn out?" Tamara demanded.

"Not so good. Sort of landed you somewhere you didn't want to go," Glock agreed. "But you got to further your education. They keep telling us we gotta get educated. Can't ever stop learning and improving ourselves."

"I don't want to do that again. I want to stay out of it this time. So, I need someone who could help out..."

Glock shook her head. "Ain't nobody gonna do that for a favor, baby girl. For something like that, you gotta have plenty of bread. *Comprende?* Rich folk, they can hire out. But people like you and me, we gotta do for ourselves."

"But I thought you might know someone..."

"Nah. You're looking at seriously hard time in the federal pen for taking care of a little problem like that. That ain't something you do for a friend."

"Not even for you?"

"Even my influence has limits. If I was out..." She licked her lips, casting a slow look over Tamara. "Maybe I'd help you out personally. But hiring a contractor... you need some serious capital."

"What if I could get it?"

"You can't."

"But what if I could?" Tamara pressed. She knew she was pushing it. Glock was going to get suspicious. She knew Tamara didn't have any skills that would translate to large amounts of money.

"You can't," Glock repeated firmly. She rocked on the back legs of the chair. "Some things you gotta do for yourself, Frenchie. Just like before."

"But I got caught last time. How would you do it? If it was you, how'd you... get rid of a little problem?"

"I wouldn't get in that kind of trouble in the first place." She shook her head. "How did you manage to...?"

"It was when I was out with Vernon... I got... mixed up with this guy..." Tamara felt her face flushing. She didn't know if it was because she was misrepresenting her relationship with Sly or because she was worried how Glock would take it. That sort of confession might just turn Glock against her. She would get jealous and stop talking to Tamara.

Glock blinked her red eyes, processing this. "This is *your* little problem?"

Tamara nodded. She swallowed, unable to find her voice for a minute. "Yeah," she agreed.

"Why don't you just tell Social Services you don't want to deal with this problem? Lots of people out there who'd be happy to take it off your hands."

"Not that easy." Tamara took a breath and let it out slowly. "Only reason I got out was to... deal with this problem. If I say I don't want to... they're going to throw me back inside."

"You always gotta try to do things the hard way, don't you?"

"The right way," Tamara argued.

"There ain't no right and wrong. I've told you before. You can't be so worried about what everyone else tells you to do.

You're out there walking around free. What makes you think you gotta stay around and deal with this little problem? Walk away. Just get out of there. You want to disappear the ki—the problem —and stay there in some foster home or halfway house? Why? You know what I told you before. They're just looking for a reason to send you back. To say you're unreformable. You want them to put you away for another six? Get outta Dodge before they do, Princess. That's what you should do."

Tamara nodded, looking down at the scarred counter. Glock's words made sense. Especially with the police and everyone else suspecting her of Olly's disappearance. It would be best just to run and never let them catch her.

She knew she should, but she couldn't bring herself just to forget about Olly and whatever had happened to him. If she disappeared, it would just confirm to everyone that she was guilty, and Olly would be forgotten forever. No one would keep looking for him after Tamara was gone.

* * *

"No luck," Bowen said, when they met Tamara after her visit with Glock. Her voice had no inflection. Not a question, but a statement of fact.

"No," Tamara agreed. "I don't think she had anything to do with it."

"A waste of a day," Timmons said with disgust.

Tamara felt like she should apologize. She bit the inside of her cheek, forcing herself to keep her mouth shut. She hadn't intentionally sent them on a wild goose chase. Glock could have been involved. Tamara had needed to be sure that Glock hadn't had anything to do with Olly's disappearance. Now she knew.

Glock was right about one thing. No one was going to kidnap a baby as a favor. If it was a kidnapping, it had to either be someone who had a direct personal grudge against Tamara or someone who had been paid a lot of money. Tamara didn't know anyone who had a lot of money to pay a contractor off. From the start, it had felt like a personal attack. Not just some random twist of fate, but something targeted.

Bowen was saying something to her. Tamara had to shake off her thoughts and focus on her.

"Sorry, what?"

"She makes a good suspect. I can see why you wanted to be sure of her, if you didn't know what happened."

"I don't know." Tamara was irritated by Bowen's bulldog-like insistence that she was the culprit in Olly's disappearance. "If I knew, I'd tell you just so I could go back to prison and get a break from you."

Timmons chuckled. Bowen gave him a dirty look. He put up his hands in a gesture of surrender. "Just means you're good at your job," he pointed out.

Bowen looked like she could bite his head off. Tamara looked down at the floor as they walked along, avoiding looking at either detective. She wondered whether they had been together for long. They didn't exactly seem to get along together.

"Spielman sounded like she and you were pretty close," Timmons suggested.

"We were cellies. Cellmates. For a couple of years."

"Ah."

"We weren't friends," Tamara said, looking sideways at him. "Everybody thinks we were friends, but we weren't. And if you think life is easy when someone like Glock likes you..." She shook her head. "Well, it's not." She opened her mouth to say something about what it had been like when Tamara had been out on parole before and had to deal with Glock, or how she'd had to keep Glock appeased when they were in juvie, but they were comments that would need deeper explanations and

Tamara wasn't willing to share that much with the detectives. She needed to keep her mouth shut, just like Glock had taught her.

She wasn't looking forward to the ride back to the Hensons' house.

NINETEEN

TAMARA KNEW SHE SHOULD get permission from Wanda before going to see Sybil. But she suspected she wouldn't get it. Sybil wasn't a felon, so she didn't fall under that restriction. On the other hand, she wasn't exactly a good influence on Tamara and had gotten her in trouble before. But that had been because of Glock's influence.

Tamara's initial visit with Wanda where her rules had been laid down seemed like a long time ago. She couldn't remember it as clearly as she could remember her initial meeting with Mr. Collins. Mr. Collins had given her a paper with all of her rules clearly printed on it. Wanda had not. They had only had a conversation in which, if Tamara remembered right, pretty much anything other than taking care of Olly was off-limits. She was sure that if Wanda could have banned her from that, she would have. And maybe she would have been right.

The visit to Sybil's house might technically be a violation, but Tamara needed to talk to her. She wanted to be sure that she hadn't gone to Sybil in some state of psychosis, asking for her help in covering up what had happened to Olly. Those missing hours disturbed Tamara. She wanted to know what had happened to Olly, but what if she had had something to do with it? What if something tragic had happened and dealing with it had just been too much for her?

Sybil opened the door and stared at Tamara, her eyes huge. Her jaw dropped open. "Tamara? I..." She blinked rapidly, like she was trying to clear her vision or wake herself up. "What are you doing here? I didn't know you were out!"

"On parole again," Tamara explained, shifting awkwardly. "Mr. Collins said he would speak for me if I reapplied, and he did, and..." She spread her arms, indicating her presence. Here she was.

"That's amazing. I didn't think they were going to let you out again so soon!" Sybil looked back over her shoulder. Tamara wondered who else was there. She had assumed that, just like every other time she'd been at Sybil's house, that Sybil would be home alone taking care of her little sisters. Just like Tamara had been left to take care of the Baker kids any time she was out of school. Was there someone else there? A boyfriend or a girl from school? Sybil's mother or stepfather?

"Is it a bad time? Should I leave?"

Sybil's eyes darted around. "Uh, no. You could come in."

But she stood blocking the doorway rather than allowing Tamara in. Tamara waited. She looked Sybil over. Some things had changed. Her makeup was not so stark. Her hair, while dark, was not dyed black like it had been when Tamara had met her a year before. She didn't have the same air of recklessness as she had then. Maybe she had learned something from their experiences. Maybe having her fingers broken by Glock or the little girls being threatened had convinced her that she wasn't such a bad girl and that she couldn't just jump into a world of rebellion and crime without consequences.

"So...?" Tamara drew out the question. Was Sybil going to let her in, or were they going to stand there on the doorstep where the whole world could see them?

"Uh... yeah... come in."

This time, Sybil stepped to the side and motioned Tamara in.

Tamara felt like she had stepped back in time. Nothing about the living room she walked into seemed to have changed in the year she had been gone. She was almost sure that even the scattered toys were the same ones as had been there the last time she had visited. She expected to see Glock there, goading and threatening her, rolling her eyes at Sybil's wannabe attitude.

"You can... sit down."

They both sat in the living room, Tamara on the couch and Sybil in the easy chair, looking at each other awkwardly.

"I didn't know you were getting out."

"I've actually... been out for a while now. I didn't think... I didn't want to bother you. Didn't really think it would be good for us to see each other."

Sybil didn't argue with the thought. She just gave a little shrug. "But now...? You're here."

"Yeah." Tamara was reassured by Sybil's reaction that she hadn't been there before. She hadn't show up out of the blue asking for help dealing with Olly. "I just... wanted to make sure you're okay. Collins said that he didn't think you were going to have to do any time. You would just have to do community service."

"Uh-huh. Community service. Counseling. Curfew. The three C's."

"Right." Tamara nodded. She swallowed, looking around the room for something else to say.

A bedroom door opened and one of the children tiptoed out to the living room to see what was going on. Tamara wasn't sure at first that it was the youngest girl. She was taller, lankier. Her hair was longer than it had been.

"Who's that?" she demanded, sheltering behind the easy chair Sybil was sitting in.

"Just a friend from school," Sybil informed her.

The little girl peeked at Tamara around the chair. Tamara was sure it was Boo. She wondered if the little girl could remember Glock breaking into the house and threatening her. Glock had sat with her in that very chair, threatening to hurt her. Tamara braced for a flashback. Seeing the little girl always made her flash back to Corrine. They looked similar and were around the same age. But instead of being thrown back into a memory of Corinne in the bathtub, struggling for life, Tamara remembered pulling Boo out of Glock's lap, defying Glock. She had protected the little girl, even knowing Glock would be angry and retaliate.

"Hi, there," Tamara said softly.

The little girl bolted like a rabbit, running back down the hall to her room and shutting the door. Tamara swallowed and looked at Sybil.

"Does she remember...?"

"I don't think so. Not exactly. She's had nightmares and stuff... they all have... but I don't think she remembers exactly what happened. She was just... sort of scared by it."

Tamara nodded. She sighed and looked around. "I shouldn't stay. I don't want to get either one of us in trouble. I just had to... make sure."

Sybil didn't object. They both stood up.

"I'm sorry," Sybil said, looking down at her feet.

"What? What for? I'm the one that got you involved in everything."

"Because... well... I mean, I listened to Glock. Did what she said. I should have just... called the cops. But I was afraid she'd hurt the girls or you, if I did."

Tamara nodded. "I know. It's okay."

Sybil leaned toward Tamara and then gave her an impulsive hug.

* * *

Tamara was unaccountably tired after the visit with Sybil. It was early; she had the full day ahead of her, but she wanted nothing so much as to just go back home and lie down and sleep all day. Her brain wanted to shut down. Going on was just too hard.

But shutting down wouldn't help Olly. If something had happened, if she'd had a psychotic break and abandoned him somewhere, then time was running out. It was probably already too late. But Tamara couldn't bear to think that she might have left him alone somewhere. She headed next to Glock's old apartment. She couldn't imagine that she would have gone there; it hadn't exactly been a safe place for her, but she had to check out every possibility. She had run away to Glock's flop before; her brain might have short-circuited and taken her back.

It had been a year and she hadn't been there many times, but her feet knew the way.

It was obvious as she drew closer that something had changed. There were boards over the windows and the entrance door. Tamara tried to swallow the lump in her throat as she got close enough to skim the pink public health notice to see that the building had been condemned. She tried the door anyway, but it was securely locked.

"Can't you read?"

Tamara whipped her head around to face the speaker. An old woman. Or a middle-aged one with a lot of experience scrounging on the streets. A homeless old bag lady. Her voice was as deep and gravelly as a man's and her tone implied that Tamara had personally insulted her by trying the door despite the public health notice.

"I... I thought I left something here."

"You left something here? The place has been closed for months. I wasn't born yesterday, you know."

"No, I was here," Tamara insisted. "A few days ago. There was a door you could get in. But I'm all turned around. Not this one... is there one in the back or the side where you can get in..."

She hadn't lived much on the streets herself, but she'd heard from enough people who had. Closed and condemned buildings always had squatters. You couldn't keep people out of them. Somewhere there was a door or a window that had been forced, allowing access. She was counting on it.

"There's no way in," the woman argued. "It's condemned."

"I wasn't born yesterday either," Tamara said, making her voice hard and threatening. "So why don't you quit trying to scam me and tell me where I can get in?"

"You didn't leave anything here."

"How do you know?"

The woman wrinkled her nose and didn't explain. But her gaze gradually turned to one side of the building.

"There?" Tamara asked, pointing. "It's the door over there, right?"

"No, you can't get in."

But Tamara was sure she was lying. She walked around the building and found a side door that, while looking like it was shut properly at first glance, had a broken catch and gave easy access. She slipped through and shut it again behind her.

It was no wonder the place had been condemned. It had been a wreck the last time Tamara had been there and probably should have been shut down years before. But people who didn't have much money needed something. Desperate for a roof over their heads, they would take whatever place they could afford, no matter how squalid. Glock had acknowledged that she didn't spend any more time there than she had to. It was just a place to crash.

Tamara was turned around, having gone in through a different door from what she was used to, so she wandered around for a few minutes, not sure which way she was facing and where Glock's old apartment was. It was quiet, not filled with the sounds of yelling and busy people like it had been when she'd been there before. It was quiet, like everyone there was listening to her. She didn't see a soul, but she knew they were there. There were smells of food cooked on hot plates, body odor, and the stomach-turning smell of rats.

Tamara found her way to the hallway Glock's apartment was in, and eventually identified the door she thought was Glock's. She hesitated with her hand on the door, stomach clenched in anticipation of what she was going to find when she opened the door. But Glock was in prison: Tamara had already confirmed that. Tamara's confidence that she had not brought Olly to this place in some kind of fugue state was getting stronger. It wasn't familiar enough. She couldn't reach any fragments of memory of it in the past few days. Her memories of the building, blurry as they were, were all old.

She took a deep breath and pushed the door open.

It hadn't exactly been well-furnished when she had been there with Glock. Paradoxically, the room seemed even smaller with no furniture. There was only a torn and stained mattress, bare of any sheets or bedding, in the far corner. It was occupied by a thin form that Tamara couldn't identify immediately by sex. Getting closer, Tamara could see it was an emaciated woman, skin covered with red patches, most of her teeth gone, eyes glazed and far away. She was, Tamara deduced from the paraphernalia littering the floor, a junkie, so far gone and swallowed up by her addiction that Tamara would be surprised if she had weeks to live. She looked days or even hours from death.

A quick glance around the bare room confirmed that Tamara had not left Olly there. Whether the woman would have even noticed another occupant, Tamara wasn't sure. But Olly wasn't there. Nor was any sign he ever had been. She turned to leave, only to find that someone had followed her in. A black man with a few gold caps on his rotting teeth stood in the doorway.

"Who are you?" he demanded. "What are you doing here? This is my house. Lila? You okay? What's this girl been doing here?"

There was no answer from Lila, if she was the woman on the mattress. The man looked toward her, and then back at Tamara again. "You do something to hurt my Lila?"

Tamara's stomach turned. He was acting as if everything was perfectly normal. As if it were normal to live in a dive like that. As if Lila doping herself to death on the dirty mattress were perfectly normal behavior. As if Tamara could do anything to the woman that could hurt her worse than she had already hurt herself.

"I was looking for my friend," Tamara said. "She's not here anymore. I heard she got arrested, but I hoped…" she trailed off and tried to slip by the man. But he wasn't that easily satisfied.

"Oh, no you don't." He grabbed her arm. "I want to know what you're doing here."

"Leave me alone," Tamara warned. She leaned toward the man, trying to get into his personal space and intimidate him, but he didn't back away.

"What the hell are you doing in my house?"

"I'm leaving," Tamara said, giving her arm a jerk so she could pass him.

"I don't think so." He showed his wide mouth of blackened, oozing teeth. "Maybe you'd like to replace Lila there. She's not as much fun as she used to be."

Rather than wasting more time on arguing, Tamara kicked out her knee as hard as she could, straight into his crotch. Not a move she'd put to much use in the all-girl juvenile facility. Her assailant howled in pain and, still holding on to Tamara's arm, took her down with him. She hit her head on the floor, making the room spin. He was down, but not out, and the two of them wrestled on the floor, Tamara trying to get up to flee and the man trying to get her under his control. Tamara hit him repeatedly, trying to claw his eyes and continuing to kick, hoping she could catch him a second time in a vulnerable spot. There was nothing she could use as a weapon. As she struggled to get to into a sitting position, the man aimed a head-butt at her face. Tamara ducked out of the way and, unable to stop the momentum of his blow, the man smashed face-first into the wall. Tamara winced at the crunch his face made when he hit it. She sprang to her feet and ran from the room.

She was almost out of the apartment building when she heard a baby cry. Tamara stopped in her tracks. Could it be Olly? She listened. The sound was soft and didn't resemble his hoarse cries, but if she'd abandoned him there and no one had discovered him to give him the care he needed, he could be very feeble. Keeping an eye out for the black man or any other potential attackers, she followed the baby's cry.

It led her to another room in another hallway. She surely wouldn't have left Olly anywhere but Glock's room... unless she'd been too confused to even know which one was Glock's. Tamara put her hand on the doorknob. It turned in her hand, but when she tried to push the door open, there seemed to be something blocking it. Tamara shoved and kicked to get it open.

"Who's there?" called a woman's voice. Hispanic accent. Scared. Young. Tamara managed to get the door open wide enough to see the woman. She held an infant at her shoulder, trying desperately to quiet him. A crying baby was a magnet for trouble. An unmistakable sound of vulnerability that drew predators.

"Who are you?" the woman asked.

"Let me see that baby."

The woman clutched it to her, shaking her head. All Tamara could see was his black hair and the size of him. Similar enough to Olly that Tamara had to see him. She had to be sure.

"I'm not going to hurt him. Just let me see."

"No. Please, leave my baby alone."

"I just want to see. I... lost my baby. I want to make sure that isn't him."

The woman's eyes widened in surprise. She was still for a

moment, looking at Tamara. Terrified that Tamara was just going to jump in and steal the baby or do something to hurt him. Finally, she moved, turning the swaddled baby around to face Tamara.

Not Olly. Too dark. His face a completely different shape. A chubby, well-fed baby, not one who had been abandoned there a few days earlier to starve to death.

Tamara nodded. "Okay. Okay, it's not my baby. I'll go."

She backed out the door, keeping her eyes on the woman. Just because she was holding a baby, that didn't mean she was unarmed. She could still pull out a weapon, shoot Tamara in the back as she retreated. Shoot first, worry about who she'd hit later.

But the woman made no attempt to draw on her and Tamara was soon out the door, her chest heaving, tears stinging her eyes.

Not there. Olly wasn't there.

TWENTY

TAMARA LONGED TO GO home. And she was worried that sooner or later, Mrs. Henson was going to call Wanda, reporting Tamara for running away. She looked at the sun in the sky. Still only midday. It had only taken a few hours to go to Sybil's and the apartment, even though it felt like it had taken all day. Bowen really thought that she could get to one of those places and back in the length of time that Mrs. Henson had been gone? On foot and carrying a baby? Even if she had been gone for three hours, which Bowen had suggested as the outside time limit to the judge, it would have been tight to get to any of the places Bowen thought that she could have dumped a baby. Or to any of the places Tamara had thought possible she could have gone to in a fugue.

She still had a couple more places to visit, but getting there on foot was getting more and more unlikely. She had pillaged the change jar at the Hensons' before leaving, hoping she would just be able to return the money when she got home, but she was going to have to break down and take the bus or she would still be out by nightfall, and Mrs. Henson would report her to Wanda for sure.

Tamara sat on a bus stop bench that she thought she'd waited on before, the previous year, though she couldn't remember which day it had been or where she was going at the time. All of her memories from when she was sick ran together in a muddle. She had walked, taken buses, and been driven by Glock and Sybil, but she couldn't remember enough of the details to keep it all straight. When the bus eventually arrived, Tamara got on, paid her fare, and watched out the window for landmarks. Though her memories were murky, she thought she could recall the location of the warehouse where Glock had held her. Back toward the Hensons', the haunt where Glock had taken those poor pets from the neighborhood to perform her gruesome work.

She pulled the cord to request the next stop and got out. It took some wandering to orient herself, and then she was there.

Tamara's chest hurt like she had pneumonia and broken ribs all over again. Her breaths came in short, shallow gasps. She had nearly died in the warehouse. She had little doubt she would have died if Sybil hadn't persuaded Glock to release her as a test of her loyalty. That had been a brilliant move. Sybil got all the props for that. Telling Glock where Tamara was actually going— not so much.

Tamara circled the warehouse, trying the doors, looking for a broken window or lock or other way in. Like with the condemned apartment building, street people and opportunists like Glock would find their way in. She found it at last, a basement window that had been kicked in that the owner of the property hadn't yet discovered. The glass was already cleared out of the way and there were tracks in the gravel that showed clear scuff marks where someone else had wormed their way into the building. It was a tight fit for Tamara to get through, and she had a petite frame. Anyone using that method of entry would need to be her size or smaller.

The basement was dark. There was no electricity, and little of the afternoon sun made its way down there. Tamara blinked, waiting for her eyes to adjust as much as they were going to, and then started a slow search of the building. It would have been faster to leave a baby and get back out. A search was far more time-consuming than a dump. The place was so large, Tamara couldn't be sure she had searched every possible hiding place. But she wasn't really looking for every possible hiding place. She was just looking for the place she would have used. Where her unconscious mind might have taken her. And that had to be the room that Glock had held her in. Maybe laying Olly on the old crates and counters Glock had pressed into use, like a lamb on a sacrificial altar. Innocent blood.

She found the stairs and went up to the main floor, where it didn't take long for her to find the main room she'd been housed in. The chair Glock had used was gone. There were no fresh tracks through the dirty floor. No human tracks, anyway. Other visitors had scurried through the space, leaving droppings and tiny hand-like footprints. But there were no new shoe prints. If Tamara had been there recently, there would have been shoe prints.

She looked around the counters and crates just to be sure, then finally retraced her steps and left the building the same way she had entered.

There was one more place she had promised herself she would check and then she could go home. She wasn't sure what she was going to tell Mrs. Henson by way of explanation. Something would occur to her by then.

* * *

Another bus ride and a lot more walking around, because Tamara didn't remember clearly where the pet food store was. She remembered the smell of the dirty dog in her arms. After a night or two in the filthy blankets Glock had brought her,

Tamara had probably smelled just as pungent as the poor mutt, if not worse. Eventually, Tamara found the sign for the pet food store. The hand lettered signs, cute illustrations, display in the window. A fun place for people who had dogs instead of children to take their furry babies for expensive treats. She'd lain the dog there, given it more of the muffin that Sybil had provided, and left it there in hopes that kind, dog-loving people would take care of it and maybe track down its original owners. She'd fought not to grow attached to the animal, but that was easier said than done. Just like she had never expected to become attached to Olly. He was supposed to just be a means to an end. A way for her to get out of juvie and work her way back into free society. But he and the stupid, smelly dog had both wormed their ways into her heart.

There was obviously no baby on the sidewalk in front of the store. He would have been discovered within minutes if left there. The store was open, but Tamara couldn't face the people inside. She couldn't ask them if she had been by there before and if she had just happened to forget her baby there. Since Tamara had already told Bowen about the store, describing it to the best of her ability, they should have already searched the block around the store for a baby in the dumpster or other sheltered location and she really didn't need to check on her own.

She walked around to the back of the building anyway. She had promised herself that she would thoroughly check out the alley behind the pet food store. Then she would allow herself to go home. Maybe she would even sleep. Sleep had been elusive since Olly had disappeared, even though Tamara was tired all the time. Whenever she lay down to sleep, she just tossed and turned and thought about Olly and how she had royally screwed up yet another chance at parole. It was only a matter of time before Wanda found something else to remand her for.

She had to climb up to look into the dumpster. She didn't

jump down inside, she just looked. There was no infant lying on top of the trash. No sound of a living child. If she had abandoned Olly there, someone would have heard him crying. Someone would have rescued him. She knew she wouldn't find anything inside. But she had promised herself she would look just to be sure. She had to be sure of all of those places. Having looked, she was pretty confident that she had been right in her story from the beginning. She had never left the house with Olly. She hadn't done anything to hurt him, either accidentally or in a moment of frustration. She hadn't left the house with him, to hide him far away where his death wouldn't be connected with her. That would have been pointless. But a person could do pointless things when desperate or dissociated from reality.

Tamara took a quick look around the rest of the back alley, then returned to the front of the building. One more bus ride back to the Hensons' house. She would tell Mrs. Henson that she had gone out for a walk. She had gone farther than she had planned, or she had gotten turned around and it had taken extra time for her to get reoriented and find her way back.

There was a figure leaning against the front of a car Tamara had seen before. She stared at the car, as if that was the most important thing, rather than the person standing there waiting for her.

"Having a little reunion tour?" Bowen asked. "Checking out all of your old haunts?"

Tamara gave a little shudder. How much did Bowen know?

"I just... I had to make sure I hadn't done anything," Tamara said. "I knew I didn't, but everyone else was so sure... I had to check any of the places I might have gone, if my brain wasn't working."

"But you didn't find anything."

Tamara looked at the front of the little pet food store. "No."

"Any insights? Anywhere else on your list?"

"No."

"So, just Sybil's house, the apartment building, the ware-house, and here."

Tamara swallowed the bile rising up in the back of her throat. She chewed on her already bitten-down thumbnail.

"How... you've been following me all day?"

"Of course. What did you expect? That we would just let you wander around wherever you liked, clean up fingerprints, destroy evidence?"

She hadn't seen anyone following her. But they had been there, all along, watching her journey from one place to the next.

"I told you I didn't do it."

Bowen frowned, her forehead creasing. "This little tour, it's not exactly the behavior of an innocent person."

"Is it the behavior of a guilty one?"

Bowen shook her head. "No. That's just the thing. If you were guilty and you didn't know we were watching, why would you come to these places? The baby isn't here. We already checked. There's no sign of him. And if you were guilty and you did know we were watching you, why would you come to these places?"

"Then what am I? Guilty or innocent?"

Bowen considered her for a moment, not giving away what was passing through her mind. "Sick. That's what I think you are. I think you're sick."

Tamara sighed. That was a step away from guilty, at least, but Bowen still thought she'd had something to do with Olly's disappearance. Tamara knew what it felt like to lose touch with reality and she didn't think that was what was happening. It felt like outside forces had conspired against her, but it didn't feel like the full-blown paranoia she'd felt when she had been preg-nant with Olly.

She leaned against the wall of the pet food store, looking once more at the spot on the sidewalk where she had left the dog a year earlier. She had come to the end of her list of the places she needed to visit on her pilgrimage, and she was exhausted. It had taken most of the day. Another wasted day. She was getting more desperate to find out what had happened to her baby with each passing day, but she was running out of ideas. The baby had simply vanished. No sign of a body, no call from a kidnapper, no logical explanation for what had happened. He was just there... and then he was gone.

Bowen was beside her. Tamara hadn't even seen her move, but she was suddenly there, gripping Tamara's arm, keeping her on her feet. "Whoa, now. Take a breath. Come sit down in the car for a minute."

Tamara tried to shake her off. "I'm fine."

"You just about ended up flat on your face. Sit down for a minute, at least."

Tamara didn't have the energy to fight back. Bowen led her over to the car and opened the back door for Tamara to sit down on the uncomfortable seats. Tamara kept her feet out the door, reminding herself that this meant she wasn't under arrest. Her feet were still outside of the car, so she was safe.

"What happened in the apartment building?" Bowen asked, watching Tamara's face.

"Nothing."

"You've got a nice shiner and you came out of there as pale as a ghost. Are you telling me you hit yourself?"

Tamara reached up to touch both eyes, not even aware of which one was swollen. She flinched away from her own touch on the right side. "I... didn't even know..."

"Fight or flight. Your body shuts everything else down to give you the resources to save yourself. What happened?"

"There was a guy..." Tamara shook her head. "He wanted... he tried to keep me there..." Tamara shuddered. She rubbed her arms, her skin crawling.

"If you hadn't come out, we would have come in looking for you."

At least she wouldn't have been trapped there until she looked like Lila.

"There was a baby there. Crying. I thought..." Tamara trailed off. "It wasn't Olly. Some Latina with her baby, squatting there... Olly wasn't there."

"No," Bowen agreed.

"Did you search there already?" Tamara rubbed her forehead, trying to sort it out.

"How could we have? You never told us about the place. It wasn't on the list of places you admitted to knowing of, was it?"

Tamara shook her head.

"Why didn't you tell me? We could have had someone there two days ago instead of having to follow behind you. A lot can happen in that length of time. Especially to an infant."

Tamara just looked down at her feet.

"Who lived there?" Bowen asked.

"Glock."

"Ah. But you already know she wasn't involved, so why go to her apartment?"

"Just to make sure... that I didn't... do something..."

Bowen looked at her watch. "I don't know when your curfew is, but you'd better be getting home. Pull your feet in and we'll drop you off."

"Not until nine." Tamara put her hands on the frame of the car to pull herself up and walk home herself, but she was exhausted. She was already in the car. Her body hurt all over. The fight with the man at the apartments had taken more out of her than she had realized. Her muscles felt like pulp.

"Put your feet in," Bowen prompted.

Instead of arguing, Tamara pulled her feet in. In the front seat where he'd been the whole time, Timmons looked over his shoulder at Tamara, his expression inscrutable. Bowen shut Tamara's door and rode shotgun.

"Where to?" Timmons asked.

"Crime scene. Drop her off."

Timmons backed the car out of the parking stall and they left the pet store behind. The last place Tamara could think of that she might have left Olly if she had really been the one that made him disappear. She turned around and looked at it again as they drove away.

TWENTY-ONE

MRS. HENSON DID NOT looked pleased when Tamara got home. She had been puttering over something in the kitchen, but when Tamara walked in the front door, she left her work.

"Come and sit down, Tamara. We need to talk."

Tamara looked longingly up the stairs toward her room. After all she had been through, she just wanted to be by herself and block out the rest of the world. The last thing she needed was to sit down and talk it through.

She reluctantly followed Mrs. Henson's example and sat down in the living room.

"Tamara... you know there are certain rules you are supposed to be following."

"Yeah."

"I don't know if you think that just because Wanda didn't get you remanded the first time she tried that she can't do it, but let me tell you, that's not the case. All she needs is one clear violation of your parole terms, and you *will* be back behind bars."

"I know."

"Then explain to me what this was all about today. You can't just disappear all day. I need to know where you are going to be, what you're doing, and when you're going to be back. I'm supposed to be supervising you; I can't do that if you don't communicate with me."

"Sorry."

"Where were you?"

"Just... walking. I had to get some air. Get away from here so I could think."

"And that's why you got picked up by the police?"

Tamara mentally cursed her luck. She had thought that she'd gotten in without Mrs. Henson seeing Bowen's unmarked car outside. "I didn't get picked up by the police. Not like that. They just saw me when I was in the neighborhood. I was tired, and they offered to drive me home. I didn't get in trouble, you can ask."

"I might just have to do that."

Tamara held her breath. She didn't actually want Mrs. Henson to call Bowen to ask what was going on. She didn't want Bowen sharing that Tamara had been visiting all of her old haunts, trying to find the place where she might have abandoned Olly. It was too messed up. Mrs. Henson would think it was sure proof that she'd done something to hurt the baby.

"If you were just out for a walk and didn't get in any trouble, why do you look like you were in a brawl?"

Tamara put a hand over her puffy eye. It told more than she wanted to share.

"This guy came after me. I don't know why. Maybe he thought I was someone else. He kept calling me Lila," Tamara embellished. "He grabbed me and wouldn't let me go. What was I supposed to do, let him kidnap or rape me?"

Mrs. Henson's eyebrows climbed up her forehead, clearly indicating her disbelief.

"It was this big black guy. He had all of these rotten teeth, and some of them had gold caps. Really nasty. I had to fight him off. I didn't even realize I had a black eye until Bowen told me."

"I see. That's very... colorful. You need to follow the rules, Tamara. I did my best to get you out on parole so that we could help you, but you need to do your part. You're lucky that the judge didn't remand you when Wanda asked. You taking care of Olly was part of the deal."

"It's not my fault he's gone. I didn't do anything to him. I didn't do anything wrong."

"It was your responsibility to look after him. Whatever happened... it was on your watch. I've never lost a baby before." Mrs. Henson's eyes brimmed with tears. "Never."

"That's not fair!"

"I've had a lot of girls through here and a lot of babies. I know it's not easy. I told you that. Some girls come here thinking it's going to be a piece of cake. Having a baby means they can get welfare benefits that they couldn't get by themselves. They figure they can do everything on their own and have whatever they want. But they find out pretty fast that babies are a lot of work, and you can't take care of a baby properly and still be out partying and acting like you're unattached."

"I know that!" Tamara growled. "I've taken care of babies before. I told you I didn't want to do it. I *told* you that!"

Mrs. Henson stared at her. She had done her best to ignore Tamara's history and her assertions that she really didn't want to take care of her baby. She had identified it as Tamara's best— probably her only—chance of getting out on parole, and she had pulled the right strings to make it happen. Tamara had accepted what fell into her lap, but she hadn't wanted it. Not from the start.

"I figured that once you were taking care of Olly, you would change your mind. Look at Cecelia, or so many of the other girls I've had here. They say they don't want to be tied down to a baby, but then... they fall in love..."

Tamara fought tears. She couldn't afford to think about Olly that way. She couldn't think about how she had started to feel about him. How he had come to mean something to her. He wasn't just a means to an end. He wasn't just a creature she was tied down to. She *had* started to fall in love with him.

But she couldn't think about that. She couldn't do that, or she wouldn't survive.

"I... it was okay. I had started to... be okay with taking care of him. But you didn't listen to me before. When I said no."

Mrs. Henson sat there for a long time, her distress clear. If she were honest with herself, she would know it was true. She would think back to the visits with Tamara and remember that Tamara had said no. She hadn't been excited about getting out to take care of Olly. They hadn't been on the same page.

"Then part of this is my fault," Mrs. Henson said finally, her voice rough with tears. "I have to take part of the blame for what happened to him."

Tamara wiped at the corners of her eyes, willing the tears to dry up and not escape. "It's not your fault. It's not my fault. I didn't do this!"

Mrs. Henson didn't acknowledge this. Tamara shook her head. Mrs. Henson was never going to believe her. No one was ever going to believe she hadn't had anything do with Olly's disappearance. She was going to be branded with another murder for the rest of her life, as surely as if a third teardrop were tattooed beside the first two.

Tamara got up and went to her room. Mrs. Henson didn't try to call her back or to apologize.

* * *

Tamara's body ached, and her head pounded unremittingly. She had taken a couple of pain pills, but they didn't seem to make any difference. She sat looking at the rest of the pills in the bottle for so long, she eventually had to take them to Nita.

"You need to hang on to them," she explained, while Nita looked at her with wide eyes and a confused frown. "I just... want to make sure I don't accidentally take too many."

"Accidentally?"

Tamara shrugged, not meeting her eyes. "I just need... I need you to keep them safe for me."

"I should tell Missus," Nita suggested.

"No. No, don't do that. They'll send me back. Just hold those for me, so I don't do something stupid. I'm okay. I am. I'm just... I want to make sure."

Nita nodded. She lowered her hand, with the bottle of pills clenched in her fist, to her side. "What about your other pills? Aren't you worried about them?"

Tamara swallowed and nodded. "I'll go get them."

She returned to her room, collected her other pill bottles, and took them to Nita as well. "I'm going to go to sleep. I just... don't want to wake up confused and take too many."

"I'll look after them," Nita agreed. "You just let me know when you are supposed to be taking them, and I'll give them to you."

"Yeah. I take them in the morning. I'll come get them then."

"Good night." Nita gave Tamara an awkward hug, holding the pill bottles in her hands the whole time. Tamara walked back out and went straight to her bed.

She thought at first that she wouldn't be able to sleep and that she was just going to toss and turn the whole night again, but she fell fitfully asleep soon enough.

TWENTY-TWO

TAMARA! WAKE UP! WAKE *up!*"

Tamara moved her head back and forth groggily, trying to remember where she was and why she was so tired. It felt like the middle of the night, but when she finally managed to pry her eyes open enough, she could see that it was bright out. Full day.

She had fallen asleep when Olly had finally dropped off and it was getting late. Mrs. Henson didn't usually have to wake her up. Tamara sat bolt upright, sending a lightning-bolt of pain through her brain. She looked over at the crib.

"Olly! Is he okay? Is he still asleep?"

Mrs. Henson stared at Tamara, her face white, her eyes wide and staring.

Tamara tried to get to her feet, but her legs were like lead and nothing was operating properly. She held on to the bedpost and the wall to support herself. When she staggered over to the crib, she hung onto the side, staring down into the empty space.

"No. Where is he? What happened?"

"Tamara, you need to sit back down." Mrs. Henson took Tamara by one arm. Nita was there too. She took Tamara's other arm, and they walked her back to the bed. She sat down, head spinning, nauseated, waiting for the explanation.

Nita's eyes too were wide with alarm. She rubbed Tamara's back in soothing circles. "I couldn't wake you up. You were so fast asleep... I was afraid that you had overdosed..."

"Overdosed," Tamara repeated. "On what?"

"I don't know. You gave me all of the pills, but I guess you could still have gone into the bathroom and drunk a bottle of cough syrup. Or you kept something in here when you gave me the rest." Nita looked around, but there was no evidence of another bottle of pills or an empty container.

Tamara was staring toward Olly's crib, trying to sort out her confused thoughts.

"Oh, no..."

Mrs. Henson looked at her.

The memories were coming back. "Oh, no... Olly's gone, isn't he?" A lump grew in Tamara's throat. "Somebody took him away."

"We don't know what happened to Olly, Tamara," Nita offered.

"I need to find him. We need to find out who did this."

Tamara lay back down on her bed. She cuddled the pillow to her and tried to pull the blankets back over herself.

"No, Tamara." Mrs. Henson pulled the blankets back with a jerk. "You need to get up. I want to know what's going on with you. How could you sleep this late when normally you can't sleep past reveille time?"

"I'm so tired. I haven't been able to sleep. I just... needed to crash." She closed her eyes. "We'll figure it out."

"No. Up you get." Mrs. Henson and Nita hauled on Tamara's arms until she was upright once more. "Walk around. Keep going, until you can wake up. We should take her to the hospital..." she suggested to Nita in a low voice.

"No... she's not acting high or whacked out..." Nita looked

sideways at Tamara while trying to keep her moving and on her feet. "Just tired. She gave me all her pills. You know she's barely had a wink of sleep since Olly..."

"Still..."

"We'll get her some coffee, make her take a shower. The hospital would just make her sit around waiting for tests all day and then send her home."

"Well... I suppose that's true. How about a shower, Tamara?" Mrs. Henson spoke loudly in Tamara's ear, making her wince and pull away.

"Just let me sit down for a minute..."

"No, you don't, girl," Nita said. "No more sleeping."

She and Mrs. Henson steered Tamara's steps out of the bedroom and into the bathroom across the hall. Deshawn was in the hallway, watching with her hand held over her mouth. No big, bright smile, for once.

Mrs. Henson started the water running. "Can you get in on your own, or do you need help getting undressed?"

Tamara pulled out of their grips and held her arms protectively over her chest. "No. I can do it myself."

"Okay. I want to hear you in that shower within five minutes, and if I don't, I'm coming back in to check on you. Understood?"

"Don't know why I can't just sleep," Tamara complained.

"Just get in."

They exited the bathroom, leaving Tamara to try to get her clothes off and get in under the shower spray.

* * *

By the time she got out of the shower, water already turning cold, Tamara was wider awake. She had really crashed. Unfortunately, her headache wasn't much better, but with a couple of cups of coffee, she might be able to face the day.

If she only knew what to do with herself.

Her job since she had gotten out of juvie had been to take care of Olly. Since his disappearance, her time had been occupied in trying to deal with the suspicion of the police and to sort out what might have happened. That hadn't gotten her anywhere, so what was she supposed to do next? Continue looking for baby Olly, when chances were, no trace of him would ever be found? Forget about him and go on with... what? School? Finding a job? She had no direction.

She put back on the same clothes she had just taken off for her shower. Soft, worn sweats and a tee. She finger-combed her wet hair, without the motivation or energy required to properly comb and style it. She didn't know when the last time was she had put on any makeup or made any attempt to make herself look nice.

She remembered Dirk telling her she looked pretty when she had been so tired and worn at the end of the day after taking care of Olly. Pretty was the last thing she was, dragged out and bone-tired. He'd obviously only been complimenting her in order to get something for himself.

Deshawn knocked on the bathroom door just as Tamara reached out to open it.

"You can have it," Tamara told her. "I'm done. But there's no hot water."

"No, I was just coming to check on you," Deshawn said. "Coffee's ready. Missus said to make sure you go down and not back to your room."

Why did she want to keep Tamara out of her room? Tamara had a fleeting memory of being kicked out of her cell at juvie so that they could search it. A common occurrence. Was Mrs. Henson going to search her room? But it had already been searched by the police; what did she think she was going to find?

Tamara didn't try to argue it, though. That would take too much energy and attention. She descended the stairs to join Mrs. Henson in the kitchen. There was no sign of Jesse, but of course there wouldn't be. He got up early to head to work and Tamara had slept in late. She wasn't sure why Nita and Deshawn were still home; it seemed to be too late in the morning for them to still be there.

"Get yourself a cup of coffee," Mrs. Henson said. "I'm sure you need it this morning."

Tamara rubbed her eyes and did as she was told. She stood leaning against the counter instead of sitting down. She didn't want to do anything that might make her more tired. No relaxing. She needed to stay alert. Not that she would accomplish anything by staying awake. What could she do?

The coffee was hot and strong. It did help to perk Tamara up a little more. Chased away some of the cobwebs.

"Do you feel better after such a nice long sleep?" Mrs. Henson suggested.

Tamara tried to raise a smile and to lie about it. But she couldn't tell Mrs. Henson how much better she felt after a good night's sleep. She couldn't muster the smile. She didn't have the energy.

"No. Feel like crap."

"Maybe you got a concussion in your fight yesterday. Maybe we should have taken you to the doctor to make sure you didn't have any swelling in your brain."

Tamara thought about it. She had hit her head at some point in the scuffle. She felt the back of her head for a lump or a tender place. Her fingers felt like they belonged to someone else and she didn't discover anything significant.

"I don't know. Don't think so."

"Do you have a headache?"

"Yeah. Horrible one."

"Dizziness? Blurred vision? We probably shouldn't have even let you sleep. People with concussions can die if you let them sleep, can't they?"

Tamara couldn't remember the details. She'd had concussions at juvie and they'd always let her sleep anyway. But that was with monitoring in the infirmary.

"I didn't die. I'll be fine."

She tried not to let her thoughts go again to overdosing on pills or pursuing some other method to release herself from her troubles. She turned to look for Nita.

"I need to take my morning meds. I gave them to Nita."

"She's gone back upstairs. You can get them from her when you're done breakfast."

Tamara looked toward the cupboard that held the breakfast cereal. The extended period of sleep had left her feeling hung over. "I don't think I can eat anything yet."

"Are you allowed to take all of your meds on an empty stomach? I think you'd better have something, at least. Just pills on top of coffee doesn't sound like a good idea."

Tamara found the bread and put a single slice in the toaster.

"What do you want on that? Jam? Honey?"

Tamara knew where everything was. If she'd wanted jam or honey, she knew where to find them. She didn't bother to answer. She nursed a second cup of coffee while she waited for the toast to pop. She nibbled it plain and dry.

"Your stomach isn't feeling well either?"

"No... just not ready to eat."

She endured Mrs. Henson's watchful eye for a few more minutes, then tossed the rest of her toast into the garbage and headed back upstairs for her pills.

* * *

She had gotten what she needed from Nita and hoped against hope that the painkillers would have a better effect than they had the previous day. She went back to her room, knowing that she needed to put on something more appropriate for the day and not just climb back in bed now that there was nobody there to monitor her.

Tamara stared into the empty crib. She waited for flashbacks to fill it with Julie's image.

But it remained empty. Completely bare.

What could possibly have happened to the baby?

She knew she hadn't planned to do anything to him, and without a plan, there was no way she could have made him disappear that fast, leaving no trace. It wasn't possible.

She reached for a stuffed toy on the dresser that Olly loved to cuddle and rub against his face. A little yellow duck. It was ugly, and Tamara hated it, but Mrs. Henson told her to get used to it. Babies attached to certain toys, and there was no way to break them of their lovies, so it was best to just accept it.

But the duck wasn't there.

Tamara stared at the dresser.

There was not a bare spot on the dresser; rather, a pacifier had been placed in the spot that the duck had previously occupied.

"Missus!" Tamara ran to the bedroom door and shouted toward the stairs. "Mrs. Henson!"

The clinking of dishes in the kitchen stopped. "Tamara? What is it?"

"Come up here! You... please come up! You have to see!"

There was silence for a moment, and then Tamara could hear Mrs. Henson's footsteps as she made her way to the stairs and began to climb. She was frowning as she came into view.

"Tamara? Are you okay? What is it?"

Wordless, Tamara motioned her into the room, and pointed to the pacifier on the dresser. Mrs. Henson shook her head, bemused. "What, Tamara? I don't understand."

"Mister Duck! Where is Mister Duck? He was right here."

Mrs. Henson looked again at the pacifier. "He must be somewhere else, Tamara. Maybe he fell behind or is in the diaper bag? I seriously don't think anyone came in here and moved him."

"They did!" Tamara insisted. "I know where he was. He was right here." She jabbed her finger toward the pacifier again. Stupid pacifier. They were supposed to stop babies from crying, but Olly hated them. Plug one of those in his mouth instead of a bottle, and he would turn bright red and scream his head off. There was no fooling the kid.

"*When* was he right there?"

"That's where I always put him. That's where he always was. Yesterday! He was there yesterday!" Tamara could hardly get the words out fast enough. She was aware that she was yelling, but she couldn't stop herself. The house around them was listening. Had one of the other foster children entered the room while Tamara was sleeping and taken the duck toy? Why? Why would any of them do that?

Tamara pushed past Mrs. Henson and hurried to the girls' room. She didn't knock on the door, just opened it and looked around, searching for the toy. Why would Nita or Deshawn take it? Why would anyone take it? Nita and Deshawn were sitting on the bed talking or, Tamara suspected, eavesdropping on what was going on.

"Where is he?" Tamara demanded, walking around the room and looking over all of the surfaces. "Where is Mister Duck?"

"Mister Duck?" Deshawn echoed. "Why would Mister Duck be in here?"

"You tell me! Why would anyone take Mister Duck?" Tamara started opening and closing drawers rapidly, looking for the toy. She kicked over piles of clothes and checked the closet, pushing aside clothes and shoes and trying to find the duck.

"Missus, what's wrong?" Deshawn asked Mrs. Henson, who had followed Tamara into the room.

"I don't know," Mrs. Henson's voice was hushed. "Tamara is upset. I don't know if it is some kind of breakdown..."

"I'm not going crazy! Somebody came into my room and took Mister Duck!"

"Why would anyone do that?" Nita chimed in.

"How the hell would I know?" Tamara screamed.

Nita's eyes got wide in surprise and hurt. Tamara knew Nita didn't deserve to be yelled at, but the rage pouring out of her was too hot to stop. Tamara retreated from the girls' room and into the boys'. If the boys were also out of school, they had gone away to do something else. The room was empty. Tamara ripped through it like a whirlwind, looking for any sign of the toy. There was still no sign of it. She moved on to the master bedroom. She was sure it wouldn't be there. What reason would Mrs. Henson have to take the stuffed toy and then gaslight her about it? She looked through all of the drawers and other hiding places she could see and went back to her own room. Mrs. Henson was back there, looking behind the dresser, under the crib and bed, being very slow and methodical. But she wasn't going to find it. Tamara knew where it had been. It had been on the dresser.

Tamara pounded down the stairs to check the rest of the house. It was eerily similar to her search for Olly after Mrs. Henson had woken her up three days ago. Finally, she stood there, in the living room, unsure of what to do next.

Mrs. Henson descended the stairs. "No luck?" she asked.

"It's not here. It's not in the house." Tamara stared at Mrs. Henson. "How could it be gone? How could someone come into the house and steal a toy? How could it be gone too?"

"I'm sure it must just be misplaced."

"You have to call the police. Get them back here. Get them to fingerprint everything. The dogs, we'll need them back too."

"They're not going to bring scent dogs in to look for a missing toy. I don't think there's anything to be concerned about, Tamara. Little things like that go missing all the time."

"Call the police."

"No, Tamara. I'm not calling the police about this."

"Then I will!"

"If you're going to persist in this, I'm going to ask for you to be evaluated. You're not behaving rationally."

"How is it not rational? First, someone comes into the house to steal Olly. Then they come back in to steal Mister Duck! This proves it! This proves that it was someone outside the house and not me."

Mrs. Henson did not agree.

"Won't you call them?" Tamara begged. "Tell them; I know they'll come to investigate. This is important!"

"No."

Tamara went to the house phone and picked it up. Mrs. Henson saw that she was dialing 9-1-1 and moved in to take it away from her. Tamara pushed her back and would not let her get close enough to snatch the phone away. The 9-1-1 operator started off with all of the calm, routine questions they were trained to ask callers, but Tamara didn't have the patience to deal with them.

"They took Mister Duck," she babbled. "You need to send someone to investigate. They took Mister Duck and left a pacifier. He'd never take a pacifier! This proves it!"

"Ma'am," the operator tried to calm her. "If I could get your name and address, that would help us to respond to your call."

"Check the caller ID," Tamara snapped. "I know it must show up on your system. You have to send someone. They've taken Mister Duck!"

"Is this a joke? Because you can be fined for abusing the emergency call system."

"It's not a joke! First they took Olly and then they took Mister Duck! You know that, don't you? They took my baby! And now they're back!"

"Who is back?"

"The kidnappers. The person who took my baby!"

"You're calling about a kidnapping?"

"Yes!"

"How old is this man? Can you spell his name for me?"

"Mister Duck isn't a man! He's stuffed duck!"

"Ma'am, you need to hang up now. This number is not to be used for jokes or crank calls. Someone who is in a real emergency—"

"Put me through... put me through to Bowen. Bowen and Simmons. Timmons. His name is Timmons. Get me one of them. They're the detectives on the case."

"The case of the stuffed duck."

"No, the case of the missing baby! Olly! Aren't you listening?"

"I'll try to get one of the detectives for you, ma'am," the operator sighed.

Tamara waited, listening to the computer keys clicking.

"Tell them it's Tamara. Tell them they came back. While I was asleep."

"Can I get your full name and address, please? We need it to file our report."

Tamara gave her the information requested. "Are they coming?" she asked impatiently. "Bowen and Timmons? Are they going to come and take fingerprints?"

"I'm still waiting for a response back. They may be out on a call or in an interview. They are not always reachable."

"Tell them it's Tamara. They know me. They know who I am."

"I have relayed that to them, ma'am."

Tamara tapped her foot. "Where are they...?"

She waited on pins and needles. Then the operator spoke. "They are en route, ma'am. They'll be there in a few minutes. Do you want me to stay on the line with you?"

"No. Thanks." Tamara blew out her breath. "If they're coming, that's okay."

She hung up the phone. Mrs. Henson was still standing there, looking at her with a puzzled, uncertain expression.

"You need to calm down now, Tamara. Sit down and take a few breaths. Can I get you something? What would help you?"

"I don't need to calm down. Don't you get it? This is big! This proves I didn't do it!"

Mrs. Henson was unconvinced. "I think we need to set up a meeting with your psychiatrist. This business has... upset you. You're not sleeping properly and you're not able to cope..."

Tamara brushed Mrs. Henson off with a motion. "You'll see."

Mrs. Henson shook her head. "Let's go wait in the living room."

Tamara followed her, but she couldn't sit down and relax like Mrs. Henson suggested. She started to pace, increasingly agitated with every minute that passed without Bowen and Timmons arriving. She muttered under her breath, a low, inaudible murmur. "Come on, come on, come on..."

Her stomach was tied in knots. She wrung her hands together. "Where are they? The dispatcher said they would just be a few minutes."

"We don't know where they are coming from. They could be across the city. There could be traffic. They might have had to finish up an interview or something else before they could come. Why don't you find something else to keep yourself busy? The time will pass faster, and you'll still be here if—when they come."

"No..."

"Sit down and relax with a book. Find something to distract yourself," Mrs. Henson persisted.

Tamara shook her head, irritated. "You can find something else to do. I'm waiting. I couldn't focus on anything else right now."

TWENTY-THREE

I T SEEMED LIKE HOURS had passed before Bowen and Timmons showed up. Tamara saw the dark car pull up in front of the house. She'd never thought she'd be happy to see that car. She went to the door and opened it, waiting for them to finish radio check-in or whatever they had to do in the car. Then they were finally walking up the sidewalk.

"Come on, come on. You have to see," Tamara insisted.

When they stepped into the living room, both detectives looked at Mrs. Henson to gauge her mood. She shrugged and shook her head. "She's very agitated. I'm afraid it's a wasted trip. I'm going to try to take her in to see someone. I don't know..." Mrs. Henson's voice was low. She glanced at Tamara, trying to talk about her without causing an explosion.

"Don't listen to her," Tamara growled. "I'm the one who called you. She didn't think it was important, but it is! Someone came in and took Mister Duck!"

Bowen's brow wrinkled, and she looked back at Mrs. Henson again. Mrs. Henson gave that shrug that Tamara had seen many times when she had started to break down in juvie. That 'I told you she's crazy' look. Then Bowen looked back at Tamara and focused on her.

"Who is Mister Duck?"

"Come upstairs and you'll see."

Bowen nodded, and motioned for Tamara to lead the way. Tamara pounded up the stairs and took her into the bedroom.

"There! Right there! I haven't touched anything since you guys were in here. Not since Olly disappeared."

Bowen surveyed the top of the dresser. "Okay... and what happened?"

"The duck was there. A stuffed toy." Tamara pointed to the pacifier. "Right there. Someone took it and put the pacifier there."

Bowen stared at the soother, frowning. "When?"

A wave of relief went through Tamara. Bowen didn't automatically jump to the conclusion that Tamara was having a nervous breakdown. She wanted to know more details. She was at least willing to suspend disbelief.

"Last night. While I was asleep."

Bowen's eyes widened slightly. She turned and looked at Timmons for his reaction. Whatever communication passed between them, Bowen made the decision to take Tamara's information seriously.

"Again, while you were asleep. Do you take sleeping pills?"

"No. I showed you all my meds. I don't take anything else. Except painkillers. I took a painkiller for my head."

"What kind of painkiller? An opioid?"

"No, no. Just Tylenol or aspirin. Nothing like that."

"I want to see the bottle they came from."

"Nita has it."

"Why does Nita have it?"

"I was... I wanted to make sure I couldn't take too much."

"You were afraid of overdosing?"

Tamara glanced toward the doorway to make sure that Mrs. Henson hadn't followed the detectives up. "Uh... yeah."

Bowen took some time considering this. "Are you considering suicide?"

"No... just... I dunno, I guess I thought of it, but not seriously... yet..."

"You know you need to do like Mrs. Henson said and see your doctor. See if you need to increase your antidepressant or switch to another one."

Tamara shrugged. "I gave Nita all of my pills. I'm not gonna do anything. What's important is Olly." Tamara pointed back at the dresser. "This proves it wasn't me!"

"I'm not sure it proves anything. You were out all day yesterday. It would have been easy to dispose of a toy along the way. The fact that it is missing—if it is—does not prove you didn't have anything to do with Olly's disappearance."

"But I didn't!"

"I want to believe that. I'm listening to what you have to say. The toy duck isn't here. I assume you've looked for it and can't find it in the rest of the house."

"Yeah. I looked everywhere. Nobody here took it. It had to be someone outside the house."

"Or someone who disposed of it outside the house." Bowen turned and motioned Timmons forward. "Do you remember it? A toy duck, there?"

Timmons squinted. "We can look at the crime scene photos. I can see it in my mind, but she's planted the suggestion, it might just be my brain trying to supply a picture."

"It was there," Tamara asserted.

"Assuming it was, why would someone take it?"

"Maybe they're trying to make everybody think I'm crazy."

"They're doing a pretty good job," Timmons offered.

Bowen glared at him. But Tamara's anger was not triggered by his comment. That was her point. If someone wanted to discredit her or to actually drive her to having a breakdown, they were playing their cards well.

"Was the pacifier here before?" Bowen asked.

Tamara thought back to the pictures Bowen had showed her. She'd said to study them, to tell them what might be missing or out of place. Tamara had done her best but hadn't been able to come up with anything. It was like a game of *Memory*, a game she used to play with Gran, where multiple objects were laid on a tray, then removed one at a time, and the players had to identify what was missing.

"He'd never take a pacifier," Tamara said. "It might have been here before, but I don't remember it."

"But he liked the duck?"

Tamara nodded. "Yes. Sometimes he'd go to sleep with it. He liked to rub his face against it."

Bowen walked over to the crib and looked down into it. She went to the dresser and looked at the miscellany scattered over it. She looked at Timmons. "If you were taking a baby, and you could take one thing with you, what would it be?"

Timmons considered. Tamara tried to look at the objects with fresh eyes. Diaper cream, wipes, teething toys, mismatched socks, a couple of board books, safety fingernail clippers, baby monitor, booger aspirator. All things that could be easily purchased. But babies were not robots. They had specific likes and dislikes. Pacifiers were one of the things babies could be very particular about. At her parenting classes, other mothers had exchanged stories about babies who would only take one particular size, shape, and brand of pacifier. Stick anything else in their mouths, and they wouldn't accept it. And a pacifier-trained baby might not calm for anything else. She looked at Bowen and saw that this was exactly what she was thinking. Tamara felt a wave of something like vertigo. Was Bowen a mother? Did she know this from kids of her own or babysitting someone else's? Or was it just common knowledge even among adults without any contact with babies?

"They'd take the paci," Tamara said. "Some babies have to have their own pacifiers, they won't accept anything else."

Timmons pursed his lips, considering this. "You think someone kidnapped Olly, and took the soother in case he wouldn't take another one?" He looked at Bowen, then his eyes shifted to Tamara. "But Olly wouldn't take it and was crying too much, so they came back for the stuffed duck?"

Bowen gave a shrug indicating it was a possibility. Tamara nodded her head vigorously. "That makes sense!" she said with relief. "I couldn't understand why they would take Mister Duck, but that makes sense! Olly's been fussy with teething. He hated the soother, so that wouldn't do them any good. If they came back looking for something that would calm him down... he liked the duck. It might help."

"Who would know that the duck was his favorite toy?" Timmons asked.

Tamara put her hand on the dresser to steady herself. With Bowen and Timmons arriving, her adrenaline rush was fading, leaving her shaky and wobbly on her feet.

"The duck... well, anyone in the family. But outside..." She shook her head, unable to think of any outsiders who might know about Mister Duck. "I don't know. No one. His foster mom before Olly came here, that's where it came from. Maybe someone at her house."

"You took it to parenting classes? Playgroup? Anything like that?"

"No. I just left it at home. I didn't want it to get lost. I just used it at night sometimes. When he was fussy and wouldn't settle.

"You didn't use it during the day? It wouldn't have been in the crib or on the blanket with him when he was asleep the day he disappeared?"

"No. Only at night, and only if he couldn't sleep without it. It was getting chewed up," Tamara explained. "It got dirty because it was light yellow, and everything showed. You couldn't just wash it off like a paci or teething ring, so I didn't like to give it to him."

"I think this is important," Bowen said to Timmons. Her attention shifted to Tamara. "Good grief, you're as white as a ghost. Sit down." She took Tamara by the arm and marched her over to the bed to make her sit. "Stay there." Turning her attention back to Timmons, she continued as if she hadn't been interrupted. "Have Janice go through the photos and send us anything with a duck or a pacifier. Let's get forensics out here to fingerprint the pacifier and dresser and see if we can get DNA off the pacifier. Doorknobs, door frames, anything someone would have had to touch to get in here at night."

"They'd wear gloves," Tamara pointed out the obvious.

"You would be amazed at how many people don't. Criminals get caught all the time because they're stupid and don't take basic precautions. And I doubt if they had gloves on at all times over the past three days. They'd be bound to handle the pacifier without gloves at some point. If they didn't wipe it down, we might be able to get a print or even transfer DNA."

Timmons pulled out his phone and tapped to dial someone back at the police station.

"And I want to know why you didn't wake up when someone walked into the room. Are you a heavy sleeper?"

"No... not usually. But last night I slept real hard. Nita couldn't wake me up this morning. Mrs. Henson did, but I was really tired." Tamara rolled her neck and dug her fingers into the sore muscles in her neck and shoulders. "I was just wrecked after yesterday. I've hardly slept since Olly disappeared, and even before that, I wasn't getting a lot. Then yesterday... all of the walking and the fight with that guy... I was just wrecked."

Bowen nodded slowly. "I still want to check those pills. What did you take before bed?"

"Tylenol. I think. Not the real stuff. Nita has it."

Bowen took a step toward the door. "How did Nita feel about Olly?"

"She loved him. She would always help if I asked her. And Deshawn too; Nita said she was baby crazy—" Tamara cut herself off. "They wouldn't do anything to Olly. Neither of them would do anything to hurt him. They wouldn't. They loved him. They liked being his aunties."

"Nita was home when he disappeared."

"No, she got home just after."

"And Deshawn?"

"She must have got home later... I don't know what time. I don't know if it was while I was still here."

Bowen headed for the door. "Keep an eye on her," she told Timmons. "She doesn't leave this room."

"It's not Nita or Deshawn," Tamara told her again. "I already checked their room. Mister Duck isn't in there."

Bowen ignored her and left the room. Tamara stayed sitting on the bed, watching Timmons as he made his phone calls to get everything rolling. She had to hold back her tears. Someone finally believed her and was following up on real clues. They couldn't put Tamara in prison if they proved someone else had taken Olly. She put her hands over her face to cover her expression as she made another realization.

If someone needed Mister Duck, that meant that Olly was still alive.

* * *

Bowen returned to the room, sealing a plastic bag containing a bottle of pills. "These are the ones? This is what you took?"

Hands still over her eyes, Tamara spread her fingers apart to have a look, then nodded. "Yeah. Just those."

"You didn't take any other pills? You take your prescriptions in the morning?"

"Uh-huh."

"And you didn't take anything to help you sleep? Even an herb or something over the counter?"

"No."

"We'll get these analyzed. See if someone drugged you to make you sleep through whatever might have happened in here."

"You already did a drug test on me the day he vanished."

"That only checks for the top ten illegal drugs that will show up in your urine. There are other drugs that are harder to detect or that we don't do field tests for."

Tamara gazed at the sealed evidence bag. "I didn't take any Tylenol the day Olly disappeared, though."

Bowen shrugged. "All we can do is follow the evidence. You took these last night, so we make sure they're not contaminated."

TWENTY-FOUR

THE NEXT FEW HOURS were a blur.

Tamara allowed Mrs. Henson to pull her away from watching the forensic technicians to have a sandwich as things started to wind down. She was starting to recover her appetite and needed something else to focus her attention on.

Mrs. Henson sat Tamara down and watched to make sure she was going to eat the sandwich.

"I don't understand all of this," she said, shaking her head. "Are you saying—are the police saying—that someone came into the house and took Olly? And then came back and took Mister Duck?"

Tamara nodded, taking a big bite and then chewing slowly. She ran her tongue over her teeth. "They looked at the pictures. Mister Duck was there, like I said, the day he... disappeared. And no paci. Today, there's suddenly no Mister Duck, but the paci is back."

"But why would anyone do that? Why would they come into the house to steal Olly?" Mrs. Henson blinked rapidly, maybe trying to hold back tears. "That doesn't make any sense."

Tamara had been focusing on how. How they had known Olly was there. How they had broken into the house. How they had entered without anyone knowing it, especially Tamara, who wasn't normally a heavy sleeper. But *why*, the motive behind the kidnapping, hadn't been at the top of her mind.

"I guess... someone who wanted a baby...?"

"People who want a baby... they go to a hospital nursery, or a park, or somewhere there are a lot of babies and crowds. They don't go into someone's house. How would they even know we had a baby here? It would have to be someone who knew that."

"You've had lots of babies here," Tamara pointed out. "Who *doesn't* know that?"

Mrs. Henson opened her mouth to respond, then closed it again. "I suppose that's true," she admitted with a little laugh. "Anyone who knows us knows what we do and that we often have babies here."

Tamara nodded. "Maybe someone thought... teen girls shouldn't be having babies. Can't take care of them properly, and that's why they're here. So, why not...?"

"You think it's someone who wanted a baby to take care of? Not something different? Not someone who wanted to hurt him?"

"They came back for the duck."

Mrs. Henson sat back against the counter, nodding. "That's something a mother would do."

"You think..." Tamara took another bite and chewed for a minute. "You think it was that other foster mom? Maybe she wanted to rescue him, take him back from me?"

"The police have already checked into her. Olly isn't there."

"Someone else who thought I shouldn't be taking care of him? Wanda? The social worker?"

"I can't imagine that they would. They deal regularly with teen moms and babies in less than ideal circumstances. What would make them break down and take Olly? You were doing okay with him. They couldn't have thought he was in imminent danger."

Mrs. Henson's words threw Tamara back in time to calling the police about the young girl babysitting for Mr. and Mrs. Baker.

It has to be tonight. It has to be now. She is in imminent danger.

Had someone felt the same way about her? That she was a danger to Olly because of what she had done to the Bakers' girls? She had taken Amy away from them to prevent them from hurting her. Had fate come a full circle?

"Tamara?"

It took Tamara a few seconds to shake off her thoughts and focus on Mrs. Henson again.

"What?"

"You need to eat."

Tamara looked down at the half-consumed sandwich lying forgotten on her plate. "Oh. Yeah."

"Are you okay? I still think we should go see someone."

"I don't need to see the shrink. I'm not going crazy, Bowen told you I was right. The duck was there before, and it's gone now. I'm not just making stuff up. I'm not having a breakdown."

Mrs. Henson sighed. "Eat your sandwich. Stay focused on the present."

Tamara scowled, picking the sandwich back up again. "I don't have flashbacks because I'm not focusing on the present."

"I didn't say that."

"You implied it. Focusing doesn't stop flashbacks."

"Just eat, Tamara. I'm worried about you. You need to keep your strength up. Pretend you're in training. Remember how you tried to eat last year when you were playing volleyball and the coach was helping you get into peak condition."

Tamara stopped eating. Coach McClure. He had gotten Holly pregnant and Holly's family wouldn't let her have an abortion. She'd had to go ahead and have her baby, just like Tamara. Just like Sly, Coach McClure had forced himself on Holly. Tamara had done everything in her power to stop McClure from hurting anyone else, but she had never intended for Glock to beat him like she had. She'd seen Coach McClure at Glock's trial. Tamara's lawyer said that he might have permanent damage, though how extensive, they didn't know. He'd looked like a monster. Thick, ropy scars snaking around his head. One eye bulging like there wasn't room for it inside the socket. He'd stared at Tamara, his expression not changing. She had no way of knowing what was hiding behind his blank face. Did it indicate that he didn't understand what was going on? Or were his malevolent thoughts just hidden behind a mask? When she'd been playing volleyball at school, those thoughts had been hidden behind friendly smiles and coaching advice and she'd been shocked to discover his relationship with Lotta.

Unlike Glock, McClure wasn't in prison. He was out, rehabbing, walking free. There were still charges pending against him for his interference with the girls, but they would probably never be brought to bear. What was the point? Few prisons were properly equipped to handle physically disabled inmates. He was no longer the threat that he had been as a high school coach.

He had to hate her for what she had done, bringing Glock there, unable to stop Glock from beating him nearly to death. She had been the one to expose him and the one to put his life in danger. If anyone wanted to hurt Tamara, it was McClure.

"But could he?" Tamara murmured, staring down at the painted flowers twined around the edge of her empty plate. Was he physically capable of sneaking into the house to kidnap a baby? Or did he have an accomplice?

"Could who what?" Mrs. Henson asked, mystified.

Tamara looked at her. "I'm done." She pushed the plate away from her. "I ate it all."

* * *

Fingerprint and DNA matches were almost instantaneous on TV, but Tamara knew from talking to other inmates that that wasn't the way it worked in the real life. Matches could take weeks or even months, and anything could happen to Olly in that time. Bowen had taken Tamara's fingerprints and a cheek swab, but she couldn't say how long it would take to sort out which of the fingerprints or transfer DNA on the pacifier were Tamara's, which were from Mrs. Henson or other members of the family, and whether any were left to be identified after that, even if they put an emergency rush on the tests because of the danger to Olly. And if the kidnapper were not already in the fingerprint or DNA databases, they had to actually find someone to match them to. Not like on TV, where such results would lead the investigators directly to the perpetrator.

When the detectives and the forensics team left, Tamara told Mrs. Henson that she needed a nap and went upstairs, taking the wireless phone for the house's landline up to her room with her. She didn't want to take the chance of anyone overhearing her.

Sybil's cell phone number was branded into Tamara's brain. Sybil was her first real friend since Gran had died. Still her only real friend. Tamara punched the digits into the wireless phone and crossed her fingers that Sybil hadn't changed her number. She held her breath, waiting for it to ring through. After several long seconds it did start ringing, rather than giving her a message that the number was out of service. Tamara waited to see if Sybil would answer it.

It had rung a lot of times and Tamara was ready to give up and hang up, when there was a click, and then Sybil's whispered words.

"Hello? Tamara?"

"Yeah. Hi."

"How are you? Is everything okay?"

Was everything okay when her baby had been kidnapped and even after everything else, she was still the prime suspect? Or did 'okay' just mean not back in juvie again yet?

"Uh... I dunno. Listen... what do you know about Coach McClure?"

She could hear Sybil's breathing before she answered. "Uh... Coach McClure? Nothing."

"You must have heard something. How he's doing now, if he's going to have to go to prison, that kind of thing."

"Um..." Sybil drew it out, in a hum, reluctant to answer.

"He's out of hospital, I know that," Tamara filled in. "Is he, like, in a rehabilitation place, or at home?"

"Home, I guess." Sybil didn't say anything else for a few long seconds. "What are you going to do?"

"I'm not going to do anything. I just want to know what you've heard." Tamara was not going to drag Sybil into the whole thing and get her in trouble. If Tamara ended up back in prison, that was one thing. She didn't want Sybil to end up there as well. "You know where he lives? His address?"

"You're going to go see him, aren't you?"

"Don't ask if you don't want the answer. Do you know his address?"

"It's probably not listed anymore; once word got out about what he'd been doing. It's not going to be in the phonebook."

"Come on, Syb. You know it, don't you?"

Tamara didn't know why Sybil would be holding back. Did she think Tamara would give her up if she got caught? Sybil should know Tamara well enough to know that she wouldn't snitch.

"Sybil..."

"You're going to go see him."

Tamara bit her lip and tried to formulate an answer that would encourage Sybil to give her the information, rather than scaring her into clamming up. Sybil knew what had happened a year ago. She had to know it had been Glock who had beaten McClure, not Tamara. And Tamara was not looking for him in order to finish the job.

"Sybil... he might have kidnapped my baby."

There was a sharp intake of breath on the other end of the phone. "What?"

"I know... I got pregnant and I had a baby while I was in juvie. When they let me out on parole, it was to take care of him. But a few days ago... someone stole him. He just vanished into thin air. And I'm thinking it has to be an enemy, someone who wanted to hurt me. And Coach McClure..."

Sybil was breathing heavily. Tamara could see Sybil in her mind's eye; leaning forward, eyes sparkling, eager for more details.

"And Coach McClure would want to get back at you for ruining his reputation and for... hurting him."

"I didn't hurt him. That was Glock. That wasn't me. I was just trying to get him to confess about what he was doing."

"So... why aren't the police checking him out?"

"Because they think I did it. They think I did something to Olly and made him disappear."

"You wouldn't do that!"

Tamara tried not to think of what she had done in the past and how frustrated and full of rage Olly could make her feel when he was fussy and would not settle. Sybil didn't know Tamara nearly as well as she thought she did. Unlike everyone else, she seemed to have forgotten what had happened to the Baker children. Tamara wasn't just a misunderstood kid who'd made some stupid mistakes. The justice system had misfired by not putting the Bakers in prison, but it hadn't been wrong to incarcerate Tamara. She had done terrible things.

"I just want to go to McClure's house. See if everything looks kosher. Make sure he doesn't have Olly. I'm not going to kill him."

"Even if he *does* have Olly?"

Tamara wasn't sure whether Sybil was afraid Tamara would kill McClure in that case or if she were prodding her to do it. Sybil had always been a strange tangle of nurturing substitute mother and bad girl groupie that Tamara couldn't quite unwind.

"Even if he has Olly," Tamara said firmly. "I'm not going to kill him. I'm not going to hurt him. If he has Olly, I'll call the detectives on the case. They can deal with him."

"Oh." Tamara could hear Sybil doing something in the background, but she didn't offer any explanation or tell Tamara where she might find Coach McClure. Teachers didn't give their home addresses to students, but Sybil had not yet protested she didn't know where McClure lived, so Tamara was hopeful that she knew something. Even if she just knew the neighborhood, that was more than Tamara had.

"You still there?" Tamara asked.

There was no answer, but more background noise. Tamara waited, glancing toward her closed bedroom door and hoping that Mrs. Henson wouldn't decide to pick up the extension to call Tamara's psychiatrist for advice or poke her head in the door to make sure Tamara was okay.

"McClure coached t-ball for kids," Sybil said, breathing heavily into the receiver. "The little girls..." She trailed off. "So he gave his address for parents to send payment to."

There were a few seconds of silence. Neither of them spoke.

"Tamara? Are you okay?"

But Tamara was still stuck on Coach McClure coaching little kids. He wouldn't have been able to take advantage of them the same way as he had the older girls. He wouldn't be meeting with them alone. They wouldn't be taking showers in the locker room. There would always be parents and volunteers around helping out and making sure nothing bad was going on.

Still, Tamara could imagine him hugging children who had hit a home run or who hadn't done well and needed comfort.

Putting his hands on them to adjust their stances. Seeing how much he could get away with right in front of their parents.

"Tamara?"

"Yeah," Tamara answered faintly. "I'm here. What's the address?"

Sybil blew her breath out. "Okay. Here it is."

Tamara grabbed the scratch pad from the table beside the bed and a pencil from the decorated pencil jar. She wrote down the address and read it back to Sybil.

"That's it," Sybil agreed. "I'm... going to get rid of this. I couldn't have given you his address if I didn't know it, could I?"

"Yeah," Tamara agreed. "Burn it. If anyone asks, I called, but you didn't have it."

* * *

Knowing that the police had followed her when she had left the house previously, Tamara was more careful. She looked out one of the front windows to try to spot anyone sitting in their car surveilling the house. She exited through the back door, keeping low behind the fence and peeking around the corner into the lane for anyone hanging around. She didn't think anyone observed her leaving, but she kept a sharp lookout for any unmarked police cars or anyone watching her more closely than they should. She didn't go to the bus stop that was the closest. They knew she didn't have a car and if she wanted to go somewhere, it would have to be on foot or by bus. The bus stop would be a natural place to watch for her.

She didn't like waiting at the bus stop farther along the route. She was exposed and vulnerable. But no one approached her, and she still didn't see any police, in uniform or plain clothes. No one paid her any attention. No one appeared to recognize her from TV. She didn't see anyone she remembered from school.

And Glock was still in prison. She wasn't going to show up this time.

Still, Tamara was relieved when the bus arrived. She got on, paid her fare, and chose an anonymous seat halfway back. She pretended to be bored; not watching anyone, not paying any attention to her surroundings, as if she took the bus every day and was familiar with the route and the people on it.

She counted the stops and paid attention to road signs when she could see them and landmarks along the way, so she would know when to get off and transfer to the next bus. She wasn't going to ask the bus driver to let her know the right stop. He might remember her if asked by the police. She didn't want to do anything to attract his attention. She would be just one face in a sea of anonymous riders.

Traveling around the city by bus was not quick. It took a couple of hours for Tamara to get to her destination and then to find the right house. McClure didn't exactly live close to the school. But then, he would have had a car and it would have been much faster for him to drive a direct route. Tamara studied the blocky house with a white brick facade. An older house, but better-maintained than the Hensons'. Having a constant stream of teenagers through the house tended to leave it looking a little worn and run down. She didn't know if McClure had any children, but the fact that he lived in a house like that made it more likely than if he had lived in a bachelor's apartment or basement suite somewhere. Tamara's stomach turned at the thought of him having children. But predators didn't always abuse their own children, did they?

She hadn't planned her approach. What if McClure was out of the house at rehab? What if his wife was home and answered the door?

Unsure of what to do, she scouted around the house first. She let herself into the back yard, standing tall and moving confidently, as if she belonged there rather than slinking around like a burglar. There was a big back deck that would be great for barbecues or just sitting together to watch the sun set. There weren't any children's toys left out in the back yard, but there was a shed they could be stored in. The shed was locked with a combination lock, but the latch was flimsy and could probably be wrenched off with a little force. There were fruit trees and flower beds, one with freshly-turned earth that looked like it had been recently planted.

Tamara moved up to the back of the house, trying to peer in through windows covered by curtains and blinds. What was McClure hiding, that every window had to be completely covered?

Unless Tamara was willing to watch the house all day to learn the routines of everyone who came and went from the house, there was no point in waiting. She just had to bite the bullet and deal with anyone who might be inside with Coach McClure.

Tamara didn't want to be seen marching in the front door, though, so she rang the back door, and then stood to the side, looking away, so that whoever answered the door would not be able to see her clearly through the peephole. They would have to open the door.

It took ringing three separate times before the door finally opened. By that time, Tamara was starting to worry that nobody was home. Then she heard the door being unlocked, and it opened a crack for the occupant to get a look at her.

Tamara whirled around to face the door and gave it a hard shove open, into the face of whoever had answered the door. There was a yelp of pain, and Tamara shoved the door again, driving him back until there was enough space for Tamara to slip in. She shut the door and faced Coach Quentin McClure.

TWENTY-FIVE

THE WORLD GAVE A lurch. Tamara was flooded with memories. Coach McClure helping her with volleyball and praising her when she did well. Criticizing her for the shape her body and health were in after three years in juvie. Angry at her for disrespecting him. Then in the showers with Lotta, manifesting his predatory nature for the first time.

Overwhelming it all was Glock beating him, bludgeoning him over and over again with a heavy trophy, as he fought back and struggled, making it go on endlessly. Blood everywhere, the sounds of the blows in her ears, her own screams at Glock to stop.

He stood before her, mere inches away, holding his nose after being hit by the door. In court, she'd seen him across the room, and his scars had been ugly at that distance. Close up, they looked worse, barely healed even though the attack had been a year before. His bulging eye creeped her out. She wasn't sure whether he could see her through it or not, it didn't team properly with his other eye to focus on her.

"What are you doing here?" he demanded.

"Looking for my baby."

His face showed neither surprise nor comprehension.

Tamara pushed past him. If there were anyone else in the house, they could be calling the police. She might have only a few minutes to search for any sign of Olly. She didn't have the time to question Coach McClure. He would only lie to her anyway.

Tamara marched into the kitchen as if she owned the place and took a quick glance around. No bottles on the counter or sink. She opened the fridge, but there was no formula. Someone had stolen Mister Duck to soothe Olly; that meant he was still alive, which meant they were feeding him. But bottles and formula could have been stored somewhere other than in the kitchen.

She went from the kitchen to the living room. It was pristine, straight out of a decorating magazine. No sign that any baby or child had ever been there. Down the hall, Tamara searched quickly through the bedrooms. One bedroom was set up with a hospital bed and some kind of pulley system. Coach McClure appeared able to move normally, but maybe appearances were deceiving. He'd needed some kind of assistance moving around or getting out of bed when he got out of hospital, even if he didn't anymore.

Tamara double-checked the closet before going on to the next bedroom. As the living room had suggested, Coach McClure was married, and the next bedroom was the master bedroom, apparently only occupied by his wife, with one bedside table empty and a wide gap in clothes in the closet. Tamara took grim satisfaction in the fact that they were no longer sleeping together. Was it only because of Coach McClure's newly acquired disabilities, or did the fact that his wife had found out about his messing around with teen girls factor into it?

Tamara didn't expect to find any sign of Olly in the master

bedroom, and she didn't. If McClure and his wife were estranged, she wouldn't have knowingly allowed him to bring Tamara's baby into the house. Tamara took a quick look in the third bedroom. Like the living room, the guest room was immaculate, with not a wrinkle in the blanket or a speck of dust on the furniture.

She took extra time in the bathroom checking for diapers, cream, or bath things. Nothing that looked like it was for a baby. She read McClure's prescription bottles, then went back out to the hall.

McClure was just then making it into the hall from the back door. He had a scowl and was red-faced with anger or exertion. He walked with difficulty, which explained why it had taken him so long to answer the back door.

"What the hell do you think you're doing?" He slurred like he was drunk, but maybe it was just brain damage from the attack.

Tamara didn't bother answering. She brushed past him in the hallway, anticipating that he wouldn't be nimble enough to stop her, and headed downstairs. Her logical brain told her that stairs would be too difficult for him, and she wouldn't find Olly or any sign of him downstairs either. But if McClure were able to get up and down stairs, that's where he would have kept the baby. Not upstairs, right under his wife's nose. If she weren't in on it as revenge for what Tamara had done, then the baby would have to be hidden somewhere out of the way. A workshop or a closet downstairs or the shed outside.

She hurried down the stairs to the basement. It was fully-developed and attractive. A family room, even though there were no kids, an office that had an air of disuse, confirming her suspicion that McClure could not get up and down stairs easily. Tamara looked through the file drawers for anything of interest. But they had surely been searched by the police the year before and there was no sign of pornography or secret files about the girls he coached or preyed upon. A neat, well-maintained cold room for food storage, with jams and preserves neatly arrayed down the rows. There was no crawlspace, no dungeon, no false wall.

Tamara let out a long breath. He wasn't there. Coach McClure hadn't taken Olly. He wasn't in the house and there wasn't any sign that he ever had been.

She went back upstairs and was again confronted by Coach McClure, apoplectic with her invasion of his privacy and his inability to keep up with her as she searched his house.

"Get out of here! You don't have any right to come here! I will report you!"

"You try that, and I'm going to say you called me, and then when I got here, you tried to assault me. I had to punch you in the nose to stop you. Who are they going to believe?"

His fists were clenched, and she knew that if he had his full faculties, he would have hit her. But he couldn't beat her in a fight. Not in the condition he was in. Tamara exited by the back door. She went to the gardening shed. She had to be sure he didn't have Olly locked in there, too weak to even cry anymore. Or already dead.

She looked around for a shovel or something to use as a tool to pry the latch from where it was anchored with a couple of short screws. All of the garden tools were apparently stored safely away in the shed. Tamara picked up a large decorative rock from the edge of one of the flower beds and, with a few smashes, the latch broke away from the shed and she could open the door.

It was neat and tidy. Rows of pots, bags of peat, bark, and lime. Garden tools hung neatly in their appointed places. There were a couple of cardboard boxes under the counter. Tamara pulled them out but found nothing of consequence. Just more gardening junk. She could hear Coach McClure bellowing out of the house at her, yelling at her to get out. There was an answering voice from a neighbor, and Tamara knew she'd better get out of there quickly before somebody who was capable of holding her and having her arrested got there.

There was nowhere else an infant could conceivably be hidden, so she took off, running out through a back gate and down the alley before the concerned neighbor could catch her.

* * *

It wasn't McClure. There had been no sign of Olly at the house. No Mister Duck. No bottles or other baby paraphernalia. Tamara walked down the street, thinking about it. Having seen how slow McClure was now and all of the pulleys around his hospital bed, she doubted he could climb the stairs at the Henson house. Not quietly enough and quickly enough that no one would be alerted. He certainly couldn't have carried Olly down the stairs.

So it wasn't him. And with him and his wife sleeping separately, she had to assume that his wife wouldn't be helping him kidnap a baby out of revenge either.

Tamara rubbed her head, thinking about it. She could go back to the Hensons' house and pretend that nothing had happened, that she'd been in her room the whole time. But Mrs. Henson had probably discovered her absence. She checked on Tamara pretty regularly. If McClure or his neighbor called the police and reported her, Wanda would be coming to pick her up and get her remanded. Breaking and entering wasn't exactly obeying her parole terms. Destruction of property. Uttering threats. Wanda would be more than happy to send her back to prison.

But if she couldn't go back to the Hensons' again, what was she going to do? She'd spent little time on the streets, just enough to know that she wasn't cut out for it and didn't want to spend an extended length of time fending for herself. Youth programs like the teen health bus were helpful, but she couldn't survive on sandwiches and condoms. Sleeping in the Bakers' back yard hadn't exactly been a solution. She'd stayed there only as long as she'd had to, and had eventually returned to Vernon and Sly, unable to manage on her own, especially with a baby to look after.

Tamara stopped walking and just stood there in the middle of the sidewalk like a statue.

The Bakers. Not only had Tamara killed Corinne and Julie on a psychotic break four years earlier, but she'd also kidnapped Amy the year before. She'd walked right into their house, taken the baby, and smashed Mr. Baker over the head to knock him out.

It would make perfect sense that they would retaliate by stealing Tamara's baby. She didn't know if Mrs. Baker had been able to get Amy back or not. Tamara had told Social Services how abusive Mrs. Baker was and had done her best to make sure that they wouldn't ever return Amy to her, but since when did Social Services make decisions based on what a teenage girl told them? They knew there was bad blood between Tamara and the Bakers. Why would they believe anything Tamara said? If Mrs. Baker hadn't been able to get her own baby back, maybe she had thought it divine retribution that she steal Tamara's baby. Even if she had gotten Amy back, maybe she'd wanted to give Tamara a taste of her own medicine. She wouldn't have had to steal any of Olly's baby gear, because she would have all of Amy's things. She would know that babies could have specific tastes in pacifiers. She would know to go back for the baby's well-worn stuffed duck when he wouldn't settle for anything else.

Unlike Coach McClure, Chrissy Baker would have no trouble creeping up and down the stairs stealthily. She walked like a cat and had startled Tamara many times with her sudden appearances. Tamara wasn't sure why she hadn't identified Mrs. Baker as a suspect before. It was the natural solution.

She didn't need to call anyone to find out where the Bakers lived. She didn't have to pound the pavement for days looking for her at strip clubs and bars. Tamara already knew where she lived, provided she hadn't moved away in the past year. It was a possibility, of course. People would know that Mr. Baker was a sex offender after everything had been aired on TV following the kidnapping. People didn't like having perverts living next door.

Only Mrs. Baker wouldn't have been identified as a sex offender, even on TV. A child beater, yes, but people didn't care so much about that. They wouldn't run her out of the neighborhood for being physically abusive.

Tamara forced herself to survey her surroundings, looking for any sign of police surveillance. They had fooled her the other day. They had followed her everywhere without her ever being aware of it. But she couldn't see any suspicious vehicles or anyone sitting watching her. Taking precautions, Tamara detoured through a couple of back alleys and didn't go to the nearest bus stops. She couldn't spot anyone tailing her.

This time, she knew she was right. It made perfect sense.

TWENTY-SIX

THE SUN WAS GETTING lower in the sky when Tamara reached the Bakers'. Still cautious, she had gotten off of the bus several stops away and had woven her way through various alleys and side streets before arriving. Mindful that the police might have come to the same conclusion as Tamara had and have surveillance on the house, she circled around and checked every car in view of the house for cops. The streets were quiet and there was no evidence of any surveillance.

Of course not; why would there be? Bowen was certain that Tamara had been the one who had lost the baby. That Tamara had done something to hurt him and then had callously disposed of him. Or that she just hadn't wanted him and had abandoned him somewhere to die. Why would they bother looking at anyone else?

Tamara looked in the living room window as she walked casually down the sidewalk in front of the house. Unlike the carefully covered windows at the McClures' house, the curtains were open, and Tamara could see most of the front room. The TV was on, but it looked like some kind of drama, rather than the sports that Mr. Baker would have been watching if he were at home. Tamara let her breath out slowly. She'd been worried that she would discover for the second time that Mr. Baker was free to walk around and live his own life however he wanted while Tamara was in prison for what she had done. If her breakdown in the courtroom when she was supposed to testify against Mr. Baker had resulted in his walking free, she didn't know if she could ever forgive herself.

He could still be out of the house, at the gym or the bar, while his wife was home on her own. But at least at that moment, it looked like only Mrs. Baker was home.

Tamara found her way around the back of the house where she would not be observed. The last time, she had been able to just walk into the house. She didn't suppose that she'd be that lucky again a second time. Mrs. Baker would know not to leave the doors unlocked even if she were home.

Tamara tried the back door, but the knob did not move. She scanned the back of the house for an open window, and instead saw the sliding doors to the patio. If Tamara had learned anything during her time in juvie, it was that patio doors were notoriously easy to break in through. A favorite weakness of many a burglar. She crept along the back of the house to the doors to check the catches and mechanisms. The door had been slid to the side to allow air in through the screen. There was a hole in the bottom corner of the screen, the kind often caused by pets or children trying to get out. Tamara inserted her fingers through the hole, grabbed the screen, and jerked on it. There was a lot of give. Tamara gave it a harder yank and doubled the size of the rip. She put her other hand in through the hole and, now able to use both hands, she ripped it right up the side, then squeezed through.

And with that, she was into the house.

Tamara looked around the kitchen. There were baby things, but were they for Olly or Amy? She checked the fridge and found regular milk, but not formula. Once babies were older than a year, they were allowed to drink regular milk. Olly was still on formula; he hadn't even started eating infant cereal yet. Tamara closed the fridge and looked for any other clues. She crept up on the living room and peeked into the room. The TV was still playing, but Mrs. Baker was not there. Since she wasn't in the kitchen either, she'd obviously gone upstairs, intending to return to the living room to watch TV in a few minutes. Tamara hesitated, unsure whether to wait there, get out, or follow Mrs. Baker upstairs.

The curtains weren't pulled all the way, which meant that anyone walking by on the street would be able to see what went on in the living room, at least partially. So that eliminated staying in the living room. Upstairs or leave?

Tamara wanted to leave, but concern for Olly drew her in too strongly. She couldn't just abandon him now that she was so close. She was there. He could be just upstairs, waiting for her. How could she ever be called a mother if she just walked away?

Tamara started up the stairs. She did her best to stay quiet, but the stairs squeaked and creaked like a haunted house. Someone should really have done something to fix that.

She stood still when she got to the top of the stairs, listening. She could hear the TV droning downstairs, but where was Mrs. Baker? In the nursery? The master bedroom? The bathtub? Tamara couldn't hear anything.

Tamara turned down the short hall toward the nursery. That was where Olly would be, wasn't it? As quietly as she could, Tamara opened the door to the baby's room. The lighting was dim, a lamp on, but not the overhead light. The smell of baby powder and cream hung in the air. Swallowing, Tamara moved to look into the crib, expecting to find Olly sleeping there. But it was empty. She forced down the waves of disappointment. He wasn't in the crib, but that didn't mean that he wasn't in the house at all. Trying to blank out the memories of Julie lying in the crib dying, Tamara turned back to the door. She was almost there. She had almost found her baby. No thanks to the police, who didn't believe her. She would show them what a good mother she was. She could find her baby when they could not. Mother's love. Mother's instinct. All of that.

She walked past the bathroom slowly, ears pricked. There was no sound of anyone there. But as she grew closer to the master bedroom, she could hear Mrs. Baker's voice, low, speaking to someone.

To Olly.

Tamara pushed the door open to face her enemy.

TWENTY-SEVEN

MRS. BAKER SAT ON the bed, her back to the wall. She had the phone in one hand, and in the other she held a handgun, pointing directly at Tamara's face.

Tamara stared in numb shock.

Christina Baker smiled at her. A cruel smile of enjoyment.

"I knew you would come back. When they said you were out on parole again, I knew you were going to come back here. You just can't stay away, can you?"

Tamara stared down the barrel of the gun. She didn't know what to do or say. She knew what the phone clutched in Mrs. Baker's other hand meant. It meant that the police were already on their way. Mrs. Baker had seen or heard her coming and had already called 9-1-1. Tamara had only seconds to evaluate the situation and make her choices.

"Where is he?" Tamara demanded hoarsely.

"You know where he is."

There was another noise, and Tamara turned her head to look at the playpen in the corner of the room. Amy stood there, holding on to the side, watching them both curiously. She was big, a toddler now, no longer a baby. Too big for a playpen. But she had probably been well-trained to stay put and not complain. Tamara took a step closer to look into the playpen to see if Olly were lying in the bottom. But he wasn't there. Just Amy.

"Where is Olly? Where's my baby?"

Mrs. Baker's eyes grew calculating. "Your baby?" she repeated in a high, fake-innocent voice. "What would I know about your baby?"

"My baby. You came, and you stole him out of my house. You have him here. Where is he?"

Mrs. Baker smiled.

"Where is he?" Tamara repeated.

"What makes you think I came into your house and stole him? You're the one breaking into people's houses. You took Amy away once and now you're here to do it again. I could shoot you dead and no one would care. *No one*. You're just some criminal who broke into my house. I'm allowed to defend myself. And no one will shed a single tear for you. You want to know why? No one cares about you. Not one person. You're worthless. You're worse than nothing. You're a drain on society. People like you should be rounded up and exterminated." She still held the gun steady, pointed at Tamara. "When people like you die, nobody mourns them. They celebrate."

Mrs. Baker was giving voice to all of Tamara's fears. Nobody wanted her. Nobody loved her. And when she was gone, nobody would even care.

Tamara fought back against the words, trying not to drown in them.

She swallowed. She needed to stay focused on what she had gone there for. Not to face down Mrs. Baker to prove her worth, but to save her baby.

"Where is Olly? What did you do to him?"

"What would I do to your baby..." Mrs. Baker mused. She got that happy little smile she used to get after beating Tamara, satisfied with herself. Tamara's blood ran cold. Was she too late? Mrs. Baker had already tortured Olly? How could she hurt an innocent baby?

"Tell me what you did!"

Mrs. Baker waggled the phone in her hand, indicating that the police dispatcher was still on the line to overhear them.

"I didn't do anything to your precious child. I have my own child to take care of, as you know. And you're not taking her away again. I'm not my husband. I'm not stupid like him. I've got the drop on *you*."

Tamara fought with her warring emotions. Her need to know what had happened to Olly. Self-preservation. Holding on to her freedom. In the end, she knew that Mrs. Baker wasn't going to tell her what she had done to Olly and where he was now. She was a demon with no conscience. Like Glock, she took pleasure in inflicting pain.

Tamara stepped back into the hallway and pulled the door shut in a quick movement, ducked in case Mrs. Baker decided to shoot through the door, and ran for it. She had to get out of there before the police showed up. There would be no way for her to talk her way out of breaking into Mrs. Baker's house.

She could hear sirens in the distance. They would create a perimeter. They would bring in tracking dogs. All Tamara could hope for was that the scent dogs would find Olly instead of her. If Olly's body were there somewhere, in the basement or the garbage or buried in the back yard, the dogs could smell it and lead the cops to it. But Tamara had only one option, and that was to run. To get outside the perimeter before they could finish setting it up.

* * *

She ran until she could go no farther. Then she walked, holding the stitch in her side and waiting for her breathing to settle down again. She stuck to the darkening side streets and cut through parks and parking lots and even through a fountain and a pond, hoping to foil the tracking dogs.

She wasn't even sure why she was running. It wasn't going to do her any good. They were going to catch her one way or another. She was going back to prison. The fact that they didn't catch her at the Bakers' house meant nothing. Mrs. Baker would tell them, and it was her word against Tamara's. Tamara had kidnapped and killed before. Why would they suspect Mrs. Baker of anything?

Tamara kept going, homing in on the one place she knew and felt safe. She knew there was no point in going back to the Hensons. They would only call the police or call Wanda and have her taken back into custody. Because it was the right thing to do. They always did the right thing and told Tamara that was for the best. But it was the only place she felt safe.

It wasn't quite dark when Tamara made it to the house. She didn't have a watch and wondered nonsensically if she had made it before her curfew. As if her curfew mattered at all anymore. Tamara stood for a moment on the sidewalk in front of the Hensons' house, looking at it with sadness. It would be the last time she stood there. The last time she would be free for a long time.

As she walked up the front walkway, a bulky shadow emerged from the tree, moving toward her. Tamara turned her head in slow motion, knowing it would be one of the cops, hiding there in darkness and waiting for her return. So predictable.

The man hit her much harder than Tamara expected. It was like running into a brick wall. Tamara cried out in protest. She wasn't resisting, so why were they being so rough? She was cold and wet and exhausted. She held her hands up at her shoulders in surrender, and the figure struck again. There was a hot, ripping pain down Tamara's side. She instinctively moved to block another blow, not understanding why he was attacking instead of simply putting her in handcuffs when her hands were held up in surrender.

There was another searing, tearing pain in her blocking arm and then her upper ribs. Then the figure was grabbing at her and falling, and Tamara fell with him. He landed hard on top of her on the ground. Tamara squirmed to get out from underneath him. As she wrenched free from him, she saw his face.

It wasn't Timmons or one of the other police officers. It was Coach McClure.

TWENTY-EIGHT

COACH MCCLURE WAS SHOUTING incomprehensibly. Tamara jumped to her feet, balanced on the balls of her feet and waiting for his next move. She knew from their encounter earlier in the day that he had difficulty moving. If she were quick, she could avoid any further damage. He'd been able to attack her only because she stood there waiting for him, thinking she was surrendering to the police.

There was an eruption of activity from the house, Jesse and Dirk hurrying belatedly to her aid, rushing toward Coach McClure as he struggled to get to his feet to renew the attack.

"Be careful!" Tamara shouted. "I think he's armed!"

They shouldn't be trying to interfere. They weren't trained fighters. With the wild sweeps of Coach McClure's arm, either one of them could get injured. It wasn't like fighting with someone who was rational and would take care to protect themselves. He was furious. His movements were jerky and unpredictable. Jesse rushed in and then jumped back when he realized that what Tamara had said was true and McClure was holding some kind of blade.

"Dirk," Jesse warned, "stay back. Look out!"

Teenage boys were not well-known for being cautious and logical and Dirk was no exception. He threw himself at Coach McClure as if he were a trained bodyguard, then stumbled back, holding his arm and looking baffled. He was no Jackie Chan.

Mrs. Henson was on the front step, calling out to find out what was going on and if they were all okay.

"Call the police," Jesse shouted back to her. "Call 9-1-1!"

But as it turned out, there was no need to call 9-1-1, as two plainclothes officers converged on the scene, with warnings of "Police! Freeze!" and "Drop your weapon!"

Not surprisingly, Coach McClure did not, and the cops reached for their weapons.

"Don't shoot him!" Tamara shouted. "He's got brain damage. He's not fast. He just caught me off-guard."

There was a split second in which she thought they were just going to ignore her and draw their guns on Coach McClure. But then they took an extra couple of beats to analyze the situation and watch Coach McClure's movements. Then they moved into a coordinated attack, one of them moving around McClure. Unable to watch them both at once, McClure had to decide which to focus his attention on, turning his back on the other. In a moment, the cop who slipped behind him managed to grab his arm and send the knife clattering to the sidewalk.

Tamara's head spun with the speed at which everything had happened. Jesse and the police officers were asking questions, demanding to know who McClure was and what had just happened. Tamara was still trying to catch her breath after the ambush. Any second, the police were going to realize that there was a warrant out for her arrest and would take her into custody.

"Are you all right, Tamara?" Jesse asked.

"He hit me pretty hard," Tamara admitted. She tried to slow her breathing to its regular pace. "I thought he was the—I didn't really see him or know what was going on at first."

"We should have somebody take a look at you."

Tamara was standing in the shadows, night quickly closing in around her. She rubbed her burning arm and drew it back slick with sweat. The air was cool but, with the sudden physical demands and adrenaline, the sweat was pouring off her. Tamara looked down at her fingers and realized they were wet not with sweat, but with blood. McClure had not just bruised her with his attack, he had managed to cut her too.

"Uh... yeah," Tamara agreed.

Jesse had been distracted watching the police pat Coach McClure down. He looked back at Tamara, having lost the train of their conversation.

"I might need stitches," Tamara told him.

Jesse looked down at the arm Tamara was examining by the light of the streetlight and swore. "Yes, that's going to need stitches. I didn't realize he got you." He waved at Mrs. Henson, who was still standing on the front steps of the house, trying to stay out of the way of the police operation and, Tamara assumed, keep everyone else in the house inside and out of the way. "Marion, get a clean towel."

He asked the police to call for an ambulance and went up to the house to claim the towel Mrs. Henson retrieved for him.

"How bad is it?" Mrs. Henson asked, her voice pitched higher than usual. "Is she going to be okay?"

"She'll be fine." Jesse returned to Tamara's side. He helped wrap the bleeding gash in a towel until the paramedics could get there. "It's a good thing you don't faint at the sight of blood."

That would definitely have complicated things. The adrenaline rush was subsiding, leaving Tamara shaky and nauseated.

"I think I should sit down."

Jesse looked around. "Why don't you sit on the bottom step," he suggested, motioning to the steps at the front door. But when he looked back at Tamara, she had folded where she was, sitting on the sidewalk and putting her head between he knees, waiting for the light-headedness to pass. She hadn't eaten since that sandwich Mrs. Henson had made her eat, and combining that with coming down from the adrenaline and her injury, she was feeling pretty light-headed.

"Or... there..." Jesse laughed. "Okay. Keep the pressure on that cut. Are you going to be okay? You're not going to pass out on me?"

"I might."

"Dirk? Can you come over here?" Jesse motioned for Dirk to join them. He reluctantly left the excitement of the police arresting McClure to see what was needed. "Can you just sit with Tamara, make sure she's okay? I'll go get some ice."

Dirk brightened at being given an important job to do. He crouched down next to Tamara. "That was pretty awesome," he told her. "You fighting off a guy with a knife? Wow. I could have disarmed him if the police hadn't come. I know how—"

Tamara had heard enough bravado in juvie to just tune him out. So many girls came in bragging about how tough or skilled they were, but when put to the test it became obvious they had little or no experience in fighting. She let all of the noise and action around her gray out, retreating inside herself to where she could think.

"Tamara? Here." Tamara jolted at the ice bag laid over the back of her neck, everything suddenly coming back into sharp focus. She swore and slapped it away, but Jesse replaced it again and held it in place.

"That's cold!" Tamara protested.

"I know it is. It should help the faintness. Just keep it in place for a few minutes."

Tamara had to admit that the dizziness and nausea both retreated with the application of the ice bag. The world remained in sharp clarity, even if that wasn't what she wanted.

A couple of police cars pulled up with their lights flashing, bright strobes slicing their way into Tamara's brain. She didn't know why they needed so many cars with McClure already in custody. She supposed one of them was probably there for her. But none of the cops came over to her, other than to get a brief recap of McClure's ambush and assure her that an ambulance was on its way to look at her arm.

The arrival of the ambulance with siren blaring and lights flashing made her head hurt that much more. Tamara readjusted the ice pack, trying to numb the pain.

The paramedics were directed over where Tamara was sitting.

"Got a boo-boo, do we?" one of them asked cheerfully.

Tamara let Jesse pull the towel back to reveal the slash down her arm. The paramedic shone his flashlight on it and gave a low whistle. "Yeah, that's going to need a little work," he agreed. "Why don't you come over to the ambulance and we'll see if we can fix you up here, or whether we need to take you in?"

He helped Tamara to her feet and supported her as he walked her over to the ambulance.

"Little wobbly, there," he observed.

Tamara swallowed, the nausea creeping back. "Yeah."

He patted the ambulance deck. "Just have a seat up there."

Tamara looked back at Jesse, then at the paramedic. "That's not the only cut."

"Okay...?"

"I can't get up there."

He looked down. "Your leg?"

"My stomach."

She tried to angle her body so that she was blocked by the paramedic from Jesse's and Dirk's view. He tugged her shirt up a little for a look. He swore.

"Royce, get the gurney out."

"She can just climb up," the other paramedic suggested,

several feet away, watching the police try to question Coach McClure.

"No, she can't. Get it out."

Royce rolled his eyes and climbed into the ambulance to pull the gurney out. The first paramedic helped Tamara lie down. For a moment, the change in position made the world recede behind a curtain of blackness, but it was only for an instant, a few throbs of her heart.

"What's your name, honey?" the first paramedic asked in a too-loud voice. He was tugging at Tamara's shirt.

"Tamara."

"Tamara, I'm Donald. We're going to get you stabilized and transported to the hospital lickety-split. Can you tell me what day it is?"

"Uh..." Tamara tried to sort out the timeline in her head. Everything had been a mess since Olly's disappearance. "Wednesday, I think. I'm not sure."

Donald didn't say whether she was right or wrong. He pulled open her shirt, neatly sliced up the front. The cool air made Tamara shiver. Royce, watching curiously, echoed Donald's reaction.

"Is it bad?" Tamara asked.

"I've seen worse," Donald said, keeping his voice light. He investigated the initial slash to Tamara's side and the stab wound high in the ribs that she had tried to deflect with her arm. "A lot of blood," he said in a low voice to Royce, "but it doesn't look like it's arterial. Call it in and get them ready for us." He looked at Tamara's face and smiled reassuringly. "We'll just get everything covered here. See if we can slow the bleeding. They'll stitch you up at the hospital, good as new."

Tamara nodded. "Okay."

As Royce got off of his call to the hospital, Donald turned to him again. "Better let her family know what's going on. Then we need to get an IV going."

To Tamara's embarrassment, Royce motioned for Jesse to join them. There was no way for her to hide her bared torso from him or to cover up the knife wounds.

"Did she faint?" Jesse asked, before reaching them. Then he took in Tamara's injuries and his eyes got wide. "I didn't know! Tamara, why didn't you tell me?"

Tamara couldn't cover herself up, so she looked away from him instead, her face burning. "Don't look," she protested.

"I'll... let Marion know. We'll meet you at the hospital?" he asked Royce.

"Yes. We're going to move her just as soon as we're able."

Jesse walked away from the stretcher, growling at Dirk to get back as the boy tried to get in for a closer look. Then he was out of Tamara's sight and hearing.

"Stay with us," Donald murmured, giving Tamara's uninjured arm a little shake. "Just hang in there."

Royce worked on inserting the IV. Tamara felt a spike of pain as it went in, but then it was gone, swallowed up by all of the competing messages from her battered body.

"First try," Royce said proudly. "Starting the solution."

Tamara closed her eyes against the continued assault of lights. In a few minutes, they were loading her into the ambulance. Donald sat and held her hand for the bumpy ride to the hospital.

* * *

Tamara was in and out of consciousness over the next few hours, too many people poking and prodding her, but not in critical enough condition for them to be in a rush to treat her. She kept waiting for the police to show up, or to wake up with Wanda next to her or her wrist handcuffed to the bed, but when morning came around, the only person by her side was Mrs. Henson. Tamara shifted her position and groaned. She felt like she'd been worked over by a whole gang, rather than just a two-minute encounter with one frail man. Mrs. Henson gave Tamara a sympathetic smile.

"How are you doing?"

"Ugh. Everything hurts. What exactly did they do to me?"

"Sewed you up. Just flesh wounds, no nerves or arteries or organs. A few weeks, and you'll be as good as new."

Every time Tamara moved, it hurt. She tried to lie as still as possible.

"What happened... to Coach McClure?" she asked eventually.

"He was arrested for assault. He'll probably be out sometime today on bail, unfortunately. I'm so sorry that happened to you."

Tamara lay still, waiting for more. But Mrs. Henson didn't make any accusations about Tamara going to McClure's house or provoking him to violence. Tamara closed her eyes, thinking about it.

"Guess he figured he owed me," she said. "Since I was... there when Glock beat him up..."

"I suppose so. He must have heard you were out. Maybe they informed him when you were being considered for parole. We'll have to be alert... keep our eyes out for him. I don't think there's any guarantee he won't try again. He didn't seem... very rational last night. He kept yelling and screaming, but none of it made any sense."

"Yeah."

"I'm afraid he's not very well. I'm not sure how the courts will decide to deal with him. Considering the charges against him, he really should be in jail already. Now with this attack..."

Tamara gave a tiny nod. "I know. They might not put him in prison because of his... injuries."

"You're a lot more calm about it than I am. Jesse had to spend all night calming me down."

"I'm part of the reason he's hurt, so... I guess it's partly my fault."

"I still don't think he should be walking around free."

"People say the same about me."

"But you're trying. You're trying to make good choices and make a contribution to society."

"Some job I'm doing."

"I know you're *trying*, Tamara."

Tamara studied Mrs. Henson's face. "But you think I did something to Olly."

Mrs. Henson's brow furrowed. "I thought that to begin with... yes. Now... I'm not so sure."

"Why not?"

"I guess... partly because of what the judge said and that the police detectives think there might be something to Mister Duck disappearing. At first, I just thought you were the most likely suspect... we all did. I just thought... when a baby goes missing from your care... you had to either be negligent or involved." She shrugged, looking away from Tamara in embarrassment. "I'm really sorry... I didn't *want* to think you had done anything wrong..."

"But I have a history."

"Unfortunately, yes. I couldn't forget that. You didn't have an easy time with Olly and you had harmed children in your care before, so of course... I had to consider it."

"And now you don't think so."

Mrs. Henson bit her lip, considering her answer. "I'm willing to consider other scenarios. Maybe whatever happened was... beyond your control."

Tamara couldn't help thinking about her analysis of everyone else in the house and the likelihood that one of them had taken Olly. Mrs. Henson was a strong suspect. She was the one who was ultimately responsible for Olly and what happened to him in Tamara's care. If she had come home to find Olly not breathing, she had a lot to lose. They might never let her have a baby in the house again. Tamara and Mrs. Henson were the strongest suspects, ahead of everyone else.

"I didn't hurt Olly. I didn't have anything to do with him disappearing."

TWENTY-NINE

BY THE END OF the day, Tamara was ready to go home. She'd had enough of white walls, nurses, and having to lie still. As sore as she was, she couldn't stay in bed any longer. She insisted on checking out, and though Mrs. Henson argued, Tamara sensed that she too just wanted to be home, so she didn't fight Tamara's early release too hard.

"I'll sleep at home," Tamara told her.

But when she got home, she was too anxious to sleep.

She didn't know what to do with herself.

Glock hadn't taken the baby. Coach McClure hadn't taken the baby.

Mrs. Baker... maybe. Tamara wasn't so sure, but she didn't think so. She had a sneaking suspicion that Mrs. Baker had only been trying to upset her. She apparently hadn't even really called the police. Mrs. Baker wanted Tamara to think that she had stolen and tortured the baby. She wanted to get back at Tamara for what she had done. But there had been no sign of an infant in the house. Amy's food and toys, but no formula. No Mister Duck. Mrs. Baker had betrayed surprise when Tamara had mentioned the disappearance of her baby. She'd been quick to take up the suggestion but, having had time to think about it, Tamara didn't think she had known anything before Tamara told her. She knew only that Tamara was out on parole. She'd been waiting for Tamara. She'd armed herself, knowing that Tamara would return at some point. Maybe Tamara had tripped an alarm when she entered the house.

Tamara couldn't go back to be sure. Not unless she was willing to get a gun herself and go back and have a real show-down with Mrs. Baker, and that was something she couldn't do. She'd rarely used anything but her hands as a weapon, and she didn't relish adding firearms charges to her record. Nor did she want to add another murder. If Tamara went back there with a gun, that's what would happen.

"You didn't take your meds this morning," Mrs. Henson commented, aware of Tamara's restless pacing around the house. "You should take them now."

"I can't take them so close to bed," Tamara said. "I'll have to wait until morning."

What she really wanted was to be clear-headed, without the effects of the meds clouding her mind. She needed all her wits and even the low-dose drugs slowed her brain too much.

"We could talk to the doctor. Maybe you could take a half dose before bed."

"No. I'll take them tomorrow," Tamara asserted.

She was out of ideas. Where else was there to go? She'd iden-tified all of the likely suspects, but she wasn't a private investi-gator like on TV. She couldn't go around solving the baby's disappearance all by herself.

"I need help," Tamara muttered to herself.

"What?" Nita was walking by and stopped short at Tamara's words. "You need help with what?"

"I can't find Olly by myself," Tamara explained. Her cheeks got hot. She hoped she didn't sound like a complete lunatic. She hoped she wasn't sliding back into psychosis. Dr. Sutherland had said that it was possible it could be triggered by stress. Having her baby stolen or killed, being accused of it, being attacked with a knife... those things were pretty stressful. Tamara thought she would recognize if she started slipping from reality again. But would she?

"Of course not," Nita agreed, touching Tamara's arm warmly. "You're not supposed to be figuring it out all by yourself. The police are supposed to be investigating."

"But they don't know... they're not getting anywhere. I thought the FBI was supposed to get involved in stuff like this. Why haven't there been any feds here to figure everything out? Wouldn't they be better than the local cops?"

Nita shrugged. "This is what we've got. *We* could help you."

Tamara shook her head. "There's nothing you can do."

"We could," Nita insisted. "I'm good at talking to people and finding things out. People like to tell me things."

"No one is going to tell you they took Olly."

Nita laughed. "No, but they might tell me something else. Who do you want me to talk to? Give me an assignment."

Tamara shook her head, rolling her eyes. "I don't know. I keep trying to figure out who could have done it, but I just keep spinning my tires. If it wasn't anyone in the family..."

Nita's eyes got wide in shock. "It's not someone in the family!"

"It could be."

"No," Nita said. "It couldn't be."

"Deshawn wants a baby."

"Deshawn couldn't take Olly. I would know. She couldn't hide anything from me." Nita laughed. "Not a baby!"

"What about Dirk?"

"What about him?"

"How well do you know him? He's new, right?"

"I know him better than you might think," Nita said, her expression becoming mischievous.

Tamara stared at her.

"What?" Nita asked.

"Really? He's been... making moves on you?"

Nita looked around carefully, then gave a shrug. "Maybe sometimes, a few minutes alone together, here and there..."

Tamara shook her head. "Unbelievable. Boys are so... so..."

Nita caught on. "You too? Oh, I'm gonna kill him now. He is so dead."

But Tamara didn't care if Dirk had been playing both of them. She wanted to know who had taken Olly. "You see...? He has secrets. He could have done something to Olly and lied to everyone about it, no one would know."

"He wasn't home. It was just you and me, remember? And before I got home from school, it was just Mrs. Henson. None of the others were around."

"Someone could have snuck in." Tamara amended her comment. "Someone *did* sneak in."

"It could have been anyone," Nita said. "But it wasn't Dirk. Why would he take Olly?"

"Maybe... because he wanted my attention, and he couldn't get it, with me taking care of Olly."

"If he was playing games with everyone, why would he take a risk just for you? He wouldn't. He's just playing the field, not looking to get involved with just one girl."

That, at least, made sense to Tamara.

"It's nobody in the family," Nita repeated firmly. "It's someone from outside. But we have to figure out who and why." Nita grabbed Tamara's hand and led her to the kitchen table. She picked up a scratch pad and pencil from Mrs. Henson's writing desk. "We'll make a list."

Mrs. Henson happened by. Or maybe she'd been keeping an ear on Tamara and Nita and had decided it was time to intervene.

"What are you girls so busy with?"

Tamara looked for a believable lie. But Nita just gave Mrs. Henson a guileless smile. "We're making a list of suspects. We're going to figure out who it was that took Olly."

Mrs. Henson opened her mouth to argue. Then she closed it again. She pulled out a chair. "Okay, who is on this list?"

* * *

Tamara didn't tell Mrs. Henson that she had already gone to Coach McClure's and Mrs. Baker's homes. She didn't think that would go over too well. Having done everything she could to eliminate the two of them as suspects, Tamara tried to approach the problem from another direction.

"Glock said it was personal. She said no one would do something like that just on a favor, and to hire someone would cost a lot of money." She hesitated. "I don't know anyone with a lot of money. So it must be personal. Revenge."

"Unless it's just someone who wanted a baby," Mrs. Henson reminded her.

"You said they would go to a hospital or park. Not here."

"No. I don't think anyone would. It would be too risky. There are a lot of people coming and going from this house. There's no crowd to blend in to. If any of us had seen a stranger in the house... well, it would just have been too dangerous."

Tamara nodded. "Yeah."

"Someone from juvie, then?" Nita suggested.

"I guess."

They both looked at her expectantly. Tamara looked down at Nita's blank sheet of paper, pencil hovering.

"Somebody from juvie," Tamara repeated.

"You must have had some people at juvie you didn't get along with," Nita said. "Places like that... I mean you can't get along with everyone, right?"

Maybe sunny Nita would have been able to. But Tamara...

she didn't make friends easily. And in juvie, especially during the time she had been pregnant, she had ended up fighting with a lot of different girls at one time or another. She wasn't even sure she could remember everyone.

"I don't know who is still incarcerated. If they're still there, then they couldn't have taken Olly."

Juvie was a revolving door. There were always people coming and going.

"Let's just get a list," Nita said. "We can worry about eliminating names afterward. We need a full list first of all."

"Ugh." Tamara let out a long breath. She thought about the gangs. She'd had clashes with both the Sharks and TMJ when she had been pregnant. Everyone who had been in the gangs during that time could be suspects. But how many of them would really retaliate against Tamara? Who would really take revenge on her when they were both free on account of some slight that had happened in juvie? There had been people who had died when she was in juvie. Their deaths had never been officially connected to her, but sometimes people knew or suspected without any proof. Sometimes they just had an intuition.

"Blacksnake," she said, just to get a name out of her head and onto the paper. Tamara had embarrassed Blacksnake more than once. Had choked her out and made a fool of her. She was the type who would hold a grudge for a long time.

Nita's pencil touched down on the paper. "Is that one word or two?"

"One, I guess. She was a Shark."

Nita looked at Tamara for a moment, then wrote down *Blacksnake*, with *Shark* beside it.

"The other Sharks," Tamara said. "Lewis. Waterson. Perez. No, not Waterson. She died."

Nita erased the beginning of Waterson's name, and wrote Perez down in its place. Tamara listed off some of the other

Sharks. Her head was hurting again. Was it really going to get her any closer to finding Olly?

"Okay," Nita said encouragingly. "This is starting to shape up. What about other gangs? Do we need to list them?"

"TMJ. The others weren't really important. Independents. They didn't usually get involved in gang politics."

"And you didn't get between any of them and the gangs? Get on someone's wrong side?"

Tamara looked out the kitchen window, even though she couldn't really see anything through it but an abbreviated view of the street. And framed in the middle of it, what looked like an unmarked police vehicle.

"Glock was an independent," she said. "She protected me while she was there."

"And did anyone resent the way that Glock protected you? Resent her or you?"

Tamara rubbed her head. "Yeah. I suppose."

"Maybe we'd better write them down too."

"Nadine... Chips..." Tamara shook her head. "I don't know their full names. How are we going to figure anything out if I don't know their real names?"

"One step at a time," Mrs. Henson advised. "Don't get ahead of yourself."

"Okay." Tamara took a deep breath and tried to stay focused on the job at hand.

"And the other gang you said," Nita prompted. "What was it?"

"TMJ. Rosie... Vernon... Brett, Tabby, Cinco... not Tabby, I forgot..."

"Vernon?" Mrs. Henson interposed. "She's the one who... was involved in the prison break?"

"Yeah." Tamara tried to focus on the possibility. "I ended up turning her and Sly in, so yeah, I'm sure she'd love to get back at me. But she's still in prison."

"And you don't think there's any way she could influence someone on the outside...?"

"Glock said no. She said no one would kidnap a baby on a favor. Too dangerous."

Mrs. Henson pursed her lips, but she nodded. Tamara looked at the long list of names Nita had already written down. And she knew it was nowhere near all of the people she might have fought with or offended when she was in juvie. But hopefully, they were the biggest ones.

"What about adults?" Nita glanced over at Mrs. Henson and then down at her paper again. "Administrators, guards, whatever..."

"Uh... most of them I got along with okay. I guess there were some I might have ticked off..."

"Should we write them down too?"

"I guess," Tamara agreed. She looked at Mrs. Henson, wondering whether she would think this was going overboard. But Mrs. Henson didn't say anything. "There have been some guards... but I don't remember all of their names. There was this woman that I think I kind of got fired her first day there..."

Mrs. Henson's eyebrows went way up. "How did you manage that?"

"She had a temper... I sort of provoked her... she sucker-punched me in front of her boss."

Mrs. Henson shook her head. Nita giggled. "That would do it."

"I don't... I don't remember her name."

"I'll just write down a note... maybe it will come to you later, or maybe we can talk to someone who will remember."

Tamara watched Nita write it down in her neat printing.

"What do we do now? Having a list isn't going to be much help. We need to find out who's still in juvie and who's out. If they're still inside, they couldn't have anything to do with Olly disappearing."

"Leave that part to me," Nita said, smiling. "I have a way with computers. I can narrow down the list. We might need to talk to someone to find out some of the full names, but I'll work with the ones we've got now. And you can tell me if you remember any others."

Tamara nodded.

"I have a few contacts," Mrs. Henson offered. "I might be able to tap them."

THIRTY

T HE COMBINATION OF BUSY days, sleepless nights, and the physically draining effects of her injuries caught up with Tamara. She fell asleep during the early evening and barely stirred throughout the night. When she awoke in the early morning, she was startled to see Mrs. Henson sitting beside the bed in a chair she'd dragged in from another room.

"Missus?" Tamara rubbed her eyes. "What happened? Did I..." She looked around her uncertainly, but nothing seemed out of place this time. "Was I sick or did something happen?"

Mrs. Henson smiled. She looked tired, but happy. "No, everything is fine. I wanted to make sure you were okay, and that nothing could happen while you were asleep. I didn't want there to be anyone in here. No chance that anyone could touch anything in here."

She looked around, her chin held at a proud angle.

"You stayed in here all night?"

"Yes."

"You stayed up? Stayed awake the whole time?"

"Yes."

Tamara was astounded. She didn't know what to say.

"Jesse had all of the locks changed and upgraded yesterday," Mrs. Henson said. "This place was locked up tighter than Fort Knox last night. But... locks can be picked, and I wanted to make sure that nothing happened to you and we didn't have any unexpected visitors."

Tamara was touched that Mrs. Henson would care about her enough to give up her sleep and keep watch.

But Tamara half-wished their nocturnal visitor had made another appearance. They were desperately short on clues. She stretched her sore body and looked at the window. Though it was still early, the sky was getting lighter and she knew her body had woken for reveille and she wouldn't be able to go back to sleep again. Or if she did, she would dream, and she couldn't face nightmares on top of what was happening in real life.

"Up for good?" Mrs. Henson asked.

"Yeah. Do you want to go to sleep?" Tamara motioned back to her bed as she got up. "If you don't want to disturb Jesse, you could sleep here."

"I'm sure he'll be up soon, if he isn't already. I'll wait until everyone is off to school. Then if I need a nap, I'll take one."

"How can you function after staying up all night? You couldn't have gotten much sleep at the hospital either."

"I've had plenty of experience with sleepless nights and catching cat-naps at the hospital. Pregnant moms, remember? Babies don't come after three hours of daylight labor." She smiled at Tamara. "Most of them don't, at any rate. There's usually at least one sleepless night when babies come, sometimes a few."

Mrs. Henson followed Tamara down the stairs to the kitchen. Jesse was there with his paper and smiled a greeting. Tamara looked over at the computer, where Nita was scrolling through a long web page dense with information.

"Have you been up all night?" Mrs. Henson asked.

Nita looked at them, gave them a wide grin and had a sip of coffee. "You bet. Made some good progress on the list, too."

She indicated the paper she had written the juvie names on. What had previously been one neat column of names was filled with symbols, lines, and cramped notes. Tamara picked it up and tried to make sense of it. Some of the names had been crossed out, with notes such as 'deceased' or 'incarcerated' beside them. Others had more extensive notes with release dates, cities, neighborhoods, or addresses. Tamara had done her best to provide Nita with full names when she could, but in a lot of cases, she'd only known a girl's last name, or perhaps a street name or prison nickname. But most of the inmate names had been filled out in full.

"How did you do this?"

"Not as hard as it looks," Nita said modestly. "There are databases you can search to find out where your friend or family member has been incarcerated. Most of them only need a last name. Even if they're out, they're still in the search results with a release date. I compare the results against searches of social networks, public records, directories... I'm pretty good."

"I never knew you could do that." Tamara shook her head, marveling at all of the information Nita had been able to pull together in one night.

"We'll use this to pull together a short list," Nita said. "There are only half a dozen who are currently free. You can let the police know who they should be checking out."

"Yeah," Tamara agreed faintly.

"You'd better have something to eat," Mrs. Henson urged. "You need to get your strength back. I made some inquiries on the adults, and I'll follow up on any of the names Nita couldn't find anything on, call in a few favors if I can. But I think we're doing really well."

* * *

It wasn't like when Tamara had been searching for the Bakers. Sly hadn't been able to find an address for them, leaving Tamara to wear out her flimsy tennis shoes asking after them. Nita had been able to find addresses for most of the girls on the short list. Mrs. Henson's credit card had been needed to find some of them, but she had declared it a small price to pay to get closer to finding out who might have taken Olly.

The most difficult thing had ended up being persuading Mrs. Henson not to just hand the list over to the police.

"They already know all of this," she reminded Mrs. Henson. "All they have to do is ask juvie, and they would give them all of this. And they have access to everyone's addresses and contact numbers. They could already have talked to all of these girls."

"But we should take it to them, point out that these are the girls who are the most suspicious."

Tamara shook her head. "The cops will just spook them."

Mrs. Henson frowned. "What else are we going to do? How can we make any progress on finding out what happened to Olly without the police? This is their investigation."

"I'll go talk to them. I thought that was why we were getting their addresses in the first place."

Nita nodded her agreement. Mrs. Henson looked at Jesse, but he appeared to be immersed in his paper, unaware of the conversation going on around the computer.

"I can talk to them," Tamara said. "It's natural. Just one juvie looking up another. I can suss them out, and if I see something suspicious or they say something, we can call Bowen and have her look into it."

Mrs. Henson's brow wrinkled. She didn't like it, but she didn't disagree immediately. "If I go with you…"

"No. I have to go by myself. I can't take my foster mom along!" She saw Mrs. Henson's eyes shift to Nita, who was leaning forward eagerly. "I'm not taking Nita, either. If I do anything like that, they'll know something is off."

"Nita's close enough to you in age, she could just be your friend... I really don't like the idea of you wandering the city interviewing suspects on your own. Besides which, you know that under your parole terms—"

"I know. I'm not supposed to have anything to do with anyone from juvie. But this is for Olly." Tamara gave Mrs. Henson a fierce look. "It's worth going back to juvie to... find out what happened."

"If you get remanded two years in a row, your chances are not good at getting early parole again. You're likely to end up serving your full sentence."

"I know."

Mrs. Henson was on the verge of giving in. She wanted to know what had happened to Olly too. If she trusted that Tamara hadn't had anything to do with his disappearance and was really trying to help, she had to let Tamara follow through on her plan. Tamara could have run away any time since Olly had disappeared, but she hadn't. She'd stayed around and done her best to help.

"You can't take Nita? I'm sure these girls wouldn't be suspicious of you just bringing a friend along..."

"No." Tamara put some force into her answer. "I'm not taking Nita into a situation that could be dangerous. I was a loner in juvie, no one is going to expect me to be with someone else on the outside. If I don't follow the same behavior, they'll feel something is off."

Mrs. Henson looked down at the page of names. "How long do you think you're going to be? Do you want me to drive you somewhere?"

"No. Thanks, but... we don't want to make anyone suspicious. Not these girls, or anyone in the neighborhood, or Bowen if she's got cops watching the house. Besides, if Wanda finds out and violates my parole... you gotta be able to say you didn't know where I was or what I was doing. Pretty hard if you drop me off."

"If you're on foot, this is a lot of ground to cover."

"I know. Better get going."

"It's early. No one will be up yet."

Tamara shook her head. "Some of them might not be in bed yet. And if some of them are working day jobs, they'll be up soon. May as well get them while I can."

Nita stood up from the computer desk, arching her back and stretching. "You be careful, girl," she warned. She gave Tamara a sideways hug. "We don't want something happening to you."

"Yeah. I will."

Jesse looked up from his paper and watched Tamara go. She wondered how much he had really heard.

THIRTY-ONE

TAMARA STUDIED NITA'S SHORT list, trying to picture where each of the addresses was. She knew the city and how to navigate the public transit a lot better than she had a year before.

One of the closest was Rosie, so Tamara decided to try her first. Rosie had been the leader of the Sharks for a period of time while Vernon had been away from juvie. She was tough and angry, quick to take action. Tamara couldn't think of very many interactions they'd had over the couple of years that Rosie had been at the facility, before a face-off with Vernon got her transferred out. Rosie was mostly engaged with running the Sharks, not an easy prospect inside prison or out. Trying to direct a loosely-organized bunch of hotheads and thugs and keep them from killing each other off was asking a lot of anyone. Even before Rosie had led the gang, she'd been one of the top echelon. Not someone who would take the time to notice a little independent like Tamara. But Tamara had to start somewhere.

She walked briskly outside, letting the cool air and her movement wake her up. She needed to be alert dealing with Rosie and the others. Any sign of weakness could have dire consequences.

Tamara's stab wounds burned. They didn't feel as bad as they had when McClure had first attacked her, and she didn't feel weak or shaky. They just hurt. But she didn't want anything to dull the pain and maybe dull her senses as well.

On the bus, she did her best to memorize the short list and each bit of information on it. She knew she shouldn't walk around with it. Girls like Rosie didn't like to have their information written down. Especially in a list that grouped her with other juvies, friend or foe. By the time Tamara got off the bus, she had memorized it as well as she was able. She tore it into small bits and shoved it down deep into a garbage can.

She walked along a block of row houses, looking at the numbers. Rosie might actually live at the address Nita had found, or she might have given a false address and live somewhere close by, keeping a watch on the fraudulent address so she would know if people were looking for her. She wasn't stupid. Tamara saw the number she was looking for and took a quick glance around for anyone watching the house and what nearby windows had a good view of it. She tried a little convenience store across the street. A mom and pop. The type who were just trying to make an honest buck and offer their community a service.

Tamara browsed through the store for a minute, watching for watchers. She walked up to the woman at the checkout till.

"Looking for someone who used to live around here."

"I don't know anyone. So sorry."

Tamara looked at her, letting her skepticism show. "You know everybody," she asserted.

The woman wavered, unsure of Tamara's motivations.

"I'm looking for a friend I did time with. Rosie Espinoza. She used to live around here."

"Eh... I don't know."

"You do know. Rosie. Espinoza. Does she live on this street?" Tamara motioned across the road. "Over there?"

The woman's eyes didn't follow her motion. They went to the side instead. Tamara took a glance around. Rosie wasn't in the store. It was pretty much empty, the early breakfast rush over, late risers not yet up. Maybe it was the direction of Rosie's real residence, then. Tamara folded her arms across her chest and stood there, giving the store owner plenty of gangster attitude. She could stand there and be intimidating all day long, if that was what the woman wanted. She could scare all of the store's business away. Maybe it was an exaggeration and a little blond girl wasn't going to scare everybody off, but Tamara exuded as much confidence as she could and waited for the woman to buckle.

"Maybe she lives here," the owner said finally. Tamara raised one eyebrow, waiting for her to go on. "Down the block. The house with the bikes in front."

"Bikes?" Tamara repeated.

She nodded. "Yes. Down there. With the bikes. I don't know if she's home. She goes out, doesn't hang around here a lot."

"What gang is she in?"

The woman lost what little color she had remaining and shook her head. Tamara decided that was probably as much as she was going to get and started to turn toward the door.

"Has she still got that baby?" she asked casually, facing away from the woman so she wouldn't see if Tamara wasn't able to maintain an impassive expression.

"Baby?" the woman's voice rose slightly. "Rosie doesn't have a baby."

"A week ago, she didn't show up with a baby?" Tamara ventured a glance back at her to watch her expression.

"No, what would she want with a baby? Not Rosie."

Tamara left without pushing it any further. The woman had sounded and looked genuinely surprised at the mention of a baby. Either Rosie had kept Olly hidden well enough not to start any rumors, or she wasn't the one.

Tamara walked down the sidewalk, looking for the bikes, and saw them almost instantly. Not bicycles, but motorbikes. The number of bikes pulled up in front of the house told Tamara that Rosie wasn't alone. The danger of approaching Rosie rose exponentially. Should Tamara just take the shop owner's word that there was no baby? Go on to the next name on the list? It wouldn't do anybody any good if she were killed at the first place she went.

Tamara hesitated about her approach. She could circle around to the back of the row of houses to look for a way to get in that was less obvious, where she might be able to get in without alerting everybody in the house of her approach. But trying to enter like a sneak thief was also a good way to get killed before even stating what it was she wanted. With a house full of bikers, she figured she'd better try the direct approach.

She took a few deep breaths before turning up the walkway and marching up to the door. Everyone outside on the street quieted and watched her approach. Tamara avoided the doorbell and pounded on the door. She needed to be bold and act as though she expected to be respected. Her instinct to be a mouse and hide in corners wouldn't do her any good.

A biker came to the door in leathers, blinking his eyes as he opened the door, affecting being tired. Tamara was sure she hadn't just woken him up. He was the guard. He was on watch. He frowned, looking Tamara over.

"Who are you?"

"French," Tamara said, stepping closer as if she expected to walk right in the door. "Here to see Rosie."

"Rosie...?"

"Oh, don't try to tell me she doesn't live here. Just get her, okay?"

"French?" He shook his head. "I don't know anyone by that name."

"Obviously."

"You're not anyone."

"You gonna bet on that? Risk Rosie getting mad when you turn me away? She's going to want to see me."

He looked her over again, trying to read everything from her clothes to her tattoos to the stitches up the long gash on her arm. She might not be dressed like a gang banger, but enough of the ingredients were there that he had to wonder who she was and if Rosie really would want to see her.

"We were in juvie," Tamara told him, parting with one more tidbit of information. "She's out, I'm out, thought I'd see how she was doing."

The guard took one step back from the door, and Tamara followed his movement, taking a step into the house. He didn't stop her and, after a minute, conceded and moved out of the way, allowing Tamara to enter. He closed the door.

"Now, who are you?" he repeated, showing her the hand cannon he'd been hiding behind the door. "For real this time."

"Juvie," Tamara repeated. "French. Is she sleeping, or what? I don't know about her, but I can't help waking up at reveille still. Can't sleep in like a kid anymore."

He gave a nod at that. She waited for him to make some kind of move.

"What's all the racket?" demanded another biker, walking into the room. He was even bigger than the first. The small living room felt crowded with just the three of them. He tinkled and clinked when he walked, with all of the chains, studs, and jewelry he wore.

"Asking for Rosie," the first said, nodding to Tamara. "Says they were in juvie together."

Tamara folded her arms and waited while the second biker examined her. He gave a shrug. "She's been inside," he observed, indicating her prison tats with his gaze rather than pointing.

"So, I should get her?"

"Better, I guess. That one is a devil if you cross her. Just tell her. Let her decide." He looked at Tamara. "What's your handle?"

"French."

"Go and see," the bigger biker told the first.

The man who had answered the door headed up the stairs, his feet landing with a crash with every step he took. When he reached the floor above, the light fixtures vibrated with each footstep.

"Pete couldn't sneak up on a deaf man," the bigger man said, shaking his head in amusement.

Tamara nodded and waited. She kept her ears pricked for any suspicious sounds. A baby's cry. Something being hidden away. Doors or windows being opened. If Olly was there, she was only going to have one chance to figure it out. She wouldn't be able to return a second time.

A few minutes passed with some discussion overhead. Tamara could hear Pete's gruff voice, but not Rosie's quieter answers. Eventually, they could hear Pete returning, until he stood at the top of the stairs.

"Send her up," he ordered.

The second biker nodded at Tamara. "Go ahead."

Tamara stood tall and took firm steps, projecting confidence she didn't have. Her legs were shaking. Her heart was racing as if she were facing down Coach McClure's knife again. She'd never been scared of Rosie in juvie; but in juvie there had always been guards on hand to break up fights before anyone got killed. The guards that Rosie had around her now were of a different ilk. They would hold Tamara still while Rosie beat her down rather than protecting her.

Pete met her at the top of the stairs, looking impatient. Maybe Tamara should have gone faster, but she was afraid that would make her look too eager, too inexperienced and unsophisticated. She was there of her own free choice. She had to look like each step was her own choice.

"In here." Pete gestured to a bedroom door. It was covered with graffiti and had a fist-sized hole in it, through which Tamara could see that there was a light on within the room, or else some of the morning sun was being allowed to filter into the room through the windows.

Tamara stopped, waiting for further instruction. She didn't have a clue what the proper protocol was for visiting a biker chick in her bedroom. Maybe it wasn't set up as a bedroom. Maybe it was her office and that was where she ran her operations from.

"Go in," Pete told her.

Tamara nodded. She twisted the door handle and pushed the door open.

The room was dim. Little light got in through the blacked-out windows. A small lamp had been turned on to provide enough light for the visit.

It was indeed a bedroom. Rosie was lying in the bed, blankets pulled up high enough to cover her to the chest, but not far enough to cover all of the intricate black tattoos that wound from her bare shoulders down into her ample breasts below the blanket. A hairy man lay beside her, studying Tamara with open interest. Tamara stared into the middle distance, trying not to stare at either one of them. The couple reminded her uncomfortably of Vernon and Sly. Their open displays of intimacy had not been a good portent for Tamara.

"Frenchie," Rosie said lazily. "This is a bit of a surprise."

Tamara cleared her throat. "Uh... yeah." She didn't have a prepared speech but had been planning just to improvise. "Sorry, I didn't mean to interrupt your..." she motioned to the two of them, her cheeks flaring with embarrassment, "...your sleep."

Rosie chuckled. "Where did you expect to find me at this hour?"

Tamara shrugged. "Can't sleep past reveille myself."

"Try staying up until reveille and *then* going to bed."

"Never tried that," Tamara admitted.

There were a few seconds of uncomfortable silence.

"You're out on parole," Rosie observed. "Didn't think they'd let you out so quick after the last time."

And Rosie didn't even know about everything that had happened after Tamara's return from her first failed attempt at parole, having been transferred almost immediately on Tamara's readmittance.

"I was lucky," she agreed.

"And what do you want from Rosie? You need to be hooked up for something?"

Tamara shifted from one foot to the other, trying to figure out how to approach the issue, or whether to say anything at all. Telling Rosie that she didn't actually want to see her after all wouldn't likely be taken well. But it was pretty obvious Rosie wasn't the one who had a grudge against her. There was no sign of Olly or any other baby. Rosie had allowed Tamara into her home, right into her most private sanctum. Tamara had to show her respect in return.

"I wondered... do you have any contact with anyone else who was in juvie with us? Anyone who is out now?"

Rosie's expression was curious. "I hear from people from time to time. But it's not like I'm having drinks with any of them. Why?"

"I have a problem... and I think it's because of something that happened in juvie... that someone from juvie is trying to... get revenge on me."

"Who?"

"I don't know."

Rosie laughed. "Well, that's a problem, isn't it?"

"I just think it's the only answer. Someone from juvie... but I don't know who or why."

Rosie nodded. "You were never in a gang or any other trouble before you ended up in juvie."

"No."

"And that guy you and Glock beat down when you were on parole, you don't think it's him?"

Tamara swallowed. Rosie knew more than Tamara had expected her to. Tamara refrained from arguing that it had only been Glock who had beaten Coach McClure, not her. She held up her arm to show off the stitches on her arm. "No... he prefers the direct approach."

Rosie's boyfriend joined in on the laughter. "So you think it's someone from juvie," Rosie said. "Someone like me." Her voice had gone from friendly to hard.

Tamara chewed on the inside of her cheek but tried to keep her bearing confident. She hadn't done anything wrong. She hadn't disrespected Rosie. She'd gone directly to her, rather than asking anyone else about her or sneaking around.

"Someone like you," she agreed. "But it's not you."

"Yeah? What makes you think that?"

Tamara desperately wanted to pace around the room, but that would make Rosie and her boyfriend edgy. They were already guarded, despite their casual appearance. Tamara had no doubt there were weapons close at hand, perhaps even under the blanket draped over them.

"I had to check," she said. "I didn't know who it might be. The thing is... someone kidnapped my baby. Last week. Came into my house and took him. And I don't know who."

Rosie's eyebrows went way up. "Your baby?"

"I had him in juvie," Tamara said, waving Rosie's surprise at this detail away. "I got out on parole to take care of him. And then someone stole him away."

"What makes you think it's someone from juvie?"

"That's the only possibility left. I've checked out everybody else."

"The father?"

"In prison."

Rosie scratched the back of her neck. "And Glock's still inside. But I'm not sure that would be her kind of thing. She's not so subtle. If it had been her, you would have known."

"She's the first one I checked. Even went to talk to her to make sure she hadn't... *influenced* someone else to do it."

"Huh. Well, you can see there's no baby around here. Though... you sure he's still alive? I mean, I didn't, but what's to say someone didn't kill him and dispose of the body the first day? Why hold him alive?"

"I don't know. But... they came back to get one of his toys, so he must still be alive."

Rosie pursed her lips and shook her head. "Unless you're looking at it wrong. Maybe coming back for the toy was a taunt. Showing you that you couldn't do anything to stop her. That you didn't even know who it was. She can just come into your home whenever she wants and take whatever she wants. It could be because she wants you to go crazy not knowing, not because she kept him alive."

Tamara's arms broke out in goosebumps. She hadn't considered that possibility. The only motive she'd been able to see for someone to take Olly's comfort object was to soothe him. Not to taunt her with their power over her.

"Do you think... that's what happened?"

"Who would keep a baby around for a week? People would get suspicious. Babies are noisy. They attract attention. They're frustrating. Unless there was a ransom note... why think he's alive instead of dead?"

Tamara blinked her eyes, trying to keep her emotional reaction to Rosie's suggestion out of her face. Nothing had changed. She didn't have any more proof that Olly was dead than that he was alive. The kidnapper was keeping him alive and stole Mister

Duck to quiet him and help him sleep better. She needed to hold that in her mind.

"Who else is on your list?" Rosie asked.

Tamara considered before telling Rosie. "You'll keep it quiet?" Tamara asked. "I don't want word getting back…"

"Why would I tell anyone? Like I say, I'm not out drinking with these girls. They're not my people." Rosie looked at the man in the bed with her. "I got my own circle of friends."

Tamara took a deep breath, weighing the costs and benefits, then told Rosie the other names on the list. Rosie's eyes widened part way through the list. "Why not Lewis?" Tamara asked, focusing on the name Rosie had reacted to. "You don't think it could be her?"

Rosie shook her head. "Just the opposite. Lewis. It fits."

"It does?"

"That chick is crazy. And she's got a big-time grudge against you."

Tamara put her hand out to brace herself on the wall. "What?"

Rosie laughed and nodded. "I totally forgot until you mentioned her. But yeah, I talked to… a friend of a friend a few weeks back. And they said she was totally messed up, she was so mad at you."

"For what?"

"You dissed her in front of her girls. Embarrassed her. I don't know the details, I was surprised that a quiet little thing like you would have done something to mess her up so bad. You were always so… invisible."

Tamara sighed. "Not when I went back after the prison break. Not when I was pregnant. I was… not very well. Did some stupid things."

"Like dissing her in front of the Sharks? Not very smart, French."

"No. I know."

"I don't know anything about any of the other girls. Maybe you pissed them all off. But I heard that Lewis had it out for you. If she heard you were out... she would be my bet."

Tamara nodded slowly. "Okay. Yeah. You know where she is?" She consulted her memorized list. "I heard she was over near the arena."

"Yeah. Something like that. That's where her family comes from. Cuban mob runs things over there."

"She's Cuban? I never knew that."

Rosie gave Tamara an odd look. "Yeah, of course. You never knew that?"

Tamara shook her head. "I never hung out with her. Don't know anything about her or her family."

"She's big-time attached to her family. Really strong on her cultural roots. Where she came from and who she is."

"Lewis doesn't sound Cuban."

"No. That's her mom's name. Daddy was some biggie in the Cuban mob."

Tamara's heart sank. It was one thing to be going up against Lewis, leader of the Sharks, when she was inside juvie. She could have been anyone on the outside. She could have been an unknown. Being a strong gang leader inside didn't always translate to being somebody when she got out. Tamara wouldn't have guessed that Rosie would be a biker chick on the outside. And she had no idea that Lewis came from Cuban mob.

"Yeah, good luck with that," Rosie said, chuckling darkly. "You might as well give up and go home now."

"I'm not giving up," Tamara snapped. "I'm going to find my baby."

"You're going to be laying in the same grave. If I was you, I'd consider getting out of town. You don't want someone like that after you."

But Tamara wasn't going to be scared away. She shook her head and looked for a polite way to disengage from the conversation with Rosie. Her exit was almost as important as her approach. Like a spider's web, getting out could be a lot harder than getting in. Rosie had decided to amuse herself by seeing what Tamara wanted. But if she decided they didn't want Tamara blabbing about something she had seen or heard while she was there, or that she had shown disrespect by showing up there uninvited in the first place, her way out might not be so smooth.

"Thank you," she told Rosie sincerely. "Knowing all that about Lewis, that's really going to help me. Maybe I can't get my baby back, but I can try."

Rosie stretched. "Never did understand the attraction of having a brat myself. Seems like it just ties you down and makes you soft."

"It wasn't something I planned. But you do kind of... get attached after a while."

The other girl shook her head. "Not gonna happen to me. I'm not gonna put my rep at risk like that. Let the rest of the masses be breeders. Not me."

Tamara gave a respectful nod. "You've worked hard for what you've got here."

Rosie nodded, looking pleased. "Yeah. You know it. This doesn't just fall into your lap." She made a gesture that encompassed the room, the house, and her bedmate. "You want something, you gotta work for it. I'm never letting any baby hold me back."

"That's smart." Tamara took a step back, putting herself just at the threshold of the bedroom. "Sorry about interrupting you. I'll get out of your way now."

Rosie chuckled. "It's been interesting, Frenchie. I always thought there was a little more under the surface than you gave away. It takes guts, showing up here."

Tamara inched back. She strained her ears and peripheral vision to locate Pete. Was he behind her? Had he gone back to guard duties on the main floor? Did he resent Tamara for being allowed upstairs for the conversation with Rosie? Tamara wasn't sure, but their attitude toward Rosie suggested she was more than just a member of the biker gang, but somewhere in the leadership. No small feat for a girl, a juvie just a few months out of prison. The man in bed with her didn't display dominance, but deference. It was Rosie who overshadowed him.

Tamara stepped back and to the side, turning so that she could still see into the room and could also see Pete, standing on guard in the hallway, waiting for her to finish. There would certainly be no sneaking into the bathroom to check out the contents of Rosie's medicine cabinet.

"I'll see you around," she told Rosie. "Thanks again."

"Frenchie." There was a snap in Rosie's voice that made Tamara turn her gaze back toward her instead of making her escape. "Don't come back here again."

"No. I won't."

"Juvie didn't make us buds. I don't owe you any favors just because we served time together."

"No," Tamara agreed. "You don't owe me anything. I appreciate you taking the time to talk to me. You could have just had me thrown out."

"Yeah," Rosie agreed. "Well, I'm always up for a little entertainment." Rosie turned her attention from Tamara to her bedmate. "Always up for anything," she purred.

Tamara headed back the way she had come, toward Pete. He had his hand on a small cannon strapped to the side of his leg. Rosie's voice floated behind her.

"Pete."

"Yeah?"

"You can let her go."

Pete's brows rose in surprise. His attitude changed to one of respect. Her heart in her throat, Tamara walked past him. For all she knew, 'let her go' could have been a code word, a phrase that actually meant the opposite. She couldn't be sure until she got out of the house. If she got out of the house. Pete didn't stop her or pull out his gun. After she passed him, he followed her down the hall and the stairs.

"She's to go," he advised the bigger man who had seen Tamara in. He was standing talking to another biker. They both turned to look at Tamara.

"Thanks," Tamara murmured to Pete as she walked by him, and then by the others, almost to the door. She could feel all of their eyes on her as she opened the front door to let herself out. She waited for the whisper of a gun sliding out of a holster, but it didn't come. She opened the door and was through it, and then she was safely outside.

People up and down the street watched her curiously, pretending they weren't. Tamara let her air out slowly, savoring the act of just breathing.

Out of the frying pan and on her way to the fire.

THIRTY-TWO

R IDING THE BUS AGAIN, Tamara's mind kept replaying the morning in juvie when she had, in response to Lewis's goading, stood up and dumped the long table they were eating breakfast on into the laps of Lewis and everyone seated on her side of the table. It had been a bad decision. Tamara came to understand later that her judgment had been impaired by the pregnancy, she had not just been emotional as most women were with their bodies reacting to the new hormonal soup, but experiencing psychosis that would later land her in the Forensic unit, so paranoid and reactive that she couldn't function in the General Population. But at the time she had dumped Lewis's breakfast into her lap, she hadn't understood what was happening to her. She had just reacted.

And that wasn't the only thing she had done to disrespect Lewis.

Tamara got off the bus and looked up and down the street. Old houses, buildings with brightly colored murals. Finding Lewis might be a little trickier than finding Rosie had been. Like with Rosie, she had an address, but if Lewis were part of an organized crime family in the community, people weren't going to be intimidated by a bit of attitude from an unknown juvenile delinquent. They would be a lot more concerned about what the family would do.

Even just walking down the street, Tamara stood out. Among all of the dark faces and black hair, she looked like an alien. People stared at her as she went by. It wasn't possible for her to disappear and be invisible.

She looked for the address Nita had put on the list. It was a legitimate address, not a made-up one. But like Rosie's, it could easily be a decoy. Somewhere Lewis and her people would have under surveillance.

She watched the house and the people on the street, trying to glean as much as she could. She couldn't help the fact that she stood out in the population. Maybe it was good that she did. Word would get to Lewis faster that a blond girl was wandering the streets. If it were Lewis who had taken Olly, she would know what that meant. She would recognize Tamara's description.

The high wail of a baby came from one of the houses. Tamara's heart immediately started to race. She knew it wasn't Olly. His raspy bass was as different as it could be. But she couldn't stop her body's reaction. She walked toward the house just to reassure herself that it wasn't Olly. In a way, it was reassuring to hear a baby. It was a family neighborhood. If there were a Cuban mob there, they wouldn't want to be starting any firefights with their children and babies in nearby houses. If they didn't use guns against Tamara, at least she had a chance to protect herself and maybe to explain what she was doing there.

Tamara paced back along the sidewalk, looking back at Lewis's given address. There was no sound of a baby there. She swallowed and walked up the cracked sidewalk blocks. As she stood there trying to decide whether she was going to ring the doorbell, she could see through the screen of the door. There were a few children's toys scattered on the floor. Not Olly's

Mister Duck. The unfamiliar toys of an older child. Superhero knock-offs. Cartoon creatures she wasn't familiar with.

Tamara pressed the doorbell, and heard it ring. In a few minutes, a young woman came to the door. At first glance, Tamara thought it was Lewis, but as the girl got closer, Tamara could see that it wasn't. She was older than Lewis, in her early twenties rather than her teens. But her coloring and features were similar to Lewis's. She opened the door a couple of inches, staring at Tamara suspiciously.

"Yeah? Who are you?"

"I'm looking for Lew—Martina. Martina, is she here?"

The woman scowled. "Martina isn't—" Her eyes suddenly widened, and she cut herself off, swearing. She tried to shut the door all the way, but Tamara was too quick. Realizing she'd been recognized, she wrenched the door open, ignoring the pain that pulsed through her knife-wounds.

"Where is she?" Tamara demanded. She forced her way in, throwing her shoulder into the woman when she tried to block Tamara's way. "You tell me where she is!" she insisted. "Where is Martina? Where is my baby?"

"You're crazy. What are you talking about? What baby?"

"Where are they?" Tamara bit off each word and stepped up into the woman's space. She wasn't tall enough to meet her eye-to-eye, but she did her best to intimidate.

"I don't know!" The woman held her hands up defensively. "You can't come into my house! I'll call the police!"

"You go right ahead. Then you can explain to them why Martina stole my baby."

She expected a retort back from the woman about her family connections. About how she could call down the forces of Cuba's mob against Tamara. But instead the woman looked cowed, like she didn't know what to do next.

A little boy ran into the room. His skin was dark, his eyes black and sparkling with mischief. He was headed for his mother, but stopped when he saw Tamara there. Tamara stepped back from the woman and grabbed the child. She held him in front of her, an arm locked under his chin.

His mother cried out. "No! Let Pedro go!"

"You can have Pedro when I get Olly. Where is he? Is he here?" Tamara could take her eyes off of the woman for only an instant at a time, trying to monitor every avenue of approach and look for signs of Olly at the same time.

"He isn't here." The woman was crying. "I don't know where he is. Martina took him away. Not here."

Tamara's heart pumped hard. "Where?"

"I don't know."

"Then you'd better find out."

"How can I? She won't tell me."

"Well, you'd better figure out a way." Tamara pulled up on the little boy's chin. "You want me to snap your little boy's neck? I can, you know." She hated using a child, just like Glock had used Sybil's sister against Tamara. Unlike Glock, Tamara didn't have any intention of actually hurting him. But his mother couldn't know that. She had to be scared enough to find out from Lewis where Olly was.

Tamara turned herself so that her back was against the nearest wall. She did not want anyone sneaking up behind her. She pointed to the teardrop tattoos on her cheek. "You know what these mean? Do you?"

The woman nodded in terror.

"You want to know who I killed? Did Martina tell you?"

Tears started to run down Pedro's mother's cheeks. Pedro himself was also crying. He'd struggled against her at first, but then he had given up and was still, hoping she would just release him.

"You already know?" Tamara demanded. "You already know I killed two little girls? They were smaller than him. So you think I'd hesitate to snap his neck?"

The woman shook her head.

"What's your name?"

She didn't answer.

"I want your name!" Tamara shouted.

"Edelira. Please, please don't hurt my Pedro."

"Is Martina your sister?"

Edelira didn't answer.

"I said, is she your sister?" Tamara raised her voice again. It was like the woman couldn't answer unless driven by terror.

"Yes. Yes, my sister."

"Then you'd better call her and tell her that her nephew is going to die if I don't get my baby back."

"I can't call her. She doesn't carry a phone."

"How could she not carry a phone?" Tamara demanded. Though of course, she didn't either. Fresh out of juvie, she had no money for one of her own and the Hensons had not given her one. But Lewis had been out longer, and she was bound to have connections and money to get herself a phone. Everyone had cell phones.

"So she cannot be tracked. So nobody can find her."

Of course not. That was how the police had caught Vernon and Sly. Whether Lewis knew that detail or not, she undoubtedly knew that the police could pinpoint a cell phone geographically. So she had taken the extreme measure of not carrying a cell phone with her.

"You can still reach her," Tamara insisted. "You know how to get ahold of her."

As if on cue, Edelira's pocket began to play music. She grabbed her phone and turned the sound off without looking at the screen.

"Who is that?"

"It is nobody."

"Who is it?" Tamara turned her wrist slightly to make it look like she was tightening her grip on Pedro's throat. "Do I have to squeeze every little answer out of you?"

Pedro responded with a whimper, grabbing Tamara's arm and trying to pull it away from his throat. If she were really choking him, he wouldn't be able to make any noise.

"It's my papi," Edelira said.

"Your father?"

Edelira nodded. A wave of apprehension rolled over Tamara. She looked out through the screen toward the street. Nobody appeared to be watching them, but she was still anxious. She stepped a little closer and kicked the inside door shut so that no one could see them.

"Is Martina with him?"

"No. I do not know."

"Is she or not?"

She cried quietly. "I don't know. Maybe."

"Call him back. Put him on speaker."

"He won't like it—"

"Do you think I care what he likes?"

But she did. She was very worried about what Lewis's father might like or not like. Did he know what his daughter had done? Did he approve it? Would he use whatever organized crime connections he had to protect her? Remove Tamara and silence her for good?

Edelira looked at Tamara for a moment, her eyes wide and frightened, unsure what she should do. Finally, she took her phone out and looked at the screen. She must have had a special ringtone set for her father. Sybil had shown Tamara how she had different rings set up for different people, laughing at the jokes behind each choice. Finally, Edelira tapped and swiped the screen. She moved to put the phone up to her ear, then met Tamara's eyes and remembered to put it on speaker. She tapped it again and held it out in front of her, between them.

Tamara listened to the phone ring through. She tried not to

be impatient about it. Edelira's papi's phone probably wasn't even ringing yet and, when it did, he might hold off on answering it to express his displeasure over her not answering when he called. Finally, after half a dozen rings, the man answered. He gave an exasperated sigh. His accent was stronger than Edelira's.

"What is going on, Edie?"

"I'm sorry. She just showed up here. I didn't know what to do!"

There was a pause as the man considered this. "Who just showed up?"

Edelira looked at Tamara, the skin around her eyes seeming stretched and pale. "The girl, Papi. The girl... looking for Martina."

"Ask him where she is," Tamara murmured.

"Is she—is Martina with you?" Edie's voice spiked even higher.

"Who is there with you? Who else is there?"

"My name is Tamara French," Tamara said more loudly. "Martina knows who I am and what I want. Send her over here."

Tamara shuffled forward with Pedro. As Martina's papi started to demand an explanation, Tamara reached over and tapped the red button on the phone screen. Edelira gave a little bleat of protest and stared down at the phone.

"Where is he?" Tamara asked. "Your papi? Where is he?" She dragged Pedro with her to look out the front window to look for any unusual activity on the street. So far, everything remained quiet. Tamara chose a new position, her back again to the wall, where she could see both the front door and the back one through the kitchen.

"He is... at his warehouse. Working. He works hard."

Tamara kicked a toy away, considering. If he worked at a warehouse, then maybe he wasn't high up in the organization. Maybe he was just a small fish. That would be good for Tamara. Maybe he wouldn't send thugs over to kill her.

"How many children do you have?" Tamara asked. The toys on the floor seemed too old for the little boy, who couldn't have been older than three or four. The others were probably at school, but she needed to be aware of the dynamics. To know what was going on before anything unexpected happened.

Edelira sniffled. "I have four," she said. "Pedro, two older, and one younger."

"So Martina brought the baby here, because you would know how to look after him."

Edelira didn't admit or deny it.

"Where are your other children?"

"At school and napping. This one is supposed to be napping too."

Pedro whined and tried to wriggle away from Tamara. She held him securely.

"Where did Martina take Olly? Why isn't he still here?"

More tears came from Edelira's eyes. "I do not know. I told her I cannot take care of another baby. And this one, he is crying all the time. I tell her he needs something familiar. A blanket or a toy, something to hold on to."

Tamara nodded. Lewis had returned to take Mister Duck. But something had happened. Olly wasn't there anymore.

"He still is forever crying," Edelira sobbed. "Martina..." Edelira choked and paused and considered her words. "I told her he needs his mami. She took him away. I don't know where. I swear, I don't know where."

"I don't care if you know. Because Martina is going to come here and she's going to tell me, isn't she?"

Edelira rubbed at her eyes and bit her knuckles, blinking at Pedro. "I don't know. What if she does not come? I can't help it if she does not come."

"She will."

"I cannot be sure. Martina is different." Edelira reached her hands out toward Pedro pleadingly. "Martina can be hard. If she doesn't want to see you…"

"She did all of this to hurt me. She'll want to see my face. She'll want to know she succeeded."

Edelira sobbed. They waited in silence. Tamara's heart grew heavier in her chest. Lewis had taken Olly away from where he would be cared for. She hadn't done that because she wanted to take care of him herself. Edelira had been unable to soothe him. Mister Duck hadn't been the answer. Olly's raucous cries grated on Lewis's nerves; Lewis was not known for her patience and forbearance. Tamara knew how frustrating Olly was. She knew the rage that Olly raised in her when he wouldn't calm down, crying and crying for no discernible reason.

Edelira sobbed, but it was not because she was afraid her sister wouldn't come.

THIRTY-THREE

WHEN THE DOOR FINALLY opened, it made all of them jump. Tamara tightened her grip on Pedro and pulled him against her. Edelira burst into fresh tears.

Lewis stood in the doorway. "What the hell are you doing in my house, French?"

"I thought it was your sister's house," Tamara countered.

Lewis looked at Pedro, at Tamara's arm around his throat. Her lips pulled away from her teeth in a snarl. "It's my house," she repeated. "My family's house."

"I'm here for my baby. Where's Olly?"

"Olly? What kind of a name is Olly?"

"Quit stalling and just tell me where he is. I'll get him and that will be the end of it. I'm probably going back to prison even if I prove I didn't do anything to him. So you've succeeded. You took away something that was mine and you get me sent back to prison. Adult prison, this time, they won't send me back to juvie."

Lewis's eyes glittered. "What makes you think I had anything to do with your baby?"

"Rumors," Tamara said, avoiding specifics. "Somebody told me you got a grudge against me." Tamara shrugged. "I thought juvie was just juvie, but I guess you figure it differently..."

Lewis advanced. Tamara squeezed her arm, really cutting Pedro's breath for the first time. Lewis stopped.

"You thought you could get away with anything," Lewis spat. "You had the guards wrapped around your little finger and you could do whatever you wanted to. You messed with me and my gang. You think you get away without any consequences?"

Tamara shook her head. "I was sick. I didn't know what I was doing. I was just reacting and..." she shrugged, not sure what to say. "You had the Sharks behind you. I was just one stupid juvie. What did you care what I did?"

"Because you made me look bad. And nobody makes me look bad in front of my girls!"

"It was a mistake."

"I warned you. I warned you that you were going to get hurt and you still didn't listen."

Tamara bit her lip. She didn't argue the point. It was true. Instead of being intimidated, she'd decided to attack. To do damage to the gang and keep them off balance until they forgot about her or decided to leave her alone.

Lewis nodded. "Yeah. I *knew* it was you. Sneaking around, pretending you were so fragile and innocent. You killed Waterson. I knew she didn't tangle with Tabby. I know my girls!"

"Yeah. You do."

"When I heard you got out on parole, I saw my chance. I could screw you up so bad you'd never forget it. When I saw you had a baby..." Lewis laughed. "It couldn't have been better."

"You knew they'd suspect me."

"Who else was there? You leave the baby-killer alone with the baby, and what do you think is going to happen? I watched the cops run in circles for hours. Could they be more pathetic?

Taking dogs out to look for his body. Looking in the trash cans. It was like watching my favorite reruns, except in real life."

"What did you do with Olly? Where is he?"

"Olly. That's got to be the worst name ever. Seriously, where did you come up with that one?"

"I didn't. Foster family called him Oliver." Tamara breathed, waiting for the images of Olivia Vernon to fade so she could go on. "So I call him Olly."

Trying to suppress the memories of what Vernon and Sly had done to her tipped Tamara over the edge. Rage welled up and spilled over. Whether Lewis had killed Olly or was only trying to provoke her, she didn't know. She didn't care. She heard Edelira cry out and felt Pedro struggling in her grasp. But her anger was overpowering.

"Let him go!" Lewis drew her gun and aimed it straight at Tamara's face. It was shiny and sleek but had heft. Tamara didn't know guns, but it looked deadly enough to her. Shock loosened Tamara's grip on Pedro. She knew she was looking death in the face and that Lewis would kill her before Tamara could kill Pedro. She could put pressure on his carotid artery instead of his windpipe, that would be faster. But still not faster than a bullet speeding toward her brain.

"Tell me where my baby is," Tamara insisted.

Tamara saw Lewis's finger tighten on the trigger. Was she really going to risk hitting her nephew? Or allowing her nephew to witness Tamara's gruesome death?

Lewis was dangerous. Tamara had known that from the start. But if Olly were dead and all Tamara had to look forward to in life was six more years of prison, maybe it didn't matter. Tamara wouldn't have to worry about making any more decisions or taking care of anyone else. She would be done.

"On the floor!" a voice thundered.

There had been enough brawls at juvie that Tamara obeyed automatically. She dropped, taking Pedro down with her. In the time it took for her to put her hands on her head, Lewis was turning around to identify the voice and determine her course of action. Lewis was a fighter and a planner. She wasn't like Tamara, quick to comply with orders.

By the time Lewis finished turning her body around, there was a sharp report. Lewis staggered back. Tamara closed her eyes and pressed her face into the floor. She hoped that Pedro was doing the same thing, because seeing his aunt shot in front of his eyes was probably more traumatizing than seeing his aunt shoot a stranger.

"Pedro, Pedro," Edelira was standing behind Tamara crying. If she didn't obey the police and get down on the floor, she was likely to be shot as well. The police would see her as a threat, even if they didn't see any weapon. She was resisting. She wouldn't listen to what she was told, so she was a danger that had to be taken care of. Tamara turned her head to look at the woman and kicked her in the shin.

"Get on the floor!" she ordered through gritted teeth.

Edelira looked at her, not processing what Tamara was telling her or why. Tamara kicked again, harder. "Get on the floor!"

Edelira started to move slowly, putting her hands behind her head like Tamara and getting down, first to her knees and then stretched out on the floor, crowded close to Tamara and Pedro. Pedro was trying to squirm out from where Tamara had him pinned. Tamara looked toward the door, over Lewis's crumpled body. Police in black vests were breaching the doorway, guns still raised, looking for additional weapons or threats. Tamara kept herself pressed to the floor, her hands in full view. As one of the cops stepped over her, she spoke to him. "There's another child sleeping somewhere. I don't think there's anyone else."

She didn't want them to be startled by a sleepy child and put a bullet in him.

He grunted and continued past her. A couple of them moved

in a coordinated pattern into the kitchen, then back into the front room and up the stairs. Other cops moved into the house. One of them stopped over Tamara, cuffing her wrists and feeling for any weapons. They pulled Pedro away from her to check him for injuries and put weeping Edelira into cuffs despite her protestations of innocence. Once they were all secured, Tamara was allowed to sit up. Bowen entered the house, her face a hard, impassive mask. She too wore a protective vest.

"Well?" she demanded. "You want to explain?"

Tamara wet her lips and tried to find an explanation that would show her in a good light. Once again, she had done everything she wasn't supposed to. Lewis lay there dead because of it.

"Lewis... she's the one who kidnapped Olly."

"You have proof of that?"

"We have to look for evidence. He was staying here for a while, so there must be baby things. Maybe his DNA."

"But you don't *have* anything."

"No... just what she said. And Edelira—" Tamara nodded to the other woman. "She was the one taking care of Olly, after Lewis took him."

"And why would Lewis have kidnapped him?"

"We were in juvie together. I embarrassed her in front of her gang. She was still mad about it, all this time later." She found it bizarre that Lewis would spend any time thinking about Tamara after getting out. She didn't have to associate with the Sharks anymore, so why care that she'd been embarrassed months before by an inmate clearly not in her right mind?

"What made you think of her?" Bowen asked. "Why did you suspect her?"

Tamara looked toward the door, the pieces slowly clicking into place. "You followed me."

"Of course we did. How else are we supposed to know what you are up to? You don't seem to see any reason to talk to us about your suspicions."

"I... I'm sorry. I was going to call you, once I knew for sure..."

"And when would that have been? After she shot you?"

"I thought... I didn't think she was going to do that."

"Yeah? Serving time with her convinced you of her gentle nature?"

Tamara grimaced. Confronting dangerous juvies without any kind of weapon hadn't exactly been a smart plan. But she had thought she was safer approaching them as a non-combatant. She'd never been comfortable using weapons. "No... no, you're right... I thought... she took Olly to hurt me. She could have shot me then. But she didn't. She took Olly instead. So... I didn't think she would."

Bowen looked down at Tamara, hands on hips. "And where *is* Olly?"

THIRTY-FOUR

AMARA LOOKED DOWN AT Lewis's body with growing realization. If what Edelira said was true, no one but Lewis knew where Olly was, and Lewis had just taken that knowledge with her to the grave. Tamara swallowed hard, trying to keep her emotions at bay.

"I don't know. She didn't say whether he was alive or dead."

Bowen nodded, her mouth a thin, grim line. "Kidnappers rarely hold someone more than a day or two alive, and then only when they're negotiating for ransom. Unless she wanted a baby of her own, which obviously wasn't the case."

"She came back for Mister Duck... he was still alive then. Edelira had him here... but Lewis took him away..."

"Chances are..." Bowen trailed off and didn't finish the thought. Maybe better not to put anything too explicit into Tamara's head.

The immediate danger past, Tamara's brain started to work through what was going to happen next. She had broken her parole rules and, whether or not Bowen charged her with obstruction of an investigation or some other nuisance charges, as soon as Wanda heard what had happened, she would have Tamara up before a judge and on her way back to prison.

Lewis was dead and there was no proof of what she had done. If they thought Tamara capable of hurting Olly and cleverly disposing of his body, frustrating all attempts to figure out how, then what was to stop Tamara from setting Lewis up as a fall guy? Bowen could keep building a circumstantial case against Tamara until they had enough to convince a jury that, once more, Tamara was guilty of murdering a child.

"I gotta use the can," Tamara said, looking into the kitchen to see if there was an adjoining bathroom on the main floor. "Can I...?"

"Not in here," Bowen said immediately. "It's a crime scene. We can't take the chance of contaminating any evidence that Olly was held here."

"I really need to..."

Bowen motioned to one of the other officers on the scene. "I need you over here, please."

The officer came over.

"I need you to take this witness and find a public restroom. Bring her back here after."

"Uh... yes, ma'am. Will do." He flicked his hand for Tamara to move forward, took her by the elbow, and escorted her out of the house. Tamara took a quick look around outside. There were plenty of neighbors watching and talking to each other. She couldn't see anyone who appeared to be upset or concerned about whatever had happened inside, only interested and excited to spread the news.

Tamara sat in the back of the police car and was quiet, watching for anything out of place. It wasn't like she thought Olly might be there, held in the arms of one of the spectators, but it wasn't totally out of the realm of possibility.

"This good?" her escort asked, pulling into the parking lot of a gas station with a convenience store.

Tamara looked it over and nodded. "Yeah, looks good," she agreed. When the cop took her out of the car, Tamara held her arms out toward him. "Can you take those off, please?"

The officer looked down at the handcuffs doubtfully. "I don't think I can do that."

"I'm not under arrest," Tamara pointed out. "Detective Bowen said I was a witness, not a detainee."

"Still..."

"I haven't been arrested. That means I can go any time."

"She said to bring you back."

"I didn't say I'm not going back. I just want to use the facilities. Listen, officer," she dropped her voice to a confidential tone. She looked at his name badge. "Officer Deluth. It's my period and I need to take care of *things*. I don't know if you've ever watched your girlfriend, but you sort of need independent use of your hands, or it can be very *messy*."

Deluth's face drained of color. He took out a handcuff key and fitted it into the cuffs. "You need to come right back out when you're done..."

"Yeah, of course. Just to warn you, though, it's going to take me a few minutes. I need to—"

He waved her to silence, not wanting to know any details. "Fine, fine," he agreed.

He tucked the handcuffs away and walked with Tamara into the convenience store and to the ladies' room door. He hesitated for a moment, indecision on his face. Deciding whether to go in with her, or at least check it out. But there were women's voices from within, so he shrugged, deciding against any further precautions.

"I'll be right here."

"Thanks."

Tamara went into the bathroom and took a look around. A couple of women talked to each other, one at the sink and the other in a stall. It was a mid-size restroom, more than two stalls but not like a movie multiplex. As usual, there was only one door in and out. The woman at the sink stopped talking, looking at Tamara.

"Something you need, honey?"

"No. I'm fine, thanks."

She went into one of the stalls and waited for the women to leave, studying out the situation while she waited impatiently for them to finish up. There were narrow windows up near the ceiling. Out of reach, but maybe still accessible...

There was a pole with a hook on the end designed to open the windows without having to use a ladder. Tamara opened the windows and examined the available options. If she climbed onto the toilet and used it to boost herself up to the walls of the cubicle stalls, she could probably then pull herself up into the open window. She wasn't any gymnast, and had never been one of the girls obsessed with exercising and strength training inside juvie, but her slim build was in her favor, both for climbing and slithering out the skinny windows.

She hadn't factored in her stab wounds before she started. Hanging, stretching, and pulling herself up ripped the healing wounds apart. Tamara managed not to cry out, though tears ran down her cheeks. It was harder and took longer than she had expected, but eventually she was able to pull herself up into the window and have a look outside.

It was both better and worse than she had hoped. The restroom windows were on the back of the building, so she wouldn't be easily observed by customers. Deluth wouldn't see her lowering herself down and escaping. But unfortunately, there was no shed, dumpster, or refrigeration unit for her to jump down onto. It was a sheer drop from the window to the ground, a ten-foot drop to the pavement.

But it was the only chance she was going to get.

Tamara didn't give herself any time to worry over it. Again ignoring the pain it caused to her wounds, she backed out of the window and hung down by her hands, stretching her body out as long as her short stature would allow. She still hung almost five feet above the ground.

She let go and tried to land in a crouch, absorbing the shock with her bent knees, but she ended up crying out and toppling over backward with the force. She swore and picked herself up. Her knee and ankle both flared with pain. All of her injuries were on fire. She looked down at the slash on her arm and saw that it was bleeding again, some of the stitches pulled through.

But if she wanted to slip away from her guard, it was Tamara's one chance. She straightened the best she could and limped down the back alley.

* * *

Tamara didn't know where to go or what to do next. She stayed out of sight, knowing they would be looking for her. Time passed slowly. Tamara held her head, searching her mind for every detail she knew about Lewis. They'd been at juvie together for a couple of years, but Tamara, not being in the Sharks, hadn't learned a lot of intimate details about her. She hadn't even known that she was Cuban, a fact that Rosie had been aware of, and Rosie had been Lewis's sworn enemy.

Lewis lived with her family or, at least, gave her sister's home as her address, and referred to it as her family's home. On kidnapping Olly, she hadn't kept him hidden, but had taken him home with her, apparently making him part of the family. Edelira had known something about where Olly had come from, recognizing Tamara on her doorstep. She was afraid of Tamara and what she would do. Lewis must have had a very close relationship with her family to have told Edelira details about Olly's origin and Tamara's past.

She had been a tough gang leader in juvie. She'd been wily, careful of Tamara's reputation as a favorite of the administration.

She knew when to pick a fight and when to keep things quiet. She'd been smart enough not to retaliate against Tamara after the breakfast incident, despite her threats. Things had become too unstable, and she had apparently guessed correctly about Tamara's involvement in Waterson's death.

Tamara closed her eyes. Strong family connection. Smart. Cautious.

Tamara would not have considered Lewis coming into the house to kidnap Olly or to get his Mister Duck cautious, but the fact that she'd gotten away with it both times without leaving a clue behind as to who had been there or how it had been done, Lewis had apparently known what she was doing and mitigated the risks.

Tamara needed to find Lewis's father. Edelira didn't know where Lewis might have taken Olly after things hadn't worked out at the house, but maybe her father would.

Officer Deluth hadn't taken Tamara out of the neighborhood, but only a few blocks away, so Tamara didn't have to walk far. A number of hours had passed since her escape, but she kept a close eye out for any police searching for her. She stopped at a group of little girls playing with handheld electronic games on the front steps of one of the houses similar to Lewis's. Tamara's Gran had never seen the point in electronic games, so Tamara had been forced to find her fun in farm chores, watching Gran's TV shows in the evening, or playing by herself or with the animals. The little girls didn't look up at her.

"Hey, did you hear what happened over at Edelira's house?" Tamara tried, acting as if they all knew each other, and she might have an interesting tidbit to share with her friends.

One of the girls, about ten years old, looked up from her game at Tamara. She frowned. "Who are you?"

"Just a friend. It was scary, huh? You heard?"

The girl looked back at her game and continued to play, disdaining the conversation.

"Cops shot Martina," one of the other girls contributed. "Not like everybody didn't know *that* was going to happen someday."

"I know," Tamara agreed. "Sooner or later..."

There were some curious glances from the other girls, but none of them were interested enough to abandon their games.

"I heard it was because of that baby," one of them contributed.

Tamara suppressed a shiver. "That baby?"

"That one that sounds like a bullfrog." Giggles from the others. "Crying all day long. It drove everybody in the neighborhood crazy!"

"Then what happened?" Tamara asked. "Where did it go?"

"You're not Cuban," one of them said. "We don't talk to people who aren't Cuban. We don't have to answer your questions."

"Oh," Tamara leaned against the railing as if she didn't care. "I thought you might have heard. But I guess not."

"She took it away." It was a little girl with short, pixie-cut hair instead of the longer hair and braids of her neighbors. "Maybe she took him back to his mami."

"Maybe..." Tamara said, her tone doubtful.

One of the older girls looked at the pixie-cut one, giving her a stern look. "We don't talk to people who aren't Cuban," she repeated.

The pixie-cut girl looked at Tamara. "She could be."

Tamara had to laugh at this herself. Certainly there was no law that said all Cubans had to have Hispanic features, but Tamara, with her fair hair, would certainly stand out among them. "I am not Cuban," she admitted. "But you don't have to listen to her. You can make your own choices."

"Yeah," the little girl confirmed, smiling at the one who had taken charge, "I can make my own choices."

There were some moments while they all exchanged brief

glances, looking up swiftly from their games and then continuing to play.

"Did Martina's dad hear what happened?" Tamara asked. "I didn't see him there."

"He knows," one of the little girls assured her, "but he hasn't gone to the house. He doesn't live there."

"He didn't go back to see Martina? To talk to the police?"

They grew more reticent. Martina's papi was apparently not a safe topic of conversation. Maybe that bore out the assertion that he was Cuban mob. They knew they weren't allowed to talk about him openly.

"He is still at the warehouse," one of them said. She let her game rest on her knees, apparently finished. "He won't go to the house while the police are there."

"Oh, the warehouse," Tamara agreed.

The girl with the short hair twirled a lock around her fingers. "He is always working. He is at the warehouse all day long. All night, sometimes. He must be a very hard worker."

"The one over there?" Tamara picked a random direction, pointing.

"No, not over there!" The little girl proceeded to locate it precisely for Tamara.

If they said that Lewis's father wouldn't leave the warehouse, they were probably right. Children on the street in a close community like that knew everything. They knew all kinds of things their families had no idea they knew about.

"I'll see you around," Tamara said. Though clearly, she wouldn't be likely to see them again. But they accepted this farewell and hunched back over their games again, talking among themselves about their scores and what they needed to do to get more points or whatever goal they were trying to achieve. Whatever interest the shooting and the scores of police at the Lewis house had garnered several hours before had been lost. They had more important things to worry about.

Tamara headed down the street, keeping her pace unhurried and trying not to attract more attention than she already did with her blond hair and white skin.

The fact that Lewis's father would not go home to talk to the police about his own daughter's death—that he hadn't shown up to protest what had happened and to rail at them and threaten to make a big stink in the media over their coming into his house and shooting his daughter down in cold blood—told her that he was working on the wrong side of the law. Even a father who was fairly uninvolved with his daughter would still protest her death, and he had not.

Tamara had no trouble finding the warehouse. She looked at the nondescript building, wondering what they were warehousing. Was it drug trade? Chop shop? Human trafficking? It could be a legitimate business, maybe laundering money for the mob. Or a front for something more sinister.

She circled the building slowly, looking at the cars parked around it. There were no police officers or guards visible watching the street. It looked just like any legitimate business in any other neighborhood.

There weren't any windows that were low enough for her to peer into. They were all farther up the walls, providing light to the interior, but not affording outsiders a look at the business. Tamara circled around to a back door to see if she could find a way to enter unobtrusively.

For a moment, she froze and was thrown back in time to when Glock had taken her to the abandoned warehouse. It was supposed to be a place for Tamara to hide out. To be safe and kept away from the eyes of Collins and anyone else who might be looking for her. But Tamara had known as soon as she had walked in there that that was not Glock's intention at all. If she'd had to stay in that warehouse for another day or two, she probably would have died there. The pneumonia she developed from having her ribs bound up too tightly, the oxycodone, the filth she had to sleep in; it wouldn't have taken long before she succumbed.

What if that was happening to Olly? What if it already had? Where would Lewis have taken him? He wouldn't settle in like part of the family, so she had banished him. She'd taken him off somewhere and probably left him to starve to death. How long would it take for an infant to starve? Tamara didn't imagine it would be more than a couple of days.

She tried the handle, but it was locked. Tamara went down to the next door, with the same results. Going any farther along the side of the warehouse would take her to the loading dock, and she didn't want everyone to see her yet. She went back the way she had come, looking for a basement window or some other way to get in, like she had gotten into the warehouse and into the condemned apartment building. Since it was being actively used, chances were that any breach would be repaired within a day or two, but all she needed was one door left carelessly unlocked.

Around the corner, Tamara tried another door and the knob miraculously turned. Tamara pushed the door open, listening for any movement within and trying to invent a good reason for walking uninvited into a warehouse. Wrong address? Right address but wrong entrance? Pretending she was looking for a job or casual labor? Asking for someone who didn't exist?

Her white skin was going to give her away. Anyone would know immediately that she wasn't there by accident.

But there was no one on the other side of the door to confront her. A hallway, probably leading to offices and bathrooms at one end and the large storage area of the warehouse at the other. Tamara picked a direction and started to creep along the hall. Her shoes, still the soft, flimsy tennis shoes she had worn at juvie, whispered over the concrete floor with barely a sound. She kept her ears strained for any security guards or other people. It was getting late in the day, and she didn't hear much activity. Maybe everybody had gone home.

Even Lewis's father, the man who practically lived at the warehouse?

It occurred to her as she got closer to her destination that she didn't know the man's name. It was going to be hard to ask for him without knowing.

The hallway opened up into the main room of the warehouse. Pallets stacked high in long rows, with aisles large enough for forklifts down the center. Tamara walked along for a minute, just looking at the boxes. Somewhere in the building, someone turned the bright overhead lights off. Tamara froze. For a minute, she was blinded by the darkness, but her eyes adjusted and there were still some dim security lights on. There were probably night guards coming on duty. They would patrol by the dimmer lights and have big heavy flashlights on their belts. Big Maglites that worked just as well as a bludgeon as a light source. Tamara needed to figure out a strategy that didn't involve being stuck all night in a warehouse.

She went to one of the big boxes and tried to pull it open. The cardboard was thicker than the stuff she'd seen before on parcels and was fastened with long industrial-size staples that could probably rip her hand apart if she managed to tear the cardboard. Tamara walked farther down the aisle until she found a box cutter. She extended the blade and dug it into one of the boxes stacked beside her. The blade was sharp, but it was still difficult to saw through enough of the thick cardboard box to pull open a flap and have a look inside.

Tamara bit back a scream when she put her face up to the hole to get a look at the contents. There was a face looking back at her. A number of faces. The box was full of doll heads. Shuddering, Tamara pulled back. Doll heads? Was it a cover-up for another trade? Or a legitimate business?

As she turned the corner and walked down the next aisle, she could see a glassed-in cluster of offices, one of them with a light still on. Tamara crept toward it. Was it Lewis's father? How would she know if it was? What was she going to say to him?

Tamara drew close enough to see that there was, in fact, a man in the still-lit office. Edelira said he worked hard. The little girls said that he sometimes stayed there all night. If there were only one person left in the warehouse offices, who else would it be?

When she reached the door, he looked up. He was clearly startled by her unexpected appearance, jerking back at first. His brows drew down. Before his lips could form the words 'who are you?' recognition flooded his features. He might not know her by sight, but he had heard enough about her that day and probably over the previous week to know who she had to be.

"You must be Martina's dad," Tamara said.

"You should not be here."

It seemed an odd response. He didn't tell her to go away. He didn't ask her why she was there. Just said she should not be there

"I want my baby."

"Do you see a baby here? Whatever happened between you and Marti, that's over now." He made a gesture like he was pushing something back over his shoulder. "She is gone, and it is over and done."

"You didn't go to the house to see her. Why not?"

"I was not a part of my children's lives. I wasn't around when they were little girls, why would she want me there when she was dead?"

Tamara took a step into the office. Her body was exhausted and screaming with pain. "I only had my baby for a few weeks. But I want him back. I have to have him back."

"I can't help you."

"Martina was here. With you. She didn't have Olly with her when she came to the house, so he must be *here*."

Looking around, Tamara saw no sign of any baby things.

Another dead end. How could Bowen have let Lewis be shot down like that? Hadn't she realized that Lewis was the only one who could lead them back to Olly? Didn't she know she was dooming Tamara to wonder forever what had happened to her baby? Whether he was alive or dead? Who had him, or whether he was buried in the cold, hard ground somewhere? Bowen should have insisted that Lewis be taken alive, even if she shot Tamara. Lewis was the one who knew.

Lewis's father gave a shrug. "What happened between you and Marti—"

"Something didn't happen between me and her. We didn't have some disagreement. She stole my baby! That isn't something that just fades away into the past!"

"Maybe Edelira can help."

"She says she doesn't know. Please, help me. I don't know where else to go. Where else did Lew—Martina spend time? Would she have left the baby with someone else? If she... wanted to get rid of him, where would she go? There must be something you can do to help me."

"I tell you the same thing I told the police. You do not see any baby here. I cannot help you."

You do not see any baby here.

Do you see a baby here?

I cannot help you.

The things that he kept repeating were intended to block Tamara, to persuade her to leave, yet he still hadn't said that Olly wasn't there. Was it a language barrier, or was he being careful not to say anything untrue, and yet not to tell her what she wanted to know?

"Where is Olly?"

"I cannot help you."

"Where is he?"

He looked at her and shook his head.

"Tell me where he is. You know, don't you? You tell me

where he is. Whether he is alive or dead," Tamara's chest hurt even just to voice the possibility, "I want to find him. I want to know where he is. I can't go back without finding him."

He still refused to answer. Tamara looked around the room. No sign of a baby. *You do not see any baby here.* She moved into the office and started looking through all of the cupboards and file drawers. Still no sign of Olly. The man made no movement to block or restrain her. Tamara looked back the way she had come. Rows upon rows of boxes. Even if she had the police force behind her, it would take days to search every box. By that time, it would be too late. Without Lewis there to point him out, Tamara had to find him herself. She was the only one who cared enough to be there. The police still believed that she'd had something to do with Olly's disappearance. Maybe they thought Lewis was her co-conspirator. Maybe they thought she was unrelated, or that Tamara had set her up as a fall guy. But they weren't there, searching through the warehouse, the one place it was most likely Lewis had hidden Olly. They thought he was dead and it was too late for anything to be done for him. Even if he were dead, Tamara couldn't bear the thought of leaving him there. Of never finding him.

Tamara walked back out into the storage area.

"Olly? Olly, baby... where are you?" She listened for any response. She didn't expect one, of course. But she desperately wanted to. Maybe if she believed in God, she could have prayed to him and he would have pointed her in the right direction. She'd heard of such miracles. But she didn't have a god to ask.

"Olly...? Olly...?" She walked up the long aisle, feeling for a tug in one particular direction. He came from her body. There should still be a connection between them. How many times had she heard of the strength of a mother's love? The special bond between mother and child? She'd started to believe it before Olly disappeared. But since he had disappeared, she hadn't once felt a tug in his direction. No special intuition or heartache led her to him.

Tamara closed her eyes. She started to hum *Hush Little Baby*.

Her baby was gone. She was going to have to accept that he was lost to her forever. She was never going to feel that warm cuddle against her body again. To smell the baby soap on his skin.

He was lost to her.

THIRTY-FIVE

BUT AS SHE RETRACED her steps along that aisle again, humming *Hush Little Baby* to herself, the tiniest sound attracted her attention. Not a cry or a rustle. Just the barest hint of a sob. She stopped short and listened.

"Olly? Olly, are you there? Where are you, baby? Mommy's here."

There was no answering cry. Tamara knew she must have imagined it. A mouse maybe, or a sob caught in her own throat. The sighing of the wind outside.

She stood still, straining every fiber of her body listening for him.

Nothing.

Tamara stood still for a long time. She started humming again. Olly never had liked her lullaby. He would quiet when Mrs. Henson hummed and sang to him, but when Tamara tried to soothe him with a song, he would kick and howl a protest.

There was another noise. Barely audible, but there. Tamara kept humming, a few words at a time, and then stopping to listen, trying to zero in on the tiny stirrings. She tried a box lid, but it was stapled securely shut. Tamara still held the box cutter in her hand. She hadn't even paid any attention to it. Had she been holding it in her hand when she talked to Lewis's father? Had he thought she was trying to threaten him?

Tamara hummed a few notes to confirm the location of the noises, then started to cut into the box. She started up high, not wanting to cut anywhere near the baby, if he were in there. She hoped it wasn't a rat or some other vermin. Looking into the box and seeing beady red eyes looking back at her after seeing the creepy doll faces in the last box might just do her in. She looked back over her shoulder to make sure that Lewis's father was not creeping up on her, intent on preventing her from discovering Lewis's secret. But he was sitting at his desk, looking over the day's records, acting as if he didn't even know she was there. Was that how he had behaved when Lewis had brought Olly there to hide him away? Looking away and pretending he knew nothing?

Tamara cut down the sides of the box, right at the corners, again trying to stay as far away from the noise as she could. She grasped the top of the flap she had cut and wrestled it down.

That box too was full of doll parts. A jumble of arms and legs poked every which way, reminding her of pictures she had seen of mass graves during the holocaust or other ethnic cleansing. She blinked, trying to sort out all of the pudgy baby arms and legs to find what she was looking for.

And then she saw him. Half-buried. Motionless. Looking like she was too late by mere minutes, carefully cutting into the box as he breathed his last. She dropped the box cutter and reached in, wrapping her fingers around him and pulling him free of the grasping hands of the unborn plastic babies.

"Come on. Come on, Olly. Show Mommy you're okay."

He was warm. His flesh was still firm under her fingers, not the empty mushiness she knew she would feel when the life force was gone.

"Olly. Olly." She held him up to her face, kissing his cheek and listening and feeling for his breath. She couldn't feel him breathing. He didn't stir or open his eyes. Tamara bent down to pick her box cutter back up and marched into the brightly-lit office.

"Now, do you see a baby?" Tamara demanded. Her voice was a snarl, hard and angry and threatening. All of those warnings about not coming between a bear and her cub came into play. This man had tried to keep her from finding her offspring. He had been prepared to let the baby die, and he might have gotten his wish. "Do you see him now? Are you going to let him die?"

The man blinked at her.

"Give me your phone."

He didn't argue, but he didn't reach into his pocket to find it, either. Tamara scanned the top of the desk. There was a wired landline, a black desk set. Tamara snatched it up and tapped 9-1-1 into the keypad. There was a recorded message saying it was an invalid extension. Tamara growled.

"Why doesn't it work?"

"You have to dial nine."

"I did."

"No, you have to dial nine before the number."

Tamara hung up, picked up the handset, and tried again. Nine and then 9-1-1. It started to ring through. Tamara's heart was racing, and her legs were shaking.

The emergency dispatcher answered, and Tamara tried to explain everything at once, stumbling over herself and probably incoherent.

Tamara turned to look at the man to make sure he wasn't going to do anything. She was holding Olly, the phone, and the box cutter, and needed to put at least one of them down. But he wasn't doing anything threatening. Again, he was working on the day's receipts and work orders, acting as if Tamara weren't even there. She put down the box cutter, well out of his reach.

"We've dispatched an ambulance," the emergency operator told Tamara.

"You should send police too." She looked at Lewis's father, but he made no sign that he heard her or intended to run.

"Someone will be there in just a few minutes. Do you know CPR?"

She'd seen it on TV, like anyone else, but was that enough? Tamara shook her head. "I don't know... I've never done it."

"I'm going to walk you through it. You need to put him down on a hard surface. Can you put him on a table or floor?"

Tamara was numb as she tried to listen to all of the instructions. Then she put down the phone and tried to do everything she had been told.

* * *

The paramedics got there first, calling out to find Tamara and arriving with their big tool boxes full of first responder supplies. They both gave her reassuring smiles, and one of them knelt down beside her, putting in the ear buds of his stethoscope to listen to Olly's chest. Tamara held her breath while he listened, afraid to make any sound that might keep him from hearing what he needed to.

"He is breathing. But it is very shallow. What happened?"

"He was abandoned here. He was in one of the boxes." Tamara glanced in the direction of the box she had pulled Olly from.

The paramedic's brows went up, but he didn't interrogate her further. "We'll want to get him on oxygen and to the hospital as quickly as we can. What about you?"

Tamara frowned. "Me? I'll come with him. He's my baby."

"No, I mean," he nodded to her arm, "you're bleeding. You need medical attention as well."

Tamara's adrenaline was still running high, so she wasn't

feeling the full impact of her injuries. She knew all of her cuts were probably bleeding just as her arm was. Her leg was hurt from her jump from the bathroom window. She was shaking all over, terrified Olly would lose his tenuous hold on life.

"I'm okay. It's Olly. Olly's the one you need to worry about."

The police made their arrival with considerably more noise and drama than the paramedics. There was shouting back and forth as they rushed into the building and tried to locate the trouble. When half a dozen of them arrived in the small office, they seemed disappointed at finding things so quiet. Tamara looked quickly over their faces, but didn't see Bowen, Timmons, or Deluth. Nobody who knew her. She pointed to Lewis's father.

"He's an accomplice in kidnapping my baby. He knew where Olly was and was just going to let him die!"

This was of more interest to the police, but when the man didn't even look up from his desk work, they looked at each other in confusion.

"Excuse me, sir... is that true? Do you want to tell us your side of the story?"

He finally looked up. "I have nothing to say to you."

"Were you complicit in a kidnapping? Did you know about this?"

Lewis's father looked down at Olly, looking so tiny and helpless on the floor. "I did not have anything to do with any kidnapping."

"Did you have knowledge of it?"

The man looked back down at his papers. "I have work to do. I'm afraid I can't help you."

The police officer questioning him had no patience for his unhelpful answers. "On your feet, please. Hands behind your head."

"You can't arrest me!" His voice was outraged.

"Stand up."

The cop patted him down and cuffed him, informing him of

his rights. A wave of relief washed over Tamara. Lewis was dead. Her father was detained and would have to explain his part in the kidnapping. And Olly... Olly was breathing. But he was still in danger.

"We're ready to move him," the paramedic told Tamara. "Do you want to carry him? Once we get him into the ambulance, we'll start him on oxygen."

Tamara looked at the paramedic uncertainly, surprised that they didn't want to put him on a stretcher to take him out to the ambulance. But she was happy enough to carry him herself. She carefully gathered him up into her arms and cuddled him against herself. She kissed the top of his head and breathed in his scent.

"Come on, Olly. Hang in here."

He didn't respond to her touch or her words. It was as if his responses to her voice when he had been trapped in the box had been a hallucination on her part. He gave no sign he knew his mother was holding him in her arms once again.

THIRTY-SIX

TAMARA HAD KNOWN THAT sooner or later, word would spread to everyone involved in the case and she would have to face the music. She had breached her parole terms. She had walked into dangerous situations, triggering the events that had gotten Lewis killed. She had escaped police custody and continued to investigate on her own.

But she had found Olly and, against all odds, found him alive. That was the only thing that mattered.

Bowen was the first one to arrive at the hospital. She faced Tamara down in a treatment room where Tamara was sitting up in bed after having her cuts stitched yet again.

"What the hell were you thinking?" she demanded, leaning in too close. "Running off like that? Walking into a situation you knew nothing about? You could have been killed. You could have gotten Olly killed."

"I needed to find him," Tamara said bullishly. She stared down at the cut on her arm, still numb with topical anesthetic, new stitches applied where the old ones had pulled away. "I'm the one who found Lewis. I was the only one who could find Olly."

"If you had told us everything you knew, we could have sorted this out a lot faster than you, and maybe Martina Lewis wouldn't be dead. Maybe we would have been able to get to Olly a few days or hours earlier, and that would have made a difference. How could you do something that would endanger him like that?"

"I didn't endanger him!"

"Because you were too stubborn to talk to me and tell me everything you knew, this investigation drew out much longer than it needed to. We could have looked into Lewis days ago, taken her into custody, and found Olly while he was still at Edelira's house. *You* put him in danger."

Tamara pressed her lips tightly together. She would never be able to convince Bowen that she, as a criminal and someone who was familiar with Lewis, was better equipped to find her and to find Olly than the entire police force. They had been to the warehouse. They had questioned Lewis's father, and they had left. They had walked right by Olly and never known it, because they didn't have enough evidence to get a search warrant and get some scent dogs in there. By the time they managed to get enough evidence, if ever, Olly would have been dead.

Not getting any further argument from Tamara, Bowen backed off.

"How are you doing?"

"I'm okay. Just waiting to find out... about Olly."

"We don't know how long he might have been abandoned in that warehouse with no nourishment... no temperature regulation... no water..."

Tears prickled in Tamara's eyes. She rubbed them away. "I hated him when I found out I was pregnant. And when he was born. I never felt anything for him when I came to live with the Hensons... just... anger, worry... I had to take care of him. That was my sentence."

Bowen gazed at her, not accusing, not making judgments for her being such a cold, uncaring parent.

"But he's my baby," Tamara said. "The longer I took care of him... even though he was so fussy all the time, I got more attached to him. I guess... I got to love him." Tamara ran her finger down the row of stitches on her arm. Her body ached. She wanted to lie down and go to sleep for a week. But more than that, she wanted to know her baby was okay. "He's mine and I love him. Then Lewis stole him away."

"It was a terrible thing to happen," Bowen said. "Made worse by the fact that you were the prime suspect in his disappearance. I'll admit that you were such a good suspect I'm still looking for ways to connect you to this. For evidence that you arranged this with Lewis." She shook her head. "But so far, all indications are that she did it all on her own. The two of you were never friends in juvie, even though you were both there at the same time. We can't find any hint of communication between the two of you once you got out."

"No. She hated me, why would she call me? Why would I call her?"

Bowen shrugged. "Just checking out all of the possibilities."

"Her dad... the guy in the warehouse... was he mob?"

"Mob?" Bowen gave a short laugh. "No, I don't think so."

Tamara had come to suspect as much.

"Who told you that?" Bowen demanded.

"Rosie... the girl I went to see before Lewis. She said Lewis's dad was Cuban mob."

"And you went to see her, and went into that warehouse, without telling anyone that? You thought you could just cross an organized crime figure?"

"I was looking for Olly. I couldn't think about that."

Bowen shook her head. "That was a stupid thing to do."

Tamara shrugged.

"So maybe this Rosie girl was just stringing you along. Or maybe

Lewis told Rosie that her dad was Cuban mob to make herself look more important. But there is no indication that he was anything more than the low-level manager of a warehouse for an imports company."

They sat for a while in silence, nothing more to say. Bowen was not leaving Tamara alone to let her run again. But Tamara didn't want to run away from Olly. Olly was more important than her continued freedom. She'd made that decision once and she wasn't going to change her mind.

After some time, Mrs. Henson got there. She peeked into the curtained area and smiled at Tamara tentatively.

"Hi... can I come in?"

She rarely bothered to ask, even when Tamara was in her own bedroom. Tamara nodded and made a motion for her to enter. There wasn't a lot of room in the small cubicle for everyone to gather, but Bowen didn't excuse herself and nobody told her she had to leave. Mrs. Henson leaned in close to Tamara and gave her a brief hug around the shoulders.

"How are you? Are you okay?"

Tamara nodded. "Still waiting to hear about Olly."

"I'm so sorry, Tamara. I'm so sorry that all of this happened to you... but especially that we suspected you. That I suspected you myself. I didn't want to, but it was the most likely scenario, especially given your history."

"I didn't just snap," Tamara said. "Even with the Bakers' kids, I didn't just snap one day because they cried too much." She'd never talked much to Mrs. Henson about what had happened at the Bakers'. "I was desperate... I thought it was the only way out. I planned it." She shook her head. "I know it was crazy. Just like the stuff I thought about Olly when I was pregnant with him was crazy. I just... listened to the wrong thoughts."

"Olly will be okay, Tamara."

"You don't know that. He could be dead already and they just haven't got around to telling me yet."

Mrs. Henson looked appropriately shocked. But she couldn't argue with the truth. Telling Tamara that Olly was going to be okay was just an empty platitude.

There was a low buzzing noise. Bowen pulled out her cell phone and looked at it. She swiped the screen and started tapping out a message. Tamara wondered again whether Bowen was a mother. Did she have kids of her own who texted her to find out what they were having for supper or if she had signed permission forms for school the next day? Did she go home and let her hair down from the sleek bun and worry about homework and bedtimes?

Mrs. Henson patted Tamara's hand, trying to calm her down. But Tamara didn't feel calmer. She wanted to slap Mrs. Henson's hand away and jump up and go find a doctor to demand what was wrong with Olly and if he was going to be okay.

Bowen was frowning at Tamara. Tamara felt a sharp stab of dread. Did they find something out that put suspicion back on Tamara again? Maybe Lewis had called the house and ended up speaking to one of the other girls before the kidnapping. That would look bad for Tamara. There would be no way of proving who it was Lewis had talked to.

"What?"

Mrs. Henson turned and looked at Bowen as well. "Did you find something out?"

"Olly was drugged. That's why he was so still. He was dehydrated too, but the reason he was unresponsive was because he'd been given something."

Tamara's anger rose. They had drugged him to keep him quiet. Lewis knew she couldn't just abandon the baby without his being found. He would cry and attract attention. So she had ensured he would stay quiet. If Olly hadn't responded to Tamara's singing, Lewis would have succeeded. By the time the drugs started to wear off, he would probably have been too weak to make noise.

"What was he given?" Mrs. Henson asked.

"Ketamine. It's an animal tranquilizer."

"And a date rape drug," Mrs. Henson said immediately.

Tamara knew the name as well. Sometimes a date rape drug, like Mrs. Henson had said. Sometimes a rave drug. Dangerous for someone to take and chance making herself vulnerable if she got the wrong dosage. It certainly wouldn't have been hard for Lewis to get on the street. "Special K," she said. "Did she put it in Olly's bottle? Is that the only way to give it to someone? Putting it in their drink?"

"No. It's injectable. That's how they give it to horses and other animals."

"If someone injected you, how would you feel?"

Bowen shrugged. "It would knock you out. You might not remember what happened afterward; it has an amnesiac effect. You'd be drowsy and confused when you woke up. Headache, nausea, sort of hung over."

Mrs. Henson got it before Bowen did. Her eyes widened. "I kept saying you were sleeping too soundly! You were never that hard to wake up."

"I couldn't remember," Tamara contributed. "I couldn't remember taking Olly up to his crib and laying down. And the night Mister Duck disappeared... I was so groggy..."

"You think Lewis injected you with Ketamine too?" Bowen asked.

"She could have."

"Yes... I suppose she could have."

"Knock, knock..." Tamara looked up at the male voice, a doctor standing at the curtain. He smiled. "You're Oliver's mother?"

Tamara clenched her fists. "Yes. That's me."

"Would you like to come see him?"

Tamara didn't need a second invitation. She kicked off the covers and jumped off of the bed, nearly collapsing when pain spiked through her ankle and knee. She rubbed her knee and steadied herself on the bed.

"Are you all right?" the doctor asked.

"I'm fine. Just take me to Olly."

She limped after him. Her visitors followed without an invitation.

Olly lay in a hospital crib, asleep, hooked up to oxygen and an IV and various other monitors. There was a lump in Tamara's throat. Were they about to tell her it was too late? They wanted permission to harvest his organs to transplant into other babies? To get her permission to unplug the machines keeping him alive?

"He's going to sleep for a while," the doctor reassured. "We're not giving him anything to bring him out of the sedation any faster. He's getting fluids and extra oxygen. We've given him a nasogastric feeding."

"He's just asleep?" Tamara asked.

"He's just asleep. Enjoy it while it lasts, because he'll probably be grumpy as heck when he wakes up."

Tamara and Mrs. Henson laughed. "He always is," Tamara agreed. She got closer to him and stroked one finger down his pudgy arm.

She had done it. She'd saved Olly.

Whatever else happened, she had done her job.

THIRTY-SEVEN

THROUGH SHEER COINCIDENCE, TAMARA ended up in front of the same judge she had faced after Olly's disappearance. The one who had refused to send her back to prison. Tamara felt one glimmer of hope. He'd refused to send her back once. Was there any chance he'd do it again? There was plenty of proof this time that Tamara had broken her parole terms. She was supposed to let Wanda know anyone she was meeting with outside the house. She wasn't supposed to be having anything to do with a convicted felon.

But maybe he would consider those technical violations that didn't really matter. She hadn't actually committed any crimes.

Wanda Brisk didn't look too pleased to be facing this judge a second time. She looked over at Tamara holding Olly and back at the judge, indecision on her face.

The judge was staring at Tamara, maybe trying to remember where he knew her from and what their previous interaction had been. Then he nodded slowly.

"Tamara French," he said, looking down at the papers in front of him for her name.

Tamara nodded.

He looked at Olly, squirming in Tamara's arms. "I gather this is the previously missing baby."

Tamara bounced him to keep him quiet and cuddled him close. "Yes. This is Olly." She turned him slightly so that the judge could see his pink, pudgy cheeks.

The judge raised an eyebrow at Wanda. "So it turns out that Miss French was not involved in the kidnapping?" He looked down at the papers. "I assume, given that kidnapping is not one of the complaints listed."

"The kidnapping would appear to have been committed by a third party. Unless the culprit was Tamara's partner, which the police have not yet been able to establish..."

"As you are aware, *this* court does not make judgments based on speculation."

Wanda nodded, her lips pressed tightly together.

The judge looked over the complaint. "It would appear that Miss French has knowingly broken a number of the terms of her parole. Would that be fair to say, Miss French?"

Tamara nodded. "Yes, your honor," she admitted. Olly fussed. She kissed him on the top of his head and bounced some more. "I was trying to find my baby. And I... I didn't trust the police to do it and broke the rules. Talked to people who might know something about it, even though they had criminal records. I didn't tell Wanda what I was doing. Or anybody," she added with a self-conscious shrug.

"Are there any police charges pending?"

"No, your honor," Wanda said.

"Are you aware of any crime that Tamara has committed of which the police are unaware?"

"No."

"It would seem to me... that these are violations of a technical nature and Miss French did follow the overall stipulation of her parole, which was to see to the welfare of her baby."

Wanda took a moment before agreeing. Tamara waited for

the other shoe to drop. She knew from the previous hearing that rejecting a parole officer's recommendation was almost never done. The same judge wasn't likely to reject Wanda's request again

He looked over the top of his glasses at Wanda. "Would you like to reconsider your recommendation?"

Wanda eventually nodded. "I suppose that all things considered... she did the best she could for the baby. But she should have communicated with me and with the police instead of going rogue."

The judge nodded in agreement. "You still need to learn to work with authority, rather than considering them your enemies, Miss French. We can do more together than alone."

Tamara nodded. She swallowed, looking over at Wanda.

The judge lifted his eyebrows. "Your recommendation, then, is that Miss French continue with probation rather than being remanded?"

Wanda obviously didn't want the judge ruling against her again. She nodded. "Yes, your honor. I think that would be what is best for Tamara... and the community."

The judge nodded and banged his gavel. He made amendments to the order in front of him, signed it, and passed it to a clerk. Tamara stood there with Olly, not sure what to do next. She had wanted to hold him, knowing it might be her last chance. But she'd beaten the odds and was again going to be returning home with Mrs. Henson. Mrs. Henson had come to the hearing to support Tamara either way. Tamara turned and walked back toward her.

* * *

Tamara and Mrs. Henson walked out of the courtroom. Wanda followed them out. Bowen was not there this time. Mrs. Arbiter was waiting in the lobby outside the courtroom, ready to take custody of Olly if Tamara were remanded. She raised her thin brows at Mrs. Henson.

"He ruled against remand?"

Mrs. Henson glanced over at Wanda, who was standing a few feet away. "She decided to change her recommendation when she saw which way the wind was blowing."

"Well, Tamara, congratulations," Mrs. Arbiter said, with a trace of a smile.

Tamara nodded. She held Olly against her for a minute and swallowed a hard lump in her throat.

"Do you think it would be better for Olly if he went back to his foster family?"

Mrs. Arbiter and Mrs. Henson looked at each other, not answering.

"I haven't been a very good mom," Tamara said. "And I'm not... ready to spend the next twenty years raising him." She tried to breathe slowly. She sniffled. "I gotta figure things out for myself. I'm not patient and when he cries, I get so scared of Mr. and Mrs. Baker hurting me... I'd do almost anything to shut him up."

"You haven't talked about this before," Mrs. Henson said.

"I thought... if I said I couldn't take care of Olly, I'd just go back to prison. But... I don't want anything to happen to him. I want him to be safe now. I don't think... I'm not ready to be a mom."

"Are you sure that's what you want?" Mrs. Henson asked. "We can get you more assistance, counseling, change your meds..."

Tamara shook her head. A tear escaped and rolled down her cheek. "I want him to have a good life. Parents who love him and are stable... who don't have connections to people like Lewis. I want him to be safe."

"Are you saying you want to give him up for adoption?" Mrs. Arbiter asked.

"Yes. That's what I wanted from the start."

"If you do, you're going to have to understand... you can't change your mind again later. You can't get him back again."

"Yeah. I know. I don't want to screw up his life." Tamara sniffled and rubbed at her eyes again. She kissed Olly on the top of his head. She started to hum *Hush Little Baby* to him very softly. Olly immediately started to kick and cried his peculiar, deep-throated cry. People turned around and looked to see what was causing the noise. Tamara laughed and shook her head at Mrs. Henson. "He really doesn't like that song."

"A good thing, too. You might never have found him."

Tamara held Olly out to Mrs. Arbiter. "Can you take him now? We packed everything he'd need."

Mrs. Arbiter took him from Tamara and tucked him, still squalling, into the carrier she had brought with her. Mrs. Henson gave Mrs. Arbiter the diaper bag. Mister Duck's head was poking out the top. Bowen had found him at Edelira's house. Tamara removed the toy and offered it to Olly, putting it into his grasp and brushing it against his face. Olly's cries slowed. He yawned widely.

Tamara straightened. Mrs. Henson gave her a squeeze around the shoulders. "You're sure this is what you want?"

"Yes." Tamara waved her fingers at Olly, eyes burning. "Bye, baby. Bye-bye."

Mrs. Arbiter didn't draw out the parting. She picked up the carrier and the diaper bag and moved away from them.

"You're not keeping him?" Wanda had moved in closer to talk to her.

Tamara clenched her teeth. "No. He needs... a better mom than I can be."

She waited for Wanda to say that since Olly was the reason she was on parole, she would be applying, once again, for

Tamara to be remanded. But she didn't. Her expression softened slightly. "I think it's for the best," she agreed.

Tamara wiped at another tear that ran down her cheek.

It was for the best. It would be a new beginning.

For both of them.

Did you enjoy this book? Reviews and recommendations are vital to making a book successful.

Please leave a review at your favorite book store or review site and share it with your friends.

Don't miss the following bonus material:
Sign up for mailing list to get a free ebook
Read a sneak preview chapter
Other books by P.D. Workman
Learn more about the author

Sign up for my mailing list at pdworkman.com and get Gluten-Free Murder for free!

PREVIEW OF RUBY,
BETWEEN THE CRACKS

CHAPTER 1

Ruby lay in Chuck's arms, listening to his deep, regular breathing. She wondered fleetingly what he did the nights she didn't see him. Sometimes it was almost a week between visits. Sometimes she saw him almost every day, but sometimes it was a long time in between.

Ruby shifted to move her arm, which was falling asleep. Chuck stirred, and the hair on his arm tickled her cheek. Ruby stroked his arm with one finger, sighing. She felt safe. The nights that she ended up alone, when she couldn't find any company, were the hardest. Cold, alone, scared... Ruby's heart pounded faster just thinking about it. Ruby turned over restlessly to face Chuck. He stirred drowsily, and his eyes opened a slit.

"Are you still awake?" he murmured.

"Mmm-hmm."

"Go to sleep. It's gotta be two in the morning."

"Three-thirty," Ruby told him.

"Mmm. Come here."

He pulled her close to his chest. Ruby tucked her head under his chin and closed her eyes. He rubbed her back for a couple of minutes before he fell asleep again. After a while, Ruby finally fell asleep as well.

* * *

Ruby awoke in the morning to an empty bed. Chuck's side was cold and empty. Ruby stretched out her sleep-cramped muscles, slid out of bed, and pulled on her t-shirt and shorts. She wandered out to the kitchen, yawning.

"Hey," Chuck greeted. "You're actually up."

He was all ready for the office. Showered, dressed, curly hair perfectly coiffed. His blue eyes were bright and alert. He smiled at her and took a sip from his coffee mug.

"Yeah," Ruby smothered another yawn. "What time is it?"

"Almost nine. I'm on my way out," he glanced toward the door.

"Mmm. To work?"

"Yeah, precious. Some of us have jobs," he teased.

"I would if anyone would hire me."

"Well then, go to school," Chuck suggested.

Ruby laughed, wrinkling her nose.

"Uh-uh. What am I going to do at school?"

"Whatever the other kids are doing."

Ruby just shook her head.

"You look after yourself," Chuck said, smiling as he looked her over, "and don't forget your jacket."

"Yeah, yeah." Ruby rolled her eyes. She glanced around and picked the jacket up off of the back of the couch.

"Seriously." Chuck's voice took on a more severe tone. "Last time you left a pair of earrings on the sink. Be more careful."

"You already told me," Ruby huffed. "Sorry, okay?"

Chuck tugged at his shirt cuffs to get them a perfect half-inch below his suit jacket.

"All right, Ruby, let's go."

Ruby put her arms around his neck and pulled him in close for a good-bye kiss.

"I'll see you around," he said softly.

"Yeah. You gonna be there tonight?" Ruby questioned, picking up her backpack.

"Maybe."

Chuck rarely committed. Sometimes he'd pick her up, and sometimes he wouldn't. He never knew ahead of time. Ruby wondered if he met someone else the other nights, policing her as carefully as he policed Ruby, to make sure that she didn't leave any sign of her presence. He had his reasons, but Ruby always wondered if he was doing more than just trying to guard his reputation. Why was it so important that there were no signs in his apartment that he had a girlfriend?

They separated in the hall, Chuck going one way and Ruby the other. Ruby wandered to the coffee shop down the street and sipped a fresh cup of coffee slowly. The boy behind the counter always paid her plenty of attention, and Ruby often wondered what kind of guy he was. He was high school or college-aged, she wasn't sure which. She'd never seen him at the high school, but she didn't hang around there very much, he might go there and she just hadn't seen him.

"Running a little late today," he commented.

"Yeah," Ruby agreed. She wasn't sure what it was about her that interested him. She never did her makeup before she got there. Sometimes, like today, she didn't even have her hair combed yet. It was just a halfway point for her, between Chuck's apartment and wherever she decided to go next.

"Doing anything special today?" the boy questioned, with an interested smile.

Ruby shrugged.

"No."

He probably was intrigued because most girls Ruby's age would really be flattered by the attention of a guy his age and fawn all over him, but Ruby really didn't care. He was actually younger than the guys she usually went with. There were only a couple of guys under twenty that she really liked. He might be a better catch than the guys Ruby's own age, but he wasn't very interesting.

"What are you taking in school?" he asked.

"I don't usually go."

"Oh. Where do you go?"

Ruby shrugged.

"Around."

She put down her mug, and he moved to refill it. Ruby shook her head and waved her hand.

"No, thanks."

Ruby got up and went to the lady's room. Unzipping her knapsack, she dug for her lipstick and other makeup. She brushed her teeth before putting on the lipstick, and brushed her hair into order. Her blond hair was straight and fine and she rarely bothered to curl or style it. She pulled it back in a pony and put an elastic around it to keep it in place. She packed her bag again and moved on.

Ruby wandered through a couple of the arcades and hangouts that she usually found company at, but things were strangely quiet. She eventually gave up, and with a sigh, decided to try the school. She arrived halfway through the morning, and joined up with a couple of the girls she knew.

Kate was plain, with no figure, a girl who desperately wanted to be popular, but no amount of makeup or trendy clothes would make her so. She didn't have the personality to join the 'in' crowd. She didn't have the money, the manner, the superficiality.

Marty was a different story. Her name was really Martha, but she preferred the less feminine form. Ruby liked her better than Kate, because Marty was more boyish, more like the guys that Ruby usually spent her time with. Of course, Marty would never be mistaken for a boy. Unlike Kate, she was an early bloomer; her figure already well-developed and she had a head of wild, dark curly hair. Marty had an easy manner, the type that attracted people to her, but didn't really care for a lot of friends or attention.

Ruby felt at ease with the two of them. They were undemanding friends, and she could spend a day with them every now and then and not have them grill her on where she'd been and what she had been doing.

"Hey, Marty," Ruby greeted, and she nodded to Kate.

"Hi, Ruby. You're just in time for math."

Ruby wrinkled her nose.

"Oh, joy. What are we doing?"

"Algebra."

Ruby shook her head. They arrived in class a couple of minutes before the second bell, and Ruby and Marty talked and watched Kate trying to flirt with Robin, the boy who sat in front of her, who she'd had a crush on for a couple months.

"He's never even going to notice her," Ruby commented, watching Robin answer Kate casually, oblivious to her body language.

"I don't even know what she sees in him," Marty commented. "Or in any guy."

"Any junior high boy," Ruby agreed.

Glancing over at them, Robin noticed Marty looking at him, and his manner changed instantly.

"Hey, Marty! How about you, what'd you think of the homework?"

Marty shrugged, and rolled her eyes at Ruby. Robin didn't seem to know how to take Ruby, and didn't say anything to her.

"Did you get A-8?" Kate asked Marty.

"Yeah."

"Can I see it?"

Marty got out her book and passed it across. Kate stared at it for a moment, and scribbled the answer down in her book. The teacher walked in and looked around. He appeared surprised to see Ruby sitting there.

"Are you still in this class?" he questioned.

"Yeah."

"Where have you been the last couple of weeks?"

"Sick." Ruby shrugged.

"You have a note from your doctor?" he demanded.

"No."

"Your mom?"

"I don't live with my mom," Ruby pointed out.

"Where do you live?"

"Foster care."

"Do you have a note from your foster parents?"

"No. You can call my social worker if you want," she suggested.

He hesitated for a moment, then shrugged it off. Too much bother.

"You're going to have a lot to catch up on. Can you get the notes from one of your friends?"

"Uh-huh."

"Okay," he moved towards the middle of the front. "Kate, do your own homework. If you don't have it by now, it won't do you any good. Anyone have any questions from the homework last night?"

Ruby stretched her legs out and looked around the room, tuning the teacher out.

* * *

At lunchtime, Ruby and the other girls went over to the senior high half of the school to look for some guys to join up with. Kate would never have been able to interest any of the guys by herself, and Marty didn't really care to, but Ruby had something that attracted the older boys.

"It's because you look so much older," Kate said. "They don't think they're dating a kid, then." She sighed. "I don't look a day older than I am. If I at least had a body like Marty..."

"You're welcome to it," Marty grumbled. "I sure don't want it. But that's not what makes the guys like Ruby. She's almost as flat as you are."

"You just look... more mature," Kate told Ruby.

Ruby shrugged.

"There's Brian. Let's see what he's doing."

Brian looked happy to see them. Tall, slim, with longish hair, he had a handsome face and was almost always smiling and relaxed.

"Hey, girls," he greeted cheerfully. "Looking for some action?"

He put his arm around Ruby's shoulders and gave her a quick hug.

"Got any plans?" Ruby questioned.

"Nope. You wanna go to my place and order a pizza?"

"Sure."

A couple of Brian's friends and Kate and Marty all agreed, so they headed for his house. Brian broke out a couple of six-packs when they got there, and they lounged around drinking and watching kid's shows on TV while they waited for the pizza.

It was almost one when the pizza delivery man got there, but nobody really cared. Missing the first class after lunch was no big deal. In another hour, though, most of them were done eating and getting set to go back to school. Ruby didn't move from her spot on the couch beside Brian.

"You going back?" she asked Brian.

"Not if you'll stick around," he said, giving her a squeeze and kissing her on top of the head.

"Good. I'll see you guys around," Ruby told Kate and Marty.

"Okay. See you later," Marty agreed.

The others went back to school. Tanner, one of Brian's

friends, stuck around for another hour watching TV with them. Then he got bored, and suggested they all go somewhere.

"The arcade?" Brian suggested.

"For a while," Ruby agreed. She knew how it would go. They'd play for a while, but Brian would be off his game from drinking for three hours, and he'd get frustrated.

Ruby played a few games herself, but the games or the booze were giving her a headache. She watched Brian play for a while, but he wasn't getting anywhere near his high scores and she could see his frustration mounting.

"Why don't we go shoot some pool," she suggested.

Brian slammed his hand down on the control panel and let the game end. He turned to face her.

"Yeah. Let's blow. I'm totally useless at this today."

Tanner had disappeared at some point. The pool hall was more relaxing. Ruby and Brian shot a leisurely game together, without caring who got the better shots or who won. Brian cajoled a jug of beer out of the management, and they smoked and drank and shot into the evening.

"You know, your friends are sort of strange," Brian commented.

Ruby smiled.

"Yeah, I know it. They're misfits, like me."

"That Marty—she gives me the creeps. I get the feeling she's got a voodoo doll somewhere with my name on it."

Ruby pictured it, and laughed.

"Don't mention it to her, she might think it's a good idea," she giggled.

"She hates me, doesn't she?"

"It's not you. She doesn't like any guys. I think she's got a short-circuit somewhere."

Brian looked thoughtful.

"No, it's more than that. She doesn't look at the other guys like she looks at me. I think it's because you like me. I think she's actually jealous."

"Jealous?" Ruby repeated, surprised. "Nah. If she was jealous, why go back to school? She could have said: 'let's go somewhere' and we could have gone somewhere without you. She could'a' skipped one afternoon of school to do something with all of us. We would've done something with her."

"She doesn't ever get you to herself, does she? Just the two of you?"

"Well, not much..." Ruby admitted. "You're nuts, you know? Marty isn't like that, she just doesn't like guys."

"Maybe... but I don't know."

They dropped the subject.

* * *

"I gotta be getting home," Brian commented, looking at his watch.

"It's not that late," Ruby protested.

He gave her a couple of gentle kisses, softening the parting.

"I know. But I got things going on tonight," he apologized.

"You gotta go home? Right now?"

"Sorry."

Ruby shrugged.

"All right."

"You want me to drop you off somewhere?" Brian suggested.

"No. I'll hang around here a while."

Brian took a glance around.

"I get nervous, you hanging around places like this by yourself," he said.

Ruby looked over the crowds.

"They're just kids, Bri'. And it's not like it's a gang hangout or something."

"I guess," he agreed reluctantly. "You look after yourself, though."

"Sure. See you 'round."

"Okay, babe."

He kissed her again briefly, and left. Ruby hung out there for a while before going to the bar where Chuck would meet her if he was picking her up. The bouncers knew her, but they never let her in because she was too young. If she was a few years older, they might have bent and let her in, but as it was, she had to stand outside. If it was cold out, they'd let her stand inside the door periodically to warm herself up, but otherwise she stood outside with the hookers, watching for Chuck.

"Hi, Ruby," Betty greeted cheerfully.

"Hi, Betty."

"How're you doing, girl?" Grace questioned.

"Good. Chuck ain't been by, has he?"

"Nope. You expecting him tonight?"

"Maybe. Saw him last night, so maybe not."

"Does he ever pay you anything?" Grace demanded.

"No. It's not like that," Ruby protested with a laugh. "I like to be with him."

"He's taking advantage of you."

"No, he's not. Any time I felt like that, I'd just stop coming here," Ruby pointed out.

"She's just too young to know the difference," Betty interposed. "She thinks she loves him."

"No..." Ruby said, frowning, "I just... like being with him. I don't like being alone."

"Well, you could get company that paid a lot better than that," Grace grumbled.

"Aw, leave her alone. She's better off not getting into this business."

Grace lit a cigarette, and they were quiet for a while. A car pulled up in front of the bar. Betty went up to talk to the driver.

"Hi, honey."

The man indicated Ruby. Betty glanced over at her.

"Oh, she's not interested, honey. But Grace or me…"

"No. Her."

"She's not working."

"I'll make it worth your while," the man said to Ruby, holding up a wad of cash.

Ruby shook her head.

"She's just waiting for her friend," Betty explained.

He screeched his tires when he pulled out, and shot down the street. Betty went back to stand with Ruby and Grace.

Grace shook her head.

"You stand there in shorts and a tee and sneakers and get more pick-ups than we do. I just don't know what you do."

"She's young. Men like 'em young," Betty said.

"I started at her age, and I never got the attention she does."

Betty looked at Ruby and shrugged.

"Some people just got what it takes."

Ruby watched for Chuck's car. If he didn't show up, she'd have to try and find somewhere else she could spend the night. But she wasn't going to take up a new profession to do it. An hour passed, and Ruby knew he wasn't going to show up. She said goodbye to the girls, and started to walk away. She got about half a block down, and a red convertible pulled up beside her.

"Hey, sweetheart."

"Not interested."

"Slow down. How'd you like to make a little cash?"

Ruby stopped and looked at him. A small, ferret-faced man in a red convertible. She'd seen him before, but she couldn't remember where. He was well dressed, but she got a bad vibe from him.

"What're you going to pay me for?" she demanded.

"To work for me," he said vaguely.

"Doin' what?"

"Leave her alone," Betty said, catching up to Ruby. "Ruby doesn't need any help from you."

The man looked at Betty.

"Stay out of it, Betty. This doesn't concern you."

"Ruby's my friend, you'd better believe it concerns me. Ruby, you ever met my boss?"

"No. Guess I haven't."

"Well, he's a snake, so stay away from him. You see this rat, you go the other way."

"Thanks."

Ruby turned and walked away. She could hear the pimp getting after Betty as she walked away, but Ruby didn't look back. The last thing she needed was to get involved in that scene. She went back to the pool hall, but no one that she knew was around. Ruby stayed there until the small hours of the morning before admitting to herself that her choices were either sleeping on the street or going home. She left the pool hall and started for home. Halfway there, a squad car pulled up beside her.

"Hi," the police officer said, through the open window.

"Hi there," Ruby acknowledged.

"A little late to be out wandering, isn't it?"

"I'm on my way home."

"How about if I drive you?" he offered.

"Yeah, okay."

"Hop in."

Ruby got into the squad car and shut the door. He pulled away from the curb.

"What's your name?"

"Ruby."

"Where do you live, Ruby?"

She gave him her address.

"Good. The name's Brown. What were you doing out so late?"

"Just hanging out." Ruby shrugged.

"There's lots of crazies out there. You shouldn't be out alone."

"I know."

"Your folks know where you are?"

"No."

"You do this often?"

Ruby shrugged.

"No. Not a lot."

Brown didn't say anything else. They pulled up to the house a few minutes later. Ruby glanced at the cop to see if he was going to insist on escorting her in and talking to her parents, but he was relaxed and didn't move to get out.

"Thanks for the lift," Ruby said.

"No problem," Brown took a business card out of his pocket. "If you're ever out late alone or need something, you call me. I'd rather be a taxi for a couple minutes then find you dead by the road somewhere."

Ruby took the card from him.

"Hey—thanks. That's cool."

She got out and went up to the house. The key was on a ring on her knapsack, and she waved at Brown and let herself in.

* * *

Ruby, Between the Cracks, Book #1 of the Between the Cracks series by P.D. Workman can be purchased at pdworkman.com

ABOUT THE AUTHOR

Award-winning and USA Today bestselling author P.D. (Pamela) Workman writes riveting mystery/suspense and young adult books dealing with mental illness, addiction, abuse, and other real-life issues. For as long as she can remember, the blank page has held an incredible allure and from a very young age she was trying to write her own books.

Workman wrote her first complete novel at the age of twelve and continued to write as a hobby for many years. She started publishing in 2013. She has won several literary awards from Library Services for Youth in Custody for her young adult fiction. She currently has over 60 published titles and can be found at pdworkman.com.

Born and raised in Alberta, Workman has been married for over 25 years and has one son.

* * *

Please visit P.D. Workman at pdworkman.com to see what else she is working on, to join her mailing list, and to link to her social networks.

* * *

If you enjoyed this book, please take the time to recommend it to other purchasers with a review or star rating and share it with your friends!

facebook.com/pdworkmanauthor

twitter.com/pdworkmanauthor

instagram.com/pdworkmanauthor

amazon.com/author/pdworkman

bookbub.com/authors/p-d-workman

goodreads.com/pdworkman

linkedin.com/in/pdworkman

pinterest.com/pdworkmanauthor

youtube.com/pdworkman